CATCHING THE EAGLE

by

Karen Charlton

CATCHING THE EAGLE

Originally published as *Catching the Eagle* (Knox Robinson Publishing 2011)

ISBN: 978-0-9928036-4-3

karencharlton1@gmail.com

Alternatively, the author can be contacted through her website:

www.karencharlton.com

Visit Karen Charlton's website to learn more about her historical novels, The Regency Reivers Series and The Detective Lavender Series, published by Famelton Publishing (a specialist, independent publisher of historical fiction and fantasy). While there, sign up for Karen Charlton's FREE monthly newsletter and join in discussion on her blog.

www.karencharlton.com

Dedicated to the memory of
my husband
Christopher John Charlton
1954 – 2013

Thank you for the journey, my love.

Praise for
CATCHING THE EAGLE

A suspense-filled page-turner

"Told with gritty realism, 'Catching The Eagle' is a suspense-filled page-turner, which spares nothing in its descriptions of the hardships and injustices suffered by the poor at the turn of the 19th century.

Its ending leaves the reader poised perfectly for the next volume – for which I can hardly wait."

Kathy Stevenson, ***The Daily Mail***

An enjoyable read

"It is a rollicking tale full of adultery, drinking, fighting, gambling.

Rich imagery, suspense and some genuinely likeable characters – as well as plenty of murky ones – make this an enjoyable read. Karen is particularly strong at capturing the Geordie dialect and recreating the rural Northumbrian world of the 1800s, where the wealthy lived in comfort and the poor struggled to make ends meet."

Laura Fraine, *Culture Magazine,* ***The Journal*** (Newcastle)

A lively tale

"When Kirkley Hall is burgled in April 1809, suspicion falls on local 'rogue', Jamie Charlton. Cleverly using information acquired from investigating her husband's family tree, Karen Charlton blends the facts into a lively tale set in the Northumbrian countryside. The depiction of poverty, squalor and oppression among the lower classes is well drawn. I particularly enjoyed Detective Lavender and his side-kick and was disappointed not to read more of them, but perhaps we'll meet again in the next book?"

Moonyeen Blakey – Author of ***The Assassin's Wife***

PROLOGUE

February 1809

A stray eagle flew east over the Cumberland border during that bitterly cold winter of 1809.

Drifting on the icy wind which came down from the hill country, it soared over a vast expanse of dark and empty beauty. For several days it glided over the silent Northumbrian borderlands; its huge shadow caressed the ruined walls of crumbling castles and the creaking, rotting stumps of ancient gibbets. The eagle plucked unsuspecting prey from the bleak, snow-covered fells and drank from remote rocky waterfalls dripping with icicle daggers.

Now, with the north wind behind it, the golden raptor sailed down into the more sheltered valleys. It drifted unobserved over squat hamlets shrouded in pearly mist where penned animals lowed and bleated hungrily through the damp morning fog.

Finally, it glided towards a copse of towering oaks near Ponteland where it landed, with barely a rustle, in the topmost branches of a tree. Gathering in its vast wings, it groomed its breast feathers and settled down to rest. Its golden eyes flicked warily onto the labourer's cottage below.

A tall man stooped and came out of the cottage doorway, his face lined with worry and tinged with malnutrition. Jamie Charlton pulled his threadbare coat tighter around his large frame and shivered as he gazed moodily into the distance.

His wife, Priscilla, followed him out into the freezing morning air clutching a shawl over her thin shoulders. Her nightgown billowed around her legs and her dishevelled, auburn hair glinted like fire in the weak morning sunlight. She touched her brooding husband gently on his arm and handed him the blue neckerchief he had forgotten.

His face erupted into a wide grin. He grabbed his wife by the buttocks and pulled her into his arms. Their lips met. They stood there, smiling, locked into their warm embrace. Her long fingers reached out and tenderly stroked the back of his thick thatch of greying hair. Eventually, he tore himself away then stepped out towards Ponteland over the frozen, black ground.

Shivering, Cilla pulled her woollen shawl tighter around her shoulders. Her own face was now etched with worry. She watched him disappear into the darkened wood before returning to the cottage and her stirring children.

Thirty feet above her, the great eagle fell into a deep and lengthy sleep.

The king of birds: nestling next to the home of one of the poorest men in England.

CHAPTER ONE

Easter Monday, 3rd April 1809

A dense, white mist enveloped Kirkley Hall at dawn and stubbornly refused to lift. Condensation dulled the leaded window panes which stared blindly across the front lawns. The birds sat mute amongst the damp, drooping leaves of the trees while indiscernible cows lowed in the fields encircling the elegant Hall. At the rear of the building a towering Lebanese cedar glistened with moisture, stretched out and disappeared entirely into the mist above.

Beneath the heavy, creaking boughs of the great tree, dozens of tenant farmers emerged out of the damp gloom, like ghosts. The new arrivals startled those who were leaving. Some came on foot, their boots and the hems of their coats clarted with mud; others rode into the courtyard, stinking of wet horse. They knocked in turn at the estate office door and sought audience with the steward in the office upstairs. With grimy hands and blackened fingernails they handed over their half-yearly rent money to Michael Aynsley and his son – who counted, recounted and recorded it carefully.

Aynsley took their money with a face as hard and rugged as a limestone outcrop. He glared at the tenants with disgust and distrust; noting any lack of deference and every missing groat. His steel-grey eyes scanned the motley group of labourers before him. He saw a shabby, ill-fed crowd of drooping shoulders and averted eyes. Beneath the grime, they looked pale and unhealthy following a hard winter of poor nutrition and scant sunlight.

There were a few though, for whom living in that harsh landscape was more profitable. For them, rent day was a chance to socialise and catch up with the local news. These richer tenants swung themselves down from their horses and traps and strode confidently into the steward's office. After handing over their money, they chatted amiably with Aynsley about the price of corn and beef and the great eagle which had been seen circling in the skies above the parish.

By four o'clock most of the rent had been collected. Aynsley and his son, Joseph, relaxed, pushed aside the ledgers and quills and ate a meal of bread, cheese and pickle, all swilled with beer. The gloom outside made the office unnaturally dark. Light came from the glowing embers of the fire, a few spluttering wax candles on the mantelpiece and the flickering oil lamps which stood in the two oak-panelled alcoves on either side of the fireplace. As the Aynsleys shuffled on the stiff-backed chairs, a dog slept peacefully on the flagstones at their feet.

The steward finished his beer and belched loudly. Ale dribbled in thin streams out of the corners of his mouth and down his shaggy beard. He wiped away these beads of moisture with his jacket sleeve and pushed back the thick mane of greying hair which framed his frowning face.

'One thousand, one hundred and fifty seven pounds, thirteen shillings and sixpence,' he said. 'Nathaniel Ogle must be bowlegged with all this brass. Over one thousand pounds for half a year's rent to keep him in the bloody lap of luxury.'

His son nodded in agreement. Neither of the men could hide their admiration for the piles of gleaming coins and stacked bank notes on the ink-stained table.

'Aye, Da,' Joseph said. 'And this is only one of his estates. Ogle must be rolling in money.'

'He is rolling in money,' Aynsley snapped. 'He's kept in feather beds, lace and fine French brandy by the likes of us.'

His coarse fingers smoothed down a pile of crackling bank notes.

'What wouldn't I give to have this much money?' he sighed.

'You've done all right, though, Da.'

'Aye, but I've worked damned hard for it, lad. Seven days a week, every week of the year, I've dragged myself out of bed to toil on Ogle's bloody farms. Aye, Sir. Nay, Sir. Anything you want, your bloody Lordship.' The permanent frown on Aynsley's face deepened. 'It was only when I left Home Farm to become steward here – at Kirkley – that I got to lie a-bed on Sundays,' he continued bitterly. 'And even then only until eight in a morning, because as his steward I now had to chivvy the bloody workforce into his damned chapel. It's easier to get these stupid heathens to work than it is to get them to prayers.'

'He's a good man though, Da…he was right concerned when Ma was dying,' Joseph said. 'He prayed for her, regular, like.'

Aynsley shrugged.

'She still died, didn't she?'

He sighed, belched and took up his quill again. All four of his sons were far too soft in his eyes – the whole lot of them. The only one of his children with any flint in them was his daughter, Sarah – and what use was that in a woman? But soft or not, his lads were the only people in this Godforsaken parish whom he could trust. He had learnt the hard way about Nathanial Ogle's chapel-going tenants.

'Right,' he growled. 'What's the full amount again? I'll enter it into the ledger and write a note to his Lordship.'

'One thousand, one hundred and fifty-seven pounds, thirteen shillings and sixpence – It's slightly down on the last yearly amount, mind.'

'That'll be because of the two empty cottages in Ogle and the empty farm in Newham.' Aynsley's quill scratched irritably across the page. 'I must see about getting that farm let. We should put up the rent as well.'

'What happened to the old farmer? Bates, wasn't it?'

'Heddon Poorhouse,' Aynsley replied sharply. 'Him and his wife. No family to take care of them when they got too old.'

He paused meditatively and a wry smile lifted the edges of his moist lips.

'Not like me, eh? I've got you to look after me when I'm drooling and pissing myself in my dotage.'

'There's a good few years left in you yet, Da,' Joseph murmured.

'Huh! I fancy a bit of peace in me old age – and no man gets any peace living with our Sarah – not even that fancy husband of hers. No, I want to end my days in front of the comfort of your hearth.'

Joseph was clearly not listening. He frowned, distracted with the figures in the ledger before him and scratched his head in confusion.

'I see Old Henry Dodds over at Wharton hasn't paid the full amount again.'

His father laughed unpleasantly and took another swig of his beer.

'Don't you worry yourself about Old Henry Dodds. We have an agreement, like.'

'What sort of an agreement?'

Aynsley paused for a moment and eyed his son shrewdly. Then he pushed the chair back and strode casually towards the stone fireplace. The dog scampered out of his way and slunk off into a corner. Aynsley placed his hands onto the edge of the mantelpiece, leaned forward and stared down into the fire. 'I let Old Henry Dodds pay part of his rent in kind,' he said.

'In kind? What could Old Henry Dodds possibly have that Mr. Ogle would want?' Joseph stared in confusion at his father.

Aynsley felt his grin stretch from ear to ear.

'Dodds has a young and very comely, second wife whom he finds he cannot satisfy.'

'So Mr. Ogle swives with her?' Joseph was startled.

'Not him – you fool,' Aynsley growled. 'Nathanial Ogle recites psalms and prays for forgiveness for his lust before mounting his own wife. Do you really think he'd be interested in riding another man's wife?'

It still took Joseph a moment or two before reality hit him.

'Why, Da! You dirty old bugger!' In the dim light from the spluttering candles, Aynsley could see his son blushing.

'You shouldn't mock the idea, Joe – especially if you fancy being steward, one day. It's a perk of the job, like,' Aynsley laughed crudely. 'You ought to ride out with me next week, when I go up to Wharton to collect the 'outstanding rent'. Dodds has also got a very bonny daughter – just coming up to fourteen – ripe for the plucking.'

'Aye, maybe so,' his son said, 'but some of us still have jealous wives.' He smiled wryly. 'Besides which, how long have you been swiving with Dodd's missus? Their daughter could be my bloody sister.'

Aynsley threw back his great, shaggy head and roared with laughter. The firelight threw the profile of a rampant lion onto the flaking walls. Joseph laughed too – but nervously. His father's lechery hovered like an unwelcome spectre between them.

There was a sharp knock at the door. Their laughter ceased abruptly. Aynsley stood up straight and resumed his customary frown.

'Come in!'

Jamie Charlton stooped and entered the room. A chill draught lifted the edges of the parchment on the table. The big labourer wore a grey carpenter's apron over his old coat and a frown across his broad face. Tension walked into the room with him.

'What the bloody hell do you want, Charlton? I sacked you years ago,' snarled Aynsley.

'Begging your pardon, Mr Aynsley, I need to measure how much wood is needed for the new sash window.'

'What are you talking about, man?' Aynsley snapped. 'Measuring windows? You drive the bloody cattle to market – you're a cattle drover. Or at least you were, until I sacked you. What window? What bloody wood?'

Jamie pointed to the hessian bag of tools slung over his shoulder and the various hammers and chisels which poked their handles out from his pockets. 'It is the instructions of Mr. Archibold, the carpenter. I'm assisting him in his work today.' His blue eyes glistened with thinly-veiled hatred as he spoke to Aynsley.

‘I’d heard that the carpenter was lodging with you and your missus over in Milburn,’ said Joseph Aynsley. ‘Giving you some work, is he?’

‘Aye.’

‘You asked Archibold to strengthen this window frame last month,’ Joseph reminded his father. ‘It’s rotten.’

‘Did I? Well, he picks a bad bloody day to choose to get around to it. I’ll have to have words with Archibold. Get on with measuring it then, Charlton, and stop your gawping. Pass me those moneybags, son – and the chest. Let’s get this money put away.’

Aynsley strode over to the table, pushed the pewter plates with the remains of their food to one side and began to gather up the hundreds of coins from the old table.

Jamie paused and watched. He had never seen anything like it. The glimmering reflection of the gold, silver and burnished metal mesmerised him. The money glinted seductively in the firelight. Golden guineas, silver sevenshilling pieces, crowns and half crowns, nickel sixpences and copper threepenny bits all dropped tantalisingly out of view into the money sacks. Metal chinked softly on metal. Each piece flashed more brilliantly than the last. He gazed longingly at the money. Transfixed.

Aynsley glanced up and caught the look on his face.

‘I said stop your gawping!’

Startled, Jamie lurched back to reality.

‘I’ll come back later,’ he stammered and moved towards the door.

‘Faster, man!’ Aynsley roared. To emphasise his displeasure, he leapt across the room and aimed a vicious kick at Jamie’s retreating backside. He missed his target – but his boot caught the back of Jamie’s thigh and knocked him off balance.

Jamie lurched forward and half-fell, half staggered, down the narrow wooden staircase into the store room below. He gritted his teeth and muttered a strangled curse.

Back outside, in the swirling fog and the gloom, he rubbed his sore leg and damned Michael Aynsley to hell. As the pain gradually subsided, he leaned back against the clammy wall, closed his eyes and indulged in a furious fantasy of revenge. He imagined what it would feel like to grind the steward’s bloodied head beneath his boot into the cobbles and horseshit of the yard.

Darkness was falling at five o’clock when Mr. Archibold, the elderly carpenter, left Kirkley Hall. He packed his treasured tools into his bag, lit his clay pipe and set off cheerfully for his lodgings at Charlton's cottage. The wisps of silvery smoke from his pipe gently merged into the swirling mist.

Jamie didn't finish until after six o'clock. He'd managed to avoid Aynsley for the rest of the afternoon and stayed behind to complete his other work after the carpenter had left. Although his thigh still ached, his good humour had returned and was heightened by the fact that he now had some money in his pocket to spend at the card tables in the smoky, warmth of the coaching inn at Newhamm Edge. As he half strolled, half limped past the dripping water pump into the yard, the oyster grey day turned into darker gunmetal. Jamie quickened his step as the card tables beckoned.

Forty minutes later Aynsley and his son left the estate office. Their lanterns cast muted shadows across the cobbles in the darkness. Aynsley inserted the iron key into the door lock and, mindful of the vast amount of money which lay hidden inside, he double-checked to make sure the door was secure.

He chatted briefly to his son and to cast a lecherous eye over the soft curves of a passing housemaid. He made a mental note to try and trap her in the laundry room the next day.

Eventually, the two men parted. Joseph Aynsley took his lantern, side-stepped the piles of dung which littered the yard and departed on foot through the muddy gloom towards the warmth of his own hearth and wife. The dog padded behind him.

The steward went to the stables where the groom had already prepared his horse. He swung into the saddle and clattered noisily across the cobbles – also on his way to Newhamm Edge Coaching Inn.

His arrangement with Nathanial Ogle was to send his employer a letter as soon as the rents were collected and to deposit the money in the bank in Newcastle the next day. The letter lay crushed in the inside pocket of his coat. Part of it read:

'...the rents have been collected and the bags of gold and silver, along with the rolls of notes, are in the wooden chest hidden behind the secret panel. The devil himself could never find it.'

As Aynsley raced into the cobbled courtyard of the coaching inn, the south-bound mail coach was already waiting. The livery stablehands were unhitching the steaming horses. In the shadows beyond the flickering light cast by the lanterns, fresh beasts waited to take their place. The blacksmith was shutting down his forge for the night and one of the parish beggars lay across a doorway, a drunken heap of stinking rags. Servants and porters bustled around the coach, struggling with the heavy trunks and valises.

The innkeeper stood on the small flight of muddied steps which led into the inn, barking out orders. His massive frame and huge, bushy sideburns filled the doorway. He nodded courteously to the steward and instructed a barmaid to fetch Aynsley a tankard of ale. While he waited, the steward joined the landlord and watched the passengers scuttle back onto the coach. Nobody wanted to travel on the outside of a coach, through an area known to be infested with nocturnal highwaymen. The murdering bands of border reivers may have vanished into the mists of time but Ponteland was still a dangerous place.

Aynsley snorted with laughter as a fat, tightly-corseted woman struggled to board the coach, hampered by her short legs and cumbersome, hooped dress. But nothing was allowed to delay the departure of the mail coaches. Two servants grabbed her opulent rear and propelled her inside in an undignified flurry of lilac satin, peacock feathers and hat boxes. Another servant then tossed up her yapping Pekinese.

Now the drivers appeared, refreshed from their suppers in the warm interior of the inn. Swathed in thick, leather coats, fingerless gloves and felt hats against the bitter cold, they were muffled up to their eyeballs in scarves. They strode purposefully towards the coach and hung lanterns on the outside of the vehicle. After climbing up onto their seats, one of them put Aynsley's letter into the leather bag which rested between them.

A hush fell over those assembled when one of the drivers took out a blunderbuss and cocked it ready for firing. Next he took up his coiled post horn and blew. The blast was ear-piercing. Beside him, the driver thrashed at the reins and yelled to the horses. The drunken beggar awoke with a scream.

The coach jolted into action, glided around and rumbled seamlessly through the narrow arched exit to the courtyard. The swaying light from its rear lantern soon disappeared into the persistent mist.

His duty done to his employer, Aynsley now thought of the pleasures which were promised him in the warm bed and between the plump, open legs of his mistress: Lottie MacDonald of Stamfordham. He swung himself back into the saddle of his horse and clattered out of the courtyard.

Through the dirty, mullioned window of the inn, Jamie Charlton glared moodily after the departing figure of the steward. He was fuddled from the brandy and a lack of food and his money was nearly all gone. The deep-seated hatred he held for Aynsley surged back through him with a vengeance. He seethed with resentment over today's latest humiliation at the end of the man's boot. The desire to waylay the steward in the gloom, knock him off his horse and smash his eyeballs into the back of his skull with a carpenter's hammer was overwhelming.

Eventually, he sighed, shoved Aynsley out of his mind and tried to find solace in his favourite pastime. He pushed the last of his coins into the centre of the table.

'Deal us another hand, Tom,' he said to one of his fellow card players. 'Give us a chance to win it back, eh?'

Over at Kirkley Hall, the gloom had thickened; the only light came from the candles which flickered behind the casement windows of the kitchen and the servant quarters. There was a low hum of voices and occasional laughter as the skeleton staff who manned the hall during the master's absence settled down to prayers, supper and an hour of relaxation before they retired for the night. The main part of the house remained, as usual, in total darkness; white dust cloths were draped like shrouds across the magnificent furniture, priceless portraits and gilded ornaments.

Just after nine, a footman took a spluttering candle around the ground floor of the hall. His footsteps echoed eerily in the deserted building. With his itchy wig tucked beneath his arm, he checked everything was secure and tested the huge bolts on the doors.

Eventually, the candles were extinguished as the staff drifted off to their attic quarters to settle down for the night. The only sounds now were those of muted snoring, distant sheep and a tiny owl who hooted softly in the drooping boughs of the magnificent cedar tree.

At the edge of the rear courtyard, a moon-shadow crept silently up towards the estate office door. With the soft ease of familiarity, it climbed deftly onto the ground floor window ledge and then pulled itself onto the flat roof above the storeroom. Hard boots scraped lightly over stone.

The nervous owlet hooted and for a brief moment the phantom paused in response.

A hundred feet above them, a large shadow glided silently across the face of the moon. The golden eagle circled slowly above their heads and landed gracefully in the topmost branches of the cedar tree. There was a flurry of terrified squawking. The other roosting birds screeched and fled. Unperturbed, the raptor drew in its huge wings and watched the human below with sharp, passionless eyes.

Confused, the intruder squatted on the flat roof and paused. He was unsure what had disturbed the creatures in the tree. He waited for a window overlooking the courtyard to be thrown up and some light-sleeping servant to cry out: 'Who goes there?'

But the event had gone unnoticed in the slumbering manor house. The great tree, with its sharp-eyed observer, settled back down again into silence.

Now the shadowy phantom on the roof moved swiftly. The abrupt crack of shattering glass echoed around the courtyard. The sash window of the office slid upwards.

Then the mysterious figure disappeared into the gloomy interior of Kirkley Hall.

CHAPTER TWO

Tuesday 4th April 1809

'Get out here, you thieving bastards! I'll have you for this! Don't think I bloody won't!'

The Kirkley servants were settled at breakfast in their dining hall when they first heard the commotion. They looked up in alarm as the enraged steward burst violently through the door. 'Which one of you thieving sods has done this?' Aynsley roared.

The servants gasped, dropped their cutlery and stared at the infuriated man.

Mr. Edwards, the butler, frowned and wiped the grease from his chin with a napkin.

'What's the matter?' he asked, annoyed.

'Get the hell out here – the lot of you!' spluttered Aynsley. 'The rent money's gone!'

'Gone? Gone where?'

Aynsley could not reply. His face was choleric, his eyes wild.

In a dignified silence, Edwards scraped back his chair, rose and followed Aynsley outside into the cold yard. The weak sunlight had pushed aside the grey clouds above and the broken office window on the first floor was now clearly visible across the courtyard. The butler's mouth tightened into a grim line.

The draught from the broken window hit them in the face as they climbed the narrow steps up to the office. The musty odour of unwashed men which usually pervaded the office was gone; it smelt unnaturally fresh. Edwards' eyes flashed to the broken window and the shards of glass lying on the wooden floor.

Aynsley pointed to the alcove beside the fireplace which had been swept clear of its books, quills and candle holders. The oak panelling at the back of the alcove had been smashed to pieces. Behind this, in the secret cavity in the wall where Aynsley kept the rent, stood a broken money chest.

The butler worked his way across the debris-strewn floor and reached into the alcove. He removed some of the jagged edges of the splintered wood and stuck his trembling arm into the gaping chasm. It was empty. The money bags were gone. All gone. Not even a groat was left. Edwards' face paled with shock. Beside him, Aynsley was purple with fury, a vein throbbing dangerously in his neck.

When they returned to the courtyard, the frightened servants had gathered outside the kitchen door and were pointing to the broken window.

'It's gone,' Edwards said gravely to the assembled staff. Many gasped audibly. Several threw their hands over their mouths in horror.

Aynsley clenched his fists. His eyes flashed from face to face as they gathered around. Unable to think rationally, he glowered viciously at all of them.

'Which one of you thieving swine has taken it?' he bawled. 'There's only you lot that knows about the secret panel. Where's the bloody rent money?'

The startled and frightened crowd all began to express their innocence at once.

'What makes you think it's any of us?' snapped the cook, indignantly. Her voice rose above the hubbub of denials from the others.

'Mrs. Hodgeson has a good point there, Aynsley,' said the butler quietly. 'Everybody in the parish knew you collected the rent money yesterday.' The clamour abated as the respected, elder servant spoke. 'In fact, everyone in the county knows that it is the custom in Northumberland to collect the first rent of the year on the first Monday after the Durham Fair,' he continued. 'The thief could be anyone from Berwick to Newcastle – and I doubt that the servants here are the only ones who knew about your hiding place.'

Incensed by the calmness of the gentle, grey-haired butler, Aynsley took an aggressive step towards him.

Unperturbed, Edwards stared him down coldly before calling out to one of the grooms: 'Harry? Saddle up man, and ride to Ponteland. Find the beadle and tell him a crime has been committed at Kirkley Hall – and don't – I repeat don't – tell anyone else what is going on. The rest of you – return to your breakfast and your duties.'

'The beadle?' Aynsley snarled. 'What's that bloody useless old fool going to do?'

'What are any of us going to do?' Edwards retorted sharply. 'You've lost Mr. Ogle's rent money, Aynsley. You are the one who is going to pay unless that money is recovered. Not us.'

With this last stinging retort, Edwards set off back across the cobbles in the direction of his own office.

As the butler calmly took control, all Aynsley could do was stand gulping like a helpless salmon tossed up onto the river bank. Bile rose to his throat and gut-wrenching nausea swamped him.

He was ruined: totally ruined.

The steward's office became a hive of activity. The beadle could think of no other course of action except to invite every person of importance in the neighbourhood, to turn up and examine the crime scene themselves. Harry the groom was despatched again and tore around the area to fetch Mr. Ogle's lawyer, the captain of the local fusiliers and several others. Everyone who gathered there could see how the thief had got in and out through the window but nobody could see any clues as to who may have done it – although plenty of accusations were made.

Eventually the captain announced that he would take a few of his men and turn over the hovels of a few known local criminals to see if anything could be found. A list of possible villains was drawn up. In the meantime, Mr. Edwards conducted a thorough search of the Hall and the servants' quarters. Aynsley's accusation that one of the servants had done it rankled the butler; he was determined that no hint of suspicion should lie at the door of any of his staff.

Michael Aynsley continued to storm around the Hall, shouting and lashing out at anyone who got in his way. It was the calmer Mr. Edwards who penned the urgent letter which was eventually despatched to Nathanial Ogle in London.

William Charlton still lived with his family at North Carter Moor Farm and he first heard about the robbery from his niece, Lizzie, who was the housemaid at Kirkley Hall. Tuesday was Lizzie's half day off and her little legs could not bring her home fast enough that day. She had covered the two miles back to the farmhouse in less than thirty minutes and was breathless with excitement when she burst through the door. William and his older brother, John, had been up most of the night calving and were resting in front of the smoke-blackened range in the kitchen when Lizzie almost fell into the room.

'Da! There's been a robbery!' she cried.

William and John were soon joined by their elderly mother, Ann, and John's wife, Susan. Everyone looked on gravely as Lizzie recounted the dramatic events at Kirkley Hall. The womenfolk were shocked and discussed the robbery in nervous whispers. However, William could barely conceal his grin and began chuckling to himself: 'It sounds to me like that bugger, Michael Aynsley, has just got his comeuppance,' he said.

His mother frowned. 'This is no laughing matter, Will. 'Tis a terrible crime – and a great sin.'

'What's going to happen to us servants?' Lizzie asked, tearfully. 'Will we all go to Morpeth Gaol?'

'Nay, child,' comforted her grandmother. 'The innocent have naught to fear – God will protect you. God always looks after the innocent.'

'Aye, tell that to the poor bugger they arrest and charge for this,' William said sharply. 'Every one of the local gentry will take this robbery personally. Their wrath will be intense and in the rush to hang someone – they might not get the right man.'

'The thief will be caught and hanged,' his brother announced firmly. 'Justice will be done and all right-thinking folks will be glad for it.'

But William did not hear the reproach in his older brother's tone. He was suddenly distracted by a worrying thought; their Jamie had been working at Kirkley Hall the day before.

After supper, when his mother, John and Susan and their seven children gathered around the table for prayers, John opened the tattered, black, family bible and preached to his family from John 10:10. William left them to it and strode across the farmyard with his brother's monotonous tones trailing behind him through the closing kitchen door:

'The thief cometh not, but for to steal, and to kill, and to destroy: I am come that they might have life and that they might have it more abundantly...'

Jamie and William Charlton were close in age and had always got along well. As the second and third sons of the old farmer at North Carter Moor, they were exempt from the pressure placed on the more serious John, who had been marked out as the natural heir to the farm since his birth. The two younger lads had spent their childhood trying to escape from their chores, roaming the fells and clambering on top of the ruined Roman Wall which skirted the boundaries of their farm. Despite the best attempts of their mother to make them literate and numerate, they would miss school and escape over the heather-swathed moors in search of adventure. Feeding themselves on purple turnips from the fields and stolen milk from indignant cows, they would shelter from bad weather in barns or down ancient mine-workings. They only went home when the weak, northern sunlight failed or when forced to join in with the daily rhythm of the farm work by their father.

Despite being tired from the calving, William wanted to warn Jamie against being too jubilant about the robbery. He was well aware of the antagonism between his brother and the steward. A cornered Aynsley would be even more dangerous than normal.

He had a good idea where he would find his brother.

Striding across Ponteland High Street towards the Seven Stars public house, he had an unwelcome encounter. Mrs. John Robson – the surgeon's wife – drove past in her dogcart. His skin flushed and he stumbled over a rut in the road. Cursing, he paused and watched Sarah go by. Proud and cold, she sat haughtily erect. Her eyes looked straight ahead.

It had been nearly nine months since she had jilted him to take up with the town's elderly surgeon but the pain still seared through him like a sheep-brand. Her face framed and shadowed by her black, silk bonnet, was impassive. The woman he had loved – still loved – passed him by without so much as a sideways glance. It hurt. As the cart rumbled by and her slim figure disappeared into the twilight, William found himself wondering, yet again, if the old surgeon managed to satisfy her in bed?

The image of a half-naked Sarah with dishevelled, auburn hair tumbling over her bare, ivory shoulders and green eyes flashing with lust, leapt into his mind. He tried to shut it out but failed. His manhood stirred uneasily in his breeches. Misery, jealousy and anger swamped him in successive waves as he thought of the old doctor parting those white thighs. That prize should have stayed his, and everyone knew it.

Damn the woman. Was she going to haunt him for ever?

Ma and Barny Shotton's Public House, the Seven Stars, was the most popular drinking place in Ponteland for the labouring men of the district. Ma Shotton kept it clean, homely and law-abiding. A roaring fire crackled and spat in the grate of the large stone fireplace and a genial hum of conversation and laughter drifted through the smoke-curled air.

It was particularly busy in Ma Shotton's that Easter Tuesday. Forced to spend hours with both the minister and their families over the Easter weekend, many of the local men had now gratefully escaped for a couple of hours to the tobacco and burnt-wood scented gloom of the tavern. Dozens of customers sat on the oak settles or were grouped around low tables on stools. They smoked pipes, played dice and talked companionably. Several large mongrels lay sleeping and scratching in between the wooden tables and spittoons. Barmaids in mob caps swirled around the tavern with jugs of ale, bottles of brandy and a cheery smile for all.

Jamie Charlton had arrived at the Seven Stars several hours earlier. He was in an excellent mood. He seemed to have plenty of money in his pocket and drank several large glasses of brandy as he caught up on the gossip.

The main topic of conversation was Sam Dale's disastrous attempt to catch the eagle the previous night. Staggering home from the public house at dusk, Sam spotted the raptor settling down to roost in a tree. The drunken labourer armed himself with a net and attempted to climb the tree and snare the bird. Unfortunately, he lost his footing and fell nearly twenty feet – disturbing the bird and breaking his leg in the process. At dawn, his worried wife found him tangled in the net and groaning in agony beneath the tree. Of the eagle, there had been no more sign since Dale had frightened it from its roost. Allegedly, it had flown off towards Kirkley.

'I'll have to look out for it and trap it,' Jamie said. 'They pay a fortune for those birds in Newcastle market.'

'Ye'll end up in Milburn Beck like the Morgan brothers,' observed his friend Tom Phillips. 'They set a net for it across the river and baited it with salmon. The damned thing was too quick for them though – it took off with the net still in its talons and dragged them both into the water.'

'No bird is going to force me to bathe,' Jamie slurred defiantly.

Tom's gaunt, pock-marked face relaxed into a toothless smile.

'Aye, Jamie. I'm sure it won't. How you doing, anyway?' He joined him at his table by the fire. 'I haven't seen you for months. How's the missus and the bairns?'

'Grand. Grand,' enthused Jamie. 'Cilla is in fine fettle and the bairns are thriving.'

Tom sighed. 'I'd like a missus and bairns like yours,' he said, wistfully.

'Aye, well they're not for sale,' Jamie smiled.

Jamie knew that Tom's chances of attracting any wife at all were very remote. Riddled with worms, Tom was small in stature and cursed with sharp features and a bad complexion. He always looked like he was only days away from starvation. He lived with his mother in a one-roomed tumbledown cottage on the edge of the parish.

Apart from his poor looks and extreme poverty, the man was also afflicted with the most appalling shyness. Everyone in the parish knew that he blushed scarlet from the roots of his thin hair to the soles of his calloused feet, if a female so much as looked at him. It was so bad that some of the crueller, more raucous women of the town took great delight in teasing him and adding to his suffering, especially if they had been drinking. It was not uncommon for them to call out after him in the street, or undo their bodice and pull out a breast to wave immodestly in his face. At this point he would always turn crimson and scurry away, the women's vicious laughter ringing in his ears.

'So is tha here in Ponteland on business then, Jamie?' Tom asked.

'Aye. That I am. And tomorrow I'm away to Morpeth to get myself a new coat.'

'A new coat?

'Aye. You can have my old one, Tom,' he offered generously. 'Mind, this has long been a bad coat, though. Not like the watch I sold you of me Da's, eh? That was a canny watch… I miss that watch.' He paused for a moment, full of sad regret. When Jamie had been penniless a couple of months ago, he had pressed Tom to buy the brass watch. They were ploughing together at the time. Jamie claimed it was the kind of pocket watch which would really impress the lasses; he claimed they'd be falling over themselves to get a look-see at it. Tom had had often complained that there been no improvement in his luck with the lasses since that day but Jamie knew he had grown rather fond of the watch.

'Ne'er mind,' Jamie said, suddenly much brighter. 'I'll buy a dozen watches now! Say! Matthew! Matthew Mackie the tailor!'

Several people looked up as he shouted across the smoky room and there was a lull in the conversation. Even the dice throwers paused in their interminable game.

A dark-haired young man looked up from his beer.

'Aye, what is it, Charlton?'

'If I get me some cloth from Morpeth, tomorrow, will you make me up a new coat?'

'Aye, I will.

'You'd best get him to pay you in advance, though, Mackie,' advised a gruff voice from a table on the right.

Laughter rippled around the bar and heads turned to watch Jamie's reaction. Rob Wilson didn't say much but when he did, men listened.

Already flushed with the alcohol, Jamie went a deeper shade of crimson, swallowed hard and slammed his glass onto the table.

'What's that supposed to mean, Wilson?'

The last of the noise fell away and silence descended as the large, disfigured ex-soldier glanced up from his hand of cards. The firelight highlighted the vivid purple battle scar which snaked up the left side of his face to his misshapen eye. The tension increased as he slowly took a sip of ale and everyone – except Jamie – was acutely aware of his missing two fingers as he raised the glass to his lips.

Fingers lost as part of a wager, Wilson always bragged.

Everyone in the parish was wary of Rob Wilson. He now kept the turnpike gate in Ponteland but during his time in the army he had fought in both India and the Americas. He was the local 'heavy man' and frequently used by folks to collect long-standing debts. His hideous facial scars were enough to frighten most debtors into paying up immediately. For those who didn't, local rumour claimed that he had perfected a catalogue of unmentionable tortures which he amassed while terrifying the black heathens on the Indian sub-continent.

'Tha knows what I mean, Charlton,' he growled, softly. 'Tha owes money to half the bloody County.'

'Not any more! Not any more!' Jamie grinned drunkenly across the bar.

'Tha still owes James Selkirk of Newcastle six pounds for some leather.'

'If you sees James Selkirk of Newcastle, Wilson – you tell him I'll call on him on Saturday with the money I owe him for the leather,' Jamie replied excitedly.

'Yeh, yeh,' growled the ex-soldier.

'What's that?' snapped Jamie. 'You don't believe me? Is my word not good enough for you?'

'After three years, Charlton, I think there's more chance of me walking across the bloody Tyne, than of you paying off your debt to James Selkirk!'

Jamie staggered drunkenly to his feet as the humiliating laughter rippled around the inn again. 'Why you…!'

Tom Philips reached up and quickly pulled the bigger man back down onto his stool.

'Calm down, Jamie! Sit down! Tha doesn't want to pick a fight with Rob Wilson – not unless you wants to meet your maker,'

'I'm not scared of him,' Jamie declared.

Tom laughed quietly. 'Now I know tha's had too much to drink. Every man in his right mind is scared of Rob Wilson. They say even Boney himself cancelled a scrap when he thought Rob Wilson were coming. Sit down, man.'

Conscious only of his stung pride, Jamie pushed off Tom and staggered back to his feet.

'Rob Wilson thinks that I have no money. Isn't that right?'

'Aye!' came a chorus of amused voices from around the room.

'Jamie…' urged Tom.

'Well, you's wrong,' he shouted. 'See here? I have gold in this pocket…'

He thrust his hands into the pocket of his breeches and pulled out handfuls of gleaming coins which he threw recklessly onto the table. Dozens of copper farthings, pennies, golden guineas and crowns rolled or skittered across the surface. You could have heard a pin drop in the stunned silence which followed.

'…and silver in this pocket,' continued the drunken man. More coins slapped down on top of the others. Now shillings, sixpences and half-crowns were added to the large heap of money. Some slithered off the glimmering pile, rolled off the table and spun around the stone floor and came to rest in the cracks between the flags or by Jamie's feet.

'Why!' gasped Tom. 'There must be twenty shillings in silver there and the Lord knows how much gold!'

'I guess that threshing at Haindykes must pay better than cobbling,' said Wilson coolly. There was amused laughter. Jamie's poor attempts at shoemaking were well known in the community. When he lost his regular position as a herdsman at Kirkley Hall, he set up a doomed cobbling business. More recently he had been employed as the barns man at Haindykes.

'Aye, that's right,' Jamie said as the laughter eventually died away. 'And you see the Queen of Spades on the table in front of you, Wilson? I'll put a guinea on her.'

A stunned silence now fell over all the drinkers and gamblers.

'I said: a guinea on the Queen of Spades.'

'A guinea!' gasped Tom. 'Who's got that kind of money to put on a card? Sit down man, before you do sommat which you'll regret.'

Jamie ignored him. 'Who'll take my bet of a guinea? You all had plenty to say a minute or two ago – why so quiet now? Is there no man here who dare match my bet of a guinea on the Queen of Spades?'

Everyone stared at him in stunned amazement.

'They all have wives and families, Jamie,' urged Tom. 'I cannot think that anyone here – even thee – has that much money to spare.'
'It's been a hard winter, man,' someone commented.
Angrily, Jamie grabbed handfuls of coins, raised them – and then let them drop back down onto the table. More rolled and fell away.
'But I have money – plenty of money – and I have had a hard winter….'
'And you can put it back in your pocket now, you daft bugger,' said a familiar voice at his elbow.

Jamie spun around. 'Will! Why if it isn't our William!' Delighted, he slapped his brother on the shoulder in greeting. His indignation and anger faded. William was conscious that the tension had eased in the tavern. Men laughed and resumed their games. There'd be no more trouble now. Jamie always made a fool of himself when he was drunk but William kept him in check and everyone knew it.
'Well met there, brother!' Jamie continued in delight. 'Will you take a glass of brandy with me? Mistress Shotton! Another glass of brandy for me brother.'
'I think you've drunk enough already,' William said sharply. 'But I'll take one with you if it'll shut up your stupid mouth. Get your money put away, man; they'll rob you as soon as look at you around here. Here – take it.'
He nodded a polite greeting at Tom Philips then the two men gathered up Jamie's money from the floor. Sensing that the drama was over for the moment, the other drinkers resumed their conversations and card games.
'I can look after myself,' Jamie slurred. 'A few thieving buggers don't frighten me. I'll crack their bloody skulls together if they try to rob me.'
'Aye, maybes so,' William replied quietly. 'But you won't be able to crack the skull of the hangman as he's slipping the noose around your neck, will you?'
James blinked and stared in confusion.
'The hangman?' he queried. 'Why? Is having a bet on the cards a hanging offence now?'
'No. Haven't heard the news?'
'News? What news?' asked Tom.
Just at that moment, one of the landlady's pretty daughters sidled over with another glass and a bottle of brandy and plonked herself down in William's lap. There was always a rush amongst the barmaids to serve him. He knew he had become quite a romantic

figure in the parish since he had been so publicly jilted by Sarah Aynsley. There were plenty of young women who had hinted that they would happily fill her place in his heart – and his bed. Ma Shotton's daughters usually pulled rank and elbowed the others out of the way in the rush to serve him.

Unfortunately, he had been up half the night calving, and besides which he had things on his mind tonight besides a quick fumble in the piss-stinking alley that ran down beside the inn. He flirted, smiled and stroked the pert breast that strained for release at the top of the girl's bodice. Then he slapped her playfully on her petticoated backside and dismissed her. Jamie grinned as he watched his brother flirting: Tom Phillips gaped in wide-eyed amazement. Disappointed, the barmaid glided away.

Now William leaned forward conspiratorially. 'There's been a robbery. A big one. Last night.'

'Where?' asked Tom, as he gently added the water to his brandy.

'Kirkley Hall. Some bugger broke in and stole all the bloody rent money.'

The jug slipped from Tom's grasp and crashed back down onto the table. The liquid slopped everywhere. Jamie's jaw dropped open.

'So that's why I'm saying you don't want to be flashing your money around at the moment, brother,' William continued. 'Or folks will think you got it all from Kirkley Hall.'

'No! You're coddin on, man?' Tom turned pale.

'As God's my witness, 'tis the truth,' William said quietly. 'Our niece Lizzie came home from the Hall and told us this afternoon. She said there was hell to pay this morning when it was discovered. Everybody's blaming everybody else – Aynsley is raging like a bull with a slashed head.'

'Who do they think took it, like?'

'There's talk of that gang – the ones who stole those horses from Trevelyan's at Wallington Hall.'

Now Tom turned even paler. 'Sir John threatened to burn out half his parish if there were any more stealing,' he stammered. His ramshackle cottage was a bit too close to Trevelyan's estate for comfort.

'Aye, maybe the thieving swine have moved over here,' William said thoughtfully. 'Look, don't fret, Tom – Ogle's not the kind to seek vengeance on innocent folk; he's not going to burn cottages containing women and bairns. Mind you, it's a big jump from stealing a few horses to taking the rent money,' mused William.

Suddenly Jamie burst out into loud and drunken laughter.
'How much?' he asked his brother. 'How much did the buggers take?'
'All of it – hundreds – possibly a thousand pounds. Lizzie said when Aynsley arrived this morning, the office had been broken into and everything taken.'
'The Lord be praised!' Jamie shouted with glee. 'Old Aynsley must be shitting himself!' He threw his head back and roared with delight at the prospect.
'Stop laughing, Jamie,' William hissed. 'This is serious.'
'Not for me 'tis not!' slurred his brother. 'I wouldn't be in Aynsley's boots for the world! This is the best news I have heard all year! God, I wish I had been there to see his face!'
'Everyone's watching you.'
'Well, let them!' laughed Jamie. 'It has made my day to hear this news,'
'It'll be no laughing matter if they arrest and hang you for this, brother. Throwing your money about like a fool only a day after the biggest robbery this county has ever known.'
William's warning fell on drunken, deaf ears. Jamie staggered to his feet. His stool crashed down onto the flagstones behind him. He was flushed. His blue eyes were glistening and unfocused. He waved his glass in the air. The amber liquid glinted attractively in the warm, orange glow from the firelight. 'Here – a toast. A toast!' he yelled suddenly to everyone in the tavern.
All heads turned – yet again – in his direction.
'A toast – do you hear? To all the thieves and robbers of Kirkley Hall! May they thrive like the devil, and plague that miserable bastard Aynsley to his death!'
A wave of laughter rippled around the Seven Stars, followed by a murmur of agreement.
'I'll drink to that!' A man clambered to his feet. 'Good for you, Jamie.'
'And I,' declared another. 'Aynsley's a bloody tyrant and a lecher – he deserves to suffer.'
A dozen or so men now stood up. They all laughed and joined in with the toast – all damning Michael Aynsley to hell.

CHAPTER THREE

Monday 10th April, 1809

Darkness had long since settled on the coaching inn at Newhamm Edge when the post horn sounded and the northbound mail coach rumbled through the archway into the courtyard. The exhausted drivers reined in the tired, steaming horses and the livery stable staff rushed to unhitch them in their well-rehearsed routine. The beaming landlord wiped his hands on his stained apron and took his usual place at the entrance to the inn, ready to welcome his guests. The northbound coach always rested at the inn overnight; few still dared to travel after dusk across the vast expanse of empty, barren fells between Northumberland and Scotland.

The passengers began to alight and picked their way across the piles of horse muck and pools of urine towards the welcoming light and warmth of the inn. Amongst them was Stephen Lavender, a Principal Officer with the Bow Street Runners. As his assistant, Constable Woods, struggled to retrieve their luggage, Lavender's sharp eyes scanned the courtyard, taking in every detail of the scene around him.

'Be it Detective Lavender?' the landlord asked as he reached the doorway.

'Yes, my good fellow,' Lavender nodded.

'They're waiting for you up at Kirkley,' continued the innkeeper. 'The trap'll be here in a minute to take you there. Would you like some refreshment, while you wait?'

The detective paused for a moment and scanned the calibre of the hostelry. Deciding that this wretched place was probably no more disease-ridden than the other filth-infested taverns which they had endured over the past few days since leaving London, he nodded in agreement. His work increasingly meant that he had to travel around Britain; no county was exempt from the most heinous crimes, it seemed. Lavender did not enjoy the coaching inns or travelling by the bone-rattling mail coaches overnight. He far preferred the more stately stage coaches. However, speed was of the essence in this case and the mail coaches were far quicker.

The landlord despatched a servant inside to prepare refreshments while the detective waited for Constable Woods. He was grateful for a chance to stand up for a while and stretch his aching limbs. 'So, you know who I am, do you?' he asked.

‘Aye, sir,’ replied the landlord. ‘Ye’r Detective Lavender, from Bow Street in Lunnen. The whole county’s been waiting for you to arrive, for these last few days.’

‘Really?’ the detective said sardonically. ‘The whole county, eh?’

The innkeeper scanned Lavender’s clothing curiously. ‘We thought you Bow Street runners wore red waistcoats and blue coats,’ he commented, clearly disappointed.

Lavender sighed. He was dressed in black from the sole of his gleaming, leather boots to the tip of his hat. Only his spotless, white cravat and glittering, silver buttons broke up the darkness of his attire. ‘That’s the horse patrol – not the thief takers,’ he explained for the twentieth time this year. ‘They wear the red waistcoats and blue coats.’

‘Do you think ye’ll find the thieving bugger who robbed Kirkley Hall?’

‘Well, I guess I’ve lost the element of surprise but let’s hope so, my good man. Let’s hope so.’

The trap didn’t turn up for another hour and it was nearly ten at night before the two men approached Kirkley Hall. They had enjoyed a good meal, warmth and some comfort at the inn but this final uncomfortable ride along rough-hewn country lanes in the bitter cold to Kirkley had damaged Lavender’s temper. He was silent and brooding.

‘At least we’ll have soft beds to sleep in tonight,’ his cockney constable said optimistically. ‘I’ll swear that last inn where we stayed had fleas in the beds.’ When Lavender didn’t reply he tried a different subject. ‘Nice, sing-song way of speaking they have round these ’ere parts,’ he observed.

‘Mmm, don’t let it fool you, my friend,’ Lavender replied at last. ‘Voices like angels but hearts as black as the devil’s.’

‘Eh?’

‘It’s true,’ the detective continued, darkly. ‘This area was the most lawless in England a century or so back. The border region between England and Scotland was plagued by gangs known as border reivers. Loyal only to their own family or clan, they would burn down the farms, and rob anyone they did not recognise as kin. Extortion, blackmail and rape were also common. Even Royalty feared to travel through Northumberland back then. Everyone was involved in thieving and robbery.’

Constable Woods gaped at him in the darkness before concluding simply: ‘It don’t seem like much has changed then, does it, sir?’

The trap swept up the front drive towards Kirkley Hall which was bathed in silver moonlight on top of the ridge in front of them. The master was now in residence and the main house had burst into life. Dozens of tallow candles had been lit in the crystal chandeliers and the ornate candelabras, which illuminated the main reception rooms. The large, rectangular windows glowed attractively in the creamy stone walls, casting pools of warm, yellow light onto the patio which fronted the building.

'That looks grand,' observed Woods.

'We've solved crimes at grander houses than this,' snapped Lavender. Then, conscious of the flapping ears of their driver, he added more tactfully: 'But I believe Kirkley Hall is just one of several country estates owned by Mr. Ogle.'

'Ooh, the front door for us today is it?' Woods said. The trap had stopped before a short flight of stone steps which led up to the imposing oak doors of the main entrance.

'We have not been elevated in status,' warned Lavender. 'This is a sign of how serious the theft is to the owner. No doubt, at the conclusion of the case, we'll be asked to leave by the back door.'

A servant led Lavender and Woods through the elegant interior of Kirkley Hall, the exhaustion and cynicism lifted from the weary detective. Unperturbed by the gilded opulence which surrounded him, he strode confidently across the marble floors to Nathanial Ogle's pale blue and gold silk drawing room. Above their heads was a blazing candle chandelier and a magnificent gold-leaf and lapis lazuli ceiling rose.

There were two men in the room: a sullen brute by the fireplace and a tiny man with a towering wig, slumped in the chair by the fire. The butler had barely finished announcing them before the little man leapt to his feet and pumped the detective's hand warmly in greeting.

'Welcome! Welcome! Thank goodness you are here, Detective. What a terrible business this is – terrible! Come and warm yourself by the fire, Constable Woods. What a dreadful cold, spring we are having.' Small, pale blue eyes peered hopefully at Lavender and Woods beneath greying eyebrows. Woods nodded politely and moved closer to inspect the naked cherubs carved on the marble fireplace which dominated the back wall of the room.

'Thank you, Mr. Ogle.' Lavender smiled. He had been prepared to bow and was somewhat bemused at the warmth of the welcome. He assessed his new employer quickly. The old fashioned wig was clearly worn for habit and to add a few inches to the height of the little man but it was at odds with the rest of his expensive clothing. His shirt collar was so high it went above his jaw line, almost framing the white face which poked out of his silk cravat.

The detective then turned his attention to the angry, mud-splattered and shaggy-haired brute beside Ogle who was shifting his weight uncomfortably from one foot to another.

'This is Aynsley, my steward,' Ogle informed him. 'He was the one who discovered the theft and who has been trying to recover the money.'

And the one who lost the money in the first place, thought Lavender. He nodded coolly in Aynsley's direction.

Lavender's face was expressionless but he was surprised to see Aynsley here. The man looked hunted and nervous – as would any servant who had just lost his master's rent money. However, Aynsley was obviously still in employment at Kirkley. Either Ogle practised Christian forgiveness to a level unknown by most of the gentry or the man was foolish beyond belief. Loyalty like this could make Lavender's job more difficult.

'A terrible business! Shocking! The Lord save us from such things!' Ogle murmured as he sank back into the gold velvet cushions of his fireside chair.

'Pleased to make your acquaintance, like, Detective,' the steward growled. He dropped his gaze before Lavender's cold, hard stare. 'Likewise, Mr. Aynsley, likewise.'

Lavender turned back to Ogle. 'I have here, in my pocket, the letter your London secretary sent to me at Bow Street.' He pulled out his black notebook and unfolded the letter. 'He apprised me of the main facts relating to the theft of the rent money. Can I ask, sir, has any of the money been recovered?'

'Alas, no,' confirmed the squire.

'What have your initial investigations into the crime revealed, Mr. Aynsley?' Aynsley's jaw dropped open slackly and he gaped.

'Nothing, Detective Lavender, nothing,' Ogle interrupted. 'That's why we need you here. How soon can you start?'

'Well, if I can have a private office to interview those who were on the premises that night…'

'Yes. Yes. You can have Aynsley's office – or my butler's – whichever suits you best.'

'…and naturally, I'd like to see the scene of the crime, as well.'

'Naturally, naturally – Aynsley will take you there at once.'

Lavender paused and the glimmer of a smile curled the edges of his lips. 'It might be better to see the crime scene in the daylight, Mr. Ogle,' he suggested slowly.

'Of course! Of course! What am I thinking?' Ogle said hurriedly. He glanced at the elaborately wrought ormolu clock in the centre of the mantelpiece. 'Oh my goodness it is ten o'clock! You must be famished – Edwards – ask Cook to rustle up some supper for these gentlemen.' The butler, who had remained inconspicuous throughout their meeting so far, now bowed and backed stiffly out of the room.

Lavender was about to decline but then he saw the look of delight on his constable's face. Woods' appetite was legendary at Bow Street. Eating two hearty suppers on an evening was no problem for his assistant, who never seemed to be bothered by the indigestion which often plagued his superior. Despite his gargantuan appetite, the stocky constable was all muscle. He led a very active life with the Bow Street horse patrol when he was not accompanying Lavender on his cases.

'We'd be grateful for some supper,' he informed Mr. Ogle. 'We'll inspect the crime scene at first light.'

'Yes. Yes. Aynsley will take you everywhere you need to go.'

Lavender nodded and unfolded the letter in his hand.

'I understand from your secretary's letter, that the monies were carefully hidden in…' he consulted the letter, '…a secret panel in the wall.'

'That's right,' Ogle confirmed. 'It was Aynsley's hiding place. He always secreted the rent money there – and other valuables – until he could get them to the bank vault. He sent me a letter – why the very night of the crime! Saying…'

Here he rose and hurried over towards an elegant side table, whose mellow patina gleamed with layers of beeswax. He pulled out a sheet of paper from the pile scattered across its glossy surface. His wig bobbed from side to side and he lifted his pince nez onto his nose as he read:

"…the rents have been collected and the bags of gold and silver, along with the rolls of notes are in the wooden chest hidden behind the secret panel. The devil himself could never find it!"'

'Ha! Well, he did!' Constable Woods interjected.

There was a pause while everyone looked curiously at Woods. The constable coughed in embarrassment over his outburst and then shrank back inside his old coat and fixed his gaze on the row of

Ogle ancestors who stared down at them from gilt frames on the silk wallpaper.

'Why I'd barely finished reading this note,' Mr. Ogle continued, 'when another one arrived from Edwards – to tell me of the robbery! Naturally, I raced here as soon as I could – and a terribly uncomfortable journey I had too!'

Not as uncomfortable as ours, I'll wager, thought Lavender. He tried to look sympathetic, however, as Ogle sank back exhausted into his plush chair by the fire.

'So what do you make of all this then, Detective?'

There was another pause and everyone now looked expectantly at Lavender. He cleared his throat.

'It is obvious to me, so far, Mr. Ogle, that the devil has had nothing to do with it.'

Ogle gasped.

'The crime has been committed by someone, or some people, who had intimate knowledge of the interior of Kirkley Hall, the Steward's Office and the secret panel in the wall. The thief, or thieves, knew exactly where to find both the office and the money.'

'But how can this be so when there were only three of us – myself, Aynsley and his son – who knew about the secret panel?' Ogle demanded.

'There was obviously one more person – if not several more people – who were privy to the location of your hiding place, Mr. Ogle,' Lavender said gently.

'But who?' demanded the Squire.

'This is what I intend to find out,' promised Lavender, his gaze fixed firmly on Michael Aynsley. 'Let's see what the morning brings, shall we?'

Tuesday 11th April, 1809

Stephen Lavender did not need much sleep and despite the stress of the journey up to Northumberland, he slept well. Washed, shaved and dressed smartly in a fresh set of clothes, he startled Dorothy Hodgeson, the cook, by appearing in the doorway of her kitchen just after six o'clock.

Insisting that he didn't want the fuss of eating in the servant's dining hall, he enjoyed a simple breakfast of kippers and honey toast at her kitchen table. Thanking Mrs. Hodgeson politely, he asked for directions to the steward's office and sent the young footman off to find him a short ladder.

Lavender ambled leisurely across the cobbled courtyard, appreciating the fresh morning air and admiring the huge cedar tree. He paused beneath the arched entrance to the yard and took in the magnificent view of the beautiful parkland which swept majestically down to the glistening River Blyth. On the other side of the valley, the darker fells rose in the distance. The sky overhead was such a vast expanse of penetrating blue it almost caught his breath in surprise. He suddenly became aware of how much his vision had been impeded by the smoke and the towering, soot-coated buildings back home in London. He almost felt awed by the dazzling, early morning brightness and the shimmering clarity of that northern sky.

Reluctantly, he dragged himself away and tried to focus his mind on the task ahead. A close examination of the outside of the steward's office revealed nothing. It was obvious to Lavender how the thief had climbed onto the flat roof but he had left no trace of himself, not even a boot print, on the scuffed and crumbling window ledge of the ground floor storeroom. He quickly realised that even a man who was half drunk would have been able to scramble up there. When the footman returned with the ladder, Lavender climbed up onto the flat roof. It had obviously been a simple matter for the burglar to smash the pane of glass in the sash window of the office, reach inside to the clasp and then lever the window upwards to gain entry.

Locking such a vast amount of money in this office showed great negligence or blind stupidity. He sighed, and then remembered where he was. The owners of the great houses in London were more security conscious and took steps to protect their property from the many intruders who lurked in the crime-ridden capital. However, out here in the shires, naivety combined with a ridiculous belief that the peasant classes knew their place and would never violate the homes of the wealthy, left most of Britain's country houses vulnerable to the opportunist thief. This, he remembered, was what kept him in a job. Even in Northumberland, once the most lawless county in England, it seemed that the nobility had become negligent about their security.

His investigation revealed absolutely nothing about the thief's identity. A piece of card had been temporarily placed over the broken pane on the inside of the glass to stop draughts; most of the shattered glass had fallen inside the office and had been swept up by a housemaid. The broken pane and the one remaining shard of shattered glass which crunched beneath the sole of his boot were the only evidence that the burglar had ever been there.

There was still no sign of the glowering Michael Aynsley or Constable Woods when he descended to the courtyard, so he sent the helpful young footman to get the butler and his keys to gain access to the steward's office.

The footman returned with the news that Mr. Edwards did not have a key – 'only Mr. Aynsley, the steward could get into the office, 'cept of course, the master, and he was still a-bed.'

At that moment, Constable Woods appeared with sleep still in the corner of his eyes and a piece of toast in his hand. He looked as if he had dressed hurriedly. Lavender dismissed the footman.

'Find out anything, sir?'

'Nothing – absolutely nothing so far. Except of course, the fact that the thief knew exactly what he was doing and where he was going. He was cocky and confident enough to do it quickly and efficiently, without leaving a trace of himself outside the building. It is obvious to me, anyone with two strong legs – and a good head for heights – could have got up there. We need to pick up the investigation on the inside of the steward's office but alas, it seems that the steward is not here, and Edwards, the butler, does not have a key.'

'Well, at least this rules him out,' Woods observed.

'Who?'

'The butler – that Edwards must be seventy if he's a day,' the constable continued, 'and the man is very shaky on his pins. He'll have not got up on the roof. No, I think that we can definitely say in this case that the butler didn't do it.'

Lavender stared at his constable in disbelief. Woods had heard the phrase 'the butler did it' at a tuppenny music hall show in Vauxhall Gardens the previous summer. Now he always made a point of humorously working the phrase into the conversation at some point during every investigation.

Suddenly, there was a thunder of hooves on the cobbles and a flurry of cursing. Michael Aynsley had finally arrived. He dismounted and snarled at the groom who took his horse. The daylight now revealed to Lavender what the soft candlelight of the previous evening had masked; Aynsley had black circles around his eyes from lack of sleep and his wind-tanned face was deeply etched with worry.

Aynsley was curt in his greeting and then led them into the storeroom and up the narrow stairs into his cluttered and functional office.

The first thing they saw when they went through the door was the broken wooden panel. However, once again the detective could discover nothing. The splintered wood had been swept up by the maid. Aynsley admitted that half the household and a large section of the rest of the parish had trooped into the office to examine the scene of the crime. Lavender sighed and realised that looking for any further evidence of the thief was pointless.

He sat down in Aynsley's chair and picked up the top sheaf of paper from the table which contained a list of names.

'Those be the names of them what was on the premises on the night of the robbery,' Aynsley told him. 'I thought it might be useful to draw up such a list.'

Lavender scanned Aynsley's scrawling handwriting.

'Who are these two at the bottom?'

'That'll be the carpenter and his mate. They were here doing repairs during the day – but they went home before dark.'

The detective nodded thoughtfully, replaced the list on the table and picked up one of the account books which lay scattered across the surface.

The steward started shifting his weight from one foot to the other.

'Thank you, Mr. Aynsley. I'm sure this list will come in most helpful. Right, I just need to ask you a few more questions and then I'll see the rest of the staff.'

'What here? In my office?' Aynsley enquired, clearly annoyed. His eyes flicked nervously across the pile of ledgers.

What is he hiding? Lavender wondered.

'You'll be more comfortable in the butler's office.'

Lavender ignored the comment. 'So, after you had taken Mr. Ogle's letter to the mail coach, at the posting inn, where did you go?' he asked.

'I don't see as that matters,' the steward snapped.

'It was the night of the robbery, Mr. Aynsley. I need to establish the whereabouts of all the staff of Kirkley Hall on that particular night.'

'So I'm a suspect now, am I?'

'No more or less than anyone else,' the detective replied. His eyes still roved leisurely over the columns of figures in the ledger.

Woods took out a notebook and dipped a quill into an inkpot at the other end of the table.

'It's a simple question, Mr. Aynsley,' Woods said. 'Where was you on the evening when Kirkley Hall was robbed?'

'Well, I drank a glass of ale at the inn,' the steward admitted reluctantly, 'and then I went to see an old friend of my wife's – Mistress Charlotte MacDonald .'

'And your wife went with you?'

'What? Nellie? Nay! My wife's been dead nigh on nine months now. No, she'd left a few pieces, a sewing box and such like for her friend – so that night I took them round to Lottie's – Mistress MacDonald's . Then I went home to my bed.'

'You live alone?' Lavender glanced up sharply.

'Aye. Since my daughter upped and married – I've lived by mesen.'

'And Mistress MacDonald will verify this alibi?'

'This what?'

'Alibi, Mr. Aynsley. Alibi. A word from Latin which describes a plea, that when the alleged act took place – you were somewhere else. In other words, that you were with Mistress MacDonald during the early part of the evening before you went home to your bed. She will say this, will she?'

'Aye, she will,' Aynsley was clearly uncomfortable.

'Fair enough. Just one more question for now. Have you and your men searched the grounds of Kirkley Hall for the money, as well as the interior of the hall?'

Aynsley threw back his great, leonine head and burst out laughing.

'What? You think the thieving bugger may have dropped it on the way out?'

'No, Mr. Aynsley,' Lavender replied patiently. 'I think he may have left behind what he didn't need. That amount of money weighs a lot and most of these bank notes…' He pointed to the information in the ledger in front of him. '…were made out to Kirkley Hall. They would have been completely useless to anyone else. If he is an intelligent man – the thief would probably have known this. If he's not an intelligent man, the thief probably wouldn't have wanted the notes anyway; most British commoners don't trust paper money.'

Aynsley paused, clearly surprised by Lavender's perception. 'We just searched the hall and the servants' quarters,' he admitted gruffly and flushed as he realised he had been negligent.

'Thank you. That is exactly what I expected.'

Aynsley turned to go but when he reached the door, Lavender called after him. 'Before you go – who do you think stole the money, Mr. Aynsley?'

'Me?'

'Yes. You.'

'I didn't think on it at first, but I'd lay a wager it was Charlton – the carpenter's mate.'

'Why's that?'

'The stupid bugger was up here messing about with the window when we were stacking the money away. He was acting oddly. The man's always broke and in debt.'

'Thank you, Mr. Aynsley. You can go now.'

Aynsley shrugged and disappeared down the stairs, Lavender rose, walked over to the broken window and watched him leave the building and cross the courtyard below.

'Seems a funny time of night to deliver sewing boxes to the local widows,' Constable Woods observed.

'It certainly does,' Lavender agreed. 'I think there might be more to the steward than just the ugly brute that meets the eye. Now, Woods, I want you to take two or three men and do a thorough search of the grounds. You're looking for one or more large sacks containing up to one thousand, one hundred pounds and any clues which the thief might have left behind of his identity. Oh, and send the butler – Edwards – in to see me.'

Woods nodded and left.

Lavender sighed, sat back down at the table and pulled out a pocketbook into which he made several notes. When he finished, he picked up yet another accounts ledger from the table and examined it closely. By the time the elderly Mr. Edwards limped painfully up the stairs to the office, a deep frown had formed across Lavender's brow.

The detective and his assistant continued to work solidly through the morning. Lavender interviewed nearly all of the staff – including the terrified little Lizzie Charlton. She refused to look at him, twisting her pinafore nervously in her hands the entire time, and answered his questions by nodding and shaking her head. Lavender made a note that the Charlton man Aynsley had accused was her Uncle Jamie, but instinct told him this frightened little girl would have been a very poor choice of accomplice for such an audacious robbery. Meanwhile, Woods obtained a large map of the grounds of Kirkley Hall and, with the help of several gardeners and gamekeepers, began a thorough and detailed search of every rhododendron bush, vegetable plot and flower bed in the park.

Back in the office, Lavender was dismissing the footman from his interview when he was interrupted by the arrival of Dorothy

Hodgeson, the cook. She bore down on him carrying a silver tea tray, stacked high with plates of fresh bread and butter, pie and fruit cake.

'Good afternoon, Detective,' she said as she handed him a plate and a napkin. 'I took the liberty of bringing you some refreshment. I thought you might enjoy a nice cup of tea while we had our little chat, like.'

'This is most kind of you, Madam.' Lavender was amused. He observed her carefully from beneath his hooded eyelids. 'It was also well anticipated. I was just about to send for you next.'

'Well, we can't have you thinking that we're all uncivilised, thieving heathens in Ponteland. What with you coming so far from Lunnen to help us, like,' she said as she poured out the steaming tea.

'The thought never crossed my mind,' he purred.

'Milk or lemon?' she asked. He pointed towards the milk jug.

'Well, we have our fair share of Godless folk here in Ponteland, of course,' she confided. 'There's many around here that I could mention who would steal the last penny from a beggar. But I can assure you, Detective Lavender, that I'm an honest, God-fearing woman. Before you ask – I was exactly where every honest, God-fearing person should have been on the night of the robbery.'

'Where's that, Mistress Hodgeson?' he queried as she handed him a cup and saucer.

'Why tucked up all cosy in me own bed with my husband, of course!'

'This is very interesting, Madam, but I am curious – just who are these people who would steal the last penny from a beggar?'

He paused and she steadily returned his gaze.

'You see, we have a dreadful crime to solve here Mistress Hodgeson,' he continued. 'I – and your employer, Mr. Ogle – would be most grateful for any help which you can give us to help catch the thief.'

She understood his meaning very well and waved her hand towards the food. 'Help yourself to a piece of pie and a couple of slices of cake, Detective Lavender, and I'll tell you all I can about the local heathens.'

'Thank you, Mistress Hodgeson…'

'For a start, you need to know the truth about that devil Aynsley….'

An hour later, Lavender took a stroll over to the walled kitchen garden to see how Woods was getting along with his search for the missing money. The weak sunlight failed to dispel the cold, but Lavender was glad to stretch his legs. Woods was hungry and looked thoroughly fed up. He was watching three gardeners as they raked about beneath a row of currant bushes next to the crumbling, grey wall.

'Any luck, Woods?'

'No, Sir. Not a thing. This is the last section – unless you want us to search the Pheasant Wood, as well?'

Lavender glanced down at the map of the grounds in Woods' hand.

'Is that a road on the other side of the wall?' he asked.

'Yes, sir, the Morpeth Road.'

'It might reveal something, yet,' Lavender said vaguely. 'According to the cook, Michael Aynsley told her last week that he had a feeling the money might turn up.'

Woods glanced sharply at his superior.

'Did he now?'

'Oh, yes – rather an odd thing to say, don't you think?'

Woods nodded in agreement.

'The interviews I have conducted have been very revealing,' Lavender continued. 'In fact, based on the allegations I have heard so far, we could probably hang half the parish – and transport the rest.'

Woods smiled.

'I can honestly say I have never heard about such a bunch of lying, thieving, fornicating rogues as the good people of Ponteland in my entire career.'

Woods laughed and was about to ask for some details when suddenly two of the gardeners began to shout and wave furiously. One of them pulled something heavy out of a tangled bush.

'Quick, Woods! That man has found something!'

They raced over towards the men and were just in time to help the gardener drag out a large, brown sack from behind the dense forest of raspberry canes. It was passed to Lavender who opened it and looked inside. A smile of relief broke out across his normally expressionless face.

'Now we are getting somewhere, Woods!' he exclaimed. 'Now we are getting somewhere!'

CHAPTER FOUR

Half an hour later Detective Lavender found the butler in the still room, and asked for an audience with Mr. Ogle. Edwards and two footmen were laying a plate of game pie, translucent white, bone china crockery and a crystal decanter onto several silver trays.

'You may have to wait,' Edwards informed him. 'He's got company.'

Lavender nodded patiently but when the butler and the footmen filed out bearing their trays, he followed them into the spacious, marbled hallway. As they disappeared into the drawing room, Lavender crossed to the front doors. A magnificent gold and black state carriage with liveried footmen waited on the gravel driveway outside.

The coat of arms of the Duke of Northumberland was emblazoned on the gleaming paintwork of the carriage door. Lavender smiled and raised an amused eyebrow. Aynsley had told him that half the county turned up at the Hall in the days following the robbery, all full of curiosity. Now Nathanial Ogle was back in residence, it would appear that the other gentrified half of the county had started to arrive at the Hall.

Lavender returned to the interior of the hallway to wait for the summons he felt would be soon. Sure enough, five minutes later he was shown into the drawing room.

Nathanial Ogle was slumped in his usual seat by the fire, where he fed lumps of game pie to his fat spaniel. Today he wore a ruffled black and yellow striped satin waistcoat which gave him the appearance of a fat bumblebee. Opposite him, an elegant woman, whom Lavender assumed to be the duchess, poured tea from the Spode teapot into china cups. She wore a simple white, muslin dress, fastened with an ornamental, gold clasp across her bosom. Small sapphires glistened on her earlobes.

By the window stood Hugh Percy, Duke of Northumberland. He held a crystal glass containing a generous measure of Madeira, which he passed restlessly from hand to hand. His features were gaunt and stern beneath his greying hair. He was soberly attired in chestnut brown coat, buff-coloured breeches and a cream, silk waistcoat. Only the diamond pin which secured the matching silk cravat and the exquisite tailoring of his coat hinted at the duke's enormous wealth.

Lavender knew that Percy had seen active service in the American Colonies with the Northumberland Fusiliers. He had earned a reputation down in London for being a no-nonsense landowner with a rough and ready manner who did not suffer fools gladly. He glowered with cold disdain when the detective was introduced. However, Lavender welcomed his presence; he suspected that he might now have an ally when it came to imparting some of his more distressing discoveries to Mr. Ogle. The duke would not be blinded by loyalty to a servant.

Lavender bowed low.

'Detective Lavender, may I introduce their graces, the Duke and Duchess of Northumberland? They are most eager to hear what your investigation has discovered pertaining to my burglary.'

Lavender bowed again. 'A pleasure to meet you both.'

'Likewise, I'm sure, Detective,' the duchess said.

'Your reputation precedes you, by the way,' the duke said. 'My wife tells me that you retrieved the Hutchinson Diamonds for the Countess of Skelton.'

'Indeed,' Lavender confirmed. 'And your reputation precedes you, Your Grace. As a young man, I was an avid follower of your campaign in our war against the rebels in America. I remember reading about your success at the battle of Long Island and how you stormed Fort Washington.'

The duke was visibly impressed. 'You are very well informed, Lavender. Just a pity though, that we won those damned battles but still lost the bloody Colony, eh?'

'Quite so, sir.'

'Now, what news have you got for Mr. Ogle?

Lavender cleared his throat. 'This morning, I went straight to the scene of the crime. I found a broken first floor window; the door to the steward's office forced; a wooden panel smashed in the office wall – and behind it a money chest ransacked…'

'A wooden wall panel smashed?' the duke interrupted, angrily. 'What new devilry is this?'

'No, he's right, Hugh,' Ogle explained. 'It was Aynsley's hiding place. He always secreted the rent money there – and other valuables – until he could get them to the bank vault. The thief smashed his way into the money.'

'You do not have a stronghold in the hall?' the duchess asked.

'Of course I do,' Ogle told her. 'It is in my chamber – but naturally I have the only key.'

There was a stunned silence for a moment. Then Hugh Percy turned back to Lavender. 'No one heard anything?'

'It appears not.'

The duke laughed sharply. 'Either you need to water down the beer you serve in the servants' hall, Nathanial, or they're covering up for each other – the lying sods. So what do you make of this then, Detective?'

'That the thief or thieves knew exactly where to find both the office and the money. Allegedly, there were only three men who knew about this – Aynsley, his son and Mr. Ogle.'

'Surely, you're not suggesting that Michael Aynsley – or his son – had anything to do with the robbery?' the squire groaned.

'It has happened before, Nathanial; landowners like us are robbed by their stewards all the time.'

'That's what I thought,' Lavender said, quick to capitalise on the duke's support. 'So I spent some time questioning Michael Aynsley.'

'How did you find him, Detective?' the duchess asked.

Lavender paused for a moment to examine the graceful and elegant woman seated on the sofa in front of the fire. Her dark, brown curls were discreetly dyed to cover up the grey but her complexion was good – only lightly powdered and rouged – unlike the over-painted dolls he so often did business with in London drawing rooms. Her dark eyes were pretty and intelligent.

'He was nervous – very nervous. In fact, one of the female servants…' Here he paused to rustle through his notebook. '…a Mistress Dorothy Hodgeson has already told me how excessively nervous Mr. Aynsley became when he heard that I had been summoned from Bow Street to investigate the case…'

'Oh, I won't have this!' Ogle bobbed up and down on his chair, like an agitated insect. 'Aynsley is a good man – a bit rough, I admit – but he and his sons have served me loyally for nearly thirty years! Why he ran the Home Farm at Thorneyford before he was steward here! Michael Aynsley is a decent, honest, God-fearing man. I cannot believe for one minute that someone I know and respect so much could have robbed me so viciously.'

'But someone has, Nathanial. Someone whom you probably know – and trust – has broken in here, into Kirkley Hall and has callously robbed you of over one thousand pounds,' said Her Grace.

'And you have to admit – it's not looking good for Aynsley,' the duke added.

Lavender decided it was now time to inform them of more of his discoveries about Michael Aynsley. 'Sadly, it wouldn't be the first time Aynsley has robbed you either, Mr. Ogle.'

'What?' gasped the startled squire.

'Explain yourself, man,' the duke demanded.

Lavender cleared his throat and glanced back down at his notes.

'I have made a cursory examination of the accounts ledgers and I am sorry to inform you that – even to my untrained eye – there are several inconsistencies.'

'So he's been fiddling the books as well, has he?' the duke enquired.

'That's right,' confirmed Lavender. 'I would recommend that a third party be brought in to Kirkley Hall to examine the accounts. It may be that he has been robbing you for years, Mr. Ogle.'

Ogle groaned and shrank back in his seat.

'And there is more, I'm afraid, Mr. Ogle. I believe Mr. Aynsley may have once been a man of good character and repute. However, I understand that since his wife died last summer he has become bitter and twisted…'

Ogle waved his hand dismissively from his chair by the fire. 'Well, grief can affect some men that way. There is much comfort to be found in prayer, of course, but not all men take this path.'

'…he has also degenerated morally and consorts with the lowest kind of women and…'

Three pairs of eyes stared at him in surprise.

'..If you will excuse me, Ma'am, for mentioning such things in your presence,' he continued, bowing slightly in the direction of the duchess. '…It is common knowledge that he keeps a mistress – the Widow MacDonald – in Stamfordham.'

The duchess, who knew all about mistresses – especially royal mistresses – tried to hide her smile.

'What! Who told you this? Why this is base slander, surely?' Ogle gasped.

'I think not,' said Lavender gently and he referred to his notes again. 'It was the servant woman Hodgeson who first mentioned it – she has been most helpful. Her comments have been verified by other persons of your household since.'

'Well, I've never heard of this. I am distressed at the thought of Aynsley's soul being in such peril! Where would a man of his station in life get the money to keep a mistress?'

There was a pause as the other three observed the distressed and confused squire. Time seemed to stand still for a moment. Lavender could hear the gentle snores of the fat dog, asleep by Ogle's feet.

'He may have stolen it from you, sir,' he said, gently.

'That's what we've been trying to tell you, Nathanial, for the last ten minutes.' The irritated duke twisted the stem of his Madeira glass in between his large fingers; the fiery, red liquid flashed in the light.

'I still cannot believe it,' Ogle sighed.

'Well, I'll be straight with you, Lavender. I'm impressed,' the duke said. 'You've found out more about Nathanial's household in the last few hours, than he's found out about them in the last ten years – and you've got a likely suspect for the robbery. I have to confess, I thought it was all the doing of a local gang, at first but you've convinced me it's this fellow. So what's the next move? Shall I summon the guard to search this Aynsley's house for the money?'

Lavender smiled. 'That won't be necessary, Sir.'

'Well, the house of the Widow MacDonald then? The lads would probably enjoy that.'

'No, that won't be necessary either,' said Lavender, dramatically. 'You see – I have already recovered the bulk of the money.'

'Good gracious!' the duchess gasped.

Ogle's jaw dropped. His small eyes widen with surprise.

'What! Are you playing with us, man?' the duke demanded.

'No, Sir. I rarely joke. Allow me to summon Constable Woods, my assistant.'

While the others looked on in amazement, he walked over to the bell pull by the fireplace and gave it two sharp tugs. Woods had obviously been waiting for the signal because it was only moments later when the door opened and the constable entered accompanied by a footman. Between them they carried the two black money sacks they had discovered amongst the raspberries. Following Lavender's directions, they placed them carefully on a rosewood table and then stepped back.

Ogle closed his gaping mouth, leapt to his feet and scurried across to the table. He was quickly joined by the duke. They opened the sacks and pulled out the banknotes and examined them.

'Good God!' the duke exclaimed.

'This is amazing! Praise the Lord!' Ogle gasped in delight.

Lavender thanked his assistant, took a piece of paper from his hand and dismissed Woods and the footman.

'You should have told us straight away, man!' the duke exclaimed.

'Is it all here?' the duchess asked.

'I couldn't tell you we had recovered the money straight away, sir,' explained Lavender, 'because I needed Woods to count it first, to find out how much was missing.'

'Missing?' Ogle snapped.

'Yes, sir, it isn't all there I'm afraid. I needed to know how much the thief has taken for himself before I returned it to you. Woods has written down the amount on this piece of paper. The robbers initially stole over one thousand, one hundred and fifty-seven pounds ...'

'I believe so,' Ogle confirmed.

'Well, he – or they – have returned just over nine hundred and ninety-five. This means that he has kept about...' He paused. His brain calculated rapidly. '...one hundred and sixty two pounds for himself – mostly the coins by the look of it.'

'Where was this found, man? And when?'

'About an hour ago, when I ordered your gardeners to undertake a thorough search of your grounds. It was found in the walled garden next to the Morpeth Road. It looks like someone has thrown these bags over the wall in the dead of the night. As Mr. Aynsley had not ordered a thorough search of the grounds following the robbery – it could have been lying in your raspberry bushes for quite a few days.'

'How did you know it would be there?'

'It was just a hunch. After all these years of working with the criminal underclass, I know how they think.'

'But I don't understand – why return any of it at all?' the duchess asked.

'Because, Ma'am, the thief – be it Aynsley or another man – has started to get worried. The enormity of what he has done, the vast amount of money he has stolen and the sheer audacity of his crime are starting to panic him now. He is obviously a local man, someone familiar with this Parish and its people. He knows that if he is to remain here, he can't spend over one thousand pounds – people would notice.

'In addition to this, he's probably worked out that it is going to be difficult to hide, especially the banknotes which are made out to Kirkley Hall. He knows it will be only a matter of time before His Grace, here, orders The Northumberland Fusiliers to raid every cottage and hovel in Ponteland and turn over every mattress and loose flagstone until they find it. So he has just kept enough to make himself 'comfortable' – without being ostentatious – and he has returned the rest.'

While Ogle continued to smooth and count his banknotes, the duke left the money boxes, drained his glass of Madeira, and gave the detective his full attention.

'This is excellent work, Lavender,' he said. 'But how much of the money did you say is still missing?'

'About one hundred and sixty-two pounds. It seems the thief has kept most of the coins – they're untraceable, of course – unlike the banknotes which would condemn him if he tried to spend them.'

'The thief could have just burned the banknotes, of course.'

'It's possible the thief is feeling guilty or frightened at what he has done,' Lavender suggested. 'He may even imagine that his punishment will be lighter – should he ever be caught – on account of the fact he has returned most of it.'

'Hah! No chance of that happening,' the duke snapped.

'One hundred and sixty-two pounds,' the duchess commented. 'Surely this is still more money than most men around here could expect to have come by honestly?'

'Yes, Ma'am.'

'So what now, Lavender?' the duke asked. 'Do we go and get the militia and arrest this Aynsley chap?'

'Not just yet, Sir. I still have a few more lines of enquiry to follow.'

'Oh, yes? And what would they be?'

'There are other suspects: a man named Charlton and a pair of brothers named Clifford. Charlton and one of the Clifford brothers used to work at Kirkley Hall. They were both dismissed from their posts and it's believed that they both hold a grudge. Both of them would have been familiar with the secret hiding place were Aynsley kept the money. The other Clifford brother, in Morpeth, is known to be a particularly nasty piece of work; he has a previous conviction for theft.'

'Charlton?' the Duke snorted derisively. 'Now why doesn't it surprise me that you've got a Charlton amongst your suspects? You'll have to be more specific, Lavender. Northumberland's full of them. It's one of the old reiving family names and there's hundreds of them – all descended from thieving swine and murderers. I'm not surprised you've got a Charlton amongst your suspects. Who is he?'

'He's called James Charlton – James Charlton of Milburn.'

At last, Ogle tore himself away from his money chests and padded back to the fireside in his velvet slippers. He looked delighted and excited; relief lit up his face.

'Yes! Yes – I remember him well! Why he's a decent man. He has a pretty wife and a young family – they attend my chapel every Sunday without fail.'

'Oh, don't tell me he's keeping a harlot in Stamfordham, as well?' The duchess smiled.

'No, Ma'am, but he has apparently spent a lot of money this past week – exactly the kind of behaviour I would expect from someone who has just illegally gained one hundred and sixty two pounds.'

'Well, there's no law against spending money, detective,' the duke joked. 'Or there would be quite a few of us in Morpeth Gaol – including my duchess!'

'Well, thank you, Hugh! I protest my innocence.'

'Only teasing, Fanny!' he grinned. 'You spend no more or less than a woman should in your position.' She smiled back at him.

Lavender cleared his throat again and interrupted. 'You are quite right, Sir. Of course, there is no law against spending money. But this man seems to have much more money than one would normally expect for a man in his situation.'

'I am led to believe that he has flaunted his money around in a manner which has attracted attention and can only be described as foolhardy in the circumstances. I need to follow this line of enquiry to discover if he is our thief.'

'Fair enough, Lavender,' the duke said. 'You're the detective. Just send word to Alnwick if you want any help from me or the fusiliers. We must be making our way home now. Come on, Fanny.'

'Thank you so much for coming – but are you sure you won't stay to dinner, Hugh?' Ogle said. 'My cook has poached a salmon for dinner, I'm sure that it will be excellent.'

'We can't, I'm afraid, Nathanial,' the duchess said. 'We're under strict instructions to return to Alnwick in time to dine with our daughters tonight. The girls are all agog to hear what's been going on down here in Ponteland.'

Reluctantly, Ogle rang the bell beside the fireplace.

'Come to think of it, most of the county is alive with excitement over this robbery,' the duke commented. 'The daughters will be fascinated to hear how Detective Lavender solved the case and retrieved the stolen rent money.'

‘Most of London will be fascinated to hear how Detective Lavender solved this case and retrieved the stolen money,’ the duchess said, as she rose gracefully. ‘Rest assured, Detective, I shall not hesitate to recommend you to any of my friends should they ever be unfortunate enough to need your services.’

Lavender bowed low to hide his smile of satisfaction. He had no doubt that relating this story would make the duchess a sensation in London’s salons and drawing rooms next season. The servants arrived with her ladyship’s fur trimmed pelisse and ostrich feathered hat.

‘Hugh – Frances – how can I thank you, for all your kindness?’ Ogle asked as they prepared to leave.

‘You can thank Detective Lavender, not us,’ the duchess suggested.

‘Actually, there is something you can do for me,’ the duke said.

‘Anything, Hugh, anything.’

‘There’s an eagle been sighted around these parts.’

‘An eagle?’

‘Yes, a big beggar – golden – I believe. Must have drifted over from Cumberland. It feeds on salmon from the river. Get your men to trap it and send it to me at Alnwick, will you?’

‘Certainly, Hugh, certainly.’

‘Right, try and cheer up now, Nathanial.’ The duke drained the last of his Madeira. ‘You’ve got most of your money back – thanks to Lavender and he seems to know what he is doing. A final word of advice though – get rid of your steward – this Aynsley chap. Nothing but trouble from what Lavender’s discovered.’

Next he turned to the detective.

‘I look forward to seeing the thieving swine who stole the rent money in the dock at the next assizes, Lavender. It will be good to have him hanged before harvest.’

CHAPTER FIVE

Lavender chose to eat his supper in Aynsley's office that evening while he re-read the statements he had collected and started on his report. The daylight was fading outside. The fire had been lit and several wax candles spluttered in the draughty corners of the room.

There was a knock on the door and Mr. Edwards, the butler, entered. 'Can I have a word, Detective?' he asked.

'Certainly,' said Lavender. He pointed towards the empty chair at the other side of the table. The senior servant had stayed out of his way for most of the day; Lavender had gained the distinct impression that the elderly man was assessing him from a distance.

'Mr. Ogle has asked if you can move your work into my office tomorrow,' the butler said as he seated himself. 'It's smaller than this, but quite comfortable.'

'Of course,' Lavender said casually. His eyes scanned the page of parchment in front of him, the quill twirled in his hand. 'Does Mr. Aynsley require his office back?'

'No,' Edwards paused. 'I trust I can rely on your discretion, this evening, Detective Lavender?'

Lavender's dark eyes fixed on the butler's face and he nodded imperceptively.'Mr. Aynsley won't be working as steward at Kirkley any more,' the butler informed him. 'However, I imagine that you foresaw that this would happen?'

Lavender replaced the ink quill into the stand. 'What has happened?'

'Mr. Ogle had a lengthy meeting with his secretary, Mr. Royce, this evening after the duke left. It would seem that Mr. Aynsley is to be removed from his position. Lord Percy is sending his own steward down to Kirkley for a while, to oversee matters until a new steward can be appointed here. The duke's steward will require this office and access to the estate accounts ledgers.'

'Ah,' Lavender tried to mask his satisfaction. 'This is portentous news indeed. Of course, it will be no hardship for me to move into another office. But how do you feel about this turn of events, Mr. Edwards?'

'I have mixed feelings, Detective Lavender,' the butler said, sadly. 'I have worked with Michael Aynsley nigh on thirty years. He has always been – how shall we say – a rough diamond, perhaps? However, he has been a good steward for Mr. Ogle and has always run this estate profitably. He was stern and never popular – but he was always fair with the hinds – as far as I could see.'

Lavender did not speak, so Edwards continued: 'His wife Nellie was a lovely and popular woman in the local community. There can be no doubt he has not coped well with his grief since she died. But he has made a huge mistake in losing the rent money – not one which can be overlooked. In fact, Mr. Ogle intends to look to him for the one hundred and sixty-two pounds which is still missing.'

'Of course, he was only following Mr. Ogle's instructions when he hid the money behind the secret wall panel,' Lavender commented. 'I understand there is a perfectly good, iron stronghold in Mr. Ogle's bedroom? Yet Mr. Ogle would never let anyone else have a key to it.'

'Ah, but Aynsley should have taken care with the money,' the butler protested. 'It was his job to secure it safely. The blame lies with him – and him alone.'

'Of course,' Lavender purred. 'So where will Mr. Aynsley go, do you think, now that his services are no longer required at Kirkley Hall? I only ask because I may need to ask further questions of him in the course of my enquiries.'

'He has tenancy of a farm at Newhamm Edge. He runs it with his two eldest sons, Mick and Joseph Aynsley.'

'Ah, yes.' Lavender referred to his notes again. 'Joseph Aynsley – he was present on the day of the robbery also. I shall need to interview him too.' And he tapped the crisp pile of signed statements which he had beside him with his long, elegant fingers. 'In fact, I was hoping a message might to be sent to him to ask him to call in here tomorrow – and Archibold the carpenter.'

'I shall send one of the servants to summon them both,' Mr. Edwards informed him.

'You cannot imagine, Detective, how grateful I am you have recovered the master's money. We are all breathing a huge sigh of relief in the servants' hall. Most of us knew Mr. Ogle would have had to make great savings to recoup the loss of a thousand pounds and we all had been worried about the security of our positions here, at Kirkley Hall.'

Lavender smiled. 'I'm glad I was able to help.'

'Now all that needs doing is to track down the thief,' Edwards continued, 'and I regard it as my first duty to assist you in any way that I can. It will be a privilege to share my office with you, sir.'

'Thank you, Mr. Edwards; this is reassuring to know. Not everyone is always so accommodating when we arrive at the scene of a crime. However, as we are sharing confidences at the moment, I will be honest with you; this burglar is going be a slippery devil to catch. He has left no trace of himself at all. It will take great cunning – and luck – to bring this fellow to justice.'

'There are many who would be disappointed to hear about this,' Edwards observed. 'Mr. Ogle does not permit gambling on these premises, of course, but I understand money has already started to change hands across the parish since news leaked out that you had recovered the rent money. Confidence in you is high; even the most cynical amongst the community are assuming that the thief will soon be caught. I understand the best odds have been laid on you arresting the thief by Friday.'

Lavender laughed. 'The duke has charged me to find the thief by the August assizes. I believe that this may be more realistic under the circumstances. It is a matter of personal pride, Mr. Edwards, that we arrest the right man. I will be thorough and I will not rush the investigation to suit anyone.'

'Well, you have my confidence, sir. If anyone can catch this thief – you can. I wish you luck with your enquiries.'

He rose stiffly to his feet and added: 'I assume Michael Aynsley will retire to his farm for the moment. Though how long he will choose to stay in this area, I cannot imagine. The man is ruined. His reputation is quite spoilt.'

Wednesday 12th April, 1809

Lavender said nothing to anyone – not even to Woods – about the information that the butler had shared with him about Aynsley's impending dismissal. However, by eight o'clock the next morning, when Aynsley rode into the rear courtyard of Kirkley Hall, there wasn't a servant in the hall who didn't know Aynsley was about to be sacked. A number of them escaped from their duties and gathered in the cobbled yard beneath the boughs of the great cedar tree, keen to enjoy the unfolding drama. Lavender and Woods completed the removal of their papers to the butler's office and then joined them.

Aynsley was taken straight to see Mr. Ogle's secretary.

Harry Robinson, the head groom turned to one of the stable lads and said: 'I wouldna bother unsaddling his 'oss, He'll be needing her again in a minute.'

Sure enough, ten minutes later a red-faced Aynsley strode angrily back into yard. Without a word to anyone, he swung himself into the saddle and thundered out of the yard. As he left, his horse's hoof clipped the rear end of Ogle's fat spaniel which was busy sniffing a pile of horse muck. The dog yelped and ran inside squealing like a pig, bearing a vivid, horseshoe-shaped weal on its arse. The assembled staff burst out laughing.

The head groom spat onto the ground. 'Good riddance to Aynsley,' he snarled.

'Aye,' muttered several others in agreement.

Twenty minutes later, the Duke of Northumberland's steward arrived at Kirkley Hall. He was a thin-boned and thin-haired man dressed entirely in black, with quick bird-like eyes, no chin, a swarthy complexion and a beak-shaped nose. His overall appearance gave the onlookers the impression of a black, two-legged crow. His presence had a sobering effect on the servants who hurriedly returned to their duties. The new steward went straight to a meeting with Mr. Ogle's secretary.

Half an hour later, the new steward, the head groomsman and two footmen carried the box containing the recovered rent money out to the trap. They were moving it to the bank vault in Newcastle. Mr. Ogle was taking no chances with security now; the groom laid a primed pistol on the wooden seat beside him.

'I heard it said that Mr. Ogle slept with that money in his bed chamber last night,' Woods informed Lavender.

'Beneath his pillow, more like,' snapped Mrs. Hodgeson, the cook.

After lunch, the new steward sought out Lavender and introduced himself. 'I'm pleased to make your acquaintance, Detective Lavender,' he said as he extended a bony, bird-like claw and shook the detective's hand. 'His Grace speaks most highly of you.'

'Thank you,' said Lavender.

'In fact, His Grace has asked me to pass on a message to you.'

'Oh?'

'He would greatly appreciate it if you would keep him informed – in writing – of any developments in this case. He has taken a particular interest in the successful capture of this thief.'

'Certainly,' agreed Lavender. 'Shall I give a copy of my report to you to pass onto His Grace?'

'That would be most satisfactory,' the steward agreed.

Once he had gone, a surprised Woods turned to Lavender and asked: 'Now what was that all about, do you think?'

'I don't think his Grace entirely trusts Mr. Ogle's judgement,' Lavender said quietly. Wood's eyes widened in surprise. 'But no word of this is to be told to the servants, do you hear?'

'Of course not but it's a bit unusual, isn't it? It's Mr. Ogle who will pay our wages after all; seems a bit wrong to send a secret report over to Alnwick Castle as well.'

'Oh, everyone is answerable to someone else,' commented Lavender, 'and ultimately, Mr. Ogle is answerable to the duke.'

Joseph Aynsley was the first of the summoned witnesses to arrive at Kirkley Hall to speak to Lavender. He was nervous and agitated and he stammered a little as he spoke. However, when questioned about the day of the robbery, he looked the detective straight in the eye and appeared to be telling the truth. He confirmed everything that his father had said – including the strange behaviour of James Charlton when he saw the heaped piles of gold and silver on the table in Aynsley's office. Joseph Aynsley claimed he had returned straight home on the night of the robbery and had remained with his family until the following morning. The first that he had known about the theft of the rent money was when his father had returned to Newhamm Edge on the evening of the next day.

Lavender and Woods put little faith into alibis provided by wives and observed Joseph Aynsley closely. They knew he could easily have been in league with the steward in the robbery and there was no doubt that the man was in awe – perhaps even fearful – of his dominant father. His voice was monotonous: his manner dull. He didn't have the sharp intellect of Michael Aynsley and would obviously be easily swayed by the older man.

Lavender and Woods were thoughtful after Joseph Aynsley had left.

'I think, we should have a word with this 'ere, James Charlton,' said Woods.

'My thoughts exactly,' Lavender agreed. 'We'll track him down tomorrow. Let's speak to this Mr. Archibold, the carpenter, first.'

The tiny carpenter arrived half an hour later. With his bulging tool bag swinging on his bony shoulder and his clay pipe clamped firmly between his yellow, nicotine-stained teeth, he stuck his head around the door of Mrs. Hodgeson's kitchen and asked to speak 'to the detective gadgie.' He trailed a line of sawdust into the butler's office.

He was as helpful as he could be but his testimony added little to what Lavender already knew. Archibold had been busy all day on the 3rd of April and had seen nothing of the steward or the gold. In fact, he had hardly been aware the rent was being collected. Although, as he pointed out: 'the fog were that thick, that ah could barely see me own hands in front of me face.'

Lavender then asked him about James Charlton, his assistant on that day. The little man burst forth with praise about the pleasant, easy-going man with whom he lodged and the kindness and excellent cooking of his wife, Cilla. Apparently, Charlton was a 'good grafter' and he had employed him, now and then, for a few days' work.

'Tha'll not find a kinder, more Christian family in the whole of the parish than those Charltons in Milburn,' he had insisted. 'I just wish I could have given the gadgie more jobs to do.'

Yes, he told Lavender, he had sent Jamie Charlton to the steward's office on the day of the robbery to measure up for the new wood for the rotten window frame. From what Charlton had said later, this hadn't pleased the steward and Charlton had returned with the job undone. No, he had not seen Charlton that evening back at his lodgings. He, himself, had retired to bed early after an excellent supper and he believed Charlton had gone out drinking in Ponteland, as was his habit.

'That carpenter Archibold were biased,' Woods observed, after the wiry, little man had left. 'It is clear he'll ne'er think badly of the man.'

'It could be the Aynsleys are biased in the opposite way; prejudiced against Charlton, in fact,' Lavender mused.

'Yes,' Woods agreed. 'I've heard it said in the servants' hall that the Charltons and Aynsleys have little time for each. There's an ongoing feud running between the two families. There are also lots of rumours circulating about this James Charlton,' he added. 'He seems to have come into quite a bit of money recently and has been flashing it about. He's a regular at the card tables, as well.'

'Mmm, a good win on the cards could easily account for a sudden increase in spending. However, a gambling habit is not what I'd expect to discover in the saintly Christian described by Archibold. I think we should talk to this Mr. James Charlton and make up our own minds about him.'

'Shall I have him summoned?' Woods asked.

'No, I think we'll pay him a visit at his home in Milburn – and while we're at it we'd better track down these Clifford rogues as well.'

Later that afternoon, when the trap had returned from Newcastle, Lavender and Woods called at the Kirkley home of John Clifford, another disgruntled ex-employee of Kirkley Hall, whose name had also been brought to Lavender's attention as a possible suspect. However, they were unable to gain entry to his ramshackle cottage, as it turned out that Clifford had contracted smallpox and was seriously ill with the disease. The man's distressed and terrified wife shouted this information out to them through the closed door. She warned them not to enter and told them to ask Doctor Robson, the surgeon, if they did not believe her. John Clifford was not expected to live out the night.

'And as for his good-for-nothing brother in Morpeth, we've no idea of his whereabouts and have not seen hide nor hair of him for six months past,' the poor woman told them. 'The last we heard he had moved away to Gateshead.'

Lavender and Woods beat a hasty retreat from Clifford's diseased home and returned to Kirkley Hall. Lavender sent Woods with Harry Robertson, the surly groom, to Morpeth to try to find out if the Morpeth Clifford brother had indeed left the area. Meanwhile, Lavender borrowed a horse and went to call on Doctor Robson in Ponteland.

The surgeon was at home and had just finished his evening meal. Lavender was shown into the wood-panelled dining room where he and his wife were finishing their desserts. He was not asked to sit down. The elderly surgeon continued to eat as Lavender explained the nature of his business. The doctor's wife was a slim, prickly looking redhead, a lot younger than her husband. She dabbed her thin lips delicately with a linen napkin and glared at the detective across the mahogany table. She reminded him vividly of someone whom he could not quite place and he was puzzled by her open hostility. That was the trouble with these close-knit rural communities, he thought; everybody was connected or related to everybody else in some way or another.

'Yes, yes,' the doctor told him. 'I remember the Clifford man. I was called there about a week ago when he first contracted the disease. He was in a bad way then with a high fever, vomiting and cramps; I'm surprised he has lasted this long.'

'His wife fears he will not last out the night.'

'No, he probably won't.' The doctor was clearly unconcerned. He held up a crystal decanter. 'Can I offer you a glass of port, Detective? This is an excellent vintage.'

'No, thank you. So is it possible that John Clifford could have been the thief who robbed Kirkley Hall?'

'I doubt it. The man could barely get out of bed a week ago – never mind climb up onto a first floor roof and burgle the hall.' The doctor poured himself a generous measure of port. 'His wife has kept me updated with the development of his papules and pustules and by all accounts, he has developed the most severe form of the disease, purpura variolosa.'

'I see.' Lavender, shuddered. 'Is there an outbreak in the parish?'

'The odd case – there's no cure of course. The only thing one can hope for is containment.'

'I have heard that a Dr. Jenner has developed something called a vaccine which allegedly gives the recipient a form of immunity to the disease,' Lavender said.

'Apparently so,' the doctor yawned. 'However, it would be a bit late for John Clifford now, by all accounts. So I guess you are going to have to look elsewhere for your burglar, Detective Lavender.' He grinned across the table at his wife and winked. 'I understand the steward of Kirkley Hall is also a suspect?'

The next moment she slammed down her cutlery, stood up abruptly and stormed out of the room.

Lavender was startled but the doctor threw back his head and laughed.

'You'll have to excuse my wife, Detective,' he explained, still laughing. 'She's been very distressed by the events surrounding this robbery. Her father is Michael Aynsley, the Kirkley Hall steward – or should I say, the late steward of Kirkley Hall?'

Woods returned to Kirkley Hall later that evening. He had discovered nothing about the whereabouts of the other Clifford brother. Everyone he had questioned had told the same story as John Clifford's wife. The man they sought had not been seen for months and was believed to now live in the Gateshead area. Although, Lavender realised, this did not preclude the man – wherever he was – from taking part in the robbery, his enquiries about the Clifford brothers had amounted to nothing.

CHAPTER SIX

Thursday 13th April, 1809

The following morning, Lavender and Woods set off early to call on James Charlton. The country lane which led from Kirkley to Milburn was little more than a rutted, mud-strewn track. As they jolted and rattled along, Lavender soon realised it probably would have been easier – and more comfortable – to have walked or ridden. It was a journey of only a few miles, so he settled back on the hard wooden seat of the trap and tried to distract himself by observing the freshness of the blossoming countryside around him.

There was no doubt spring came later to this part of the world than to London but the verges of this Northumbrian lane, and the meadows beside it, were thick with promise. Shy creatures scurried away into the undergrowth as they approached, and sought safety behind the fresh shoots of ivy and curling ferns. Primroses sprouted vividly at the base of the bursting hawthorn and hazel. Everything was entwined with the fresh growth of honeysuckle. In the fields, he could see the muted yellow of cowslips between the swathes of lush grass and the woolly legs of gambolling lambs. Above them, huge flocks of birds glided noisily across the sky.

They approached Milburn through a copse of oaks which towered above them. A carpet of fallen leaves muffled the clip of the horse's hooves. The sunlight was filtered through the canopy of fresh green leaves high above their heads, casting their faces into shadow and creating a soft dappled effect on the glossy haunches of the chestnut horse.

Milburn consisted of just a few scattered stone and thatched cottages. The common land surrounding the hamlet had been cleared and divided into strips for the cottagers to grow herbs and vegetables. They were mostly bare apart from a couple of pig sties, although one or two showed signs of careful tilling. Here and there a few rows of spindly, green shoots suggested carrots, onion and wild beans. A solitary man in an old jacket and a blue neckerchief hoed his strip. Several cows and a couple of calves grazed contentedly on the other side of the road in the swaying grass of the meadow which fell away down to the mill stream.

The trap drew up outside Charlton's stone cottage. They could see it was a modest home of only a couple of rooms, with an overgrown garden to the front. The budding stems and brown thorns of a climbing rose clambered up the wall beside the partially open door.

A spiral of smoke curled away from the chimney into the clear blue sky above. The delightful smell of freshly baked bread wafted in their direction.

'Well, at least there's someone at home,' Woods observed.

They climbed down stiffly from the swaying vehicle, and sent a flurry of chickens squawking along the dusty track and onto the rickety fence which surrounded the tangled garden. In the tumbling confusion of daffodils, herbs, currant bushes and vegetables, a child's face suddenly appeared, framed with red curls and a dirty white bonnet. Seconds later, up popped another – identical to the last. Both girls were wide-eyed, and kneeling amongst the plants.

'What devil's trick is this?' Woods exclaimed.

Lavender smiled. 'Unusual isn't it? Twins rarely survive the birth. Is your father at home, little miss?'

Neither child answered. Behind them, the gaping door swung wide open and a tall, very beautiful woman appeared. She wiped her floury hands on her apron and pushed back a wisp of gleaming, copper-coloured hair which had escaped from beneath her cap. Her large, green eyes flicked nervously across the faces of the two strange men before her.

'Are you wanting to see Jamie?' she asked.

'Mistress Charlton?' Lavender asked pleasantly. She nodded. 'We're looking for your husband, James Charlton. Is he at home?'

'He be out in the fields. Hannah, Mary – go fetch your da.' The two girls needed no second bidding. They were up from their knees in a second, flew out of the gate and sped off towards the fields. Their boots clattered over the stony path and red pigtails streamed behind them.

'Pretty gals, them,' Woods observed.

'I'm Detective Lavender from Bow Street in London, Mistress Charlton. This is Constable Woods. We are investigating the theft of the rent money from Kirkley Hall.'

'You'd better come inside then,' Cilla said calmly.

They followed her into the cottage. Lavender glanced around; he was keen to have a good look around before Charlton arrived.

The door led straight into the main living area, which was dominated by the stone fireplace and a wooden table in the centre of the room. There was one padded armchair in front of the fire. At the other side of the hearth stood an ancient yew settle, scattered with colourful homemade cushions. A soot-blackened rag rug lay on the floor. Along the entire back wall of the room was an oak dresser crammed and cluttered with pots, pans, baking ingredients, knitting and sewing equipment and just about everything else the family owned. The table was covered with an appetising array of freshly made bread, pies and pastries.

Sitting on one of the wooden chairs at the table was a thin-faced woman who rose hurriedly as they entered.

'I'd best be getting along,' she said.

'Take these into the bedroom, will you Mary?' Cilla said quietly, ignoring her friend's embarrassment. She scooped up a pile of bulky, brown paper parcels from the dresser and deposited them into the other woman's arms.

The woman pushed open the door on the back wall with her foot and carried the parcels away. For a brief second, Lavender was able to see several beds in the darkened room. A man's coat hung on the outside of a wardrobe door.

Cilla now began to move the food from the table into the space created on the dresser. Lavender observed her dispassionately as she glided around the room. The faded blue dress she wore beneath her apron, had lines of needle marks running from the dark stains beneath her armpits down to her waist. It had obviously been let in and out several times – probably to accommodate her expanding waistline during her pregnancies. As if on cue, an infant whimpered in the back room. She paused and listened but the sleepy child seemed to settle again.

The woman was stunningly attractive, but even in the darkened kitchen of the cottage he could see the fine lines around her eyes and the hint of grey at her temples. This magnificent red-headed beauty was starting to lose her looks. How old would she be? Thirty perhaps? She was past her prime. Another five years of child-bearing, and the poverty and malnutrition which dogged her class would age her prematurely.

The woman Mary reappeared from the bedroom and moved towards the front door. She reached for her shawl from the back of the chair. Lavender and Woods stepped out of her way.

'I'll be seeing you, Cilla,' she said as she left. 'Thank you for the money for the butter – I'll get you some change for that note as soon as I can.' With this she gave Lavender and Woods a filthy look and then disappeared out of the cottage door.

Cilla gestured the men towards the spindly chairs at the table.

'Take a seat,' she said. 'Jamie'll not be long; he's close by.'

Lavender sat down and began to remove his gloves. He continued to scan the room. He saw nothing unusual for a labourer's cottage: second-hand furniture, patched furnishings and pewter plates. There was another door off the kitchen which led to a small scullery. Cilla carried her baking implements into this side room and Lavender observed a large, uncooked ham sitting on a plate on top of a cupboard.

This family eats well at the moment, he thought.

'Can I get you a cup of tea?' Cilla asked when she returned. The two men accepted and watched as she picked up a teaspoon and a battered, tin tea caddy. She measured out the leaves carefully, and then dropped them into a chipped, brown teapot. Next she reached for the iron kettle which sat on the hearthstones and set it back over the fire to boil.

Suddenly, they heard voices and footsteps in the garden outside. The light in the cottage dimmed as a tall, broad man paused in the doorway.

'Good morning, Mr. Charlton. I'm Detective Lavender from Bow Street in London. I've come to ask you some questions about your movements on the day of the Kirkley Hall robbery.'

The big labourer nodded and stepped into the room, his vivid, blue eyes flicked sharply from Lavender to Woods and then back again. His thick hair and sideburns had once been black; now they were streaked with grey. He had a broad forehead, wide features and a stubborn jawline. His lined face was tanned and weathered from working in the fields; it shone with sweat.

'Aye, anything we can do to help you is fine,' Charlton said. 'We were right shocked to hear that Mr. Ogle's money had been taken – weren't we, Cilla?' She nodded silently.

The twin girls and a thin, black-haired lad of about eight had followed Charlton into the cottage. One of the girls limped slightly, as if her boot chafed her foot. Suddenly, Lavender noticed that the boots were brand new.

Cilla shooed the children back outside.

Charlton took off his coat and grabbed a grey, threadbare towel from the dresser. He wiped his sweaty face and sat down opposite Lavender. Woods took out some sheets of paper, a pot of ink and a quill and prepared to write Charlton's statement.

'You used to work at Kirkley Hall, did you not?'

'Aye, I were a herdsman there for nigh on four years,' Jamie confirmed. Lavender noticed that Charlton's shirt was hand-stitched and wearing thin.

'I used to take the cattle to market in Newcastle: feed them; birth them and doctor them. I left there about four years ago.'

'Though we still worship at Kirkley chapel,' his wife added quietly.

Lavender paused for a moment and observed the big man sharply from beneath his hooded eyes. He got the distinct impression James Charlton had been expecting him and had already rehearsed this speech. Lavender wondered how he could rattle him.

'Why?'

'Why what?'

'Why did you leave such a good position?'

Charlton laughed a little and glanced across the room towards his wife: 'Well, I've no doubt you've heard Aynsley's side of the story, so I'll not hide it from you, Detective. I was sacked for poor time-keeping. It were just after the twins were born. Cilla and I didn't get a good night's sleep for two years – I were always tired and late.'

'And how did you feel about that?'

'Eh?' Charlton looked baffled. His grip tightened on the towel in his hand, the taut skin on his large knuckles gleamed white beneath the grime.

'Did you feel that you were treated unfairly by the steward of Kirkley Hall? Do you hold a grudge?'

'What – hold a grudge about that? Lord help us man, it were years ago. There's a lot of water passed under the bridge since then. Life moves on.'

Lavender paused and waited. He didn't believe him. There was something which flashed across the man's face when Aynsley's name was mentioned; an almost imperceptible tightening of his jaw muscles. The silence hung heavy in the overcrowded room. The only sound was Cilla, slowly stirring the tea with a spoon.

The technique worked. Charlton felt awkward in the silence and began to bluster. 'Look, I'm not saying that I like Aynsley – you'll be hard pressed to find any bugger who does, in these here parts – but no, I don't hold any bad feeling about what happened four years ago. I've got other things on my mind.'

Cilla placed a jug of milk and a chipped bowl of steaming, brown tea in front of Lavender. He nodded politely in her direction.

'So how do you live now?' he asked Charlton. 'What work do you do?'

'Oh, we get by. I have a few cows of me own – you can see them out there.' He gestured towards the door. 'There's the chickens, the pig and a patch of land. I do the odd day's work here and there for the local farmers: ploughing, threshing, haymaking and the like.

Mind you, I've been working as the barn man up at Haindykes for a few weeks now.'

'We have a couple of lodgers, as well,' Cilla interjected.

That explains all the beds in the crowded back room, thought Lavender. With lodgers sleeping in the tiny garrets upstairs, the children must sleep in the back room with their parents.

'We've had a local carpenter staying with us – for nigh on six weeks,' Charlton informed him. 'He's only just gone back to Maften. It were right handy; he took me on as his assistant and paid me well to help him.'

'How much work did he give you?' Lavender thought about the new boots on the children and the shopping parcels, lying in the next room on the patchwork eiderdown.

'Now and then,' Jamie said. 'He's been working on the new Hall they're building down the lane – here in Milburn. Yes, we get by well enough, and we thank the Lord every day for his bounty. Cilla, hinny, are there some pastries these gentlemen could have with their tea? My wife's an excellent cook, Detective – I'm a very lucky man.'

Cilla placed a tea plate of jam tarts in front of the men. 'Help yourself, Constable, they'll be right tasty,' Charlton said. Woods, who had just finished heaping four spoons of sugar into his tea, needed no second invitation.

'What were you doing on the day of the robbery?' Lavender asked.

'There were no work for Mr. Archibold at Milburn Hall that day, so he'd gone to Kirkley Hall to do a few jobs for the steward. He finished off some new cupboards for the laundry room and repaired a couple of rotten sash windows,' said Charlton. 'I weren't needed at Haindykes either, so I went with him to help.'

'Where were these rotten windows?'

'One was in a small bedroom – and one in the steward's office. But as I'm sure Aynsley's already told you, he wasn't best pleased when I went to measure the window up for the wood. I'd interrupted him counting out the money.'

'What happened?'

Charlton glanced across the room towards his wife. He hesitated before he replied. 'The bastard kicked me down the stairs.'

'Oh, Jamie!'

Cilla's shock was genuine. Charlton hadn't wanted to admit his humiliation in front of his wife.

'Oh, that were nothing unusual for Aynsley. Don't forget I used to work for him regular for four years. He thought nothing about kicking his workers around. And if he weren't assaulting the men – he was molesting their wives,' he added darkly.

Lavender pounced. 'Has he ever molested yours?'

Jamie flushed with anger. 'Aye. Not that it is any of your business.'

'Is the child asleep in the back room, Michael Aynsley's bastard?

Woods gasped and choked on his jam tart.

Charlton rose to his feet and slammed his fist down on the table in fury. 'No, he ain't, God damn you!' he yelled. 'And I'll thank you to never suggest that again! Aynsley tried to fondle her one day – tried to put his hand up her skirt – that's all!'

Woods was now also on his feet. Lavender stared calmly up at the big labourer. 'What happened?' he asked.

'One of the neighbours heard her screaming and ran to help her,' Charlton snapped. He breathed heavily. His face was flushed and contorted with anger.

Lavender glanced over towards Cilla: 'Is this true?'

'As God's my witness,' she replied quietly. 'Sit down Jamie, the detective is only asking a few questions.'

There was another strained pause. Then Charlton laughed awkwardly. His anger subsided and he dropped back down onto his chair. 'You'll have to forgive me, Detective – I'm a passionate man when it comes to my family.'

'So I see, Mr. Charlton,' Lavender said, sardonically. 'I suppose we should have been grateful that Michael Aynsley never tried to maul one of your daughters.'

'I wouldn't have put it past him to try,' Jamie growled.

Lavender decided to change tack. 'There's only one more thing I need to establish.'

'Oh?'

'Your movements after you left work at Kirkley Hall on Easter Monday. Where did you go?'

'Why I came straight home – here to my family.'

Charlton stared him straight in the eyes. To his right, Lavender sensed that Cilla had stiffened.

'So you came straight home?'

'Aye.'

Lavender and Woods watched the big labourer closely; they both knew he was lying. Charlton's blue eyes never wavered. His ability to lie without flinching was impressive. Lavender decided this was neither the time, nor the place, to challenge his account.

'I think this is all we need to know – for now,' he concluded briskly. 'If you could please place your mark on the document the constable has been writing, we'll be able to get on our way. It's just an account of what you have told us regarding your movements.'

'I don't use a mark,' Charlton said proudly. 'I can sign me own name, like – and read an all.'

'Well, that doesn't surprise me.' Lavender's tone was ironic. 'I'd already worked out that you were a very clever man.'

Jamie took the piece of parchment from Constable Woods and read it to himself, his lips moved slowly as he absorbed the words. He was pleased to see Woods had not included any mention of Aynsley molesting Cilla but he hesitated when he realised Woods had included the fact that Aynsley had kicked him down the stairs. 'I don't like this,' he growled and tapped the parchment with his forefinger. 'It makes me look a fool.'

'On the contrary, Mr. Charlton,' Lavender reassured him. 'If anything it goes worse for Michael Aynsley – who completely forgot to mention his brutality in his own statement.'

Jamie glanced up sharply. 'Well, if you put it like that…' he said. 'There are those who think Michael Aynsley knows more about this crime than he's letting on.'

'Are there?' Lavender feigned surprise.

'Aye, the town's full of talk about him,' Jamie confirmed. 'There's many say he stole the rent money himself.' Then he took up the quill, and slowly scrawled his name at the bottom of the sheet.

The detective and his assistant took their leave. Rather than drive straight back to the hall, Lavender suggested that they took a walk down beside the stream, out of earshot of the groom. Walking in silence, they followed an overgrown path beside the freezing water, pushing aside the towering foxgloves. Lavender was in deep thought and barely noticed the nettles, red campion and gypsy lace which lashed at his legs. Eventually they reached an ancient stone bridge and clambered up to lean against the crumbling parapet. Lavender stared down into the brackish water below, which swirled icily through a bed of weeds. As he waited for the brooding detective to break the silence, Woods shivered in the cold breeze and fastened up the buttons on his coat.

'Let's discuss what we've found out so far,' Lavender said eventually. 'For a start, do you think it was a man or a woman who burgled Kirkley Hall on Easter Monday?'

'Why – a man!' Woods was startled. 'I mean, a woman could have helped him, I suppose – but it would have taken some strength to have smashed the wooden panel in the steward's office. A woman couldn't have done it.'

'Do you think Charlton did it, Woods?'

'It's hard to say, sir. He seems a decent, friendly fellah but the family are as poor as church mice and he's got no regular income.' He paused for a moment. 'We'll have to speak to the farmer at Haindykes about how much he pays him. There's no doubt in my mind, that the man's got a grudge against the bloody steward – not that I blame him, like.'

'Charlton says there are a lot of rumours circulating in the parish that Aynsley stole the money.'

'Yes, and Charlton probably started them all,' Woods concluded shrewdly.

'What about the rest of the staff at Kirkley Hall?' Lavender asked. 'You've spent several days with them. What do you think?'

'There's no one who stands out as particularly guilty. That groom Robertson is a miserable old bugger but we can hardly clap him in gaol for that. Truth is, when it comes to servants, they usually find their own way to rob their masters: they fiddle the books or short change a shopkeeper on their master's behalf. To be honest sir, burglary seems a bit of a risk when there are so many easier ways for a hired help to rob their rich master. Many of the Kirkley staff confessed they were afeard for their jobs after the robbery, so why cut off your nose to spite yourself?'

'What about Michael Aynsley? Are we right to suspect him?'

Woods sighed: 'I don't think he did it neither.'

'Why's that?'

'For the same reason, I don't think any of the Kirkley Hall staff did it. He was on to too much of a good thing working there. I know he behaved oddly and said daft things just after the robbery – and I know he has that fancy woman to keep. But if you'll excuse me pointing this out, sir – all women are expensive to keep. You are a bachelor man, Detective, and are not used to women – I've been married nigh on fifteen years and I can assure you that wives – mistresses – why, they're all as expensive as each other.'

Lavender hid his smile as Woods continued.

'Besides which, he has no other expenses – his children are all married off and settled and he'll have a fair amount stashed away, by now, I shouldn't wonder after farming and working at Kirkley for thirty years.'

'What about the fact that there was only him, and his son, who knew about the secret compartment behind the wood panelling?'

'That's nonsense, sir, if you don't mind me saying so. Three days at Kirkley Hall and I've realised there's not a thing those servants don't know about what is going on in the Hall. Several of them have as good as told me they already knew where Aynsley stashed the money.'

'Which brings us back to James Charlton,' Lavender said slowly. 'He worked there for four years, so no doubt he knew about the secret compartment behind the panelling too. Did you see those parcels, Woods? And the food in the house and the child's new boots?'

Woods thought for a moment.

'I didn't see the boots but I did notice a man's brand new coat hung in the bedroom.'

Lavender glanced at him sharply.

'Are you sure?'

'Aye, sir, I think I got more of a look see than you did – I were in a better position. It were a dapper coat with silver buttons and all. When that woman Mary opened the bedroom door – it were a brand spanking new coat that were hanging on the wardrobe door. Obviously he's keeping it for best and just wears his old one for farming his strip. Then there were the twenty shilling note, as well…'

'What twenty shilling note?'

'The one the other woman took out of the cottage with her – it were for payment for the butter, she said. She pocketed it quickly when we come in. She were going to get some change for Mistress Charlton, she said.'

'You've done well.' Lavender was impressed. 'So, despite having no regular work, our casual labourer, James Charlton, has been on a bit of a spending spree for himself and his family and still has enough money left to pay for the butter with a twenty shilling note and not to fret about the change.'

'Just the kind of thing you'd expect from a man who'd just stolen over one hundred and sixty pounds of rent money,' Woods observed shrewdly. 'He lied about where he were the night of the robbery, as well.'

The two men paused for a moment while they mulled over their shared discoveries about Charlton.

'What we going to do, sir?' Woods asked eventually. 'Do we get him arrested and have the gaolers torture a confession out of him?'

A flicker of repugnance swept across Lavender's face. Torture was common but it was not something he advocated. In fact, he tried to avoid it whenever possible. To him, it was a sign of failure – an admission that all other methods of detecting the criminal had failed.

'Even with a confession, we need more evidence than a new coat to convict Charlton of this crime – a lot more evidence. We need to know where all his money has come from and what he was doing the night of the crime. I suppose that it is possible, he also could have been visiting a whore on the night of the robbery – he wouldn't have wanted to mention that in front of his wife.'

'He doesn't look the type to be an adulterer. He seems right fond of his family.' A broad grin broke out across Wood's face. 'Mind you, sir, if you prove me wrong and Charlton does have some little doxy stashed away for a bit of swiving on the side, then I'm moving up North. They all seem to be bloody at it up here...'

Lavender wasn't listening. He was watching the drama in the heavens above them. He took a sharp intake of breath and pointed upwards into the pale, blue sky. 'My God, Woods! Look at that!'

An enormous bird dived and soared on the air currents. With its wings tucked in, it dropped out of the sky hundreds of feet above them. Lit by the weak sunlight, it gleamed like a golden ball as it plummeted towards the earth. Then – after briefly opening its wings – the bird shot upwards again; only to repeat the deep undulating dives, over two or three miles, in a spectacular display.

'What is it?' Woods asked.

'It's the golden eagle,' Lavender explained. 'This is some kind of territorial display – probably for the benefit of the other birds of prey in the area.'

'Is that the bird the duke wants captured?'

'I presume so. I can't imagine there are any more of them around here. They're native to Scotland and Cumberland – not this part of England. My God! Woods – just look at it!'

Lavender was transfixed by the magnificent creature. His hand shaded his eyes as he followed the raptor's silhouette as it glided gracefully across the face of the mid-day sun.

'What a beauty,' Woods murmured. 'The duke's offered a ten pound reward for its capture.'

'Has he now?' An idea began to form in Lavender's mind.

‘Mind you,’ Woods commented, his own eyes still fixed on the bird. ‘I doubt if anyone will trap it – it looks too bloody smart to get caught.’

‘Oh you never know,’ Lavender said, cryptically. His mind now raced with possibilities. ‘I’m sure that when the duke wants something caught – it usually gets caught.’

CHAPTER SEVEN

Lavender decided that there was not much more he could do in Ponteland at the moment and he resolved to return to London the next evening. Woods was to stay behind to keep his ears open for news of the missing Clifford brother and to continue to collect information and evidence about James Charlton. Lavender intended to return within a fortnight to review the case and relieve Woods.

He knew their investigation now needed to move beyond the confines of Kirkley Hall and out into the community. Instinct told him that his best informants about James Charlton were probably the regulars at the man's favourite two public houses. So it was with some sadness that Woods packed his bag and left the comfort of the Hall, and the excellence of Mrs. Hodgeson's cooking, to take a room with a lumpy mattress and a damp smell at the Coaching Inn at Newhamm Edge. The plan was for him to spend his evenings here – or at Ma Shotton's – eating his supper and mixing with the regular drinkers of the inn, gleaning whatever information he could.

Woods was also instructed to keep a high profile and let it be known within Ponteland that he wished to interview every single one of Mr. Ogle's tenants who had come to pay rent at the hall on Easter Monday.

'All of 'em?' Woods gasped. 'I'll need six months, never mind two weeks!'

'It's just a cover story,' Lavender explained patiently. 'Your real purpose is to keep your ears open for any information about Charlton, Clifford – or Aynsley. You will also need to frequent Ma Shotton's establishment on a regular basis to quench your thirst.'

'Ah, now you're talking!' Woods grinned. 'I'll probably be a right drunken sop by the time you return, mind you!'

'You will need to discipline yourself with the ale and the strong spirits,' Lavender said sharply. 'For you have another task. While you idle your time away waiting for informants to come through the door of the office, I want you to make a neat copy of my report. We need another copy to send to the duke.'

Woods groaned inwardly at the thought of all the writing but couldn't hide his pleasure with the overall arrangement.

Lavender had complete trust in him. Woods had a good memory for detail and a sharp nose for a lead. In addition to this, despite his obvious link with the famous Bow Street, he had an easy way with the common folk and could quickly get them to trust him and to confide in him.

Woods did not disappoint him. When Lavender returned just over two weeks later, his constable had plenty of news for him.

They ordered supper and went into a private dining room in the coaching inn to discuss the case. A warm fire glowed in the hearth and they ate an excellent dinner of beef stew and dumplings washed down with several large glasses of the landlord's best Madeira.

Woods confirmed that John Clifford had died a couple of days after Lavender's departure for London and had since been buried in a pauper's grave. This part of the investigation had yielded nothing. However, new evidence had come to light about James Charlton.

'Firstly,' Woods claimed, 'Charlton did not go home to his wife the night of the robbery, as he claimed; he was seen drinking and gambling here at Newhamm Edge. As far as I can gather, he stayed late, lost a lot of money at the card tables and then staggered home, drunk.'

'Mmm, drunk and penniless – definitely the right frame of mind for a bit of opportunistic thieving,' Lavender observed as he stabbed at his meat.

'Secondly,' Woods continued, 'the man was in Ma Shotton's the day after the burglary, throwing money around like water. I've also got a statement from a tailor…' Woods paused while he referred to his black pocketbook, '…one Matthew Mackie, who claims that Charlton approached him the same night about a new coat. Mackie made the coat and Charlton paid him the next week in cash.'

'This is good evidence,' Lavender told him. 'What about the new boots the children were wearing? Any leads on the boots?'

'Ah, we'll have to discount the boots, sir. It turns out that Charlton was trained as a cobbler. He could have made them himself – they will never hold up in court as evidence of his spending.'

'Pity.'

'But I was paid a visit by that 'friend' of Mistress Charlton's who provides her with the butter: Mary Hall.'

'The same woman whom we saw in Charlton's cottage?' the detective asked in surprise. His fork was suspended half way to his mouth. 'I thought she was a friend of the wife?'

'Maybe so, but she was one of the first people through the door of the office at Kirkley Hall after you'd gone. She threw some more light on that twenty shilling note which Mistress Charlton gave her to pay for the butter. The week before Easter she had asked Priscilla

Charlton for the money for the butter, only to be told there was no money in the house apart from fifteen pounds which they needed to pay for a new cow. During this conversation, Mistress Charlton also let slip that the family had run up nearly fifteen pounds' worth of debts over the winter.'

'Mary Hall didn't call on the Charltons again until, coincidentally, the day we visited the house. She asked for eleven shillings for the butter money and this time Mistress Charlton gave her the twenty shilling note. She told her to bring her the change whenever it was convenient. Mary Hall knew that the Charltons had already bought the new cow and she was surprised to see they still had so much money. Cilla Charlton was unconcerned about getting the change back quickly. Hall claimed that when Mistress Charlton went to fetch the twenty shilling note, she pulled it out of a brown pot containing a whole handful of banknotes. She couldn't count how much was there but claims this wad of notes was bulky.'

'Hmm, further evidence that Charlton had more money than one would normally expect for a man in his situation,' Lavender murmured.

'Anyway,' Woods continued. He had begun to bristle with pride. 'After what she told me about the Charltons' debts, I decided to extend our enquiries to the local shopkeepers – in Ponteland and hereabouts.'

'Oh?' Lavender smiled. 'And what did you uncover?'

'I discovered James Charlton had been a very busy man the week following the burglary at Kirkley Hall…' he referred again to his pocket book. 'On Easter Tuesday, last, he paid Mr. Harbottle, a draper in Ponteland, a bill which amounted to thirteen shillings and five pence. He said James Charlton called in at past twelve in the forenoon and paid him with a twenty shilling banknote.'

'Another banknote?' Lavender interjected.

'Yes, and Mr. Harbottle was most helpful. He also alerted me to the fact that Charlton had also run up debts with a butcher in Morpeth called Edward Chaloner and with another shopkeeper in Ponteland, a Mistress Sarah Kyle.'

'Did you call on them both?'

'I did. The butcher confirmed that Charlton had called on him at his stall at Newcastle market on Saturday 8th April last, and paid him the sum of two pounds, one shilling and sixpence, being the amount of his bill. Mistress Kyle was more reluctant to talk to me – one of Charlton's younger brothers is shortly to wed her niece.'

'A summons to appear at the summer assizes will loosen her tongue,' Lavender snapped. 'Family loyalty holds no sway with the magistrates.'

'She did confirm, however, that James Charlton owed her no money at the present time,' continued Woods. 'The draper, Harbottle, had been sure that Charlton's debt to her had been for over three pounds in the winter, so we can assume this bill has been settled recently as well.'

Lavender leaned back in his chair and stared at the smooth Madeira in his glass. It glowed like a liquid jewel in the reddish glow from the firelight.

It was all beginning to add up: thirteen shillings and five pence for the draper; two pounds one shilling and sixpence for the butcher; the eleven shillings for the butter and over three pounds for the reluctant Mistress Kyle. It was still nowhere near the fifteen pounds of unpaid debt which the sly Mary Hall had suggested the Charltons owed. In fact, it barely amounted to seven pounds, but it was moving closer. All this was on top of the new cow, the new coat – and God only knows what was in those parcels. It was time to set the trap.

Woods waited patiently at the other side of the table for his employer to respond. When Lavender finally raised his eyes from his wine goblet and spoke, his words caught Woods by surprise.

'Did the duke ever get his eagle?' he asked. 'Was it successfully snared?'

'I'm not sure. I don't think so…though I have heard that the reward for its capture was raised to fifteen pounds. There have been many who have tried to snare it. Is it significant?'

'Fifteen pounds for a wild bird,' Lavender said slowly. 'What price would Mr. Ogle offer for the capture of his thief, do you think?'

'Ah, you think Ogle might offer a reward for those turning in James Charlton?'

'Quite so,' Lavender confirmed. 'A two hundred pound reward for information leading to the arrest and conviction of this criminal should bring in a flurry of further witnesses. Blood is only as thick as water when there's money like that to be gained; I'm quite sure Mistress Kyle will be one of the first in the queue with her information. I shall call on Mr. Ogle tomorrow and track down a magistrate for an arrest warrant for James Charlton. You, my friend, can return home to London – and your family – on the next available coach.'

Woods breathed a huge sigh of relief at that last bit of news.

'I have to confess, it'll be good to see the missus and the rest of the family again. By the way, Ogle returned to his Southampton estate last week – you'll have to write to him about the reward. And you can take this bloody thing, an all,' Woods pushed a bulky sheaf of paper across the table towards Lavender. 'It's a copy of your report for the duke – with extra details of my discoveries.'

Lavender looked down at pages of legible but shaky writing before him and smiled. He pictured his constable hunched over the paper, squinting and cursing in the dim light of guttering candles and painstakingly copying out the report.

'You have done well, Constable Woods,' he said at last. 'Very well. You have discovered valuable new leads for us in this investigation. Although I still don't feel we have enough to convict the man yet, I feel confident enough to have him arrested and questioned at Morpeth Gaol. We already know that he has lied to us about his whereabouts on the night of the burglary, and that in itself is enough to have him picked up and questioned further. Let's see how confident and sure of himself James Charlton continues to be after he has been rotting in Morpeth Goal for a while.'

Wednesday 17th May, 1809

Armed with an arrest warrant, Lavender, Captain Wentworth and a platoon of foot soldiers arrived at James Charlton's cottage in Milburn before dawn. They burst into the darkened cottage to discover that no one was at home. The fire was burnt out in the grate and the only evidence of life in the quiet hamlet was a distressed cow which lowed forlornly in the meadow beside the stream.

Not one to miss an opportunity, Lavender instructed the fusiliers to strike their tinder boxes, light candles and lanterns and search the place for stashed money and any items newly purchased. Meanwhile, he hammered on the door of the neighbours to question them about the whereabouts of Charlton and his family.

He discovered that Charlton and his wife had set out an hour before. They had gone to sell a pair of calves at Morpeth cattle market. Charlton had borrowed a horse and cart from a friend for the journey and they had ridden off in style with the bullocks tied to the back and trotting along behind them.

Unfortunately, this was all he discovered. Apart from a brown, earthenware pot with a few coppers, the soldiers had found nothing in the cottage. Mattresses had been turned over and ripped open, the rugs had been swept from the floor and the flagstones examined for evidence of secret hiding places but all to no avail. Even a close examination of the stinking privy and the soot-lined chimney breast, had revealed nothing. With a sinking heart, Lavender realised that a thief as clever as the one who had robbed Kirkley Hall was not going to leave the best part of one hundred and sixty pounds lying around to incriminate himself.

Disappointed, he remounted his horse and asked Captain Wentworth to regroup his men for the long march to Morpeth in pursuit of the Charltons.

'Never mind, sir,' the Captain said. 'At least when we arrest him at Morpeth cattle market, we will only have to drag him a few hundred yards to the gaol.'

It was late morning when they eventually arrived at Morpeth market. The town heaved. They could hear the racket made by over a thousand head of cattle from a mile away as they approached. The beasts lowed, the dogs barked, the drovers and drunks cursed and shouted. The rank smell was the next thing that hit Lavender and his party. The temperature had been rising steadily all morning and with it so had the stench from the sweltering animals and their excrement. As their horses clipped along the narrow streets at the edge of town, past patient flocks of tethered sheep, Lavender fumbled in his coat pocket for his perfumed handkerchief. It was another minute or so before they turned a corner and rode into the market place itself.

As the crowds surged around him, Lavender surveyed the chaos with dismay. Even from horseback it would be impossible to find Charlton in that writhing pack.

The Captain informed him that most of the livestock would have been sold off by nine that morning. This left the farmers, the workers and the drovers to enjoy the rest of the day in the twenty-six public houses of the town – or to spend their profits at the crowded market stalls. There was clearly a good deal of excessive drinking associated with market day in Morpeth, Lavender observed. As the adults milled – or staggered – around the stalls, packs of boys raced in between them, gathering up sacks full of manure. Beggars draped in rags followed the wealthy. Gaudily dressed whores gathered in groups outside the public houses. Here and there, discharged and limbless soldiers stood awkwardly on their crutches begging, their scarlet uniforms now faded like the fire in their eyes.

The Captain and his fusiliers paused respectfully beside Lavender, awaiting his instructions. He realised too late that they should have stayed at Charlton's cottage and waited for his return. He was just about to admit his mistake when a familiar, mocking voice hailed him from the pavement outside The George and Dragon.

'Found your thief yet, Detective?'

It was Michael Aynsley. Lavender could just hear him above the din. A flagon of ale was clutched in one hand; the other rested on his hip in a stance of defiance. Beer dribbled down Aynsley's beard and ran onto his stained waistcoat. He grinned contemptuously at the detective.

Around him stood a gang of powerfully built, hard-featured men attired in the dirty, thick jackets, neck cloths and collarless shirts of farmers. They looked on in cruel amusement. Their sharp eyes darted from Aynsley's face to Lavender's and enjoyed his discomfort.

Lavender's quick brain raced. Maybe this situation could be turned to his advantage. If there was one man in this heaving marketplace who would be aware of James Charlton, it was his nemesis, Michael Aynsley.

'Actually, I'm just on my way to arrest him…' Lavender replied cautiously. He never even got to finish his sentence.

'Well, if it's that bloody, half-wit Charlton, you're looking for,' Aynsley interrupted, 'he's over at the main auction ring with his missus and his brothers.'

'Thank you.' Lavender smiled. 'You have no idea how helpful you have just been.' He picked up the reins of his horse and urged her forward.

'What? Are you serious, like? You're going to arrest Charlton?'

Lavender ignored him and pressed forward.

Aynsley downed the last of his beer, and tossed his empty tankard aside. 'Come on lads – I wouldn't miss this for the world!'

Then he – and several of his mates – whistled to their dogs and began to follow the horses and the fusiliers, as they pushed their way through the milling crowds.

Priscilla and Jamie Charlton were in high spirits and thoroughly enjoying their day out. Cilla had wanted to accompany Jamie when he brought the calves to sell at the market so he had borrowed their neighbour's old horse and rickety cart to transport her in style. The children had been despatched the previous day into the care of their grandmother and their Aunt Susan at North Carter Moor.

Jamie had sold both calves for a good price. They had picked up a few provisions and a smart black bonnet with green silk ribbons for Cilla. Then he had given the rest of the money to her for safe-keeping.

His brothers, John and William, had driven down a herd of cattle from North Carter Moor to sell. Eventually, the three brothers and Cilla met up to discuss market prices and family business. An empty barrel was rolled over for Cilla to perch on between them, and they leaned against the railings of a sheep pen, deep in discussion. William's two exhausted sheepdogs slept at her feet. Their mother's health, her spasmodic rheumatism and the quack remedies she kept buying to cure it, was their first topic of conversation. The surprising development that their younger brother, Henry, was courting Grocer Kyle's niece was the second. They then moved on to the inability of one of their sisters' husbands to keep a pig alive.

William noticed how healthy his brother and sister-in-law looked; the miserable aura of poverty which had haunted their features all winter had now disappeared. Jamie's gaunt face had filled out and glowed with ruddy, good health. His clothes looked like they fitted him. This, combined with his smart new coat, gave him an air of shabby respectability.

'Why that's a charming new bonnet you're wearing, Cilla, hinny,' he told her.

She blushed and told him that Jamie had just bought it for her.

'Well, it suits you, lass,' he informed her. 'You're by far the bonniest lass in the whole of Morpeth today.'

'Tshh, Will,' she chided, laughing. 'Look around you – there's dozens of prettier women than me here.'

'I have eyes only for you, Cilla. It has been the greatest tragedy of my life that my useless saphead of a brother plucked you out of Corbridge before I got a chance to find you.'

'Well, her twin sister, Bella, is still unmarried if you fancy one of your own,' Jamie informed him, laughing.

'Alas,' William replied. 'I fear poor Bella would pale into insignificance beside her twin.'

Jamie and Cilla laughed but beside them John stiffened uncomfortably. William was an outrageous flirt with both of his brothers' wives but whereas Jamie was always amused, John was not. Irritated, the farmer took his leave and went off to a committee meeting at The Black Bull.

'What committee is he attending this time?' Jamie asked as they watched John's stiff, black-coated back disappear into the crowd.

'Oh, no doubt it's another one aimed at increasing the chapel-going and reducing the drinking in the parish of Ponteland.' William grinned and winked.

'So, what will you do for the rest of the day?' Cilla asked him.

'Well, I was going to take a glass or two of brandy in The Kings Arms with my brother – but I see he has far better company already than I...'

Cilla blushed again. She had always loved William like she had loved her own brother. He never failed to cheer her up, or to compliment her in some way when they met. Jamie, meanwhile, suffered a pang of disappointment about the lost drinking opportunity but he knew he could not leave his wife alone in those heaving and drunken crowds.

'...so I shall just have to have a drink with Archie Musgrave, instead,' William continued.

'Your friend from Corbridge way?' Jamie asked with a flash of jealousy.

'Aye, he's doing well. His new farm yields far more crops and produce than he expected.'

'Does he still pester you to go and work with him?' Cilla asked.

'Yes,' William said simply. 'He's hoping to buy more land and wants me to join him as a partner in the farm.'

During those lonely years William had spent in Newcastle with their elderly uncle in his chandlery business, Archie Musgrove had been his closest friend. They had been two country lads, lost in the alien world of the city. William had amassed a respectable amount of money during this time – and could have easily afforded to buy the lease of his own farm. However, he had returned to North Carter Moor to help John when their father had died and he had then become embroiled in that disastrous relationship with Sarah Aynsley. He had been tempted to go and work with Archie after Sarah had jilted him – even now, he hadn't completely abandoned the idea.

'I don't know why you don't take him up on his offer,' Jamie said. He had recovered his good humour. 'There's nothing to keep you at North Carter Moor, and our John's prayers and bible readings must be enough to drive a sane man to the asylum.'

'Ah, but then I'd rarely get to see my favourite brother and sister-in-law,' he smiled. Jamie and Cilla were pleased; Cilla flashed him a dazzling smile.

'More likely, you'd miss our ma's cooking too much!' Jamie laughed. 'We all know you're still tied to her apron strings! Get away with you, man – you'd have us believe anything!'

They all laughed and then Jamie turned back to his brother. 'We are thinking of buying another pig,' he said. 'Will you step up to the stall with me and give us your opinion, like?'

William's face fell and he hesitated. Jamie and Cilla could see there was something amiss. 'You should stop spending your money so freely, man,' William advised him quietly.

'Why? What's the matter?'

''Tis this damned robbery business at Kirkley Hall.'

'Oh, that,' Cilla said dismissively. 'Have they not found their thief yet?'

'Nay,' William replied – part of him did not want to frighten Cilla but he did not see how he could avoid it. 'Our Lizzie tells us they're close to arresting someone. That constable they got up from London to track down the thief has made out that Jamie is the main suspect.'

He turned to his brother now: 'He's done nothing but ask questions about you for the past month. Your name is mentioned often.'

'It always was!' Jamie said irritably. 'It'll be Aynsley who has started it. Aynsley has always hated the ground that I walked upon. He's allus bad-mouthed me.'

'Look, I've told you before: stop spending money and drawing attention to yourself,' William persisted. 'Leave the pig. Go home and keep your head down.'

Jamie burst out laughing. 'Don't be such a bloody fool, man! I've done nothing wrong.'

'It'll be no laughing matter if they arrest you for this crime, Jamie – innocent or not. Have you thought about what would happen to Cilla and the bairns if you were detained in Morpeth Gaol for even a few weeks?'

'Get away with you,' Jamie replied. 'As God's my witness, I'm innocent of this.'

'Do you think that will matter to the likes of Ogle and the duke?' William snapped, 'Do you think they'll really care if they send an innocent man to the gallows – or to Botany Bay? Someone has had the gall to break into Kirkley Hall – the local manor – the 'big house'. And they've stolen the rent money from under the noses of the gentry themselves! Somebody will swing for this crime after the summer assizes – and do you think they'll care if it's the right gadgie?' His voice had started to rise in frustration.

Jamie paused in his protestations of innocence. The smile had dropped from his face but William knew he was not convinced. 'I just wish you hadn't flashed your money around so much recently,' he said. 'You've made yourself the number one suspect – not Aynsley.'

Suddenly Cilla was on her feet and by their side, pointing through the crowd.

'I think you may be too late with your warning, Will,' she whispered. 'Look yonder.'

'What is it?'

''Tis the fusiliers – about a dozen of them. That London detective's leading them this way on a horse.'

She was right. The crowd ahead of them parted to make way for the red-coated soldiers and the two men on horseback. William could see their steel bayonets glinting ominously in the sunlight.

'Bloody Hell!' Jamie laughed. 'Would you believe it? Look who's with them – it's Aynsley! He leads them – not the Detective.'

'Aynsley?' William suddenly felt worried.

To his horror, Jamie began to shout out. 'Aynsley! Michael Aynsley!'

'For God's sake, Jamie, don't!'

'Have you taken the King's Shilling then, Aynsley?' Jamie yelled at the top of his voice. There was a ripple of laughter in the crowd around them. Everyone had paused in their business to watch the approach of the fusiliers.

'Here's hoping as much,' someone commented. There was more laughter.

'For God's sake, the pair of you – be quiet!' William hissed.

Aynsley had heard Jamie's voice and scanned the crowd for him. He was not hard to spot; the Charlton brothers stood a head taller than most.

'There he is!' he yelled.

'This way, men!' Captain Wentworth urged his horse forward. The crowd parted and the soldiers raced through: a crimson stream of well-fed muscle and lethal, glinting steel.

'I think they're after you, Jamie,' William hissed urgently. 'Slip away, man. I'll try and hold them off.'

'What? You against a dozen fusiliers, Will?' Jamie laughed undaunted. 'I've heard everything now!'

'They've come for you, brother,' William snapped. His voice rose with panic. 'Make a run for it, while ye've still got chance!'

‘I’m damned if I’ll run from Aynsley,’ Jamie snarled and stood his ground. His hatred of Aynsley blinded him to all reason.

‘Think of your family, Jamie! Cilla – and the bairns…’

‘There he is! Arrest him, men!’

The soldiers rushed forward, shoved William and Priscilla viciously out of the way and seized Jamie. He struggled violently as they lunged at him.

Cilla screamed – and Jamie struggled even more.

There was a flash of gunmetal as one of the soldiers raised his musket and brought the barrel crashing down into Jamie’s face. It smashed into his cheekbone with a sickening crunch and blood spurted from his nose like a fountain. Instinctively, William and Cilla lurched forward to help him.

Cilla was thrown back onto the ground. She curled into a ball, clutched her belly and screamed.

Two soldiers leapt in front of William. One of them jabbed him violently in the balls with his musket. The other gave him a glancing blow on the side of his head. He cried out and doubled over in agony, his eyes streamed with water and blood. All around them, the crowd recoiled in shock and anger and yelled out in protest. Aynsley and his cronies cheered and brayed.

Now William’s two snarling dogs leapt into the fray. With their hackles raised, they launched themselves at the redcoats. One was kicked out of the way but the other clamped his jaws onto the leg of a soldier. The razor sharp teeth tore through his flesh and the soldier added his screams to the rest. Another fusilier rushed forward to help his comrade; his bayonet fixed – his intention obvious.

This was too much for a crowd of farmers. Several strong pairs of grimy hands grabbed hold of the valuable dogs by their scruffs and hauled them out of sight and out of danger.

‘Charlton? James Charlton of Milburn?’ the Captain yelled above the noise.

Jamie was in no condition to answer. Stunned by the blow to his head, he was on his knees spitting out blood onto the cobbles. His arms were pinned behind him.

‘I’ve orders to arrest thee and take thee to Morpeth Gaol.’

‘On what charge?’ William yelled hoarsely. He had dropped onto the ground, half blinded with rage, blood and the excruciating pain in his balls.

‘Tha knows on what bloody charge, Will Charlton,’ Aynsley snarled.

'The theft of the rent money from Kirkley Hall,' the Captain confirmed. 'Now clap him in irons and take him to the gaol!'

The crowd around them gasped in surprise.

''Tis a lie!' William yelled, as he struggled to get to his feet. 'You've got the wrong man – it's Aynsley you should arrest!'

'Any trouble from you – and you can join your brother in gaol,' the Captain said coldly. The soldiers shoved William back down onto his knees again. As the fusiliers clapped the great iron restraints onto Jamie's wrists, the bleeding and dazed prisoner started to come to his senses. He lifted his head.

'Will – don't fight them!' he yelled. His face was bloodied and swollen; his voice almost unrecognisable. 'I need you to go to North Carter Moor – tell our John – get me a barrister. Tell him I'm innocent, Will. I never did nothing.'

'Aye,' Aynsley snarled sarcastically, 'and I'm the Prince Regent.'

Another wave of laughter swept through the crowd. It wasn't just Aynsley's cronies who laughed now. Drunkards had poured out of the public houses in their dozens to watch the fusiliers arrest the burglar of Kirkley Hall. The peaceful marketplace was filled with a seething mob; half protested about the brutality of the fusiliers – half egged them on.

'May you rot in hell, Aynsley!' Jamie screamed as he was dragged through the jeering crowd. William felt a wave of humiliation for his brother sweep through him – quickly followed by a wave of anger. He brushed away his womanish tears with the back of his sleeve.

'You've got the wrong man, Detective!' he yelled in desperation. 'All the parish knows it's Aynsley that's done it! He's the thief!'

Michael Aynsley glared contemptuously at William and moved towards him. William breathed heavily and tensed – expecting another blow. He knew he was in no condition to fight off Aynsley. The steward came right up to him. William could smell the ale-reeking breath as Aynsley leered into his face and spat at him. William recoiled but Aynsley had turned away.

'Now don't you be fretting over that pretty young wife of yours, Charlton,' he yelled at Jamie's disappearing back. 'I'll make sure she's cared for – give her lots of comfort, eh!'

'You evil bastard, Aynsley!' William groaned, 'I'll see you dead for that.'

His threat was lost in the raucous laughter of the mob. Another searing jab of pain shot through William's groin which bent him almost double. He collapsed in misery onto the ground. He was so absorbed in his own agony, he did not see Aynsley stop in his tracks as he bore down on Cilla.

Aynsley's daughter, Sarah Robson, had gone to Cilla's aid and stood protectively over her. She gave her father a withering glare. He paused. Father and daughter stared coldly at each other; their eyes locked in mutual dislike. Then Aynsley shrugged and turned back to his mates.

'Let's get a drink at the Black Bull, lads, to celebrate the capture of the thief who robbed Kirkley Hall.'

'Aye,' one of his cronies agreed. 'You'll probably get your job back now, Aynsley.'

CHAPTER EIGHT

It took William several minutes to regain his numbed senses. His head was swimming. The crowd in the marketplace moved in a dream-like rhythm and spoke in muted voices. He was vaguely aware that there were two men around him: one of them rolled the empty barrel over to him and gently helped him to sit down; the other pushed a flask of brandy into his hand. He drank deeply. As the fiery liquid hit the back of his throat, his brain leapt back into action. His eyes focused and his ears were once more assaulted with the rowdy noise of the market place.

'Easy lad,' a friendly voice said. 'You have had a bit of a shock, I'm thinking. Those fusiliers were out of order – there were no need to rough you all up.'

He finally recognised the two men standing by him. They were fellow chapel-goers from Kirkley; two older, black-coated and grey-haired Samaritans.

He nodded, not daring to trust his own voice yet, and handed back the flask to its owner. He took off his neckerchief and wiped the blood off his face as well as he could.

Clearing the moisture from his eyes, he searched for Cilla. She still lay on the ground, moaning. The crowd had thinned between them. There were several women grouped around her: some crouched on the ground holding her hand; others stroked her forehead. Most of them had their backs to him but he recognised one of them as the wife of the man who had given him the brandy. Another looked like a woman of quality with her navy riding habit and bonnet. At any other time, when he did not feel so wretched, he would have been moved by the kindness of the folks around him.

'Your wife is in a bad way.'

'It's my brother's wife,' he said automatically. 'Him that was arrested.' He tried to get to his feet but the pain forced him back down again.

Now the woman in the navy bonnet turned her head around and looked at him. He realised with shock that it was Sarah Aynsley.

Bloody hell, he thought angrily. What's she doing here?

She stood up and came over. She looked different somehow, thinner. Fine lines had formed around her eyes. The confident and glowing steward's daughter had changed; her face was white and tense.

'Cilla is losing the bairn, Will,' she said gently. 'She's been bleeding – though we think it has stopped for now. You'll have to get her inside somewhere…you can't move her like this.'

'What bairn? What are you talking about?' he snapped, confused.

'She's in the first months – or was in the first months – of a pregnancy,' Sarah explained carefully. 'I guess she and Jamie had not told you and the rest of the family yet?'

His brain raced as he tried to make sense of it all and a new wave of nausea washed over him. So now Cilla would lose a bairn as well? Could today get any worse? Sarah was an easy target for his frustration and anger.

'How do you know, Sarah Aynsley?' he snarled at her. 'You've never had a bairn in your life.'

'Easy, lad!' cautioned one of the men around him. 'She's only trying to help.'

One of the other women left Cilla's side and joined them. He recognised her as one of his mother's friends from chapel.

'Maybes Mistress Robson hasn't had a bairn, Will,' she chided gently. 'But the lass knows what she's talking about. Cilla is losing her child.'

'Well, maybe so,' he snapped. His voice rose in anger. 'But she's still her father's daughter. Were you proud of his performance back then?'

'Aye,' someone murmured behind him. 'That were shocking, that.'

'Staying behind to gloat, are you – Mistress Robson?'

There was an awkward silence. Sarah's pale face flushed.

'I can see you don't want my help at the moment, Will,' she said. 'So I'll go. But if there is anything else, either I, or my husband, Doctor Robson, can do to help ….'

Cilla screamed.

Ignoring Sarah, William climbed off the barrel and limped over to where Cilla writhed on the cobbles. He winced with every step. Cilla looked terrible. Her eyes were narrowed and glazed with pain; her skin clammy and drained of colour. He averted his gaze from the bloody stain which seeped across the front of her skirts.

'The horse and cart, Will,' she gasped in between contractions. 'Get me into the cart. Get me home.' Then she screwed up her eyes and screamed again.

'You cannot take her all the way back to Milburn,' said the elderly woman at his elbow. His mind raced.

'How long has she got before the bairn comes away?'

'It'll be a few hours yet. She's only just started, poor lass.'

'I'll take her to me mother at North Carter Moor,' he said. There was a murmur of approval. It would be a shorter journey.

The decision made, he set off painfully in the direction of The Queen's Arms where he knew Jamie had stabled his neighbour's horse. The man with the brandy fell into step besides him: 'I'll give you a hand, lad.'

They worked quickly and in silence as they hitched the old horse to the cart. The nag looked like it was ready for the knackers' yard and the cart swayed and creaked ominously as he swung himself up onto the driver's seat. It felt as if it would collapse under him at any moment.

Trust Jamie to set out on a journey with his pregnant wife in a contraption like this, he thought irritably. The man lives his life on a wing and a prayer.

They were back at the marketplace within minutes. He scooped Cilla up as if she were a feather and gently laid her in the back of it. The women tried to make her as comfortable as possible. He glanced around for Sarah Robson but she had disappeared. He climbed back into the driver's seat and prepared to set off. The elderly man, who had helped him, paused to speak before they left.

'She could ha' been a lot worse, lad.'

'What do you mean?'

'One of them fusiliers went to kick your sister-in-law when she were knocked to the ground – that Doctor's wife threw herself in between them, and stared him down. She's a plucky woman, her – and she stopped her da from interfering wi' the lass.'

William nodded and felt some of his anger with Sarah abate. Sarah and Cilla had always been fond of each other, he now remembered. He regretted his harshness.

'Don't worry about your brother,' the man added just before he drove away. 'If he's innocent as he claimed, God won't let him go to the gallows. God knows the truth and protects those who believe in him.'

I only wish I could believe that, William thought, as he urged the horse forward.

Jamie Charlton's humiliation on the streets of Morpeth did not last very long. Morpeth Gaol was situated just off the marketplace. It took only five minutes to drag him to the prison.

He was shoved roughly into the damp, stinking building and then herded through the gloom into one of the cages which divided the ground floor of the tower. He sank onto a pile of filthy straw. Shocked, exhausted and racked with pain, he closed his eyes and tried to close his mind to the agony in his face and jaw.

Lavender observed him dispassionately. He sensed that Charlton was not the kind of man who would conveniently roll over and confess to the crime he had committed; it would take pain, discomfort and suffering to make him more amenable. He decided to wait to interview him until the following day. Let him suffer his first wretched night in gaol.

He completed the necessary paperwork with the old gaoler and left instructions that Charlton was to have no visitors, before he joined Captain Wentworth for a meal in The Turk's Head.

The journey back to North Carter Moor seemed interminable.

William drove the horse forward as carefully as he could along the rutted lane but every time the wagon lurched it seemed to send a new jolt of pain through the suffering woman in the back of the cart. He tried to put his worry about Jamie out of his mind for the moment and concentrate on Cilla. He tried to soothe her and reassure her.

'Stop fretting, Will,' she managed to say at one point between her sobs. 'I've had worse than this with the other bairns.'

Relieved, he tentatively tried a joke about their predicament. 'Well, I've delivered a fair few calves in my time, Cilla. If push comes to shove I can hop into the back there and give you a hand.'

There was a strangled laugh from behind him. 'You come anywhere near me and I'll throw sommat at you.'

'I was only coddin on, hinny,' he said gently. However, he was mentally weighing up his ability to help her if the bairn came away before they got back to the farm. He was more familiar with a woman's physiology than an unmarried man probably should be but he doubted he had the expertise to help her effectively. Concerned, he urged the horse on a little faster.

'Don't try to make me laugh, Will,' she said. 'It hurts when I laugh.'

He drove on in silence, his face grim.

Cilla's pains seemed to ease slightly as they neared the farm and her groaning became more muted. He was moved by her strength and courage.

When they finally pulled up in the farmyard of North Carter Moor he shouted urgently for his mother and John's wife, Susan. The women ran out of the kitchen with the children clattering at their heels. As he scooped Cilla up into his arms and carried her inside, he told them in a few brief sentences what had happened. His mother and Susan gasped with shock, but wiped their hands on their aprons and went straight into action. Ann ordered him to carry Cilla upstairs to her bedroom and his eldest niece, Minnie, was dispatched for fresh sheets, towels and hot water.

By the time he had laid Cilla gently onto his mother's bed, Ann, who was known for her quick temper and forthright views, had begun to react to the news. She pronounced that the detective and Nathanial Ogle were both 'idiots and fools', and next raged about the evilness of 'the lecher, Michael Aynsley'. Then in a flurry of indignation, she swept William away towards the door.

'Get tha face washed, Will, the blood's frightening the bairns as much as Cilla's screams.' She shut the door firmly in his face and turned back to give what comfort or help she could to 'poor Cilla' as the baby came away.

Relief flooded over him as he realised he was now excluded. He took himself to the kitchen, warmed himself awhile and gulped down the scalding cup of sweet tea pushed into his hand by one of his nieces.

Next he took himself off to the privy and the washhouse to inspect his own injuries. His balls were badly bruised and swollen and when he started to urinate, a fresh wave of pain shot through him. Thankfully, the cut on the side of his head was relatively superficial. A splash of water, a bite to eat and another strong cup of tea, and he began to feel more like himself.

He decided to take the horse and cart back to Jamie's neighbours in Milburn. He would let nine-year-old Jack go with him. Cilla's younger children had been unable to grasp the seriousness of what had happened to either their mother or their father but her son was scared and followed him around, pale-faced and frightened. William felt for the lad. There would just be time to round up Jamie's cattle and herd them back to North Carter Moor before milking time. Jack came with him willingly – glad to escape from the muffled groans of his mother and the ceaseless chatter of his sisters. He questioned his uncle about his father, and William tried to explain as gently as he could what had happened. 'Don't fret, lad,' he said. 'It's all a mistake. Your Da will be home before you know it.'

The boy still looked scared and said very little. William gave him the reins to help take his mind off things.

They took the cart back first. Jamie and Cilla's neighbours were good folks and were horrified at the news; they had been worried sick ever since the fusiliers had arrived that morning and turned over Jamie's cottage. Yes, they would take care of the pig and chickens for a few days, while the Charlton family decided what was to be done.

Leaving young Jack outside, William entered his brother's home with a deep sense of foreboding. The wreckage he found angered and horrified him as much as the fusiliers' brutality at the arrest in Morpeth. Nearly every stick of furniture was smashed. All the mattresses – even the children's – had been ripped open. The stuffing had been yanked out and was now settled in piles around the room amongst the broken crockery and trampled toys. The soldiers had left no nook or cranny unexplored in their bid to find evidence of the crime. Cilla's flower vase had been turned upside down and then hurled to the floor, where it lay shattered in the piles of soot which they had brought down from the chimney. Indigo bluebells lay scattered at his feet.

If you did steal the damned rent money, William thought grimly. *I hope you had the good sense to hide it well, brother.*

He tried to shake the anger off and went to the larder. He took all the food he could find and dropped it into his bag. Cilla and the bairns would have to stay at North Carter Moor for a while, whether his elder brother liked it or not. No doubt John would moan constantly about the extra mouths he had to feed. A sack full of bread, flour, cheese and ham might shut him up for a couple of days at least. He thought about trying to take a few personal effects, bits of clothing for Cilla and the bairns but then he dismissed the idea. It was not his place to rummage through Cilla's undergarments. No doubt his mother and Susan would come down later and sort all that out. No doubt they would try to sort out the mess in the cottage, as well.

His final act was to find the little-used cottage key. Once word got out about Jamie's arrest, the cottage would be vulnerable to looters. There were always those who came like carrion crows to help themselves to the pickings following someone else's misfortune.

The key was underneath Cilla's mantelpiece clock which lay smashed on the floor, its coils and springs protruding like the innards of a gutted pig. He knew the clock hadn't worked for years, but Cilla had been sentimentally attached to it because it had once belonged to her dead father. Now it was ruined. A fresh wave of fury swept through him and he stormed out of the cottage.

He locked the door and sent young Jack scurrying off to Jamie's strip to pull up some cabbage shoots to feed the pig. He scattered some corn for the hens and then rounded up Jamie's small herd of cows to take back to North Carter Moor for milking. He hoped the walk back to the farm would calm some of his rage and give him time to think.

On his return, he found that his eldest brother, John, was now at home – and he was not in a good mood either.

John had enjoyed an excellent meal and a constructive meeting at The Black Bull with other sober, respected and chapel-going landowners from the local parish. In fact, they had even discussed the possibility of financing a Temperance Hotel in Ponteland, a project close to John Charlton's heart. Feeling rejuvenated and glowing with religious fervour, he had stepped out of The Black Bull, only to be told, by nearly everyone he met, that his brother Jamie had been arrested and dragged off to Morpeth Gaol for the robbery at Kirkley Hall.

Burning with shame and fury, he had thundered back to the farm on his horse. When he arrived home, it was to hear the unwelcome news that his sister-in-law was ill upstairs losing a bairn. On top of this, all the women of his household were in a state of considerable distraction and were totally preoccupied with Cilla with no interest in him, or his needs, at all.

'What in God's name has been going on?' he demanded when William walked into the kitchen. William briefly told him the facts of what had happened and then left him alone to mull them over. He felt it wiser to wait until the evening to engage John in a lengthy discussion about what was to be done.

Supper that night was a further disaster. Abandoned by Ann and Susan, whatever it was that had been in the pot over the fire had now burnt to a blackened pulp.

'What is the use of keeping a houseful of women, if I can't even get a decent supper?' John moaned.

Finally, accepting that no-one in his farm had any sympathy for his plight at all, the farmer of Carter Moor sighed and sought refuge with a platter of cold meats, cheese and bread in the sanctuary of the farm's parlour.

A dull and rather drab room, it was rarely used except for Christmas, Easter and funerals. The room smelt damp and contained a mismatched collection of uncomfortable furniture which had been passed down from one generation of Charlton farmers to another. An ancient Tudor settle stood side by side with pale, bow-legged Queen Anne tables and winged chairs, all thick with dust. The colours on the tapestry upholstery had been rubbed away to grey by dozens of Charlton bottoms and faded by the decades of sunlight which had streamed through the leaded panes in the mullioned window. Several dour-looking ancestors – their names long forgotten – glared down from the walls in chipped gilt frames. A collection of ugly pottery dogs lined the mantelpiece where a plain mahogany clock took centre stage.

Outside, across the valley, the sun was beginning to set into a soft, reddish glow along the ridge which still bore sections of the ancient Roman wall. William struck his tinder box and lit a couple of candles and a fire in the grate beneath the carved Jacobean fireplace. Then he settled down to eat with his brother. Although he had his own two-roomed cottage attached to the stables, he ate with the family and was welcome to come and go in the main farmhouse whenever he pleased.

They were not to be alone for long. News of Jamie's arrest had spread quickly around the parish. John and William had only just lit their pipes, when their other brother, Henry, burst angrily through the door. Henry lodged in Ponteland close to his work, but when he'd heard about Jamie he he'd come straight back to North Carter Moor Farm. Hot-headed and young, Henry was incensed with the treatment meted out to Jamie. He raged about the injustice and demanded to know what the family planned to do about Jamie's arrest.

'We have to send money for his keep,' William announced. 'Though God only knows, how much of it will be actually spent on feeding Jamie. The gaolers are bigger thieves than the prisoners.'

'It sounds as if he may need to see a doctor as well,' Henry commentated. 'Do you think they may have broken his jaw?'

'I couldn't say for certain,' William admitted. 'But one thing's for sure, lying in chains in gaol tonight he's in a lot of pain. He took a good beating.'

There was an uncomfortable silence as the men in the room each pictured Jamie's wretchedness. While they were feeling guilty, William decided to push his advantage.

'We'll have to keep Cilla and the bairns here,' he added. 'Ma's already said that Cilla and the girls can have her room. I'll take young John with me to sleep in my cottage. She'll not be able to pay the rent on her own home while Jamie's in gaol.'

'Can't she go to her own family?' John suggested sourly.

'Hardly,' William said. 'Her mother and sister are naught but paupers since her father died. They'd starve.'

'That sister of hers is worse than a pauper – or so I've heard,' Henry sniggered.

'We'll have none of that tap room talk here,' John snapped.

Henry raised an eyebrow but fell quiet. In the silence that followed William realised that they had all heard the shocking rumours coming out of Corbridge about Cilla's twin sister, Bella. Allegedly, she had taken up whoring to feed herself and their mother. William watched his brothers shuffle uncomfortably. They avoided each other's eyes. He casually wondered if either of them had taken a trip over to Corbridge to try her out. When he had first heard the gossip he had considered it himself for a while. There was something appealing about the thought of lying with a woman who was the spitting image of the beautiful Cilla. His manhood stirred in his breeches. The movement sent violent stabs of pain racing through his injured groin. It brought him sharply back to reality.

'That's no place for Jamie's daughters to live,' he snapped, while trying not to wince.

'So I'm to take in another four mouths to feed?' John moaned.

'Aye,' His mother was framed in the doorway. 'And be thankful it's only four – Cilla's lost the bairn now.'

They all turned. Henry rose from his seat to greet her. His mother had removed her bloodied apron and washed her hands and face before coming to talk to the men. William got up to give her his chair but she shook her head. She preferred to remain standing by the fire. She rested her arms across the high mantel and stared down thoughtfully into the flames. The men waited for her to speak.

Although plagued in the winter by her rheumatism, Ann Charlton was a sprightly woman in her sixties. From healthy farming stock herself and with an intelligent mind of her own, she had breezed into life at North Carter Moor as a young bride nearly fifty years ago and had quickly established herself as a force to be reckoned with. Worshipped by her late husband and adored by her seven surviving children, she was known for her sharp insight, common sense and outspoken manner.

''Tis a shame about the bairn,' Henry snapped. 'That'll be Aynsley's fault, an all.''Don't go on about it,' William warned. 'Our Jamie's going to be mad enough when he gets out of gaol –

he'll be after Aynsley's blood for the part he played in this. Talk of the dead bairn will just inflame him even more.'

''Tis probably for the best.' Ann Charlton's tone was matter-of-fact. ''Tis too soon after her last bairn – and Cilla may need to work now.'

'I think we need to settle what we will do to help Jamie,' William said. He was encouraged by his mother's presence. He knew she would back him when John started to object. 'Jamie'll need food and money – and he's asked for a barrister.'

'A barrister!' John gasped in predictable horror. 'Is there no end to the man's needs?'

'Folks like us, don't employ lawyer types!' Henry said in surprise.

'Folks like us don't get arrested and falsely accused of crimes they didn't commit,' snapped Ann Charlton, who was clearly in no mood for argument tonight. Her three sons fell silent.

'If our Jamie needs a barrister to prove his innocence – then we'll all pay for one for him. I have some money put by which your father left for me, as you all know. We'll go round the whole family. Everyone can give something – including your sisters and their husbands.'

'I'm saving to get wed,' Henry protested.

Ann spun around sharply on her youngest son. 'Your nuptials might have to wait till after the assizes, Henry – and you'll have to spend less money in Ma Shotton's, Will. Do any of you want your brother's death on your conscience because you were too tight to help out? Do you, John? Can any of you really think to carry on enjoying yourselves when our Jamie's life is in danger?'

The thought of Jamie swinging on the gallows sent an icy shock through William. The men fell silent. Sensing her advantage, Ann pressed her point home.

'This thing will affect all of us. Not one of us will be able to hold our heads up in this parish again if Jamie is hanged for thieving.' Her words seemed to strike home with her eldest son; John sat up straighter and looked thoughtful.

'This family is respected hereabouts – and that's how it's going to stay,' she continued. 'We've looked after our own since the time of the reivers and that is how we will carry on. We've never had a Charlton hanged yet – and we're not going to have one now – not my son,' she finished firmly.

Not quite true, thought William.

There had been one Thomas Charlton, a cousin of their father's, who had supported the wrong side during the Jacobite rebellion and who had been hanged for his misjudgement. William tactfully decided this was not the time to remind her of the rebellious Thomas.

'And as for Cilla and the bairns – my grandchildren – they need our protection now – from both Aynsley and the malicious tongues that wag in this parish. Aynsley has already tried to rape the poor lass once and they'll starve if we don't feed them. So Cilla and the bairns can have my room for as long as it takes. I'll move into Lizzie's bed in Minnie's room. Cilla will be up and about in a few days and will earn her keep.'

There was a short silence while the men digested her words.

'There is no doubt of his innocence, is there?' Henry queried.

'What do you mean?'

'I mean, he didn't steal it, did he? He's always been a bit wild has our Jamie: he ran away from his apprenticeship and lost his position at Kirkley Hall. Is it possible he could be guilty?'

William thought his mother would explode in rage but she did not. Instead, she and the rest all turned and looked at him. As Jamie's closest friend and confidante, they expected him to know the truth.

'Of course, he's innocent!' he declared laughing. 'Our Jamie's no thief!'

That sealed it. Decisions were made about money, Cilla and the children. Then John ordered the entire family to gather in the kitchen. The children were rounded up and everyone stood quietly around the kitchen table, while John read out Psalm 23, said prayers and beseeched God to keep Jamie strong and safe in his hour of need:

'Though I walk through the valley of the shadow of death, I will fear no evil: for thou art with me; thy rod and thy staff they comfort me. Thou preparest a table before me in the presence of mine enemies: thou anointest my head with oil; my cup runneth over…'

Meanwhile, upstairs in her mother-in-law's bed, Cilla wept for her wronged husband and grieved for her lost baby.

CHAPTER NINE

Thursday 18th May, 1809

Filthy, dishevelled and disorientated, Jamie was dragged into the dank office in Morpeth Gaol and forced down into a seat opposite Detective Lavender. The thin-faced policeman observed him coldly from beneath his hooded eyes. Jamie's swollen face throbbed and was stained and encrusted with dried blood. The pain had kept him awake most of the night. He had a livid black eye and suspected that his cheekbone was shattered. His mouth gaped open and dribbled saliva. He asked for water.

'Give him some,' Lavender instructed the two turnkeys.

Jamie drank and sighed as the liquid eased the pain in his parched throat. Behind his bruised face and bloodshot eyes, his brain raced. His overwhelming instinct was to rise up and wrap his chains around the interfering neck of that fool of a detective. Keep your temper, lad, he warned himself – or this bastard'll have you.

'You're in here, Charlton, because you're a liar and a thief,' Lavender began.

'I'm no thief,' Jamie mumbled. He was promptly cuffed on the back of the head by one of the turnkeys. 'You listen to the Detective, you,' the thug informed him, 'and keep your gob shut.'

'As I was saying,' Lavender continued, 'you're a liar.' He pointed to the notes in front of him. 'In your previous statement, you told us that on the night of the robbery at Kirkley Hall, you left your work and went straight home. That was a lie. You went drinking to the Coaching Inn at Newhamm Edge. You stayed late, lost a lot of money at the card tables and then staggered out quite drunk.'

'So?' Jamie challenged him. 'I didn't want me wife to know I'd been gambling again. Is it against the law now to have a few drinks and a game of cards?' The turnkeys moved forward again to hit him but Lavender held up his hand to stop them.

'No, but it proves you're a liar. And as for being a thief? Well, that is obvious. The night after the Kirkley Hall robbery you were seen by several witnesses in the Seven Stars in Ponteland, throwing money around like water and even trying to bet a guinea on another game of cards.'

'Oh, that,' Jamie muttered.

'In addition to this,' the detective continued, 'I have statements from several good citizens, to the effect that the week after the robbery you went round half of Ponteland and paid off debt after debt – to the sum of nearly seven pounds – and you were seen in Newcastle making several purchases on the Saturday following the robbery.'

'You've been busy.' Jamie spat the words from his swollen mouth. The turnkeys bristled behind him.

'So tell me, Charlton – without lying, if you please,' Lavender continued, 'from where does a poor man, who loses at the card table on a Monday night, suddenly get this kind of money? You had far more money than one would expect for a man in your situation – where did it come from?'

Jamie made a disparaging noise and replied calmly: 'From my regular job – and the sale of my stock.'

Lavender laughed. 'I doubt that. You went to Kirkley Hall, broke in and stole the rent money. Then the very next day – the very next week – you started spending money like water – just like the fool you are.'

'No, I didn't. I never robbed Kirkley Hall.'

'Yes, you did! How else can you – such a poor man – explain having so much money immediately after the robbery? There's only one conclusion which I can come to – and there's only one conclusion which the jury will come to just before they sentence you to hang. You're guilty as charged.'

There was a pause. Jamie knew that Lavender and the turnkeys were waiting to see what effect the mention of hanging would have on him.

'Well, there's always been the sale calves, you see.' he said. 'I'd made a bit of money selling the calves.'

'Calves?' Lavender's dark eyes narrowed.

'Aye, they're fetching nearly three pounds per beast at the moment.'

'Selling a couple of calves will not explain all those debts paid off and the amount of money you spent the week after the robbery.'

'No,' Jamie agreed. 'But it weren't just two calves. You see…two of my cows had twins.'

'Twins?'

'Aye, two sets in one year – that's rare good fortune and then – would you believe it? My third cow went and had another set! That's six calves, this year. We sold the last of them only yesterday, here at Morpeth meat market.'

There was another pause while the Detective digested this information. He was frowning; this news was obviously unwelcome to him. 'There must be something in the water in Milburn,' he eventually snarled sarcastically. 'And I suppose you have receipts for the sale of all these animals?'

Jamie's malformed mouth twitched painfully now into a grotesque grin.

'Aye – and I can give you the name of the man I sold them to, an all!'

The fecundity of Charlton's livestock was to prove a bitter blow for Detective Lavender. Armed with the details given to him by the big labourer, he quickly established that in this instance at least, Jamie Charlton was telling the truth. The calves had brought him nearly nine pounds in income in the two months before the robbery. When he took into consideration the income Charlton earned from his work as a barn man at Haindykes, Lavender realised that the evidence which he and Woods had of gathered about Charlton's apparent wealth, the week after the robbery, was now not enough to secure a conviction.

Everything now rested on the success of the reward in bringing forward more witnesses of Charlton's lavish spending in the weeks following the robbery. Here, too, Lavender was to be frustrated. Two days later, he received a letter from Mr. Ogle's secretary in London. It informed him that Mr. Ogle had serious doubts about advertising a reward for further information appertaining to the arrest and conviction of the Kirkley Hall robber. Was it really necessary to go to further expense? By now, surely the detective must have the suspect, Charlton, in custody? No doubt he would be convicted for the crime at the next assizes? Therefore, Mr. Ogle did not see the necessity of such a radical step as offering a two hundred pound reward.

Cursing the foolishness of his employer, Lavender sat down to write a letter to the duke. He updated him about the details of Charlton's arrest and implored him to intervene with his neighbour.

The next week William managed to bribe the guards and gain access to his brother. The family had sent Jamie food and money for his keep but so far no one had been able to see him.

William entered the formidable old gaol with some trepidation. The large, ground floor room was dark and rank with the smell of unwashed bodies and human faeces. He sniffed tentatively but could not detect the sickly, sweet odour of the dreaded gaol fever. Water dripped down the bare stone walls, rats scurried along their edges and there was a constant background murmur of the low, dispirited conversation of the prisoners, interspersed with the occasional sob and shriek from the women incarcerated in the next room.

The ground floor of the building was divided up by metal cages. The wide-set bars allowed the prisoners to talk to each other with ease as they lay, or sat slumped, on the piles of mouldy straw in their cages. Beside each man lay a pewter plate and mug. Each plate had been licked clean and was crawling with flies. The cage doors were secured with rusty, iron padlocks, the keys to which jangled rhythmically from the belt of the sniffing gaoler as he shuffled across the filthy flagstones. As William passed each cage, heads turned and stared. The dull eyes of the dregs of society followed his progress.

The ancient gaoler stopped at the end cage. 'He's in 'ere,' the old man told him. 'Charlton? You've got a visitor.'

Jamie scrambled to his feet and came over to the bars. His chains rattled as he moved.

'Five minutes,' snarled the gaoler.

'Here's another crown to make it fifteen.' William held out a coin.

'Ten then,' conceded the man, and he wiped his hand across his running nose and shuffled away.

Despite the wretched conditions and his swollen and bruised face, Jamie was in good health and spirits. 'Will! It's good to see you. Have you got any scran?' He grinned at William through the gloom.

'Aye…'

'Well, stop your gawping and give us it 'ere.'

William pulled out a parcel from the pocket of his greatcoat. It was fresh bread and chicken wrapped in newspaper. With a sharp rattle of his chains, Jamie snatched the food out of his brother's hands and unwrapped it. 'It costs extra to have the chains removed,' was all Jamie said before he started devouring the chicken.

'Ma's sent a pie as well,' William informed him. His voice echoed strangely in the ancient stone room. 'But your gaoler's taken that, along with two guineas of our John's money, for your upkeep. John says to tell you he can't visit you because it cost so much to bribe the guard but that he'll spare no expense on your barrister…'

William's voice faded as he watched his brother gulping down the food. Jamie barely acknowledged the message from their elder brother. Silently, William passed him his own brandy flask. Jamie drank deeply to swill down the chicken and then paused before he started on the bread.

'How are Cilla and the bairns?

'She is fine – they're all fine…' William said and paused.

Jamie sensed his hesitation. His eyes flashed to William's face.

'What's happened?'

'She lost the bairn she was carrying.'

Disappointment and pain flash swept across Jamie's features. Then he took a deep breath and said simply: 'Perhaps it's for the best. The other bairns? You say they are all well?'

William nodded.

'They're thriving; John's taken them in at North Carter Moor.'

'Good,' snapped Jamie. 'At least they're safe from Aynsley there.'

'Aye, John looks after them proper. He's going to get you the best barrister money can buy, as well. Ma's made all the family chip in, like, with the expense.'

Jamie nodded. 'Our ma's been good,' he mumbled in between mouthfuls. 'She's sent me a bit of food along most days – though no doubt that damned gaoler has eaten much of it.'

'Many in the chapel and in the Parish are behind you, Jamie,' William said quietly. He was conscious of the echoing walls and the dozens of ears listening to their conversation. 'Most were upset to hear what had happened to you. They had a collection for you and Cilla last Sunday at the chapel. I can see it is hard, like, but you mustn't get yourself down-hearted.'

Jamie grinned again.

'I know, Will,' he said, confidently. 'It won't be for long – they've got nothing on me. That detective gadgie – he's got no evidence I did the bloody robbery. I'll be out of this hellhole soon and back home with Cilla and the bairns.'

William decided to change the subject at this point. Jamie and his family would not be going home to the cottage in Milburn. That was the one thing which John had put his foot down about; he would not continue to pay the rent on Jamie's cottage while he was in gaol and Cilla was at the farm. Between them, the Charltons had packed up everything they could save from the carnage left by the fusiliers and moved Jamie and Pricilla's few remaining possessions into the back of the barn at North Carter Moor. The family would just have to start over again when he was released from prison.

'So, who are these devils with whom you share this flea-ridden hellhole?' he asked with forced joviality. He pointed to the pathetic-looking creature, clad in rags, slumped on the floor of the next cage. 'Who's that gadgie, moaning to himself over there?'

'Him? Why that's Frank Wilson of Darras Hall. He's charged with committing an unnatural act with a mare.' Jamie winked.

William laughed. 'I'd like to have seen that! Most of our mares would have kicked the hell out of him. Why does he moan so? Is there gaol fever in here?'

'No, he's just a lunatic,' Jamie replied, calmly. 'He's probably the most harmless soul in here, mind. Just don't 'whinny' as you walk past his cage when you leave.'

William laughed again.

'The rest are a right bunch of evil bastards,' Jamie scowled. 'Horse thieves, pickpockets and highwaymen.'

Suddenly William was uneasily conscious of the other men in the cages. Eyes bored into his back like daggers. The hairs rose on the back of his neck.

'What's the caterwauling in the next room?'

'That? That's the women – if you can recognise them as such. A bigger bunch of wild, pox-ridden trollops you never did see. There's a deranged girl in there. She's the one who wails. She's charged with murdering her bairn and throwing the body into the privy.'

William stopped smiling now. Conscious that his time was nearly up, he moved closer to his brother.

'It's good to see you are all right, Jamie,' he said softly.

'You too, Will.'

'I was afeard they might have…might have…'

'What? Tortured me?' Jamie said casually. 'No. Not yet. There's been talk of it, mind – the gaolers want to use the thumb screws. They want me to confess to the robbery but the detective says I'll need my thumbs to hold the quill when I sign my confession.'

William gasped in shock and tried to imagine what it would be like. The excruciating agony which intensified with each turn of the screw, until finally, the top of your thumbs exploded into a useless pulp of blood and flesh.

He felt worried when he left. Jamie's cheerful confidence belied the danger which surrounded his brother on every side. Half-starved, vulnerable to fever and dysentery, surrounded by sadistic gaolers and hardened criminals who would think nothing of blinding him for a stale crust of bread, Jamie was in more danger than he had ever been in his life. Reluctantly, William said 'farewell' and followed the shuffling gaoler back out into the sunlight, doubling his resolve to help Jamie.

At last, Lavender succeeded in gaining permission from Nathanial Ogle to place the reward notice in the Newcastle Courier. Lavender had no idea what had passed between the duke and Mr. Ogle after His Grace had received the detective's letter but he surmised that his duplicity was now out in the open.

The letter he received from Ogle's secretary was short and curt. Lavender was to dictate the wording of the advert to the steward and then send in his bill for the services he had rendered in solving the mystery of the robbery at Kirkley Hall. From now on, Ogle's secretary and the new steward at Kirkley Hall would handle this matter themselves; they needed no more help from Bow Street detectives.

Lavender was not surprised by this turn of events but he was seriously concerned about the future of the case. He had no faith in Nathanial Ogle.

Back at North Carter Moor, Cilla was recovering from the miscarriage and the shock of losing her husband to Morpeth Gaol. She had been listless and depressed for some weeks after Jamie's arrest and the loss of her child. As May moved into June and eventually into the stagnant heat of July, where the air was heavy with the scent of violets and wild garlic, she found herself feeling more hopeful and a little more energetic.

She and the children did what they could to help around the farm. She also tried her best to keep them from annoying their Uncle John. She rose in the cool of dawn. With baby William strapped to her back, she joined in the milking in the misty riverside meadow, where flies crawled lazily across her hands as she pulled on the soft, pink teats. As the temperature soared at mid-day and the air over the fells shimmered in a haze, she sought refuge from the burning sun in the dairy. Here she helped Ann and Susan and joined in the conversations about the family and the problems caused by the heat. Once again in the evening, she would follow the family down to the meadows to milk the sweltering cows, which had spent the day following the movement of what little shade was afforded by the few parched trees.

Slowly, Cilla tried to pick up the pieces of her life. Every Saturday night she would bathe her children and lay out their best clothes ready for chapel the next morning. Surrounded and protected by her husband's extended family, she and the bairns were able to walk quietly into the chapel and slip into an oak pew without too much comment from the rest of the congregation. She kept her head down and her eyes averted from curious stares. She taught her children the same humility. She avoided going out alone in public and on the rare occasions when she was jeered at in the street, she never responded and always walked calmly away.

Her serenity and grace did not go unnoticed – although, some mistook it for aloofness. William was acutely aware that his sister-in-law's quiet humility was her protection from the rest of the world.

The hot weather of July threatened to break as black clouds gathered ominously at the end of the valley on their third and final day of late-haymaking. John Charlton stopped the older children from attending school and chivvied the whole family down to the insect-swarming fields. He and William scythed down the final acres of lush, flowering grass, while the women and children racked it into rows and stacked it for drying. Cilla worked tirelessly at the backbreaking job, pausing only occasionally to wipe the beads of sweat from her face or to chide the twins for trampling the grass.

As she worked, strands of silky hair escaped from her bonnet and drifted down around her face and onto the smooth, lightly freckled skin of her elegant neck and shoulders. The sunlight reflected on its gleaming copper and dazzled the eyes of William Charlton as he straightened up to wipe the streaming sweat from his face. He watched her surreptitiously as she gazed lovingly down at his toddling little namesake. He found he envied the bairn when she took him to her breast.

The weather did not break. The brooding stormclouds slunk away beyond the ridge of the fells, and took their malevolence with them. They left behind their cool underbellies which rolled down the valley sides in a welcome breeze. The hay was piled into stacks to protect it from the morning dew and the weary family milked the cows and then returned exhausted to the farm to complete their other chores.

After supper and prayers, the children were put to bed and Cilla sought William out at his cottage, as she often did on these long summer evenings, to sit awhile and talk of Jamie.

He was outside on the step with young Jack. They were trying to mend the remains of a chair when she approached. She perched on the edge of the old stone trough and watched them. His large hands suddenly felt clumsy and he hesitated with the unfamiliar carpenter's tools he had borrowed.

'That's one of our chairs, isn't it Will?' she said quietly.

It was. She had handled the news of the destruction of her home and property with the same fortitude which had helped her bear the arrest and imprisonment of her husband. The family had done what they could to darn, patch and mend her possessions during the days she was abed recovering from the miscarriage, but not all of it could be rescued.

'We're trying to save it, Ma,' Jack said.

'I don't think there's much hope for it, mind' confessed William, sadly. 'I think we'll have to get the doctor to pronounce this one dead and get the parson to bury it.'

Young Jack laughed and asked what prayers the parson would say for a dead chair.

'I don't rightly know,' William informed him. 'You'll have to ask your Uncle John about that – but I think the sermon would be a bit wooden.'

They laughed and joked a while more with the child. Then the boy was sent to bed. He hugged his mother and William ruffled his hair affectionately as he clambered past him and disappeared into the cottage.

'Don't forget to mention your Da in your prayers,' William reminded him.

'I never do,' the boy shouted back as he vanished into the building.

'You're so good with him,' Cilla said simply. 'I owe you all so much.'

'Nonsense, hinny,' he replied. 'You and Jamie would have done the same for us.'

'We would have tried…' she began. The rest of her words remained unsaid. They both knew she and Jamie would never have been able to afford to do much to aid other family members. The words hovered briefly between them and then vanished into the balmy evening air. There was no awkwardness between them now. She moved over and sat down on the step beside him.

Suddenly he was overwhelmed with a strong desire to reach over and pull her curvaceous body over to his. Desperate to keep his hands occupied, he picked up his tools again.

'Your ma said she can't remember the last time you took yourself down to the ale houses of Ponteland,' she commented, mischievously. 'She thinks you might be finally heeding the minister's words about the evils of drink.'

'She can hope,' he said, winking. 'There's no harm in hoping.'

'Is it because of us, Will?' she half-whispered. 'Is it because of the cost of keeping me, Jamie and the bairns, that you can no longer afford a drink?'

It was, of course. They were all feeling the pinch this summer. His younger brother, Henry, had postponed his wedding to Grocer Kyle's niece.

'Nay, hinny, I just prefer the company I find at home, these days,' he said. 'Your son is a fine lad, Cilla. He's the best company an old bachelor like me could have – and his ma is good to have around, an' all.'

She blushed at the unexpected compliment and said: 'You're so good with Jack. Thanks to your instruction, he's now real canny with the stock.'

'Aye, we'll make a fine herdsman of him yet,' he announced.

'Jamie hopes he will get a fine position in life,' she confided. 'What with him being so bookish, and all; he's talked of him working in an office in Newcastle.'

William grimaced. 'It's a damn lonely life in Newcastle,' he said grimly. 'My ma had high hopes for me, as well. I often wonder what she thought when I came back here to work with our John.'

'Your ma adores you.' Cilla smiled. It had long been suspected in the family that Ann Charlton favoured her third son above all the others. Although this had caused some friction and jealousy amongst the brothers when they were bairns, it was more a topic for gentle ribbing now that they were men.

'It was alright at first when I came back,' William continued. 'I was to stay for a while and help John settle into the farm after our Da died. Then I took up with Sarah, and we were to get our own farm nearby – when a good one came vacant.'

Cilla stayed silent. It wasn't often he talked about that painful period in his life. Suddenly he felt awkward. 'Of course it all came to nothing,' he concluded sharply. 'So, I often wonder if Ma is disappointed that I am still here? Any illiterate cow herder could do my job.'

'Your ma knows – like we all did – that you needed some time after Sarah disappointed you so,' Cilla said gently.

William gave a sharp laugh. 'Time, eh? That's what you thought I needed?'

'You'll find another lass soon, William,' she said softly. 'Although she was my friend once, I have to say Sarah Aynsley proved she were not good enough for you.'

'Not good enough?' he queried. 'How so?'

'You know exactly what I mean, Will – going off like that with the old Doctor after she were promised to you.'

'She had a better offer, Cilla, that's all,' he said coldly. 'She had an offer of marriage from a rich, professional man with a large, comfortable house and stables. There was no way – not even with a small farm of my own – I could compete with that. Wouldn't you have done the same?'

She gazed thoughtfully at him through her emerald eyes. They were so close he could smell the sweet scent of her. Their faces – and lips – were only inches apart.

'Jamie and I were young and very much in love,' she told him. 'I have never so much as looked at another man since the day we took a fancy to each other at Stranghow fair…'

'I know you haven't, hinny,' he said. He felt ashamed of the lecherous feelings he was harbouring towards her but he continued to press his point home. He needed to know.

'If a rich man had come to you with a promise of a fine and comfortable life as a doctor's wife – would our Jamie have ever stood a chance of wedding you in Stamfordham church?'

'I would still have married Jamie,' she smiled, her face radiated happiness with the memories of those early years. But suddenly it clouded over; despair swamped her features and a catch caught at her voice. 'But now? Now I could be a widow by the autumn; a widow with four young children to feed. I don't know how this has come to pass, William – or why God wants to test us so. But in the autumn, if they hang Jamie – I think I'll have to be grateful for any man who'll take me on.'

The mention of Jamie and hanging in the same sentence had the same effect on William as if someone had drenched him with a pail of cold water. With his ardour now well and truly extinguished, he grimaced and inched slightly away from her.

'Don't fret,' he said, trying to smile. 'We'll get Jamie out of gaol and back in your arms before then.'

'Oh, he'll have some explaining to do before he's welcomed back into my arms,' she joked. 'He won't get off that lightly. By the time I've finished with him, he may wish himself back in Morpeth Gaol.'

She laughed and he laughed with her. 'I don't think my idiot of a brother is good enough for you, Cilla.'

'Well, just remember to tell him that, the next time you see him; he needs reminding now and then.'

'I will,' he promised.

The sun started to set and the sky began to streak with vermillion, rose and scarlet layers. Cilla and William sat in amiable silence, watching the darkness fall. As the glowing orb sank beneath the distant ridge, the fells darkened to maroon. Trees became black silhouettes on the horizon against the vast red canvas of the sky. The birds fell silent in the hedgerows and the animals settled in the fields and barns.

That night William slept fitfully in his bed. He tossed and turned for hours while his mind struggled with his burgeoning feelings for his brother's wife. As the minutes of the night crept slowly away, he started to fantasise about how Cilla would have reacted if he had reached out for her. In his dreams, they showed no restraint.

He imagined her walking sensuously towards him, her hips swaying and her unpinned hair tumbling erotically around her shoulders. She would take his roving hand in hers and guide it up underneath her skirts, over the stocking tops to the cool, soft skin at the top of her thigh and the moist place of pleasure above them. He would pull open her bodice and bury his face in her ample breasts before sucking on her erect nipples like a bairn. Then she would lead him over to the barn where she would lay down in the sweet smelling hay, raise her skirts and let him take her…over and over again….

His balls throbbed painfully as his accursed imagination explored every soft inch and moist fold of Cilla's voluptuous body. Groaning, he recited the words of Leviticus over and over in his mind: *'And if a man shall take his brother's wife, it is an unclean thing: he hath uncovered his brother's nakedness…'*

It was nearly dawn before he finally fell into a restless sleep.

CHAPTER TEN

Sunday 9th July 1809

After chapel William and John often retired to the cool of the dark parlour to rest and read the newspaper. Today William slumped into a faded winged chair and closed his eyes. He was exhausted. His nights were haunted with dreams of a lifeless Jamie swinging by the neck from a gibbet. In a vicious twist of his imagination, sometimes he would see himself lunging into Cilla's naked body on the ground below the gallows.

He had just begun to nod off when John slapped him awake with the newspaper and thrust it into his hands. 'What on earth does this mean?' John demanded.

William hauled himself upright and struggled to focus his bleary eyes on the *Newcastle Courant.* He glanced down at an advert in the *Hue & Cry* section:

'Two hundred Pounds Reward

Whereas the office of Kirkley Hall, in the Parish of Ponteland, in the County of Northumberland, was during the night of Monday, the 3rd day of April now last, broken into, and upwards of £1000 taken there out. Whoever therefore will, after this notice, apprehend the offender or offenders, so as he, she, or they may be brought to conviction, shall be paid a Reward of TWO HUNDRED POUNDS upon his, her or their conviction by applying to Nathanial Ogle Esq. of Kirkley.'

William's brain struggled to make sense of what he was reading and he wrestled with a growing sense of unease.

'I don't understand,' he said.

'Neither do I,' John confessed irritably.

William paused for a moment, his mind racing.

'Well, I don't think it is bad news,' he said finally. 'In fact, I think it means that Jamie's barrister was correct when he said the Bow Street Detective had not got sufficient evidence to bring a case against him. They must be quite desperate for information if they are offering two hundred pounds – yes! That's what it means – they are desperate for information.'

John stared at him alarmed.

'Information about Jamie?'

'Aye – but others, as well. Don't forget John Clifford and his brother were also suspected at one time – and they've never tracked down Clifford's brother. He's disappeared off the face of the earth. Maybe at last they're widening the net – trying to find the real thief instead of just picking on our Jamie.'

He felt John relax slightly beside him.

'This is good news, then?'

'The best,' William reassured him. 'It might bring forth information about the real thief.'

'Jamie needs to know about this.'

'Aye,' William agreed. 'It will cheer him up no end.'

His mother had been allowed into the gaol, the previous week, and had noticed that Jamie's spirits seemed low. The family had been concerned.

'I'll go to Morpeth as soon as we've fetched in the last of the hay,' he volunteered.

'Good,' John said grimly. 'Because as soon as Jamie's out of gaol and back in his own home with that wife of his; the better for all of us.'

It was several days before William was able to find time to go to Morpeth.

The finished hay was pitchforked into carts in large, golden piles and 'pinned' into small stacks with long pins and ropes. It was taken into the barns where it was pitched again onto a raised floor to continue drying. John Charlton's older daughters and young Jack led the Clydesdale horses and their swaying carts. Slowly they tramped between the acres and acres of fields and the barns with their ever growing mountains of sweet-smelling animal fodder. The adults stood at both ends of this route, wielding their pitchforks in the backbreaking routine.

On the last day of haymaking, when the barn doors were slammed shut and the exhausted horses unhitched from the cart, William went down the tree-lined river to wash away the sweat. The evening was hot; the slow flowing water enticing. He removed his boots, stripped off his clammy shirt and dived headfirst into the cold river. For several minutes he swam beneath the dappled green light of the trees and floated with the current. He sighed with pleasure as his overheated body began to ripple with shivers.

It was not until he clambered back onto the mossy bank, with his soaking breeches clinging to his thighs, that he realised he had forgotten to bring a cloth to dry himself. As always, young Jack was within shouting distance. He hailed the boy and sent him to fetch a cloth from the farm. Meanwhile he picked up the bar of tar soap and washed and rinsed himself.

It was Cilla who reappeared with the cloth.

Clutching it in one hand, she moved gracefully towards him, her hips swaying like the reeds in the river. The top button was undone on her bodice. Her free hand nervously smoothed down the apron over her old dress. He could see the faint line of perspiration on her forehead below the gleaming swirls of her luxurious, copper hair. She brushed the moisture away with the back of her hand. Her eyes widened at the sight of his naked chest and shoulders and flicked longingly over his bulging biceps and muscled torso. Glistening with water in the blinding sunlight, he stood up to his full height and waited for her to reach him.

She came so close he could smell the musky scent of her. Her mouth widened slightly and he watched the pink tip of her tongue appear and lick the inside of those soft lips. Their eyes met and they saw each other's desire. She flushed and breathed quicker.

She didn't hand him the towel; she started to wipe him down with it instead.

She was touching him.

He forced himself to stand still, savouring the lightness of her touch, her scent, her closeness. Then his manhood hardened in his breeches. Instinctively, he grabbed her wrist and pulled her to his naked chest. Their bodies clashed and his eyes hovered above hers, flaming with passion. Slowly, their lips moved together…but the moment was shattered.

Suddenly, one of the twins appeared. She squealed about some slight injury she had received from her sister and demanded her mother's attention. The inconsolable child launched herself at her mother's skirts and knocked William and Cilla apart. Cilla struggled to calm her.

The moment was gone.

Always there were her children – or the spectre of his damned brother – to come between them. Frustrated, disappointed and overwhelmed with conflicting emotions, William took the cloth from Cilla's hand and dried himself. Without a word to anyone, he returned to his cottage, changed into fresh clothes and stomped off down to Ma Shotton's to get drunk.

When William did eventually make it to Morpeth to see Jamie, he found his brother greatly changed.

As the date for the assizes drew closer, the gaol housed more and more prisoners awaiting trial. Jamie now shared his cage with two other men and the buzz of the flies and the smell of unwashed bodies, urine and faeces was overpowering in the midsummer heat. William felt like vomiting.

When Jamie came over the side of the cage, William was shocked by the state of him. He had lost a lot of weight. His soiled shirt and breeches hung loosely about large, bony frame and his filthy, bearded face was pinched and grey.

'Jamie? Is that you?' he gasped.

'What?' his brother said sadly. 'You think you're seeing a ghost? I haven't been hung yet, Will.'

'No, but you've…shrunk.'

'Aye, and so would you, with no decent food – and flies crawling and crapping over what little they give us. Have you brought any?'

Silently, William handed over the parcel of food and watched Jamie tear at it with his teeth. Despite the heat, his brother shivered. Once again William found himself wondering about gaol fever. 'You look cold,' he observed.

'Aye, it's the damp. God, how I wish I could escape the damp. What is the date? July? Yes? Look at me – I'm shivering. Always shivering. Damp seeps up from the stone floor below – and drips on you from above. No matter where you twist or turn, it still finds you. It seeps into your very bones.'

William handed him a brandy flask. Suddenly, he realised what was missing. 'Where's your coat?' He was surprised; he knew what that coat meant to his brother. Jamie jerked his thumb towards one of his cell mates. A thin, balding man was sprawled out arrogantly at the back of the cell. He wore Jamie's coat.

'What the…? Away! Give my brother back his coat!'

The man just laughed and told him to go to hell.

Furious, William grabbed the bars of the cage as if he was going to shake them down – but Jamie leaned forward and hushed him.

'Leave it, Will,' he said insistently. 'That's the way of things in here.'

'What do you mean?'

'The ones who come in new are fit and well fed,' Jamie explained quietly. 'They take from the ones who have been in gaol for a while. Then, when they become ravaged by the poor food and the fever – new prisoners take from them as well.'

'It's theft,' William growled. 'Just bloody theft.'

'Aye, well, we're all thieves of one kind or another, in here,' Jamie said. The sad resignation in his voice alarmed William even more than the stolen coat.

'Who is that bastard, anyway?'

'His name's Taylerson. He's charged with horse stealing.'

'Scum,' William snapped. 'Hey, Taylerson, you hear me, man? You're a thieving swine.'

Taylerson, who was laid back on the filthy straw grinning, made no response. The third occupant of the cell turned his back on them and shifted closer to the edge, as if to distance himself from the argument.

'You'd better give our Jamie his coat back, man, or else I'll be waiting for you on the outside.'

Now Taylerson laughed.

'He won't be coming out,' Jamie explained. 'This is his third time in front of the magistrates – they are sure to hang him this time.'

'Good riddance then,' William concluded loudly.

'He reckons on me joining him on the scaffold, Will. He wants to be my marra. He thinks it'll be comforting, like, to die with a mate – side by side, dancing together on the end of our ropes.'

William was aghast. What the hell was going on in here?

'Don't talk of hanging, Jamie – you're not going to the gallows. John's got you the best barrister money can buy. I can see it is hard, like, but you mustn't get yourself down-hearted…'

'Oh, I'm to come out am I?' His brother's voice was strangely dull and flat. His eyes were dead in his grey face.

What had these bastards done to him?

'Course you are, man!'

'You hear that, Taylerson?' he said. 'It seems if my kith and kin are to have their way – then I'm not to join you on the gallows.'

Jamie swirled the brandy round in the hip flask and took another long drink.

'Aye, I heard,' Taylerson said. 'Must be grand to have so many looking out for you on the outside.'

'Your barrister says that it'll never even get to trial,' William told Jamie.

'Not get to trial? Then what is this 'hearing' I'm to attend in August?'

'The lawyer says 'tis just a hearing, like – to see if there's enough evidence to try you proper. He reckons they have got nothing on you.' His voice dropped to a whisper and he pulled the news sheet out of his pocket. He hated the lack of privacy in this place.

'See...here...'

'Why it's the front page of the *Newcastle Courant!*' Jamie said in surprise.

'Aye,' confirmed William. 'I smuggled it in to show you how desperate Ogle and the Detective are.'

'What does it say?'

'What? Forgotten how to read now, have you? Stop being so helpless man, hold it up to the light and see for yourself.'

Jamie did what he was told. His chains rattled as he held up the thin news sheet and read. Silence fell in the gaol, as dozens of muttering prisoners ceased their talk and watched the Charlton brothers curiously.

'Two hundred pounds reward?' Jamie queried at last.

'What?' Taylerson exclaimed from the other side of the cell.

'Two hundred pounds reward,' Jamie repeated in a horrified voice. 'That's what it says. For information which says I did the bloody robbery.'

Taylerson burst out laughing.

'No, Jamie, man, not you,' William insisted quickly. 'It's a reward leading to the capture of the real thief. They're desperate – they've not got enough evidence to try you and are casting about, desperate like, to try and get more information about anyone who might have committed the robbery.'

Horrified, he realised too late that he had made a mistake showing Jamie the newspaper. The misery which seeped out of the very walls of this gaol was deeply rooted in his brother's soul; this news could send him spiralling down again into the black hell of his own mind.

'I'd heard that tha were a right famous thief, Charlton,' Taylerson goaded, laughing. 'They'd sed that afore I were sent to share a cell wi' you. I sees now they weren't lying!'

'Damn you, Taylerson!' William snapped. 'Look Jamie, it's canny news – not bad.'

'It is?'

'It means they do not have any real evidence against you.'

Jamie was not convinced.

'Maybes not today, they don't have any evidence against me,' he said. His voice started to rise with panic. 'But by the end of the week – half of the bloody parish will be beating a path to Kirkley Hall to try to claim the reward! Who will care if the greedy bastards are telling the truth, or not?'

'Have faith, Jamie,' William begged him. 'Have faith!'

Jamie was past himself and despair threatened to swamp him.

'I'm done for, Will! I'm done for!'

'No, you're not, man!'

'I am!' Jamie half sobbed, half shouted. He grabbed the iron bars which rose between them and shook them furiously. Then he slammed his head against them. His forehead erupted into bloody weals and the banging echoed round the sinister stone walls of the gaol.

William grabbed Jamie's bony shoulders through the cage bars and held him steady. It was too late; the turnkeys had heard the racket and hurried towards them. 'We'll think of sommat,' he whispered. 'Hold fast, Jamie. Hold fast. We'll work this out.'

'Our John,' Jamie said frantically. 'Yes, that's it – Brother John. No one will doubt the word of the farmer of North Carter Moor! He must give evidence in court – say he loaned me some money. Then no one will be able to blame me for paying them bills.'

'Talk sense, man,' William whispered urgently. 'You know damn well, John will never perjure himself in court – or tell a lie in the sight of God.'

'Get yourself outta 'ere now,' one of the gaolers snarled at William. Reluctantly, he started to move towards the exit.

'He has to!' Jamie yelled desperately from his cage. 'Our John must stand up for me in court!'

For one awful minute William thought his distraught brother was going to launch himself at the cage bars again. While one gaoler bundled William out of the prison, the other moved menacingly towards Jamie.

'Hold fast,' William yelled over his shoulder as he was pushed roughly out of the door. 'Have faith, Jamie. We'll work this out somehow. I'll be damned if I'll see my brother hang for a crime he didn't commit!'

William flung himself in corner of The King's Arms in Morpeth and ordered a brandy. Avoiding the curious stares of the other drinkers, he threw back a couple of glasses before he took out his pipe and tobacco and tried to think clearly. His visit to the gaol had unnerved him; Jamie's terrible misery and sense of panic had brought down his own spirits and confidence.

As William thought more about the reward he realised that Jamie was probably right; it was designed to bring in more evidence about him – not widen the net to catch the real thief of Kirkley Hall. The authorities were going down the easiest road; not the one that led to justice. William and Jamie shared a cynical regard for the integrity of their neighbours. The news of the reward would spread round the county like a disease, infecting the desperate and poverty-stricken population with its corruption. Dozens of them would beat a hasty path to the Kirkley Hall steward's office, eager to put in their claim for a share of the reward.

He knew from the lawyer that there was no hard evidence connecting Jamie to the crime. However, Jamie's debts had been extensive and his behaviour in the week following the robbery had been downright foolish. Only a blethering idiot would go on such a spending spree in the days after the biggest robbery in the county. The evidence against him was circumstantial but strong. Unfortunately, it would be even stronger by the time the steward's office had finished with their promise of a reward. He chewed on the end of his clay pipe and stared absentmindedly through the mullioned window out into the marketplace. He was damned if he would let his brother hang. But what to do?

Next, William tried to dispassionately deal with his feelings for Cilla and the unmistakeable attraction that had sprung up between them.

Jamie's arrest had thrown them together at Carter Moor. She was lonely, unhappy, constantly snapped at by his brother John and humiliated by the catcalls and stares of their cruellest neighbours. She had found comfort in his sympathetic company and was desperate for protection in a hostile world – and he, sad clod pole that he was, had let himself fall for her gentle beauty and grace. The conversations which they had shared on those balmy summer evenings had revealed to him a woman whom he knew he could love. Caring, gentle and quietly amusing, she was as beautiful on the inside as she was on the outside.

But at the end of the day she was Jamie's wife.

If their John caught even the slightest sense of the smouldering attraction between himself and Cilla, he would throw both of them out of the farm and have them denounced from every pulpit in the parish for lechery and adultery. The damning words of Leviticus and the threat of God and hell fire meant little to William. He paid lip service to religious doctrine and lived by his own code. But part of his code was honouring the bond which he shared with his wretched brother. And it was this code which stayed his hand; the hand that yearned to reach out for Cilla.

Jamie was depending upon him to protect his family – not to ruin it. The freedom which they were all working so hard to achieve would mean nothing to the man if he returned home to find his beloved wife lying in his brother's arms – or carrying William's bairn in her fertile womb.

But what to do?

Sighing, he resolved to double his efforts to help his brother. He would also find himself a decent whore and avoid being alone with Cilla.

It was while he was in this depressed state of resignation that Archie Musgrave suddenly joined him in the tavern. He was pleased to see his old friend and welcomed him warmly.

Archie was a slight man of medium build with warm brown eyes. His friendly face was framed by a flopping mop of chestnut hair and bushy sideburns. His geniality and easy manners belied the quick brain and burning ambition behind those sympathetic eyes. Archie's friendship in Newcastle had gone a long way to ease the loneliness William had felt when he was sent to work for his elderly uncle in the town.

For half an hour they chatted amiably about farming issues and the prices they were getting for their livestock and grain. Archie had been orphaned in his early twenties and had used his inheritance to buy the lease of a small farm back in his native Corbridge. William had missed his company when he had left Newcastle to return to Corbridge. Now as then, Archie's presence helped to lift the gloom which threatened to swamp him.

Inevitably, the conversation drifted to the forthcoming trial of William's brother. Even on his remote farm above Corbridge, Archie had heard about Jamie's arrest and imprisonment for the burglary at Kirkley Hall.

William told him the details and Archie listened sympathetically.

'Seems to me, you could do with getting away from Ponteland for a while. I have to say you were looking right down when I first saw you.'

'Aye, I was,' William said smiling. 'Is this another offer of some work up at Thorn Tree, Archie?'

'I won't deny that I could do with an extra pair of hands and I think you could do with a change of scenery.'

'Maybe after the trial; I'm needed here at the moment. My family needs me.'

'Aye, I've often thought that,' commented Archie wryly. 'That your family was very needy.'

'There speaks an only child of deceased parents,' William retorted.

Archie grinned. 'Oh, I have an elderly aunt. She can be very demanding. She demands every now and then that I go and take a cup of tea with her in Newcastle – but I will own that I probably don't know what it must be like for you with that troublesome family of yours.'

'I'll confess that sometimes I liken them to a spider's web,' William confided. 'Sometimes I feel like I'm just a bloody fly trapped in the middle of it all.' They keep sending out sticky threads to draw me back into their problems and petty squabbles.'

Archie thought for a moment and slowly sipped at his ale. 'I think your family is more like one of them darned ugly creatures that the fishermen used to land on Newcastle quayside from time to time.'

'What?'

'You know – the beast with eight arms that they would toss back into the water.'

'An octopus?'

'Aye, that was it. Ugly buggers they were. Yes, your family is like an octopus sending out its arms…'

'Tentacles.'

'…Tentacles then, to trap you and pull you back to them. If one of the tentacles doesn't get you: then one of the others surely will. First of all, you went back to Carter Moor because your ma and eldest brother needed you after your da died – now your other brother has reached out for your help. I think you'll never get a life of your own Will, unless you can break away from their reach and let the tide take you to some other part of the sea.'

William smiled at the analogy. 'You think that if I wash up on the beach named 'Thorn Tree Farm' near Corbridge, then I will be alright?'

'Aye. Of course, you will! Mind, there's something else about these octopus beasts which reminds me of your family, Will.'

'What's that?'

Archie looked serious now and said quietly: ''Tis said that when they want to confuse their prey and enemies they squirt out a black ink which blinds all around them.'

'What's your meaning, Archie?'

'Are you absolutely sure you can trust your brother, Jamie? What if he has squirted the blinding ink into your eyes? Does he speak the truth when he tells you that he is an innocent man?'

Nathanial Ogle may have thought he had finished with the services of the Bow Street detective, however, the duke was determined to keep Lavender involved in the case until its successful conclusion. He instructed his steward to keep the detective informed of all developments.

Dutifully, the steward sent Lavender two letters to his London office. The first told him that the reward notice had been successful in bringing forward further evidence of Jamie Charlton's spending spree in the week following the robbery. In total, the steward at Kirkley Hall now had over sixty witnesses whom he could call on to give evidence of Charlton's poverty before Easter 1809 and of his apparent wealth in the weeks after the robbery.

In addition to this, amongst all the wild tales and the hearsay was the strong evidence which had eluded Lavender and Woods for so long. Rob Wilson, the debt collector, had come forward with the news that in the week following the robbery, James Charlton had paid off a bill for six pounds worth of leather which he had owed Mr. Selkirk of Newcastle. A few days later, Elizabeth Selkirk, the wife of the man himself, arrived at Kirkley Hall to confirm this information and give her statement. Another Newcastle stall holder gave evidence that Jamie Charlton had spent nearly three pounds on sheeting on the Saturday following the robbery.

The steward confidently told Lavender they had now got their man. The purchases aside, they now had evidence that Charlton had paid off more than sixteen pounds worth of debt during the week after the robbery.

The steward's second letter informed him of a more worrying development.

Michael Aynsley had written to Mr. Ogle demanding the right to present the case to the magistrates. Still resentful about his dismissal from his position at Kirkley Hall, Aynsley claimed his reputation had been ruined by the events following the burglary. He demanded the right to publicly prosecute the Kirkley Hall burglar. He believed that this public act would vindicate him in the eyes of his neighbours and fellow parishioners. There was no doubt in Lavender's mind Michael Aynsley was also motivated by the reward; he was also after a share of the money. Unfortunately, Nathanial Ogle had agreed. Michael Aynsley was to present the evidence against James Charlton at the initial hearing.

Lavender was seriously alarmed.

CHAPTER ELEVEN

3rd August, 1809

The courtroom was packed as Cilla, flanked by Ann and John Charlton, joined the crowd of spectators. She followed the others to seats in the public gallery, trying to avoid the curious stares and whispers of the crowd. Silently, she cursed her distinctive head of auburn hair which made it so easy for others to identify her in a crowd.

The voice of Mistress Maun, the parish dressmaker stood out above the whispering, shuffling and coughing behind them.

'That be his wife,' the old gossip informed those closest to her. 'He won't say 'nay' to her at all. Gets everything she wants does Cilla Charlton – owt she asks for.'

'Why that ain't natural in a husband!' the woman next to her said. 'No wonder the poor gadgie has found himself here!' There was a murmur of agreement from those around her.

Cilla felt her mother-in-law go rigid beside her.

'Remind me never to invite that Maun woman into my kitchen for a cup of tea again,' Ann hissed through her teeth.

Cilla, who was more used to the comments, just smiled slightly. She had been determined to accompany John and Ann to the hearing but she was scared. She wished William was here but he had disappeared from the farm shortly after milking that morning and no-one knew where he had gone.

The weather outside was sweltering. Tunnels of sunlight streamed in through the dirty, mullioned windows onto the gnarled, wooden benches. Cobwebs dripped down from the rafters above the mixed jumble of humanity which made up the spectators. Wealthy town merchants and their wives were forced to sit shoulder to shoulder with the working men and women of Ponteland. Their silk-skirted thighs brushed against coarse, worsted breeches. The gentry dabbed their noses with handkerchiefs perfumed with bergamot and rosemary to dilute the stench of unwashed bodies and ward off contagious fevers. Ostrich feathers, sprouting from velvet bonnets, swayed dangerously in the eyeline of those seated on the back rows, threatening to obscure their vision. A small argument broke out amongst the crowd.

'Them wi' big hats should sit at back…' someone suggested.

A hush fell as the emaciated and cowed figure of Jamie Charlton came blinking into the bright light of the court and pushed into the dock. He was dirty, coatless and despite the heat, he hugged his arms to himself as if he was cold. He didn't look up and his face was almost completely hidden behind the straggly, grey beard which covered it.

Cilla let out a gasp of shock when she saw the pathetic state of her husband. She stared at him sadly, her eyes full of compassion. All around her, the spectators glanced curiously from her face to Jamie's bowed head.

'I thought he was supposed to be a big man?' someone commented in the public gallery, clearly disappointed.

The crowd were soon distracted by the surprise appearance of Michael Aynsley at the prosecution stand. He wore his church clothes; his waistcoat was adorned with a gold pocket watch. His unruly hair had been cut and smoothed back. He even appeared to have made some attempt to trim his bushy sideburns. Murmurs of derision greeted his arrival. At the back of the public gallery someone booed.

Then everyone stood as Northumberland's three magistrates filed into their courtroom. Thomas Clennell Esq., the chairman, led the Reverend Fredrick Ekins and George Fenwick Esq. to their seats at the bench.

'Their role is to examine all the evidence gathered,' John explained to his mother and sister-in-law. 'They must decide whether it is sufficient to send Jamie to trial by jury in front of the visiting circuit judges later this month.'

'So we might have to go through this all again?' Ann queried. John never had chance to reply because the usher demanded silence. The clerk of the court stood up to begin proceedings:

'Your Worships, ladies and gentlemen. This court is now to begin the examination of the evidence in the case of 'The King versus James Charlton of Milburn', in the said county of Northumberland, on this the 3rd day of August, in the year of our lord one thousand, eight hundred and nine.'

'The said James Charlton, labourer, is charged before us on the oath of Michael Aynsley of Newhamm Edge, with the suspicion of breaking into the dwelling house of Nathanial Ogle Esq. of Kirkley in the night between the 3rd and 4th days of April 1809 and feloniously stealing, taking and carrying away from the said dwelling house monies in circulating bankers' notes and cash the amount in value of one thousand one hundred and fifty seven pounds, thirteen shillings and six pence. How do you so plead?'

There was a pause until one of the gaolers nudged Jamie in the ribs. 'Not guilty,' he mumbled.

'Speak up, man,' demanded the clerk.

'Not guilty!' he shouted loudly.

There was a ripple of laughter in the gallery, which stopped abruptly when Michael Aynsley stood up to give his evidence. The crowd bristled with anticipation. Jamie glowered at him from the dock. Aynsley scowled back, coughed and then read out his statement:

'I, Michael Aynsley, do hereby swear that on Easter Monday last, I received the rents of Nathanial Ogle Esq…'

The man had lost nothing of his authority. No one tittered at him as he confidently snarled out the information about rent day. The crowd in the gallery remained silent and hung on his every word; the Ponteland contingent was sullen.

'The rent received amounted to one thousand one hundred and fifty seven pounds, thirteen shillings and sixpence and I kept a note of this in a ledger. The money was then deposited in a chest and hidden behind a panel in the estate office.

The prisoner, James Charlton, was employed at Kirkley that day and he was seen coming into the office upon an errand at which time the chest was open. He well knew the office at Kirkley as he was previously employed at the estate as a cattle herder.

The next morning I was informed that the office had been broken into, and the whole of the money stolen, taken and carried away.

Since this time two parcels of notes have been found near a gate in the grounds of Kirkley Hall on the 8th April, containing just over nine hundred and ninety five pounds.

Since the said robbery, James Charlton has been in possession of money and paid off bills he owed to a large amount, more so than a person in his situation in life could reasonably be supposed to come by honestly. Therefore, this informant has cause to suspect and does suspect the said James Charlton was concerned in the said robbery.'

'Call the first witness,' the clerk instructed Aynsley.

Cilla noticed that at this point, a small portion of Aynsley's confidence seemed to leave him. He hesitated slightly before the huge pile of documents which lay on the table. Every one of the witnesses was present that day in case they would be needed to give evidence in a later trial. Cilla realised Aynsley could not decide where to start.

Eventually, the steward called the three gardeners who had helped Lavender and Woods retrieve the stolen money from beneath the currant bush at Kirkley Hall. As the third gardener left the stand, the spectators in the gallery began to shuffle with boredom on the hard wooden benches.

Magistrate Clennell decided it was time to intervene. 'Mr. Aynsley, I think a little discretion is called for in your selection of witnesses. I understand you could call over sixty witnesses, is that correct?'

'Yes, Your Worship.'

'I think we have now firmly established that Detective Lavender and these men found the bulk of the missing rent money beneath a currant bush so perhaps we should move onto evidence which actually incriminates the defendant? Otherwise we may find ourselves here for the rest of the week and the defendant will have to wait until next year's assizes to go to trial.'

Aynsley flushed with embarrassment, while the public smirked and giggled at his discomfort.

'Yes, certainly, sir,' Aynsley blustered. 'I have just one more to call – Ralph Spoors.'

Ralph Spoors was a belligerent old gardener from Kirkley who took the oath and although he could not read, declined the clerk's offer to read out his statement, declaring that he had a good memory of what he had told the detective gadgie. He took the stand and announced that:

'I, Ralph Spoors, do hereby swear that on 8th April last, I was just enjoying me dinner when I was called upon by Mr. Lavender, that detective gadgie from Lunnen, to gan and watch him take up that money as was found thrown over the garden wall. As me dinner was about to turn cold, I refused.'

The court room erupted into a roar of laughter and Michael Aynsley turned red with a mixture of anger and embarrassment. This was not what Spoors had previously told Lavender. While the public were distracted and chattered amongst themselves, Mr. Clennell called the Clerk of the Court to the bar for a private word.

'This fellow – Aynsley – he's not trained as a lawyer I take it?'

'Oh no, sir, he's Mr. Ogle's late steward.'

'What is he doing presenting the evidence for the prosecution?'

'It was Mr. Nathanial Ogle's idea,' the clerk explained. 'Apparently, at one time Mr. Aynsley himself was under suspicion of committing this crime. Now Mr. Ogle thinks it might help clear Aynsley's reputation if he was seen prosecuting James Charlton.'

‘’Tis more likely it will ensure that the case is lost,’ Mr. Clennell observed dryly. ‘Oh, pray proceed, Clerk.’

The next batch of witnesses were the shopkeepers and traders to whom Charlton had been indebted before the robbery and who were so quickly repaid following the theft of the rent money. Among them was Tom Philips, Jamie’s friend to whom he had sold his father’s watch when he was desperate for money in February.

Philips now seemed to regret his decision to betray Jamie; he looked decidedly unhappy. Beads of perspiration dripped from his forehead. His discomfiture was not helped by the fact that Jamie’s ice blue eyes fixed him in an unblinking stare. The other Charltons in the room watched dispassionately as Phillips tugged nervously at his thin coat and gave his evidence in a voice which was barely audible.

‘Our Jamie should take more care about whom he chooses to befriend,’ John Charlton observed quietly as Phillips scurried back to his seat.

‘He has been tempted by the reward – like the rest of them,’ Ann said cynically.

John Harbottle, the Ponteland draper, was next to take the stand and swear on the greasy Bible. ‘I swear that the prisoner, James Charlton of Milburn, has lately dealt at my shop and between Christmas and Easter last, got goods to the amount of thirteen shillings and five pence. The said James Charlton then called in on Easter Tuesday last, at past twelve in the forenoon and paid me the above mentioned bill by giving me a twenty shilling banknote.’

Michael Aynsley, whose confidence had clearly returned somewhat during the last half an hour, decided to question Mr. Harbottle further. ‘Is it true, Mr. Harbottle, that you had cause one time to refuse credit to the defendant?’

‘Yes, sir,’ Harbottle confirmed. ‘It had come to my attention that Charlton owed money to half of the county. So I had stopped his credit at thirteen shillings and five pence. I was very surprised when he turned up that Tuesday to make good the debt.’

A new wave of excitement swept through the court when Rob Wilson, the turnpike keeper took the stand.

‘I, Robert Wilson, swear that I knows the prisoner James Charlton, and that some months ago I was asked by one James Selkirk a currier of the town, to see if I could procure payment of a debt of six pounds fourteen shillings an four pence halfpenny due to the said James Selkirk for leather. The debt was great longstanding and I was authorised to say that he may pay it off at twenty shillings at a time…'

A curious Mr. Clennell was prompted to ask for clarification at this point. 'Mr. Wilson, didn't you say that you were the keeper of the turnpike gate in Ponteland?'

'Yes, Your Worship.'

'Well, I do not understand. Why were you collecting debts for James Selkirk?'

'It's a service that I offer to help out friends, like,' Wilson explained. He grinned and his scarred faced distorted.

'No doubt, out of the goodness of your heart?'

'Aye, I've long been disposed to offer charity.'

The spectators from Ponteland could barely contain their laughter.

'Yes, you do look like a gentle, giving soul,' Clennell observed ironically. He was now beginning to understand. 'Pray continue.'

'Anyhow, when I telled James Charlton that he could pay off the debt at twenty shillings a time; he telled me that he could not do it. And that once he had got the money made up, but that he had got into cards again and had lost it all.'

The public gallery took a sharp collective intake of breath. Many glanced at Cilla; a flush of red now tinged the milky whiteness of her face and neck.

'So on Easter Tuesday last, I was in Ma Shotton's public house at Ponteland about three o'clock and Charlton asked me if I was gannin to Newcastle. When I said 'Aye,' he said that I might let Mr. Selkirk know that he would now pay the bill all at once.'

Elizabeth Selkirk then took the stand and confirmed that James Charlton had indeed called at her husband's shop in Newcastle on the Saturday following the robbery and had paid off the debt of over six pounds which had been outstanding since October 1806.

Next to speak was Matthew Mackie, the young tailor who had made Charlton's coat. He held his statement in shaking hands and read quickly.

'I, Matthew Mackie, do swear that on Easter Tuesday last, about three o' clock in the afternoon. I went to Ma Shotton's public house in Ponteland and was there approached by James Charlton of Milburn…'

'Was the entire parish in Mistress Shotton's public house on Easter Tuesday?' interrupted Mr. Clennell, sarcastically.

The young tailor turned white and looked like he was about to flee from the stand. 'I don't rightly know,' he stammered. 'Charlton asked me to make him a coat, to which I agreed. There were other people within the house playing at cards…'

'Mistress Shotton's public house is a very popular and respectable establishment,' Michael Aynsley told the magistrate.

'Mmm, popular maybe, but I tend to think that strong drink and gambling rarely make for a respectable establishment, Mr. Aynsley. Pray continue, Mr. Mackie.'

'As I said, there were other people within the house playing at cards and James Charlton frequently offered to bet a guinea but no person offered to accept the same. Then the prisoner started to brag that he had plenty of money and he put his hand into his left hand breeches pocket and produced some gold. I think I saw three or four half guineas and several seven shilling pieces. After which he put his hand into the other breeches pocket and produced a great quantity of silver, upwards of twenty shillings…'

'Oh, Jamie,' Cilla moaned softly.

As the rest of the witnesses gave their evidence, the painful poverty of the Charltons was laid bare in the minutest detail for the salacious enjoyment of their neighbours. The warm courtroom became heavy and airless. The spectators fanned themselves with whatever they had to hand. The heat was also clearly too much for the magistrate Reverend Ekins, who nodded off to sleep.

Through it all, Cilla maintained her dignified poise while she listened intently. Ann's strained face displayed a range of emotions but her dour eldest son displayed none.

The last witness whom Aynsley called was Sarah Kyle, the Ponteland shopkeeper who had been summoned against her will, to add her evidence to the growing tally against Charlton. She took the stand defiantly, glared at Michael Aynsley with undisguised contempt and rapidly read from her statement.

'I know the prisoner James Charlton. He frequently dealt at my shop for goods for which he got credit. On Saturday 8th April 1809 he called and paid up his account which amounted to three pounds and one half penny. He paid me with three one pound notes and a coin.'

Aynsley decided to question this witness further. 'Three pounds, Mistress Kyle! That is a huge amount of credit to give to a common labourer, is it not?'

'Maybes so, Mr. Aynsley, but his younger brother, Henry, is about to marry with my

niece. I thought they was a decent family, like…in fact...' she finished with growing confidence, '…I still do. I can no more understand how anyone can believe Jamie Charlton robbed Kirkley Hall than they would believe that I did it!'

'Are you aware, Madam,' demanded Clennell, 'that you are here as a witness for the prosecution? It is not appropriate for you to show support for the defendant.'

But the little woman was not going to be cowed by a mere magistrate. Bristling with indignation, she stretched herself up to her full height, which was something less than five feet, and stared straight back at the chairman.

'Well, no one ever said nowt about that,' she informed him angrily. 'I was just told I had to come here – against my will, I might add – swear on the Bible, and tell the truth about the debt which Jamie and Cilla had run up at my shop and that's what I've done. If he don't like my answers,' she jabbed her finger in the direction of Michael Aynsley, 'then he shouldn't ask the questions then, should he?'

There wasn't anyone in the room whose jaw hadn't now dropped open in either shock or delight – including Mr. Clennell. He snapped his mouth shut and sat up straighter.

'I think, Mistress Kyle, you had better sit down,' he said sternly. 'I am undecided whether to have you committed to the gaol for contempt, or to applaud you for your forthright honesty. I suggest you sit – before I go with the first thought.' With a rustle of starched, indignant petticoats, Sarah Kyle marched back to her seat.

Ann Charlton was impressed. 'If her niece has half the character of Sarah Kyle then our Harry has chosen himself a good wife,' she announced.

'If the niece is anything like the aunt,' John retorted, 'she'll make Henry's life a living hell.'

A short break was held before the court began to examine the evidence for the defence but with Sarah Kyle, the damage to the prosecution case had already commenced. There was something about the tiny woman's support for Jamie Charlton which had touched a nerve with everyone in the room. Previously, it had seemed that nothing could have lifted the suspicion which had surrounded the impoverished labourer. Now the outcome of this hearing was by no means certain and the crowd waited expectantly to hear the evidence for the defence.

Back at North Carter Moor, nine year-old Jack Charlton felt restless. Unlike his three younger siblings, he knew what was happening in the courtroom in Newcastle. He had wanted to go but the adults had insisted he stayed at the farm with the other children and Aunt Susan. Normally he would have shadowed his Uncle Will around the farm but William was not there so the lad was left to his own devices. He felt frightened and unhappy as he tried to imagine what was happening to his father. North Carter Moor had never felt so boring and restrictive as it did on that sweltering August day.

When his aunt called them for lunch he took his food out into the shady woods to eat. He walked towards Milburn, curious to see what had happened to his old home. The woods were deliciously cool and tranquil after the hot, overcrowded farm. The air was rich with the heady fragrance of pine, wild garlic and soft, warm earth. He started to feel better and swung a large stick by his side, slashing at the ferns and decapitating the purple heads of giant foxgloves. As he neared the hamlet he left the path and dodged between the trailing fronds of a willow tree and a blackthorn bush to take a short cut to his old home.

A few steps later he stopped dead – unsure of what to do.

Five yards away, in a clearing between the trees, the great eagle was on the ground, eyeing him warily. Its golden plumage blended so well with the bracken-covered woodland floor that if it hadn't been for a slight, nervous twitch of its head, Jack would probably have never seen it. The boy paused and watched. He expected that any moment the bird would unfurl its huge wings and take flight – or even lunge out and attack him – but the eagle just stared back at the child with unblinking, deadened eyes.

Over the past few months, Jack had spent hours watching this incredible creature as it soared across the treetops near his home. He knew it never remained on the ground for any longer than the few seconds it took to catch and kill a hare. His instincts told him something was badly wrong.

Cautiously, he took a few steps closer. He saw the rotting dove carcasses scattered in front of the eagle. A few more steps – and he saw the trap glinting evilly in the sunlight.

He gasped in horror. The bird bridled its feathers and opened its sharp, yellow beak in a silent warning.

Jack knew all about the traps which the gamekeepers laid to catch deer and deter poachers. He knew that those powerful jaws could easily break the leg of a child, never mind a bird. If the steel teeth of the trap had failed to snap the leg bone, then the muscles would be shredded and the veins severed. It was a wonder the creature had not already bled to death. Its chances of survival were slim. Grimly, he remembered the calf which had been born with no mouth at the farm; his Uncle William had killed it to put it out of its misery.

He wondered how long the eagle had been trapped there in excruciating agony. It had obviously devoured the flesh off the doves which had been used to lure it down from the tree tops. The bony carcasses were evidence of that. It could have been here for days. Then another thought struck him; the men who had laid the trap could be back at any minute. If he was going to do something, he would have to move quickly.

He pulled the bread and meat from his pocket and threw it just in front of the bird. The starving creature never hesitated. It snatched up the food and gulped it down.

While the bird was temporarily distracted, Jack carefully moved to one side. He wanted a better view of the damaged leg. He was relieved to see it was only partially trapped. Two talons of the huge claw were caught in the teeth. Some sharpened instinct for survival must have made it pull away just in time. How they hadn't been completely severed, he didn't know – but they hadn't. They obviously remained attached to its claw. He didn't know if an eagle could survive in the wild with two talons dangling uselessly – but he guessed that it could. However, his relief was short lived. He felt like retching when he saw the shredded flesh and sinew on the talons above the trap; the eagle had been trying to chew off its own talons in a bid to free itself.

He sat down and tried to think. Ten feet away from him was an ensnared and dangerous wild animal which stood over half of his height. It had a beak like a cut throat razor, incredible strength and vicious claws with a span greater than his father's hand. At any moment, the men who had laid the trap could return.

Still the young lad was determined. Somehow he would free the eagle and return him to the wild. As he sat and pondered, the giant bird seemed to relax. It waited patiently for the lad's next move.

CHAPTER TWELVE

The barrister whom John had employed for Jamie's defence was a calm, reassuring, pleasant man in his fifties called Blake. William had been concerned that Blake was too quietly spoken to be taken seriously but John's instincts proved to be right. Mr. Blake soon had the crowd hanging on his every word. He informed the magistrates and the assembled crowd that James Charlton was the victim of a terrible coincidence. He called him a hard-working, God-fearing family man and stressed that Charlton had had plenty of casual work that spring.

His first witness was Mr. Thomas Gillespy, the farmer from Haindykes. Gillespy confirmed that Charlton had been his barn man, got his victuals from the farm kitchen, always behaved well and had made plenty of money. Another witness, Joseph Emmerson, whose shop fronted the barn at Haindykes, claimed he saw James Charlton turn up for work as usual the day after the robbery. Hardly the behaviour of a man who had just acquired over one thousand pounds, suggested Mr. Blake.

Next the barrister called on the Charltons' two lodgers to confirm the amount of rent they had paid to Cilla Charlton in the months leading up to the robbery. Then Mr. Blake made much of Jamie's good fortune with his small herd of cows which had all borne twin calves that spring – doubling the income which he would normally have expected to receive at this time of year. The Morpeth meat trader who had bought the calves was called to the witness stand and handed over documentation to prove the purchase.

Cilla listened to everything with an expression of slight surprise. After being maligned for so long, she could barely believe others were now prepared to stand up on their behalf. Jamie looked similarly surprised.

Finally, Mr. Blake announced that in addition to all of the above, James Charlton had also just borrowed some money from his brother, William, in order to pay back Mr. Selkirk of Newcastle for the leather and he would call William Charlton as his final witness.

This announcement stunned Cilla and she turned pale. She had no idea that William had become involved.

John turned on her sharply. 'Did you put William up to this?' he hissed.

Jamie's expression never altered as William rose to his feet from amongst the crowd of witnesses and walked confidently to the stand.

Cilla could not believe they had not been aware of his presence, seated as he had been, quietly against the wall at the back of the crowd.

'Now there's a big fellah,' a woman whispered suggestively, at the back of the gallery to the amusement of those around her. As the other women giggled lewdly, irritation flashed across Ann Charlton's face but she never turned around. Her eyes were fixed on her favourite son.

William took the oath and made pretence of kissing the battered old bible. Then he announced clearly:

'I, William Charlton, servant in husbandry, of North Carter Moor in the parish of Ponteland, do swear that I lent my brother, James Charlton, the sum of ten pounds. My brother came to the farm for this money on the morning that I was going to help at ploughing day at William Potts' farm at Boney Hill. But what day of the month it was I cannot recollect.'

There was snort of disbelief from Michael Aynsley.

'Thank you, Mr. Charlton,' Mr. Blake said. 'But can I just clarify a few details? You told me your brother borrowed the money with the clear intention of repaying Mr. Selkirk of Newcastle for the leather, is that so?'

'It is,' William said confidently. 'He had long been worried about this outstanding debt and his wife had urged him to pay it. But when he realised that he had a third set of twin calves to sell this spring, he approached me, in confidence, for a loan. I was happy to help him. He was confident that when he sold the calves he would be able to repay a large part of the loan at once.' Here he paused and glanced at Jamie who stared back, expressionless. 'My brother believed his luck had turned, and that his fortunes were on the way up.'

The spectators in the court listened intently as William spoke. Many of them sat back and murmured with satisfaction when he had finished his testimony.

Michael Aynsley had listened to William's evidence with a look of complete frustration and mounting anger on his face. He rose angrily to his feet as Mr. Blake dismissed William Charlton from the stand.

'Excuse me, Your Worship. May I question this witness?

'I don't see why not,' Mr. Clennell said. 'You there – fellow – return to the witness stand.' Reluctantly, William returned. A confrontation with Aynsley was obviously not something he had anticipated.

Aynsley cleared his throat. The difficulty of dealing with the feisty Sarah Kyle had clearly made him cautious. Cilla realised that none of this had proved to be as easy as Aynsley had expected and, like everyone else from Ponteland, Aynsley was acutely aware that William was the cleverest of the Charltons from North Carter Moor.

'Right. You are William Charlton of North Carter Moor, are you not?' Aynsley began pompously.

'You know damned well I am, Aynsley,' William snapped.

When the laughter in the courtroom had subsided, Mr. Clennell decided to intervene.

'Mr. Charlton. Answer the questions Mr. Aynsley asks either 'Aye' or 'Nay.' Any more contempt or swearing – and I shall have you clapped in irons, do you understand me?

'Aye,' William muttered.

Clennell eyed him coldly. After a pause he indicated to Aynsley to proceed.

Aynsley, moved closer to the witness stand. 'You say that you loaned your brother ten pounds, is that right?'

'Aye.'

'That you gave it him on ploughing day at Potts' farm?'

'Aye.'

'Well, I don't believe you,' the ex-steward snarled. He thrust his face into William's. 'I think you're a right pair of liars – you and him! You've got together and made up this tale to save him from hanging!'

The court erupted into exclamations of surprise, indignation and excitement.

'Go to Hell!' William snarled and glared straight back into the steward's eyes. Aynsley was so close William, Cilla realised that he would be able to smell his reeking breath. She grimaced as she remembered that time Aynsley had tried to force himself on her; she vividly remembered the smell of his breath.

Mr. Clennell rapped furiously with his gavel and the Reverend Ekins jerked awake.

'Order! Order! I will have order in this court,' the chairman shouted. Eventually the noise subsided and Clennell turned his anger onto Aynsley. 'Mr. Aynsley you asked if you could question the witness – not accuse him of perjury. You may continue on the understanding that you restrict yourself to questions only. Do I make myself clear?

'Yes, sir,' Aynsley snapped. He continued to glare at William. 'Where did you get the ten pounds from?' he demanded.

'I took it from my savings; I have a bit put by.'

'Savings?

'Aye.'

'What savings?' spat Aynsley. 'How does a man like you get savings? You work with the livestock for your elder brother at the farm, don't you?

'You know I do.' William's voice was now dangerously quiet. 'And it is from years of good honest work that I've got my savings. But of course, I have no wife, nor bairns to keep…nor a fancy woman in Stamfordham.'

'Why you…!'

While most of those present had no understanding of this latest comment, the Ponteland section of the audience knew that William was referring to Aynsley's whore. Another eruption of ribald laughter rippled around the courtroom. The crowd were loving it.

'Any more disturbances from the public gallery and I will have the court cleared!' yelled the infuriated magistrate.

Michael Aynsley was red in the face with anger; a muscle twitched in his thick, bull-like neck. But he would not give up; he knew how to rile cocky buggers like Charlton.

'So when did you say you loaned your brother this ten pounds?'

'It was the ploughing day at William Potts' up at Boney Hill.'

'Which day was that?'

'I don't rightly know.'

'You don't know?'

'No. I have no need to keep a track of the date. It's the seasons which dictate my work – not the date.'

'So you have no idea if you loaned him the money just before – or just after – the robbery on the 3rd April?'

'No.'

'How convenient. Is Mr. William Potts here, so we can ask him when his ploughing day was?'

'I understand that he has taken to his bed with a fever.'

'Again – how convenient. Tell me, Charlton. Can a cow herder like you read and write?'

'You know I can, Aynsley.'

'And can a cow herder like you, count? Or do you leave the sums to your sheep dogs – do they do the counting for you?' There was another ripple of laughter in the courtroom.

William clenched and unclenched his fists. 'I can count, yes.'

'So, can you tell the court how much debt your brother paid off the week after the robbery?'

William hesitated. He clearly had no idea where this line of questioning was going and neither did Cilla.

'I couldn't rightly say…'

'Oh, surely you can, Charlton? You've just heard witness after witness come to the stand and give evidence that your brother gave them money during the week after the robbery. So how much in total did they claim he gave them?'

'I don't know,' William persisted stubbornly.

'What is your point, Mr. Aynsley?' Mr. Clennell asked.

'The point is, sir, we have just heard evidence that James Charlton paid off a total of sixteen pounds four shillings and sixpence halfpenny in the five days after the robbery – and we have no idea how much he spent in Newcastle the following week. But we have heard evidence that he spent three pounds on bed sheets alone.'

Aynsley paused dramatically to let his audience digest this information. Then he turned sharply back to William. 'So it really doesn't matter if you stand up here and perjure yourself for him, Charlton – he will hang anyway. Your paltry ten pounds is not enough. There's only one thing which explains where he suddenly got all of the money from – he robbed Kirkley Hall!'

'Ah,' William said calmly. 'But it were the second load of money that I'd loaned him.'

'What!'

'It were the second load of money that I'd loaned him,' William continued blithely. 'He had come for another ten pounds earlier that month.'

'You barefaced, bloody liar!' Aynsley spat out the words one by one.

'Mr. Aynsley!' the magistrate warned. 'I'll have no swearing from you either.'

'He's lying!' Aynsley snapped.

'It's new evidence,' the clerk muttered.

'It is no lie,' William insisted. 'It is true. But I never thought to mention it before because all anybody wanted to hear about was the money I loaned him around Easter…'

Aynsley exploded. 'You're a liar, William Charlton! May you rot in hell with your useless thieving brother!'

'Sod off, Aynsley!' William replied gleefully. 'Everyone knows you're the real thief – that it were you who robbed your own office in Kirkley Hall!'

The courtroom now erupted into chaos. Many of the public leapt to their feet – shouting in anger at – or in support of – William's accusation. Aynsley roared like a bull and moved towards William in the dock, screaming: 'Slanderer! Slanderer!' Joseph Aynsley rose to restrain his furious father but it was the court bailiffs who got to William first. They elbowed Aynsley out of the way, hauled William out of the dock and dragged him in front of the magistrates' bench. Clennell said a few short sharp words which no one could hear beneath the shouting of the mob and then the gaolers from Newcastle Keep came forward and dragged William out of the room. Next, the bailiffs began to clear the public gallery, roughly ejecting the crowd.

Cilla's eyes never left her husband's face. Jamie remained serene as mayhem exploded around him and his own eyes never left William's face. As he was dragged past, William grinned and winked at Jamie. Jamie winked back. Then the edges of his dry and cracked mouth flicked up into a broad grin.

Back in the woods outside Milburn, young Jack Charlton had an idea.

First, he found a long, slender branch. Then he lifted his shirt and started to undo the string which held up his breeches. He knew from his reading that the rich folks who kept birds of prey in their big houses put leather hoods over the creature's eyes to calm them. Well, he had no leather hood but he reckoned he might be able to slip his breeches over the eagle's head with the help of the long stick.

'You'd better be good,' he said softly to the bird as he stepped out of his trousers. 'Ma'll kill me if you rip them.'

Cautiously, he circled round to the back of the bird but this gave him no advantage. The eagle merely swivelled its head and watched him with his cold, unblinking, golden eyes. Sighing, Jack decided to risk it anyway. Dropping to his haunches, he reached out with his stick. He kept his hand as steady as he could and slowly inched the dangling breeches towards the raptor's head.

Unbelievably, it worked. The eagle allowed the ragged trousers to be dropped over its head and then just sat there, silent and still.

Now Jack moved swiftly. Within seconds he was beside the creature – so close he could smell its earthy smell, hear its breathing and feel the warmth of its feathered body next to his own. He pulled with all his strength to open the jaws of the trap. It groaned in protest but opened up a fraction of an inch. Pouring with sweat at the exertion, Jack struggled to hold the lethal device open. The eagle remained silent and still.

‘Move you daft bugger,’ the boy hissed between his teeth. He nudged the mass of silky plumage with his shoulder.

Instantly, the subdued eagle came back to life and jerked its talons free. It half hopped, half stumbled away.

Now Jack was able to release his grip. The trap sprang back shut with a resounding clang which sent every roosting bird in the copse screeching into the sky. Alarmed at the noise, the great bird now struggled to free itself from the child’s clothing and take flight. Shaking its head, it snatched at the garment with its claw in a frenzy. It unfurled its great wings and whipped Jack smartly across the face as the lad scrambled frantically out of the way. As he dived behind a tree, Jack managed to snatch the dangling leg of his breeches and pull them off the raptor’s head.

The great bird was finally free. It paused for a second, blinking in the sunlight and looked straight at the boy, its golden eyes now blazing with fire.

Jack stared back. ‘Now gan and set me Da free,’ he said. ‘You lucky bird.’

The next second, the eagle leapt into the air and wheeled upwards into the tree canopy on its stiff wings.

It was damaged and starving but alive and free.

The gaolers returned Jamie Charlton to the squalor and stench of Newcastle Keep while the magistrates deliberated on the evidence that had been presented to them. Several men were crammed together into the dark stone cells with their soot-blackened walls. A tiny, barred window, ten feet above the straw-strewn floor, was the only source of light. Jamie had been transferred to Newcastle Keep with William Taylerson, the horse thief, and was sharing a cell with him. As the ancient door slammed shut behind him, he sank to the floor with his head in his hands.

His mind raced as he tried to make sense of the morning’s events. Was there enough evidence to send him to a full trial with the circuit judge? As every second passed, he became more and more convinced that there was. For a few brief hours out there, in the gloomy courtroom above the cells, he had started to regain some hope. He had allowed himself to be distracted by Mr. Blake’s staunch defence, the conviction of Sarah Kyle’s argument with Aynsley, and the unexpected and dramatic testimony of his brother.

Now back in his stinking cell, Jamie’s courage began to fail him and depression washed over him again in wave after wave. In desperation, he began to pray.

Taylerson, who was relentless in his goading, burst out laughing. 'What you doing, man? Are you praying?'

Jamie ignored him and tried to concentrate: '…those that trespass against us. Lead us not into temptation…'

'Bit late for that now, Charlton. You've already been tempted and done your trespassing. You trespassed all over Kirkley Hall.'

'For thine is the kingdom, the power and the glory…'

'…and now the court's sitting and deciding whether you walks free – or walks with me to the gallows.'

'For ever and ever…'

'Praying's not gannin to help you now, man.'

Finally Jamie snapped. 'Oh, for Christ's sake, Taylerson! Can't you ever leave me alone?'

'I think you needs a bit of company, right now.'

'Well, I don't.'

'When a gadgie starts praying in here, it usually means that the magistrates is out, making their minds up.'

'They've only just finished giving evidence against me…' Jamie blurted out. He buried his head in his hands and his voice broke. '…there were over sixty witnesses willing to speak out against me! Sixty!'

'Sixty?' Taylerson exclaimed in genuine surprise. 'Well, I heard tell that you were right famous – the gadgie who robbed the big house. I see that now.'

'I'm not as famous as Nathanial Ogle's two hundred pound reward,' Jamie replied bitterly. 'That will be why they are all so keen to damn me! Thank God my brother spoke out for me, in defence.'

'And don't you trust him?'

'Of course I trust him!'

'So why are you praying then? You don't need God if you've got kith an' kin who'll stand up for you.'

'I'm praying because they want to hang this crime on me – guilty or not. I'm praying because the man who presented the evidence against me is the man who hates me the most in the world. And I'm praying because... because I don't want to die…and I think that God'll be the only one as can help me now…' His voice trailed away hopelessly.

'I'm an innocent man but God help me if this goes to full trial,' Jamie murmured quietly. 'This hearing has been bad enough. In front of the bar – I have no doubt that my own conscience will condemn me…'

Taylerson had heard him. 'If your conscience is clear, why need your conscience condemn you?' he asked. He never got an answer. The next second, there was a sharp bang on the cell door and the iron grid was slid roughly to one side.

'Charlton? James Charlton?' It was the gaoler.

Jamie's chains rattled as he scrambled desperately to his feet. He shivered violently and struggled to control his voice.

'Yes! Yes! I'm here! What says the court?'

'Mr. Blake has sent me to tell you that there are no bills found against you.'

There was a stunned silence in the dank gaol cell as the two prisoners absorbed the news.

'Them magistrates have come to the conclusion that there was no real evidence to suggest you had robbed Kirkley Hall – only evidence that you had spent a lot of money.'

Jamie sank back down to the filthy floor.

'Oh, thank the Lord! Thank God! Thank you Lord for this deliverance…!' he gasped. He could barely believe it.

'As soon as I can get an opportunity,' the disembodied voice from the other side of the metal grille said, 'I'll come and knock your irons off.'

'Thank you! Thank you!' Jamie was almost too emotional to speak.

Taylerson watched him from the other side of the cell in silence. The disappointment was etched deeply into his haggard face. The man was an illiterate, emotionless brute who had no friends, family or visitors and who had been in and out of gaol since he was a child. The appalling physical conditions never seemed to bother him but he had become obsessed with the horror of being alone at the end.

'I guess we're not to hang together then, Charlton?' he said at last.

'No. You can take that walk on your own, you pathetic bastard,' Jamie snapped. 'Oh. Thank God for this deliverance!'

'You'll be gannin home for a quiet life now, eh?' the other man said morosely. 'With your missus and the bairns?'

'Quiet?' Jamie said sharply. 'I don't think so, man. I've wasted three months of my life in this hellhole – and it's down to the evil and spite of Michael Aynsley I was put here. I reckon it's time to get even now. Aynsley had better watch his back…I want vengeance.'

It was another twenty minutes before the turnkeys returned to strike off Jamie's leg irons. As the door swung open, two gaolers entered.

William was pushed roughly into the cell ahead of them. He leant against the wall, grinning. He was in his shirt sleeves and wore chains on his wrists. The two brothers stared at each other; the silent understanding which had descended on them in the court room was still in place.

'One Charlton in: one Charlton out. Your ma must be so proud of you boys,' one of the turnkeys goaded cheerfully. 'That's two sons she's got in gaol right now.'

Taylerson stumbled awkwardly to his feet. 'What's this? Taylerson asked nervously. He licked his parched lips and jerked a thumb towards William. 'What's he doing 'ere?'

William eyed the horse thief coldly.

'Hasn't James Charlton told you?' the gaoler asked. 'His idiot of a brother got himself a two week sentence for contempt of court while he were giving evidence. The magistrates said he were to take his brother's place in a cell.'

'He can't come in here, with me!' said Taylerson in a panic. 'I'll not have him in here with me!'

'I don't blame you, Taylerson,' the turnkey said with mock sympathy. 'I'm bloody well sick to death of the Charlton family and all. But if his worship says he's to take his place – then he's to take his place. What the magistrates says – goes.'

He turned to Jamie and shoved a coat he had been carrying into his arms. 'Your brother's also insisted on giving you his coat to gan home in. A mighty fine gesture of brotherly love, methinks. Now get the hell out of here, Jamie Charlton, afore we changes our minds.'

Jamie paused as he moved towards the door and turned to William. 'Are you going to be alright?' he asked.

'Of course I am,' William replied, and winked again. 'Just tell our Ma to keep the food coming for another couple of weeks.'

'I can't thank you enough.'

'Well, don't try,' William interrupted sharply. 'I'll see you on the outside in two weeks.' The next second, Jamie and the gaolers had gone. The cell door slammed shut behind them throwing the cramped space into gloomy darkness.

William stared hard at the cowering man, who cringed against the clammy wall at the back of the cell. Taylerson looked terrified.

'Now what were it our Jamie said?' William leaned forward and hissed viciously into the other man's ear. 'The ones that come in new, are fit and well fed.... and take from the ones who have been in gaol for a while.'

The next second William had Taylerson by the throat. He banged the horse thief's head back against the wall. Taylerson squealed like a pig but William had him in a vice-like grip. Taylerson tried to scream out for help but William just squeezed harder.

'Now give me back my brother's coat, you pathetic bastard,' he hissed. 'Or I'll choke you till you faint like a lass.'

Ann Charlton burst into hysterical tears when she saw William arrested by the bailiffs and dragged out of the courtroom. John Charlton chivvied Cilla and his distraught mother out of the door as all around them the courtroom descended into anarchy. They stumbled out into the blazing sunshine and down the grey stone steps of the courthouse, drifting instinctively towards the shade of a large sycamore tree. Beside them the busy road heaved with swaying wagons and rumbling carriages. The stench from the river was overwhelming but the women were barely conscious of it. They tried to comfort each other while a grim-faced John went in search of Mr. Blake, their solicitor.

When he returned he was flushed and excited. 'Jamie's to be freed!' he told them. 'There were no bills found against him! We can meet him at the gate of the Keep.'

Cilla's hand fluttered to her heart. She swallowed hard. Her mouth was parched. She barely heard her mother-in-law demand: 'But what of William?

It was over. Jamie was coming home. Cilla burst into tears of relief. Ann Charlton put a comforting arm around her shoulders. 'But what of William?' the older woman said again.

John frowned. 'He's to spend two weeks in gaol for contempt of court.'

Ann's hand flew over her mouth in horror. Now Cilla reached out to comfort her.

'Mr. Blake said our William had come to see him privately, a few days ago and had told him about the loan,' John told them. 'Apparently, Jamie had asked William never to tell a soul he had borrowed money from him, which is why William had not mentioned it before. It seems William was concerned about the case and had realised that it was wise to disclose the facts about the loan so they could be used by the defence.'

Cilla glanced slyly at her brother-in-law's face. It was clear from his tone and the tightness of his mouth that John did not believe a word of this story.

They waited quietly for Jamie in the stifling heat by the gate of Newcastle Keep. Cilla was wracked with a mixture of nerves and excitement. She had waited so long for this moment she could hardly believe it was here. The last three months had been the longest in her life. Ann Charlton was quieter; her thoughts were now obviously with William, imprisoned somewhere deep inside these grim and blackened walls.

Eventually, Jamie staggered blinking out of the gate of Newcastle Keep and fell into Cilla's open arms. He was even more emaciated and filthy close up, and seemed only half the man she had known before. She stroked his face and sobbed with joy.

But Jamie's filthy and dishevelled appearance did not appear to bother his older children. When they finally returned to North Carter Moor, the twins threw themselves squealing with delight into their father's arms, demanding that the exhausted man threw them up into the air in their time-honoured game. Jack was also clearly overjoyed to Jamie again. After throwing himself into his Da's arms in an uncharacteristic show of affection, he ran whooping around the farm house with his arms out like a huge hawk, shouting something incomprehensible about a 'lucky bird'.

Only toddler William held back, hiding his face in his mother's skirts, fearful of the stinking, bearded man he did not recognise.

CHAPTER THIRTEEN

The relentless rhythm of rural life meant there was little time for celebration or for Jamie to gently regain his strength. They needed to fetch the harvest in. With William in gaol, North Carter Moor was now a man down. Even in his prime, Jamie had never been a match for William when it came to hard work, physical strength and concentration on the job. Now he was a shell of the man he had been, but nevertheless he picked up a scythe and took his brother's place in the fields.

Yet, when William strode out of Newcastle Keep two weeks later – proudly bearing Jamie's precious coat in his arms – the experience hardly seemed to have touched him.

With William's return, the mood lifted instantly at North Carter Moor. Ann started smiling again and John breathed a visible sigh of relief. After a hearty meal prepared by his delighted mother and a good bathe in the river, Will changed his clothes and persuaded Jamie to go with him for a celebratory drink to Ma Shotton's.

'Don't get drunk,' snapped John. 'You both are needed in the fields tomorrow at dawn.'

Apart from two trips to chapel to thank God for his release, Jamie had not left the farm in two weeks. A fortnight of good home cooking had started to put flesh back on his bones but he was still struggling to cope with the psychological effects of his incarceration. As they strode across the parched fields of stubble towards the flickering lights and smoking chimneys of Ponteland in the gathering dusk, a fox barked in a nearby copse. Jamie flinched at the sudden noise.

He stopped dead on the threshold of the Seven Stars when he saw Michael Aynsley's two eldest sons inside the inn but William pushed him firmly forward.

There was a flurry of excitement amongst the regulars when the Charlton brothers walked in together. Many of the men shouted out support – and some even offered to buy them drinks. Several – who obviously still believed that Jamie was guilty – laughed and clapped him on the back and told him that he was a 'lucky sod to have got away with it!'

Their younger brother, Henry, was already there with his friends. He invited Will and Jamie over to join them at their table. This took them nearer to the glaring Aynsley brothers who watched the Charltons sullenly from their table by the fireplace.

For a while the two groups of men studiously ignored each other but two weeks of surviving in Newcastle Keep had hardened William and made him more susceptible to the effects of a couple of glasses of brandy.

'Mick? Joe?' he shouted across to Aynsley's sons. His eyes shone with alcohol and mischief. 'Will you not join us in celebrating our Jamie's release from gaol?'

The public house fell silent. Everyone in the inn now turned towards the two groups of men and waited for the Aynsleys' reaction.

Mick Aynsley snorted into his ale. 'I'd rather have a toast with the devil himself!' he declared hotly.

'Well, unfortunately, I don't see your father here tonight.' William said grinning 'How is the old devil, by the way?'

Laughter rippled around the tavern and both the Aynsley brothers stiffened with anger.

'Very droll – just watch yourself, Charlton,' growled Mick Aynsley.

'Why? Why should I?' asked William defiantly. 'What can you – or your damned father – ever do, or say, that'll ever bother me again?'

''Tis very likely that our da with take you to court for that slanderous allegation you made about him.'

'What are you talking about?' William goaded innocently. 'Do you mean the statement I made about his fancy woman? Or is it my claim that your da is the real thief of Kirkley Hall which bothers you? That's not slander, Mick – it's the truth!'

The inn reacted with a mixture of cheers and shouts.

The eldest Aynsley brother stood up and yelled over the noise: 'Aye! You dared to say that – when we all knows the real thief is your Jamie!'

'Well, I've got some news for you and your da,' William informed them loudly. The noise abated in the tap room as everyone strained to hear. 'If your da knew anything about the law – which from his pathetic performance in that Newcastle courtroom I can see he does not – he would know that accusations made by a witness under oath, cannot be charged as slander.'

'Oh, sod off, Charlton,' snapped Mick Aynsley. He finished off his drink and threw the tankard down into the grate of the fireplace. Its clanging reverberated around the tavern.

'Come on Joe,' he said to his sibling. 'Let's gan and get ourselves some better company in the Blackbird, this place has become the haunt of nowt but stinking gaolbirds and felons.'

Henry Charlton moved to block the Aynsleys as they made to leave, but Jamie pulled his angry younger brother back down to his seat and stood up himself. 'While we're talking about slander,' he suddenly announced. 'You might as well all know that I will be taking both Joseph and Michael Aynsley Senior to court at the next assizes for slandering my good name with that ridiculous charge. And in view of what you've just said, Mick Aynsley – in this crowded public house full of witnesses – you can also expect a summons to appear in the dock alongside your da and brother!'

The pub erupted into laughter at the thought that Mick Aynsley had just landed himself in court. Mick Aynsley mouthed some obscenity before he stormed angrily out of the tavern. If the hour had been any later or the men any younger, the argument may have erupted into a fight but it had not. The drama was over. The drinkers settled back down to relight their pipes and resume their ceaseless clattering games of dice and cards.

His anger spent, William was silent. Mick Aynsley's words had struck home.

He could pretend he did not care – but he did. He and his brother had been in gaol. No matter how innocent Jamie was, their reputations were now both soiled, and suspicion would always hover over them. In addition to this, they had dragged their whole family down with them; the Charlton name would never be as respected as it once was.

Desperate to shake off this black mood, William picked up his glass and toasted his brother's acquittal. Young Henry and his pals were only too pleased to join him in the toast.

'So that's the vengeance Taylerson told me you were threatening in your last hour in gaol, is it?' William asked Jamie. 'To take the Aynsleys to court for slander?'

'Aye,' Jamie replied, 'revenge is a dish best served cold. So how is that miserable old horse-stealer Taylerson, anyway?'

'He's a worried man,' William informed him. 'He was found guilty at trial and sentenced to hang. As it's his third offence, the judge was not inclined to clemency and will not be recommending that his sentence be commuted to transportation. Taylerson will hang in the new year.'

'Then good riddance to bad rubbish,' Jamie declared coldly.

The Charltons worked from dawn till dusk to gather in the harvest, and sometimes they worked at night, by the silver light of the moon and their swaying lanterns. Other members of the family, Henry and their sisters, all came and helped out whenever they could find time away from their own work and responsibilities. Each one of them was drawn back to the land where they had been raised by the strong family bond and some ancient deep-rooted fealty to the rich and steaming earth. Terrified that the good weather would break at any moment, John Charlton drove them all on towards exhaustion, as field after field of swaying golden corn was slain beneath the rippling blades of their scythes and then pitch-forked into the stacks. It was back-breaking work. At lunchtime, Ann Charlton and the youngest children would appear in the fields with armfuls of bread, pickles, cheese and jugs of water. The harvesters would throw themselves onto the piles of fresh straw and devour the food quickly. They only had a few brief minutes to rest their aching limbs before John chided them to their feet again.

Buoyed by Jamie's successful acquittal, the mood of the family remained high. No one laughed and joked as much as Jamie and Cilla. While he did not to begrudge them their happiness, William could not help being swamped by jealousy whenever Cilla touched her husband or stared lovingly into his eyes. Part of him began to doubt that those intimate moments he had shared with Cilla had ever existed, but his common sense breathed a sigh of relief that they had never acted on their lust.

One evening she appeared by the river bank again while he was washing away the dirt and sweat. This time Jamie was stood beside him, chattering away in his usual manner. William was aware that Cilla's beautiful eyes were flitting backwards and forwards, comparing the physique of the two brothers. He knew what she was thinking; Jamie cut a poor figure beside him.

The weather held and the harvest neared its end. Now, the family started to relax and to look forward to the harvest festival. This year it was to coincide with the long-awaited marriage of Henry to Sara Kyle. The banns had already been called.

The children busied themselves collecting luscious wild berries for fruit pies and the last of the summer's flowers for decorating the house and tables. They wove corn dollies in the time-honoured tradition and tied them on long poles to hang from the rafters of the barns. Kern babies were fashioned from the last sheaves of wheat to be cut. They were bundled, dressed in white and trimmed with coloured ribbons to represent the spring. The children saved them to decorate the bride's table; the bride who carried a spring baby in her womb.

The first of their wheat was sent to the miller. When it returned they baked into soft, moist lammas loaves. Vegetables were ripped up from the ground and they stripped the fruit from the trees. Everything was piled high next to the pot sink in the farm kitchen, ready for peeling and stewing. Two fat geese were slaughtered and stuffed with apples for the feast. Mutton was roasted in herbs.

Two evenings before the wedding, Jamie, William and young Jack began to behave furtively and then disappeared out into the dark, moonless night.

When she entered her kitchen at dawn, Ann Charlton was stunned to find three large, fresh salmon glistening on the wooden table. She frowned. 'I'm not even going to ask whose estate you have poached them from!' she said to her bleary eyed sons and grandson. They grinned at her across the room.

'I thought you two had seen enough of the inside of gaol?' John Charlton chided his brothers, humourlessly. 'What a poor example to set the young lad.'

But not even John's ill humour could dampen the excitement about this year's harvest celebrations. The day of Henry's wedding was a true family celebration. Every one of Ann Charlton's seven surviving children – all accompanied by their spouses and children – arrived for the ceremony at the squat stone church next to the river in Ponteland. Even young Lizzie had managed to get the day off from her duties as housemaid at Kirkley Hall. She arrived resplendent in a brand new dress and bonnet. This irritated her jealous sisters who pulled at their faded hand-me-downs and it worried her religious father, for whom pride was a deadly sin.

'She always was my prettiest grand-daughter,' Ann Charlton whispered conspiratorially to William.

'Oh, I don't know about that,' William replied. 'I think Cilla's flame-haired twin daughters will cause mayhem amongst the young lads in this parish in a few years' time.'

Ann just smiled.

The Kyle family was far smaller than the Charlton tribe but the little shopkeeper, Sarah Kyle, had been determined to contribute to the wedding feast of her niece; a young woman whom she had raised from an infant. A wagon had been packed with hampers of cold ham, pickles, pastries and homemade seed cake. Decorated with garlands of wild flowers and colourful ribbons, it trundled behind the wedding party as they returned to North Carter Moor.

The two families walked back together, chatting amiably in the gentle sunlight as they weaved their way along the poppy-lined lanes. Alongside them the hedgerows were weighed down with the weight of fruit and berries. It wasn't long before most of the children had stained and smeared their faces, fingers and clothes with blackberry juice.

At the head of the parade walked the delighted bride and groom. Henry was resplendent in a new coat; Sara, the bride, was bedecked with a beautiful wreath of laurel and vivid rowan berries. As she walked, she stroked the gentle swelling of her stomach beneath her muslin dress. They might have had to wait until the expense of the trial was over before they could afford their wedding, but Henry and Sara Charlton had not waited for anything else.

William fell into step with his mother as they walked. He marked quietly and with satisfaction that she looked contented. 'Are you happy, Ma?' he asked.

'Never more so,' Ann replied. 'It has been a difficult year – what with Jamie and Cilla's troubles – but it has ended well. We have been blessed – Praise the Lord. Our Henry is now wed to a good lass – and we have more of this to look forward to next year.'

'How so?' he asked.

'The miller's son, Alan Reed, has approached our John,' his mother informed him. 'He has asked if he can walk out with our Minnie – John's eldest. Of course, we've all known that he has been sweet on her for a while now but this will be a good match for her.'

'What? Little Minnie?' William was genuinely surprised about this news of his eldest niece. 'It hardly seems two minutes since I was dangling her in my lap!'

'Well, she's grown to a woman now, Will,' Ann reminded him. ''Twill be a good match for her.'

'Aye,' he agreed. 'A miller's wife will never starve.'

'Well, she most likely will be wed before you are.' Ann cast a sly glance in his direction.

'Most likely,' he grinned. He knew only too well what was coming next.

But before his mother could launch into yet another lecture about how it was about time he stopped gallivanting about with the local wenches and found himself a decent wife, they were distracted by the delighted shouts from the crowd behind.

The Kyles' horse-drawn wagon pushed itself forwards through the crowd. Jamie was stood on the back of the cart, shouting and waving theatrically at the wedding party. He too was decorated with gaily-coloured ribbons and bits of rag; a sheaf of corn hung round his neck on string and on his greying head balanced an old straw hat that sprouted corn and wilting flowers. Behind the wagon marched a group of the children with painted cardboard sickles slung over their shoulders. Cilla followed them, smiling proudly.

'Hookey! Hookey!' Jamie shouted.

'Hookey! Hookey!' the children echoed.

The laughing crowd gathered around.

'Trust our, Jamie!' Ann said and smiled fondly. 'He never passes over a chance to play the clown!'

'Friends, neighbours and family,' Jamie said confidently. 'As we all are aware, our John is the real master of the harvest....'

'Get yourself on the cart, John!' William shouted.

'Aye, you'd look good with a few flowers and ribbons,' Henry suggested.

The revellers shouted out encouragement but John Charlton smiled and shook his head.

'...but being the shy type that he is...' Jamie continued, 'we cannot persuade him to take part.' There were mock groans of disappointment from the crowd.

'Shame!'

'So you'll have to make do with me as lord of the harvest – and the bairns as the little reapers.'

'Sing us the song!' Henry yelled.

'Aye! Get the bairns to sing us the song!' chorused the crowd.

An expectant hush fell amongst all those gathered. The children cleared their throats and with tremulous little voices began to sing the song which Cilla had rehearsed with them.

'Hookey, hookey, we have shorn,
And we have bound,
And we have brought harvest
Home to town...'

A great cheer rose amongst the crowd and there was much clapping. Jamie had to wave his arms for silence. 'Give the bairns a chance,' he chided humorously. 'They haven't finished yet!'

Once more quiet descended, and the young Charltons warbled out another verse:

'Merry, merry, merry, cheery, cheery, cheery,
Trowle the black bowl to me;
Hey derry, derry, with a poupe and a lerry,
I'll trowle it again to thee...'

Applause again broke out amongst the adults and Jamie handed down a large, black bowl to the children. They ran laughing and squealing through the crowd, begging for groats, ha'pennies, sweetmeats and boiled spice.

'He home returns, with hookey cry, with sheaves full lade abundantly.' Ann Charlton smiled. 'That's our Jamie.'

'It certainly is,' William agreed.

'Now good friends,' Jamie shouted. 'When the bairns have returned the bowl to me…'

'Watch it, bairns!' someone interrupted. 'He'll steal your sweetmeats and hide them with the rest of the Kirkley Hall rent money!'

William nearly choked with laughing. The rest of the crowd was bent double and whooping with merriment at the joke. Only the children were confused.

Jamie pretended to look hurt. 'I'll pretend you never said that, Abel Wilson,' he said. 'Right, there still be plenty of room on my cart for any lasses who want to ride with the master of the harvest. Who wants to ride with the master of the harvest?' He made several rude sexual gestures and gyrated his hips crudely to accompany his words. The crowd loved it. When none of the women moved to join him on the cart his face fell in mock sadness.

'What? Are there no takers? Well, in that case, I'd better just offer a lift to those lasses who are already with child.'

The bride was lifted, giggling, onto the back of the wagon by the men.

'There's still plenty of room for any lasses who want to be with child!' the irrepressible Jamie continued.

'Oh sod it,' said William. He moved forward, scooped up Cilla in his arms and swept her into the back of the wagon with Jamie. 'Get a move on brother,' he said. 'Or else we'll all starve to death in this lane.'

'Hookey, hookey, hookey!' Jamie slurred lasciviously, as he gyrated hips again. Another great roar of laughter went up from the crowd. Cilla blushed prettily and even their John smiled.

Suddenly, everyone's attention was ripped away from the theatricals on the back of the wagon. They glanced upwards and gasped. Delighted hands were raised – all pointed skywards.

Above their heads the eagle wheeled and soared in a fantastic aerobatic display – a freshly caught salmon dangled from its fearsome talons. It circled above them and then, gathering up its tremendous wings, it dived down like a golden arrow. The crowd watched in awe as it soared back up into the sky again.

Young Jack screamed and whooped for joy. 'He's here! He's here! Our lucky bird is here!'

'They say it's a good luck bird,' someone said in the crowd.

'It's brought you a salmon for your wedding feast, Henry!'

'Aye, 'tis good luck for the bride and groom!'

'I can't believe that bird is still at large,' William said to his mother. 'I thought every man in the parish had tried to trap it to claim the reward.'

''Tis too wily to be trapped,' Ann Charlton said.

'A bit like our Jamie,' William observed thoughtfully.

'We'll not dwell on that today,' his mother informed him. 'That is all behind us now.'

Eventually, the eagle glided back towards the Milburn woods. With an increased feeling of well-being and contentment, the two families continued to wend their way back to North Carter Moor for the wedding feast and more Harvest Festival games.

William noticed that young Jack, who had shouted himself hoarse, was the last to leave. When the raptor finally disappeared from sight, the boy wiped tears of happiness from his eyes with the back of his sleeve before following his family to the farm.

As the light faded and the luminous harvest moon crept upwards into the cold night sky, a coatless and hungry William Taylerson shivered in his cell. He brooded about the bitterly cold winter months ahead that he would suffer in that miserable gaol, and the long drop on the gallows which would end it all. To take his mind off his grim future, he started to tell his latest cell mate the story of James Charlton and the Kirkley Hall robbery. It was obvious to the other prisoners that Taylerson had become obsessed with Charlton; he talked constantly about the time he had shared a cell with him. Those who would listen to his strange, repetitive and rambling monotone were becoming fewer and fewer – newly imprisoned young Wilf Oliver was the exception to the rule.

'...he were discharged when no bills were found against him,' the horse thief finally explained. 'That means that there weren't enough evidence to send him to trial.'

There was a pause as Oliver absorbed the news of Charlton's lucky escape.

'But did he do it?' he asked, at last.

'Of course he did,' Taylerson replied, slowly. 'He told me himself in Newcastle Keep after they'd announced he were to be released. He were right cocky, like, and thought he'd got away with it. He said that the rent money he had kept had got him nicely through his troubles – but that he had done it all right.'

'Well, he got away with it all,' the younger man said, clearly impressed. ''Tis a pity 'is luck did not rub off on you – he left you behind to swing at the end of a rope.'

'Ah, well,' said Taylerson. 'I'm thinking of bringing him in again.'

'What?' The younger man was startled.

'I reckon if I tells the court what I knows, I can gain me own liberty,' Taylerson explained.

Oliver stared at him in surprise and distaste – and shivered slightly.

'Would you, for the value of your own liberty, hang another man?' he asked slowly.

There was a pause as Taylerson glanced up at the barred window of the cell. He watched the gleaming harvest moon sail freely in the black, velvet sky.

'Aye,' he replied, 'I would. Liberty is sweet.'

CHAPTER FOURTEEN

The weather started to change almost immediately after Henry's wedding.

There was a sharp chill in the air and vaporous mists began to drift across the top of the fields. It seemed that overnight the trees had all changed colour together, transforming the sides of the valley into a vivid autumnal patchwork quilt of gleaming gold and orange. Red squirrels scurried around and collected fallen acorns from the drifting piles of leaves at the base of the oaks. Great flocks of birds wheeled noisily above the tree canopy as they gathered for migration.

A sense of urgency began to spread through the parish. Everything had to be ready before the first onslaught of the winter; all the repairs which had stood idle through the summer must now be attended to. The women folk pulled their shawls tighter around their cold shoulders and busied themselves with their knitting needles. Winter clothing was patched and darned. Whistling shepherds and their dogs brought the flocks down from the high fells to the lower pastures. The men hurried to repair leaking roofs, draughty windows and damaged fences. The countryside echoed with the dull, thudding sound of axe on wood as trees were felled and logs gathered in for winter fuel. Wagons, stacked high with provisions, rumbled constantly along the winding lanes and roads from Newcastle and Morpeth, through glittering copper and bronze tunnels formed by the beech hedges and overhanging oak branches. Everyone stocked up with whatever they could afford – all desperate to prepare for the months ahead which often brought dangerous drifts of snow and blinding blizzards that could cut off their community for weeks at a time.

Then the weather started to become unpredictable; it swung dramatically between violent rainstorms and heavy fogs. With the change in weather came a change at North Carter Moor.

Jamie knew that John could not support his family through the bleak winter months so he approached Tom Gillespy, the farmer at Haindykes and asked for his old job back. Gillespy, who had given evidence on Jamie's behalf at the trial, was a man who was prepared to put his money where his mouth was; he agreed.

'I have some bad news, like,' Jamie told John and William that evening as they sat smoking their pipes in the parlour. His brothers looked up, concerned.

‘I am really grateful, John, for all the assistance that you have rendered to me and mine this year, but I’m going have to leave off working for you soon.’

The North Carter Moor farmer could barely contain his delight at the news. After hearing about Jamie’s return to Haindykes, John casually mentioned that there was a good chance he could also have his old cottage back in Milburn.

Jamie frowned and looked irritated.

‘Nathanial Ogle will never rent a cottage to me again,’ he said. ‘He’ll not want me as a tenant.’

‘Oh, but he will – he does,’ John said. He almost fell over his words in his excitement. ‘I took the liberty of mentioning your cottage – which still stands empty, by the way – when I bumped into the steward at the meat market last Wednesday.’

‘It’s still empty?’ queried Jamie. ‘Why is that? ’Twas a good home for a family.’

‘There’s no one to rent it,’ said John sadly. ‘All the young folk are moving south towards the towns and cities. The streets of Newcastle, Sunderland and Durham are paved with gold – so they say. Take Bates’ farm,’ John continued, ‘it’s been empty for over a year since the old couple were carted off to the workhouse. Prime farm land all turned to fallow…’

Jamie interrupted him. ‘What did the steward say about my cottage in Milburn?’

‘He agreed with me, that you had not been found guilty of the robbery and were therefore as innocent as any other man in the parish. He said that you could have your cottage back at the old rent.’

Jamie suspected that John was stretching the truth somewhat with that first sentence; however, it was welcome news. Jamie went to the Kirkley Hall steward’s office, and signed for the lease. Then he and Cilla began to collect together the essential household items which they would need to start again and added them to the few items they had left in the barn. A buzz of excitement seemed to sweep around North Carter Moor; the whole family was excited about the move.

The whole family that is, except one.

William viewed the prospect of Jamie and Cilla’s departure with nothing but gloom. He’d enjoyed Jamie’s company over the last two months. Young Jack had shared his tiny cottage since May and he had become really fond of the lad. Even the twins were amusing in their fearless, self-absorbed and lively way. The boredom of evening prayers and the lengthy sermons of Brother John were bearable with Jamie winking irreverently at him from the other side of the kitchen or fidgeting beside him in the parlour. Jamie's family had lifted the dour gloom from North Carter Moor and made it a far pleasanter place to live. William dreaded the boredom, the hushed quiet and the religiosity which he knew would once again descend on the farm following their departure.

The prospect of Cilla leaving also left William feeling depressed. Since Jamie had returned he had accepted the inevitable and acknowledged that she could never be his. But he had taken comfort in the warmth of her brilliant smile when he flirted with her and enjoyed watching her as she glided sensuously around the farm. A small voice inside his head told William it was for the best if Jamie and Cilla left; it was right he had resisted the urge to lay with his brother's wife and it was for the best that she and Jamie were leaving.

When they were gone William's loneliness was intense. He became moody and apathetic and dragged himself through his daily chores in a black cloud of misery.

'He's missing our Jamie,' he heard his mother whisper to John's wife.

If only you knew, he thought to himself.

The first blizzard of winter hit Ponteland with a vengeance. Five days of continuous snow swirled menacingly in a bitter wind. It filled the lanes between the hedgerows and buried the farm in a deadly white blanket. Several times a day John and William braved the elements. Muffled in shapeless layers of clothing they dug their way out through the blizzard to the well and to the animals. Barely able to see their frozen hands and the spades in front of them, they forced open the barn doors against the weight of the snow and smashed the ice which had formed on the troughs. John's shivering daughters slithered behind them, unsteady on the ice and carrying lanterns which only just illuminated the freezing gloom of the barns. The family pressed themselves close to the matted, shaggy-haired sides of the cows for warmth and blew on their numb and trembling hands to warm them and before they milked the beasts. The cattle stamped impatiently and exhaled billowing clouds of white steam into the ice cold air with every breath they took.

After five days, the biting wind subsided, the sky cleared, and a weak sun rose up tentatively into a pale blue sky behind the skeletal oaks in the copse. Thawing water began to drip from the trees and eaves of the farmhouse. The men worked frantically in the lull to clear away as much as they could before the next onslaught.

That evening, despite his aching limbs, William decided to brave a trip down to Ma Shotton's Ponteland.

'You're mad,' John told him coldly as he prepared to go. 'If you slip and break a leg in this, you'll be dead before we find you in the morning.'

This was not an idle comment but William knew that the close confinement of the farm, the whining of the children, the boredom and the dull, empty ache he felt inside were getting him down. He sought the warmth, companionship and brandy offered by the public house.

'Just take care,' his mother warned him, 'stick to the lanes and don't drink too much.'

He minded her words well enough as he trudged through the snowdrifts to Ponteland. Every large rock and tree stump along that rough lane was now hidden from sight and waiting to trip him. All paths and tracks had disappeared and even the hedgerows were just indiscriminate white lumps in an endless sea of white fields. In the rare patches where the snow had drifted away, the corn stubble and grass had frozen into long, spiky shards which crunched beneath his boots like broken glass. He did the journey from memory and glanced at the sky to see if it had filled with snowclouds again. He was grateful to see the silver moon start to rise into a clear but darkening sky.

On arriving at the Seven Stars, it quickly became apparent to William that he was not the only one glad to escape from home for a couple of hours. Through the smoky interior he saw Jamie and Henry. As William breathed in the familiar smell of alcohol fumes, pipe tobacco, unwashed bodies and wet dog, he felt his tension start to slip away. He slumped down on a stool next to his brothers, threw back his drink and sighed with growing contentment.

Unfortunately, Mick and Joseph Aynsley had also decided to venture out in the thaw. They were gathered around a table by the door with a few of their mates.

It wasn't long before the bickering started up again. It was Jamie who started it this time. Ugly rumours had been circulating in the parish about Michael Aynsley.

'Say Mick, Mick Aynsley – is it true your da's had a seizure?' Jamie yelled across the crowded bar.

The Aynsleys ignored him so Jamie turned to his family and announced loudly: 'They say he fell down near dead after mounting his whore and that he's been dribbling and pissing himself ever since.'

Everyone who had heard him sniggered crudely.

Mick Aynsley stared hard at Jamie and spat onto the straw-strewn floor beside him. 'Me da's fine,' he replied icily. 'And even if he'd had a seizure, the old man would still have no trouble kicking you up the backside, Charlton – just like he used to do.'

There were howls of laughter at this retort. Jamie flushed at the memory of his treatment at the end of the steward's boot.

'Your da's not the steward any more,' William told him loudly. 'His days of kicking anyone around are long gone. He was dismissed from Kirkley Hall, remember? Dismissed in disgrace. Your bastard of a father is in no position to bully anyone any more.'

A cruel smile widened on Mick Aynsley's face. 'Aye, maybes so, Will Charlton,' he said slowly. 'Maybes our father won't be able to reduce a man to tears no more – but one glance from our baby sister, Sarah – and you'll be blubbing like a bairn!'

William was across the room like a shot and wiped the grin off Mick Aynsley's face with a ferocious punch. Mick flew backwards off his stool but he leapt back to his feet like a cat. For one moment, there was a stunned silence in the tavern as everyone watched him spit blood onto the floor.

The next second, Joe Aynsley and the rest of their companions rose angrily to their feet. Jamie and Henry Charlton leapt noisily across the tap-room to support William and launched themselves into the fight. Some of the drinkers shifted quickly out of the way as the two families laid into each other but many rolled up their sleeves and joined in.

Bar stools and glasses sailed through the air, crashed down around their heads, and shattered into pieces on the flagstones. Ma Shotton screamed and cursed them all. She and her barmaids grabbed brooms and began to whack the lot of them in an attempt to get them out of the door.

Mick Aynsley's first punch found its mark on William's right eye. His second hammered into his rib cage. Blood spurted down William's face. Half blinded, he lashed out furiously and caught Mick another glancing blow to the head. He heard the cheekbone crack. Mick launched himself at William and the two men were locked in a ferocious battle of strength next to the open door. William had his left hand round Mick's throat. Mick was trying to gouge his eyes and kick him in the balls.

Suddenly, the wall disappeared behind them. They fell through the open doorway and rolled outside in the frozen slush. William twisted as they fell and Mick ended up beneath him – his head cracked down hard on the black ice. William staggered to his feet, swayed as the pain from his ribs seared through him and then he booted Mick repeatedly in the side.

Beside him Jamie hurled Joe out of the door and several other pairs of grappling men fell or staggered out with them.

A lantern was thrown into a nearby haycart which blazed into life. The flames cast the grotesque shadows of battling demons onto the dark walls of the houses which lined the street. Sash windows were thrown up in the bedchambers above, and the pub's neighbours shouted and screamed at the chaos below.

William felt a pair of strong arms hauling him away from Mick Aynsley's limp body.

'Enough now, lad, enough.' It was Rob Wilson. His massive hands held William's shoulders like a vice. He was probably the only man in the parish strong enough to have stopped him from killing Mick.

Panting heavily, William allowed himself to be pulled back. Joe Aynsley took advantage of the break, to dash over and yank his dazed brother to his feet. Mick clutched his head and the two of them limped and staggered off down the road; Mick was nearly bent double.

William eye throbbed painfully and the blood trickled down his face but his opponent was in a lot worse state than he was.

'Enough,' Wilson said again. 'He got what he deserved. You fight well, man. You ought to sign up to fight those bloody French; Wellington would welcome a man like you.'

'I might just do that,' William said as he spat the blood out of his mouth. He didn't take his eyes off the retreating backs of the Aynsleys.

'You might have to,' Wilson observed quietly. 'The Aynsleys will have the beadle onto you by tomorrow.'

William said nothing. His eyes were still fixed on the spot where the Aynsley brothers had disappeared into the night. Around him the noise had begun to abate; Aynsleys' cronies had abandoned their skirmishes with the Charltons and took flight down the other end of the street. They had been outnumbered in the end. The enduring unpopularity of the old steward, Michael Aynsley, had ensured that most of the tavern had sided with the Charltons.

'And I always thought you were the placid one, Will Charlton,' Wilson was saying behind him. 'Has sommat got into you, lad?'

Still William said nothing.

Suddenly, Jamie was at his side, shouting. He laughed and thumped him on the back in glee. William winced in pain but stood his ground.

'A drink!' Jamie yelled. 'A drink to celebrate!'

But Ma Shotton had slammed shut the door of her public house and shot home the bolts. In a daze, William followed his flushed and agitated family down the slush-filled street to The Blackbird. But news of the fight had spread like wildfire and they found the doors of both The Blackbird and The Diamond barred to them. Half the town seemed to be up out of their beds, watching them from doorways or windows.

The other men were still overwrought and animated; they compared injuries and continued to relive every blow and punch thrown over and over again. As his own adrenaline began to subside, William felt a wave of misery sweep over him.

What a fool he had just made of himself. Now the whole parish would be gossiping about how Will Charlton still held a candle for Sarah Aynsley.

Tearing himself away from his jubilant brothers, he staggered back home across the moon-swathed fields. Still fired by his anger, he drove himself recklessly forward, no longer aware of the difficult terrain he travelled. By the time he had reached Carter Moor, the brandy had worn off – as had most of his anger – and his face was throbbing.

John was still up, poring over his accounts ledgers at the kitchen table. The sight of William's bloodied and swollen face made him slam his books shut. He was furious.

'What next?' he yelled. 'You get yourself thrown in gaol – and then start brawling in the streets! What shame will you heap on this family next?'

Roused by John's yelling, their mother ventured into the kitchen. She attempted to clean William up and tend to his injuries. He brushed her off and sat and prodded at the dying embers of the fire with the poker.

'I'm on a committee pledged to uphold the peace and stamp out lawlessness in this parish!' John raged beside him. 'Yet my own brothers seem determined to ruin me!'

William did not care. All he could think about was their Jamie returning home to Milburn and having his wounds tenderly dressed by Cilla. Would she then lay with him?

God, how he wished he had a woman right now.

'You'll have to disappear for a while,' John snapped. 'They'll be up to arrest you in the morning. Lie low for a while. Get yourself to bed – and then head off over to sister Anne's at dawn.'

'He'll never get to Corbridge in weather like this!' their mother exclaimed.

'He'll get there,' John snarled. 'It's still thawing.' He stormed off to bed.

'You're so like your da,' Ann Charlton said fondly to William. 'I've lost count of the number of times he got into a brawl in Ponteland. I was forever patching him up when he got home.'

William set off for Corbridge at first light. The pain in his bruised ribs had subsided but he had a black eye, a throbbing head and an aching jaw. The snow was melting fast and with a bit of care he was able to wend himself along the tracks made by the wheels of the carts which had gone before him. He sighed; it was going to be a long fifteen miles with not much cheer at the end of it. The prospect of spending a few days with his eldest sister and her husband was a miserable one. This was as good a time as any to take Archie Musgrave up on his offer, he reasoned.

As he trudged on, step after step, Rob Wilson's words still rang in his brain: 'I always thought you were the placid one, Will Charlton. Has sommat got into you, lad?'

Placid?

Stupid more like, he decided. He knew he had to get himself sorted out....but how? He wondered if John would hold his job open for him, for when he returned. Then he asked himself if he actually cared?

Once he was along the main road which ran beside the river, he was able to hitch a lift with an old man in a wagon who trundled up behind him. The driver was taciturn and muffled with layers of scarves and a hat which enveloped all his features except his eyes. William brooded silently as they slithered along the road.

From his elevated position on the wagon he caught the odd glimpse of the black Tyne as it surged towards Newcastle and the German Sea. The edges of the river were iced over, trapping the frozen reeds and trailing tendrils of the bankside willows like iron prison bars. Cold and confused waterfowl skittered amongst them on the ice. They squawked mournfully. William knew how they felt.

They stopped occasionally to clear the drifts or let the bigger, faster stagecoaches past but they made good time and reached Corbridge just after eleven. As he tramped through the slush of the broad main street of the town he decided to get himself something to eat and drink at the Angel before asking directions to Archie's farm.

As William crossed the ancient bridge which arched over the Tyne, he stopped dead in his tracks.

Cilla was there. She was standing outside the public house, laughing and gossiping with a group of other women.

He felt his stomach lurch. His fuddled brain struggled to make sense of it. Then he remembered that her twin sister, Bella Nimmo, lived in Corbridge. He also remembered that allegedly Bella had turned to whoring, to feed herself and her pauper mother.

It was some years since William had last seen Cilla's twin and at this distance Bella was strikingly like her sister. However, on closer inspection he could see that her beauty was fading. Her hair was badly dyed. She was thinner and her face was lined with poverty and hunger. Her eyes shifted from one passing man to another. She wore a thin and faded blue jacket and a dirty green dress which was too short. The jacket was clearly not warm enough, because she hugged her arms to her sides and stamped her feet to ward off the cold. One of the other women passed her a brandy flask and she drank deeply.

He started to contemplate what it would be like to lay with her. The resemblance to her sister was uncanny. Would it ease his demons if he lay with Cilla's twin? Or would it just make him feel even more wretched?

But he was not to find out – that day at least. A friendly hand clapped him on his shoulder and a familiar male voice whispered in his ear: 'You don't want no truck with them doxies, every last one them has the pox.'

It was Archie Musgrave. William smiled for the first time in days.

CHAPTER FIFTEEN

'Thank you for warning me, Archie – I'll keep that in mind,' William said. He turned around and shook his old friend by the hand. 'And well met,' he added. 'I was just on my way up to your farm. I've decided to take you up on your offer.'

'Excellent!' Archie beamed. 'Will you come and have a bite to eat with me first, Will? I was just on my way to the Angel.'

'Aye, I was just going there, myself.'

Archie's eyes flickered over the bruises on William's face. 'Looks like you have been in a bit of trouble, my friend.'

William nodded.

'What were it about?'

'A woman,' William replied dully.

Archie's eyes widened and he laughed. 'I think you had better come inside and tell your Uncle Archie all about it,' he joked. 'It seems to me that living in Ponteland gets more and more dangerous by the week!'

As they moved towards the Angel, he glanced back at the whores milling outside the tavern. An old soldier, with one leg amputated beneath the knee, had joined the girls. He passed over some coins to Bella. She bit on the coin to make sure it was genuine, pocketed it, and then linked her arm through the soldier's. They set off unsteadily towards Middle Street. His crutch tapped excitedly on the cobbles as they went. Beneath the frayed hem of her skirt, her ripped petticoat and laddered stockings were visible. Glancing down at her exposed ankles, he could see tiny specks of lily-white skin peeping through the rents.

Archie followed his gaze again and grinned. 'Judging by the mess of your face, I think that you should keep away from the fairer sex for a while.'

William managed a grimacing smile.

The men ate a good lunch of lamb hotpot, swilled down with several glasses of ale. They mopped up the gravy with generous chunks of freshly baked bread. As the good food and the crackling fire in the grate warmed his frozen body, William felt himself relax. He told Archie about the dramatic events of the summer: Jamie's arrest and subsequent release; his own imprisonment for contempt and the friction with the Aynsleys.

'Aye, I'd heard ye'd had some trouble,' his friend said softly. 'Looking at your face, it seems it ain't over yet.'

William touched his swollen eye. It was tender. 'Our John's banished me to our sister Anne's until all the fuss dies down.'

'So you're in Corbridge looking for somewhere to hide out for a while, are you?'

'Aye.'

'Well you might as well come and stay with me up at my farm as bother your sister. I could always do with an extra pair of hands and I'd welcome your company.'

William gladly accepted his offer. Thorn Tree Farm consisted of three hundred acres of exposed and sloping fields, all of which were blanketed with snow. The soil was thinner here than in Ponteland and the wind more biting on the unsheltered slopes; there was little tree cover.

The old, ramshackle farmhouse was dirty and untidy; there seemed to be more farm equipment inside the kitchen than in the barn. Yet despite its prickly name, Thorn Tree Farm was warm and welcoming. In addition to this, Archie felt no need to hold prayers after supper or to ban strong spirits from the farm. He kept a stock of good brandy.

For the next three weeks William helped Archie with his stock. Archie had nearly a hundred pregnant ewes milling heavily around in his barns.

They'll be hard work in a couple of months, William thought.

His routine was similar to the one he had left at North Carter Moor but he enjoyed it more at Thorn Tree Farm. Archie was good company and so was 'Old George', his labourer. William appreciated being away from his family with their interminable problems and their complicated lives and relationships.

The thaw continued and on Sunday he went with Archie down to church in Corbridge. Afterwards, Archie took him to visit their nearest neighbours, the Milburns. Like William's own father, old Joshua Milburn had borne too many sons. But he had solved the problem by despatching three of them, at different intervals, over to the Americas to make their fortune there. It seemed that his plan had worked; the family received regular letters back from their three sons about their extensive farms in the rich and fertile New World.

The Milburns treated Archie like a son and fussed over William like an honoured guest. They pressed all kinds of food and beverages onto them. After they had drunk and eaten their fill, Jenny, the Milburns' daughter, read out the latest letter from her brothers in America. Archie appeared to be enraptured by Jenny Milburn and hung on every word which tripped from her soft lips.

William was also impressed with the girl's prettiness and her obvious intelligence.

'I'll be there soon, Will,' Archie said, when Jenny had finished and laid down the letter in her lap.

'Sorry?'

'New England or the prairies.' Archie sighed wistfully. ''Tis my ambition to emigrate – there's an easy fortune to be made out there. Imagine it, Will – thousands and thousands of acres just waiting to be claimed.'

'If the hostile natives, wolves and vicious winters will let you!' William laughed and turned to Joshua Milburn. 'Your son writes as if he has found the Garden of Eden but I have heard it is a very harsh life, beset with problems.'

The bold man nodded. 'Aye, they've had a problem or two with extreme weather and the natives.'

'That'll not put me off!' said Archie. 'As soon as I've built up a bit of cash from farming here, I'm away to the New World – and young Jenny here will marry me and come along to see her brothers!'

The whole family whooped with delight at this idea. Jenny blushed modestly on her stool. William smiled.

William's heart was heavy as the time came for him to return to North Carter Moor. On the last day of his stay, the sky was pastel blue. The combination of winter sunlight and the retreating ice was dazzling. Archie took him over to the western boundary of the farm. He pointed to a ruined farmhouse and a whole swathe of unbroken snow which stretched endlessly towards the horizon.

'What do you, think?' he asked.

'About what?'

''Tis another 200 acres. It's been abandoned for years. No one will take on the lease because the cottage which goes with it has all but collapsed.'

'Oh, yes?' William said. He had an inkling about what was coming next.

'The lease is cheap – and the rent,' Archie told him. 'You could get it for a song and then come in with me. We'd live together at my place and work both pieces of land together. You would be a part-owner of the farm. We'd make a fortune, man – I'd be on a ship to America before I know it – and you could come with me if you wanted.'

William stared into Archie's hopeful and friendly face and then glanced back at the Promised Land in front of him. He was not daft.

The ground beneath all the snow would be a nightmare to work on. It was overgrown, full of stones and riddled with tree stumps which would need clearing but Archie was offering him the chance to work on his own land. It was also the opportunity he needed to escape from the misery of North Carter Moor. None of it would be easy on these bleak and desolate fells; the lambing in a couple of months would be hell for a start. Yet it felt right. As long as he could keep his hands off Bella Nimmo's skinny arse in Corbridge he knew he would be fine.

'We'd best pay a visit to the estate office this morning and see about that lease then,' he said finally.

'You mean it?' shouted Archie in delight. 'You'll come in with me?'

'We'd also best find a solicitor and get an agreement drawn up.'

Archie grabbed his hand and pumped it vigorously up and down.

'You'll not regret it, Will. You'll not regret it!'

'I think I already am!' Will laughed as he tried to extricate his hand from the enthusiastic and painful grip of his friend. They talked for a while, making plans, sharing ideas. Then suddenly Archie changed the subject.

'There's just one thing, though, Will.'

'What?'

'That Milburn lass – Jenny.

'Oh, aye?'

I was wondering when she would crop up, thought William.

'I knows how you are with the lasses, Will – and I knows how they are with you – but this one is special. I wouldn't mind her for myself.'

William laughed.

'You've nothing to worry about there,' he informed his friend. 'I've had enough of women to last me a lifetime.'

In Morpeth Gaol the shivering and wretched William Taylerson grew more and more desperate. His pathetic appeal for clemency to the Prince Regent had been rejected and he was due to hang in the New Year. Every day he beseeched the turnkeys to tell the authorities that he had news for them regarding the Kirkley Hall mystery but they just laughed back in his face and told him to shut his bloody mouth.

In the darkness of the freezing gaol, the short days and long nights blended into one. Often they lost track of the date and time. Several men died that winter from malnutrition and the bitter cold. The survivors were a pitiful bunch; they stamped their frozen feet, blew on their numb hands and huddled under thin blankets in the filthy straw in a desperate attempt to ward off the cold.

Taylerson became more and more agitated as the time of his execution drew near. Then one day they came for him.

The ancient gaoler shuffled along, sniffing as usual and wiping his nose on the back of his sleeve. Behind him came one of his muscle-bound assistants carrying a lantern. The keys rattled in the lock and the rusty cage door grated open with a screech.

Taylerson had been sleeping fitfully. The noise woke him and for a moment the light which shone in his face, blinded him.

'Taylerson?'

'What?'

'Get to your feet, man!'

Taylerson struggled to understand what was happening – or did not want to. He hid his face behind his eyes and cowered on the floor.

'Taylerson?' the gaoler yelled again. 'For Christ's sake – get to your feet!'

'Why?'

'You'll know soon enough. You're to come with me.'

Taylerson's voice now rose sharply with fear. 'Why? Where are you taking me?'

'For God's sake man, get to your bloody feet!' the exasperated gaoler growled. 'Unless you want us to come in there and drag you out?'

'Look at Taylerson!' one of the other prisoners said. 'He's as scared as a bloody lass!'

'Aye,' young Wilf Oliver commented. 'So much for the hard man of Morpeth!'

'He thinks you're taking him to hang him!'

At the mention of hanging, Taylerson now erupted into total panic. He scurried like a rat to the other side of the cage and clung onto the bars with all his might.

'No! No!' he squealed. 'It's not time. I'm to have me last scran – canny good bait before I die…' His voice broke in a choking sob and he banged his head in anguish on the bars.

The gaolers and many inmates now burst out laughing. It was not often that they got a performance like that. Most prisoners just crapped themselves when they were taken to the gallows.

The old gaoler wiped the tears of laughter and a stream of snot from his face. 'Stop your bletherin, man! I'm not taking you to the gallows – yet. In fact, if you plays your cards right with these gadgies of the law – you might not hang at all.'

'Why?' Taylerson was trembling.

Suddenly everyone was interested.

'What gadgies?' Wilf Oliver demanded.

'There's some gentlemen, magistrates like, as wants a word with you about your old marra and cell mate, James Charlton.'

'Eh?' Taylerson was unsure if he had heard correctly. 'What do they want to know?'

'Anything you can tell them, I'm thinking,' the younger turnkey replied. 'Charlton's caused nowt but trouble and mischief since his release. There's a few would be happy to see him back in here.'

There was a disgruntled murmur from the other men in the cages.

Taylerson started to rise to his feet.

'Is there still that reward that Mr. Ogle was offering for information, like?'

The murmur from the other prisoners now rose to a growl.

'What?' Wilf Oliver yelled. 'Are we to be set upon each other now? Like dogs?

'Aye!' The ancient gaoler laughed. 'You're all nought but stinking dogs, anyway!'

'Don't do it, Taylerson!' another prisoner shouted. 'They want you to say that he telled you that he did the crime!'

Taylerson attempted to brush some of the dirt off his thin coat. The moment he had been waiting for had come and he knew it. He pushed back his matted hair from his eyes and half smiled. His black and gaping teeth made him look demonic.

'Aye, maybe so,' he said softly.

'Charlton's blood'll be on your hands if you damn him!' Wilf Oliver yelled.

'Move yourself,' the gaoler said.

'Would you hang another gadgie, just for your own liberty?' another prisoner asked.

'Aye, damn right I would,' Taylerson replied slyly. 'I've said it often enough: liberty is sweet.'

'Then you'd better watch yourself when you get back, you blabber-mouthed bastard!' someone growled.

When William finally managed to get home, it was to find out that the Aynsleys had brought no writ against him. They kept away from the taverns of Ponteland and were rarely seen outside their farm. Rumours continued to circulate in the parish about the old steward, Michael Aynsley. Everyone knew he had had a seizure of some kind.

Jamie was gleeful. 'I just hope the old bastard lives long enough for me to bring a writ against him for slander at the next assizes,' he told William. He was convinced that the Aynsleys were afraid of running into the Charlton brothers again after their beating.

William was not too sure about this. He suspected that if it was true that Michael Aynsley was seriously ill then his family had more important things on their minds than their feud with the Charltons. He had privately resolved that even if Mick Aynsley hit him over the head with a fence post he would not fight with him any more.

There was one Aynsley though, who was still regularly seen out and about in her trap in the slush-filled lanes of the parish: Sarah Robson, née Aynsley.

One afternoon when William was passing the empty farm which used to belong to Bates family, he saw her approaching. For once, the woman did not stare icily ahead. In fact, she was regarding him rather curiously.

Damn it, he thought. Instinctively, he reached out, grabbed the bridle and pulled her horse to a standstill.

Sarah turned pale, gripped her whip and raised it slightly.

'Don't worry yourself, Sarah,' he soothed. 'I'm not going to hurt you.'

'I should think not, Will Charlton.'

'I know you're busy with your father and all that…' he said, and paused to see if she would correct him. She didn't.

'I just wanted a few minutes of your time to explain a few things to you. I've got some news.'

'What news?' she demanded.

'I'm leaving, Sarah – leaving the parish.'

Her mouth dropped open in surprise. 'Well, that is news!' she conceded. 'But we can't talk here, folks might see us together. Half the parish is already gossiping about us again – after your little outburst in the Seven Stars.'

'Aye,' he grinned. 'How is your brother by the way? Has his head mended yet?'

'He'll live,' she snapped brusquely. 'But no thanks to you.'

'Look, drive the trap up the lane to Bates' Farm,' he instructed her. 'I'll cut across the fields and come in the back door – that way we can talk without compromising your reputation.'

She paused for a moment and then, much to his surprise, nodded in agreement. 'Very well,' she said. 'But this had better be important – and none of your tricks, Will Charlton.'

She flicked the whip expertly across the horse's flanks – inches away from William's face. The trap pulled away. It was only when she had gone that he realised how quickly she had acquiesced to his request. He was surprised. She was more than capable of using the whip on him if she had been in the mood; Sarah had always been her father's daughter. Did she think the rumours were true, he wondered? Was she hoping that he would declare his love for her again, so that she could pour scorn on his feelings once more?

As he traipsed across the muddy field towards the farm, he remembered the day Sarah had sought him out in the cattle byre to end their betrothal. Foolishly, he had thought that she'd come for another romp in the hay and he'd reached out for her. She had side-stepped him, told him she intended to marry the surgeon and then pleaded with him to understand why she was jilting him. Surely, he must see why this was such a good chance for her?

He had not been able to speak or look at her. He'd turned his back coldly, desperate to hide the pain and the womanish tears which welled up in his eyes. She'd walked away, leaving him a shell of a man.

He found her in the gloomy kitchen of the deserted farm. She had started a small fire in the grate. The farmhouse had been uninhabited for two years. It stank of misery, damp and despair. Apart from a wooden table in the centre of the room, there was only one broken chair and a smashed cup on the dusty floor to suggest that anyone had ever lived here. As he entered, a few dry autumn leaves swirled around on the flagstones until he shut out the wind. Where Sarah had found the kindling and wood for a fire he couldn't imagine; only a farmer's daughter would be so practical. She was wasted as a cossetted surgeon's wife.

He glanced around and took in the bleak, lifeless room which hid a ghost in every cobwebbed corner. He remembered coming here with her and Jamie and her brothers when they were youngsters. The gentle old farmer and his wife had been childless and had always been kind to the roving packs of neighbourhood children when they had turned up in the farmyard. They would ply the children with warm milk and biscuits.

'What happened to old farmer Bates and his missus?' he asked.

'Heddon Poorhouse,' she informed him blandly. 'They were kept apart in separate wards. She died quite soon. He lingered on for a few months longer. They say he sobbed himself to sleep every night calling out for her. They'd been together for nigh-on fifty years.'

A wave of sadness swept over him; that was no way and no place for such a kind couple to die.

'So, Will,' Sarah said, provocatively, as she pulled back on her gloves. 'What is so important that you decide to waylay me in the lanes of Ponteland?' The lightness of her tone lifted the mood which threatened to swamp him.

'It were impulse, Sarah.' He smiled. 'And well you know it. If I had decided to 'waylay' you – you would be on your back by now.' He added with a wink.

She stared straight back at him, smiling. Her own eyes never wavered from his.

'But those days are long gone,' he concluded a little sadly before changing tack. 'I wanted the opportunity to thank you for your assistance last May – when our Jamie was arrested in Morpeth.'

She looked confused. Then she remembered. 'Oh, it was nothing. Those soldiers were barbaric. I'm just sorry that I couldn't have done more to help poor Cilla. I understand she went on to lose the bairn?'

'Aye, she did,' he confirmed. 'I was later told you threw yourself in front of her, to stop one of those bastards kicking her when she was on the ground. You may have saved her life. God knows what damage their boots may have done.'

'Anyone else would have done the same.'

No, they wouldn't, he thought. There's not many women with your spirit, Sarah.

'I also wanted to tell you that – despite any rumours you may have heard – I am moving on with my life. I have taken on the lease of a farm up in Corbridge. It has two hundred acres attached and I will work it with Archie Musgrave.'

Her eyes widened with surprise and she questioned him briefly about the details. 'Well, good luck to you,' she finally said. 'Though I can't say for sure whether I'm pleased or sorry you are leaving.'

A shadow he didn't understand passed over her face.

'I thought you would have been glad to see the back of me. I'll bet that your husband will be; no man likes his wife's former lover hovering around the parish.'

'My husband has always been indifferent to you,' she informed him sadly. 'It never even bothered him that I had lain with you before we wed. However, you caused me a lot of trouble when you accused my father of being the Kirkley Hall robber in court last summer – I find it hard to forgive you that.'

'Caused you trouble? How so?'

'It's the world I move in now, Will,' she told him. 'I help the vicar's wife, I take tea with the schoolmaster's wife and the wives of solicitors and other doctors – it is hard to be accepted by them. Being branded the daughter of a common thief by you last summer didn't help me at all.'

He stared at her in surprise. He'd heard that Sarah entertained Surgeon Robson's gouty friends as if she had been born to grace mahogany dining tables and pick food from Dresden crockery. He had often imagined her pouring wine from crystal decanters and wielding a silver fish fork. He had often heard common folk grumble that Sarah Aynsley had 'got above herself' but he knew how driven she was, how ambitious and determined. It had never occurred to him before that she might have struggled to be accepted by the class she had married into.

'It sounds a lonely world that you move in now,' he commentated.

'It is,' she said simply, and turned away from him towards the fire.

He took a deep breath.

'Well, you made your choice,' he said as gently as he could. 'You had a choice and you chose the surgeon.'

She did not respond. She continued to stare down into the fire in the grate. The glow illuminated the deep sadness etched across her face. She looked miserable and frustrated.

'I'd get yourself with child, Sarah,' he advised. 'Have a bairn to keep you company and occupy your days.'

'I wish I could have a bairn,' she said in a voice which was barely audible. 'But it is not possible to become with child by a husband who does not…who cannot…'

William was stunned. So that was it was it? The old surgeon did not, or could not, swive with his wife?

For a moment he had an incredible urge to laugh out loud, but he bit it back. All that time he had wasted, jealously imagining their lovemaking. All those anguished nights he had tossed and turned in his own bed, picturing her in the doctor's arms. Yet, if Sarah could be believed, none of that was happening. He shook his head at his own foolishness.

'So what did he marry you for then?'

She shrugged her narrow shoulders. 'I don't know… companionship perhaps? Someone to run his home – his surgery? Or maybe because I was the only woman in the parish who had never heard the rumours about his childless first marriage.' She sounded bitter. Cheated.

'Well, I'm sorry for your unhappiness, Sarah,' he said and he shifted uncomfortably. Thoughts of Thorn Tree Farm, Archie and the New World now flashed across his mind. This was why he was leaving, he reminded himself – to get away from the complicated spider's web of the lives which lay across this parish. Everyone's tortured life was intertwined with everyone else's.

God, I need to get away.

'I cannot think what advice to give you…,' he said at last.

'I didn't come here for you to give me advice, Will Charlton.'

'No? What then?'

She turned swiftly and moved towards him until she was inches away from his face. He could smell her perfume and the sweetness of her breath.

'I don't want you to give me advice, Will. I want you to give me a bairn.'

His eyes widened with surprise.

'You are a good man. I know that,' she continued quickly. 'You've always been discreet about what has passed between us when I was betrothed to you. Now you are going away. You will have a new life, new adventures, new friends – and new women. What does it matter to you what you leave behind here in Ponteland?'

My God, she's begging for it! he realised with a start.

'Do this for me, Will – give me a child before you go.'

Her voice quickened. For the first time, she seemed to realise that he might not agree. 'I know you still care a bit about me; you wouldn't have thumped our Mick, if you didn't…'

Her voice trailed away and she stared up at him, her eyes desperate and pleading.

'What am I?' he teased softly. 'Some kind of stud ram to be picked up, used and then discarded when it's all over?'

She never replied. Her lips sought his, and she kissed him with a desperation which aroused him. He felt the passion swell within him. He took her in his arms and kissed her back. He felt her soft warmth and the smoothness of her mouth, her cheeks, her neck beneath his lips. He moved upwards and gently sucked on her ear lobe. She moaned softly.

'I'll do this for you, Sarah,' he whispered in her ear. 'But you need to know that there is – was – another woman I'm fond of.

Whatever you have heard rumoured about you and me, is false; that's ancient history now.'

But she didn't seem to hear or care. She breathed quickly. Her fingers fumbled with the buttons on his breeches and his manhood leapt into action like a bloody fusilier. Moving over to the table, with Sarah clamped to his side, he swiped away the years of accumulated dirt and filth with the sleeve of his free arm.

He swung her up onto the edge of the table, raised the soft material of her skirts and searched for the opening in her undergarments. As his hand brushed against the smooth skin of her inner thigh, she moaned again.

Then he lunged forward and took her.

CHAPTER SIXTEEN

William Taylerson was dragged outside into the market square at Morpeth. The low winter sunlight blinded him after so long in the dank gaol. His weakened legs struggled to move and he stumbled over his ankle chains as the gaolers pulled him over to The Black Bull public house. The crowds parted to let the two gaolers and the filthy prisoner past. Inside the Black Bull Taylerson's starving stomach lurched when the smell of roast beef hit his nostrils. He was bundled into a private side parlour where he felt the surging heat from a log fire smart against his frozen skin. Finally, he was pushed down into a chair facing a wooden table. He panted heavily from the exertion after months of inactivity but relished the warmth seeping into his bones.

Make this last as long as possible, lad, he told himself.

He took in his surroundings as quickly as he could; this meeting could mean the difference between life and death.

Besides the two gaolers, there were four other men in the room. All of them still wore their coats – as if none of them intended to stay long. One of them was the grey-haired, steely-eyed magistrate who had sent him to trial: Thomas Clennell. Another sat at the end of the table, a quill poised in his hand. A scribe thought Taylerson and he dismissed him as unimportant.

Taylerson did not recognise the other two men in the room but when they spoke their accents marked them out as foreigners, men from down south. One of them was clean-shaven and thin-faced. Apart from his spotless white cravat, he was dressed plainly in black from his hat to the tip of his polished black boots. He leaned casually against the wall by the window and observed Taylerson dispassionately from beneath his hooded eyelids.

Magistrate Clennell cleared his throat and eyed him coldly from the other side of the table with undisguised contempt. 'I understand that you have something to tell us, Taylerson.' His voice was as hard as granite. 'Something about the robbery at Kirkley Hall?'

'I want some scran –' Taylerson said firmly. His mouth was parched. '– and a drink.'

'You are in no position to make demands!' Clennell snapped. Taylerson shrank down into his chair but his eyes held the gaze of the furious magistrate. The smell of the roasting meat was driving him mad.

‘Oh, get him some food and ale,’ the Londoner by the window said. ‘It might loosen his tongue.’ The gaoler hurried out to the tap room.

Taylerson’s head turned at the sound of the alien accent. He had no idea who the gadgie was, but he recognised authority when he saw it.

Sarah was quiet when they’d finished their lovemaking; she wouldn’t look at William. She turned away and smoothed down her clothes. A wisp of her hair had escaped from her pins and dangled down, jauntily bobbing across her face. She struggled to pin it back up without a mirror so William moved across and tenderly secured it for her.

‘Who is she?’ she asked.

He shook his head and moved away to put out the fire.

She replaced her gloves and straightened her bonnet. Together they walked out to her trap, and he helped her to climb up onto the swaying vehicle.

‘If it doesn’t take the first time,’ he grinned wickedly, ‘we might have to do it again.’

She didn’t smile back.

‘After all, I never got you with child when I lay with you before,’ he persisted.

‘I made sure that you didn’t get me with child, back then,’ she informed him icily. Her haughtiness had returned. His passionate lover had gone. The doctor’s wife was back.

He shrugged and slapped the horse across its haunches. The beast pulled away, taking Sarah Aynsley out of his life – again.

He stood for a moment and watched her drive away. He thought about how she had ruined his life for years with that one decision – and how she had ruined her own. He thought about what could have been. But the memories no longer stirred up much emotion in him. He was glad for this. He shrugged and walked back into the cottage to check that the fire was out in the grate.

The beef, bread and ale came quickly and Taylerson fell on it like a man possessed. A mixture of meat juices and beer slid unchecked down his chin. The others watched dispassionately as the starving man ate like an animal. He devoured every last scrap of the meal.

‘So, the robbery at Kirkley Hall?’ said Clennell at last.

‘Charlton did it,’ Taylerson mumbled. His mouth was still full of food.

'He told you this?'

'Aye,' Taylerson confirmed. 'In so many words.'

'What words? What words did he use? Start from the beginning and tell us what he said.'

'Well, we started talking about Stockton,' began the horse thief in his well-rehearsed speech. 'I'm from Stockton, see? And so is Charlton's missus…'

'We don't need your life history, man,' the Londoner interrupted sharply. 'Get to the point.'

So Taylerson told them. Bit by bit, line by line, he gave his long, rambling statement about the conversation he had had with James Charlton in Newcastle Keep while they were waiting for the gaoler to come and remove Charlton's leg irons. Taylerson spoke slowly while the scribe recorded every word that he said.

'There had been no bills found against him at the hearing, see,' Taylerson explained. 'He thought he had been found 'not guilty' and could never be charged again with the crime. So 'e opened up to me.'

'Double jeopardy,' Clennell murmured, as he read back through Taylerson's statement. 'He was wrong. That was no trial – just a preliminary hearing. Double jeopardy does not apply.' He glanced up quickly from the sheaves of paper and fixed the prisoner with a piercing glare. 'You will be prepared to stand up in court and give this statement?' he demanded.

'Aye, if I'm still alive,' Taylerson replied.

'Still alive?'

'Well, I'm sentenced to hang, aren't I? Sommat needs to be done about that,' Taylerson explained. 'And I'll need decent food and clothing, a comfy bed to sleep in and a fire, of course – if I'm to survive this winter.'

The other men in the room stared at him in disbelief.

'Otherwise, I might be dead by the time of the summer assizes,' Taylerson continued. 'Like them other poor stiffs they's hauled out of the gaol this winter.'

Clennell turned his attention to the two gaolers. 'Is this true? Have prisoners died in Morpeth Gaol this winter?'

The old gaoler shuffled uncomfortably. 'Aye, there's been one or two.'

A grim silence descended on the room as the men absorbed the news.

'I guess that we're lucky you're still alive to give a statement, Taylerson,' the Londoner said in a voice heavy with irony.

'Make sure that from now on this prisoner receives three meals a day, a bed to sleep in and a fire in his grate,' Clennell said sternly to the gaolers. 'Do you understand me?'

'Aye, sir,' the gaolers replied. 'Who'll pay fer it?'

'Charge it to Nathanial Ogle,' Clennell said.

Taylerson felt hope surge inside him. 'And of course, I'll want me liberty in exchange for me testimony,' he announced.

Another stunned silence descended on the room as the men weighed up his demand. But Taylerson heard the muffled laughter from the tap room across the corridor and the slow, rhythmic ticking of the old grandfather clock which stood in the corner.

'Liberty!' the startled magistrate exclaimed. 'Don't be ridiculous there, man! You are a convicted felon due to hang. If you are lucky you might find your sentence commuted to transportation, for the service you are rendering the crown…but liberty? Pah!'

'Well, that might give me a problem.'

'Problem? What sort of problem?'

'You see, the other felons, don't take kindly to a snitch – and they've made it plain that they've already got it in for me, coming here today, like…'

'Is this true?' Clennell barked. 'Have there been threats?'

'Aye, there's been one or two.' mumbled the gaoler.

'You see, your worship…if I give evidence then I'm a marked man. It isn't worth opening my gob unless I'm promised me liberty – them bastards inside Morpeth Gaol will have me by the throat as soon as look at me. It might not be this week, or next….but I've no doubt the bastards will do for me long afore I get transported to them there colonies.'

'Has there ever been an instance of prisoners murdering each other in Morpeth Gaol?' Lavender asked the gaolers.

The old man cleared his throat nervously.

'Let me guess,' interrupted the Londoner. 'There's been one or two?'

The gaoler nodded.

'How?' snapped Clennell.

'They tend to wait till the marked man is asleep. Then they slide a noose – perhaps a belt or a bit of stiff wire – through the bars of the cage over his head and pull.' The gaoler demonstrated the strangulation to illustrate his words. 'We don't find them till the next day.'

'I've heard enough,' Clennell snapped. 'Take this man back to the gaol – and keep him alive – while we decide what to do.'

The gaolers sprang into action. They dragged Taylerson to his feet and pushed him out of the door.

'Don't forget me liberty!' he yelled over his shoulder as he was hauled away.

Detective Stephen Lavender opened one of the casement windows to let out some of the sickening stench which Taylerson and his gaolers had brought with them. He watched them drag the wretched creature back across the cobbled marketplace towards the gaol. The whole episode left him feeling nauseous. He had serious misgivings about using informants; it was the last resort when all other methods of crime detection had failed. Behind him, Constable Woods shuffled uncomfortably on his hard-back chair.

Clennell sent the clerk out on some errand and the three remaining men were quiet for a minute while they digested the information which Taylerson had given them.

Eventually, Lavender sighed and slumped down into a chair. 'Do we believe him?' he asked.

'It doesn't matter if we believe him or not,' Clennell growled. 'It is for the jury to decide if he is telling the truth.'

'Taylerson is a condemned felon. He'll say anything to avoid the gallows,' Woods commented.

'I know that,' the magistrate snapped. 'But the thief, James Charlton, is still at large in the parish – and causing trouble. Taylerson's statement could bring him in again.'

Lavender just shook his head: 'There was not enough evidence to send him to a full trial last summer.'

'Yes. Nigh on sixty witnesses you found to speak against him,' Clennell sneered. 'And it still was not enough to send him to trial by jury. If we do not use Taylerson we need more evidence.'

'There is no more evidence to be found,' Woods said. 'Our investigation of Charlton was most thorough.'

The magistrate eyed him coldly. The constable was unabashed and stared straight back. Clennell turned to the detective. 'Lavender, do you think James Charlton robbed Kirkley Hall, or don't you?'

'I would have liked more time to have pursued other lines of enquiry. There were the Clifton brothers for example. One of them died of smallpox shortly after the robbery but the other one eluded arrest…'

'And is now long gone,' Clennell interrupted. 'Do you think that Charlton did it or not?'

'Yes,' Lavender said finally. 'I was convinced he had committed the crime.'
'Then that settles it. We'll bring him back in again and send him to trial by jury with Taylerson's statement.'
'It will still be one man's word against that of another,' Woods protested. 'The jury may still not convict him.'
'I guarantee you that a jury of his peers in Newcastle will convict him,' Clennell informed him coldly.
Woods fell silent. Lavender sighed. Clennell was right. The jury would be made up of the local landed gentry and prosperous middle classes. Not one of them would be Charlton's 'peer'. They would move as one to denounce him and uphold the rights and privileges of the wealthy. James Charlton's fate was sealed; it was only a matter of time before he was sentenced to hang for the robbery at Kirkley Hall.

The old lawyer William had hired in Corbridge to draw up the agreement between him and Archie worked on the deed as slowly as he walked on his gout-ridden legs. The weeks of waiting dragged on past Christmas and into the New Year. Then another vicious snowstorm raged for three days and North Carter Moor was snowed in again. William was desperate to move to Corbridge but nature and a dozy lawyer had decreed that he had to wait until the end of January to leave. Finally, he was able to round up the small herd of cattle which he had bred from the stock left to him by his father and set off with his dogs on the long trek to Corbridge. John had agreed to bring the rest of his possessions over later that week in the cart. William was excited at the prospect of showing off his new farm to his older brother.
The parting from his mother was emotional. 'Now come on, Ma,' he said as she sobbed in his arms. 'I'm only moving to Corbridge – you'll still see plenty of me. It's not as if I'm being transported to New South Wales.'
'Don't joke about that,' chided Ann as she wiped her streaming face in her apron.
As North Carter Moor Farm faded into the distance behind him, William breathed a huge sigh of relief. He knew he was doing the right thing.
His only regret was that he had not seen Sarah again since their coupling at Bates' Farm. He wanted to reassure himself that she would be alright. He had no regrets about what he had done but in the cold light of day he had started to worry about her. Her plan to

conceive a child with him had been madness. If her husband was impotent, how would she explain her pregnancy? The man sounded like an indifferent husband but accepting another man's bairn as your own was not something any man would do lightly. He was a doctor, for Christ's sake, he would soon be able to work out that any child she conceived was not his. However, one thing William knew from bitter experience was that Sarah was a survivor – and an ambitious one at that. If she had got what she wanted then somehow, knowing Sarah, she would make it work.

He sighed and shrugged off all thoughts of Sarah Robson. A whole new life lay ahead of him and he refused to let those in the past drag him back. He remembered Archie's description of his family as an octopus with flailing tentacles reaching out to drag him down into the murky depths; Sarah was just another tentacle of the beast.

Life at Thorn Tree Farm was every bit as hard as William had expected it to be. He arrived at the start of the lambing season and for the next six weeks worked around the clock with Archie and Old George to bring the new flock into the world.

When the time came for the first batch of ewes to lamb, the men let them out into a field to give them more room. The heavy animals slithered across the icy ground, enjoying the extra space after months of being cramped in the barn. The weak winter sunlight shone down on their dirty bloated bodies as they sought out the frozen grass beneath the lingering snow. The field soon became trampled and stained red as one steaming bundle of life after another slithered onto the ground. With their coat pockets bulging with jars of lubricant and heavy metal tongs, the men moved swiftly from one struggling creature to another; checking for those who needed assistance and coaxing stubborn ewes to nurse. Whenever there was a lull in the birthing, the men would slither around the ice and shovel up the slippery, bloodied afterbirth before it could attract foxes. This continued day after day. The men took it in turns to drag their exhausted bodies inside for a couple of hours' sleep and a bite to eat. By nightfall they had the whole flock back inside the barn; the new lambs snuggled in fresh straw next to their mothers' teats. Yet even then the birthing would continue. Always someone had to watch the sheep. Often they would have to wake each other in the night to get assistance. Day and night became blurred to William as the barns started to fill to bursting point with their enlarged flock and he became more and more exhausted.

No sooner had the lambing finished, than they started on the tilling and ploughing. They cleared the overgrown acres on the newly purchased two hundred acres; it was back-breaking work. Yet William had never enjoyed anything as much in his life. The sense of achievement he felt as he worked his own fields was overwhelming.

Weather permitting, he visited the Corbridge taverns with Archie and the two men attended church every Sunday. They got into the habit of spending the remainder of the Sabbath with the Milburn family at their farm. After a good home-cooked meal, Archie would continue his shy courtship of Jenny Milburn, while William would read the latest edition of the *Newcastle Courant* and chat to Joshua Milburn. He was grateful for the chance to rest his aching body in a comfortable armchair and often would fall asleep in front of the Milburns' crackling parlour fire.

Thanks to the constant stream of traffic between Corbridge and Ponteland, William received regular letters from his mother who kept him informed of the news. He waited until Archie and George had gone to bed, then he would sit with a glass of brandy and read her letters in private by the light of a couple of guttering candles. He smiled at the petty squabbles and jealousies she recounted and was glad of the fact that he was no longer required to take sides.

Other news was more substantial. His younger brother, Henry, was now the proud father of a baby girl. The miller's son had asked for the hand in marriage of John's eldest daughter, Minnie – and Cilla was expecting another bairn later in the year.

This last piece of news was no surprise. Both Cilla and Jamie had often talked sadly of the bairn they had lost on the day of Jamie's arrest. Despite their poverty, they had been determined to have another child. According to his dour eldest brother, Jamie and Cilla had been at it like rabbits when Jamie had been first released from gaol. Even the thick walls of North Carter Moor had not protected John and his family from the embarrassment of their noisy lovemaking. He sighed but then cheered up when he realised that he hadn't thought about Cilla for over a week – until he had got this letter.

However, it was the postscript to a letter he received in March which caused him the most concern:

'You need to know also, Will, that the surgeon and Sarah Robson are also expecting a bairn later in the year and that there are wicked rumours in the parish that the child is yours. Our John is very angry at the slander. I thank Heaven that you have moved on

with your life and pray to God that you continue to find success and contentment over in Corbridge...'

He stared into the dying embers of the fire and tried to work out how he felt about this news. He had half expected to hear that Sarah was with child, but the fact that their secret was out worried him. He struggled to understand how this had happened but then shrugged sadly; even the trees and hedgerows had eyes and ears in Ponteland.

There was no doubt that rumours like this would make Sarah's life harder. She would find it more difficult to be accepted by the class she had married into and although her husband may have turned a blind eye to the mysterious conception of the child, he may not stand by her in the face of such pernicious gossip. For a moment, he tried to imagine what would happen if the doctor threw her out. One thing was for sure, Archie's face would be a picture if his destitute and pregnant lover turned up at the door of Thorn Tree Farm.

Sighing, he folded the letter and secreted it in the pocket of his breeches. He began to dampen down the fire. There was nothing he could do except carry on as normal. Any contact he had with Sarah to try to find out what was happening in her life would probably be rebuffed by Sarah herself and would only fan the flames of the gossip.

As he climbed the stairs to bed that night, he realised something which made him smile. The thought that he had planted a little cuckoo in the old surgeon's nest gave him a small glow of satisfaction. The man had stolen his woman away from him, broken his heart and dented his pride. Revenge was sweet.

What goes around comes around, he thought to himself as he fell asleep.

Meanwhile, in Morpeth Gaol, William Taylerson was living a life of comparative luxury. His stay of execution was still in force. He received regular meals and had been given his own cell on the second floor, well away from the other murderous prisoners. This cell was usually reserved for the richest and most successful criminals who could afford to pay for their own bed, a fire and an upholstered chair to sit in. But Clennell's insistence that Taylerson was well-treated had thrown the Morpeth gaolers into a panic. They did not have anywhere else in the overcrowded gaol to keep him separate from the others apart from this one upstairs cell. So the smug forger, who was enjoying the comforts of this private cell – and who had paid out a lot of money for the privilege of using it –

was forcibly ejected down the stone stairs into the freezing cages below.

As Taylerson's body recovered from months of deprivation and starvation in the warmth of his new cell, his shattered wits also began to reform and sharpen.

He had been stunned to find out it had been that London detective who had interviewed him along with Clennell. It was the proof he needed to confirm what he had always suspected – that catching the Kirkley Hall robber was important to the upper classes. With nothing else to do except sit and think all day, Taylerson continued to work on his story and stuck rigidly to his declaration that he would only give evidence against Charlton in exchange for his liberty.

CHAPTER SEVENTEEN

Cilla was concerned about her son, Jack.

He was a big lad – like all the Charlton males – and had a healthy appetite. He went off to his school in Ponteland every day clutching as much scran as she could spare. On the days when he did not attend school, he would disappear off into the woods with half the contents of her small pantry. He had become secretive and a bit moody. Despite his size, she knew that he was too placid to stick up for himself. She had learnt that the local lads thought it was a great game to pile on top of Jack and try to get him onto the floor. He often came home filthy and bruised from this silly game with his clothes ripped. Whenever she questioned him about it the lad clammed up or got stroppy.

Cilla was struggling to cope with her pregnancy and the demands of the other young children. She had been very sick for months now and was exhausted beyond belief.

'You want me to do what?' Jamie asked. He was late home from work and they were eating alone in the kitchen. The piece of rye bread he was using to mop up his gravy was suspended mid-air as he paused in surprise at her request.

'I want you to follow him tomorrow when he disappears into the woods.'

'For God's sake hinny, don't you think I've got enough to do with my time?'

'Jamie, I'm sure he is being cruelly treated. I think the other boys take food from him – and money.'

'What money? Are we missing any money?'

'I don't know – I'm not sure,' she said frowning. She slowly took down the earthenware pot from the dresser and peered inside it. Any movement these days seemed to leave her short of breath.

'He's always been one for sneaking off on his own with a book into the woods,' Jamie reminded her.

'He never takes a book no more,' she informed him, tearfully. 'Look Jamie, I've got a fancy that something is wrong. It might just be my condition – but would you humour me, please and follow him tomorrow and find out what happens?'

He kissed the top of her head.

'If it'll set your mind at rest, hinny, I'll do it.'

So it was that a mildly amused Jamie followed his young son into the woods the next day. He kept a discreet distance from the lad and saw no sign of the neighbourhood children.

He had no worries about Jack. As far as he was concerned, Jack was just a growing lad who was eating his mother out of house and home. However, he was a bit concerned about Cilla whom he knew was struggling to cope with this latest pregnancy. She had become fanciful of late. It seemed a small price to pay to put her mind at rest about her firstborn.

Jack veered off the main path and headed to a remote spot near to the river bank. The agile lad nipped quickly through the undergrowth; Jamie had trouble keeping up with him. By the time he had pushed his way through the briars, ferns and hazel to the very edge of the wood Jack was a good thirty yards ahead of him.

The lad broke cover and appeared to be laying down a good part of his food parcel beside a stunted thorn tree at the bend in the river. Jack moved back about ten feet away from the food and sat on a moss-covered boulder as if he was waiting for something. Jamie moved back into the shadows of a large sycamore tree and waited.

Otters, he thought and smiled. The lad's found a holt and has been feeding them. I hope he's careful – them little buggers have sharp teeth.

Suddenly, the sky darkened above him and the smile was wiped off Jamie's face. The eagle momentarily blocked out the sunlight as it swooped down towards his son. The hairs stood up on the back of Jamie's neck at the sound of the deep, rhythmic beat of its huge wings. The wily raptor landed on the old thorn tree next to Jack and eyed the boy suspiciously. The tree swayed precariously beneath its weight.

Jamie swore under his breath and fought back his urge to yell out a warning. This was no curious otter but a wild beast over half his son's height with vicious claws and a razor-sharp beak. One swipe of its wings alone could break the lad's arm. Yet Jack seemed completely at ease and just sat there, relaxed and smiling.

Now Jack encouraged the eagle to drop onto the ground – where it would be most vulnerable for capture – to take the food. It worked. A moment later, oblivious of danger, the bird hopped down onto the bank and began to devour the bread and meat.

Jamie's fear now turned to amazement. Like everyone else, he had often seen the bird soaring across the sky in search of food but he had never seen the creature this close before. He doubted anyone had.

Half the parish had tried to trap it for the twenty pound reward: half revered it like a sign from God. It was the 'lucky bird' – the bringer of happiness and prosperity. Young mothers held up their new-born children for it to bless as it circled on the thermals above them. Discarded eagle feathers were gleefully collected by the local children and sold for tuppence each. They were displayed above kitchen fireplaces to ward off evil and bring luck to the home. Jamie had fantasised many times himself about trapping the bird; the reward money would buy him two new cows.

Now he marvelled at the bond which the golden-brown bird shared with his son.

Jack threw the raptor another few morsels of food, in the same way he would toss grain to the chickens back home, and then he began to chatter to the great creature. His voice drifted down to Jamie on the breeze but he could not hear the words.

The eagle ate the food but was in no hurry to depart; it preened its glossy feathers with its hooked yellow beak. It remained on the ground next to the chattering child for what seemed like an age. Jamie had a strange fancy that the raptor was enjoying his son's company as much as the lad clearly enjoyed being with the bird.

Could it be lonely? he wondered. *So far away from its home and the rest of its kind?*

He remembered being a child and escaping from the overcrowded farmhouse to go to the barn to talk to a toothless old sheepdog. That dog had been his friend when his brothers had turned against him. His heart had been broken when his da killed the crippled animal became it was too old to work any more. Now his lad had found his own confidante.

A searing cramp shot down Jamie's left leg from the unnatural half-crouching position he had assumed in the shadows. He gritted his teeth and backed away into the muffled darkness of the wood with the silence and stealth of an experienced poacher.

As he limped home, he concocted a story to put Cilla's mind at rest.

I'll keep your secret, son, he promised silently.

At Easter, William decided to remain at Thorn Tree Farm while Archie went to visit his only relative, an aged aunt in Newcastle. Old George had some woman stashed away at nearby Bavington and also disappeared for a few days.

As William went down to pay the rent money at the estate office, he couldn't help but remember that it had been Easter Monday the previous year when Kirkley Hall had been robbed and all their troubles had begun. The burglary was fading into history now; life had moved on and folks did not talk about it any more, except occasionally as the mysterious robbery at Kirkley.

Overall, when William reflected on the events of the past twelve months, he felt pleased with the way life had turned out. Even the pain of his unspoken feelings for Cilla had served its purpose; it had pushed him away from his humdrum life at Kirkley and forced him into independence.

The weather was balmy and warm – the complete opposite of the fog-drenched Easter of the previous year. He removed his coat as he walked back from Corbridge. As he neared the farm, he climbed onto a stone wall around one of his fields and watched his fat lambs gambol and play. His faithful dogs dropped obediently to the ground by his feet, their tongues lolled out of their open mouths. His savings were depleted after paying for the lease and the rent on his share of the farm but soon it would be time to reap the benefit of all his hard work. Lambs would be sold at market and the harvest gathered and sold. He tried to work out how long it would be before he started to show a profit. Not this year, but next year, perhaps?

Believing he was alone, he took his shirt off and let the warm sun lick his skin with its gentle tongue. He had lost a bit of fat with the poorer diet and harder work up at Thorn Tree but he suspected that he had gained a few more muscles. He was in good shape and he knew it.

What a pity there are no lasses up here to appreciate it, he thought.

Then all of a sudden there was.

Jenny Milburn appeared at his side, a wicker basket slung over her arm and a beaming smile spread across her pretty face. 'What a nice view,' she laughed.

Startled and embarrassed, William leapt down from the wall and landed on the tail of one of his dogs. The animal yelped in pain and set off a stampede of fat lambs which raced in thundering circles around the field. The other dog now leapt to his feet, barked furiously and made ready to give chase.

'Down!' William roared as he struggled to get his arms back into his shirt. 'Damn it, you bloody mutts! Get down, will you!'

Jenny Milburn threw back her pretty head and laughed and laughed. The sunlight danced and sparkled in her hair.

William blushed. As the noise and the panic of the comical animals subsided, he glanced up from fumbling with his buttons to see Jenny's face radiant with laughter. 'I'm sorry,' he said. 'I thought I was alone – I never intended to embarrass you.'

'You didn't,' she said, simply. 'Don't forget, Mr. Charlton, I have grown up with a houseful of brothers.'

'Aye, so did I, Miss Milburn,' he said. 'But that doesn't mean I like to see them with their shirts off.'

'When I said 'nice view', I was referring to this,' she lied merrily and pointed down the hillside at the valley below. The countryside was bursting with promise and sprouting verdant new life. Below them the patchwork fields fell down the slopes of the hills towards the tree-lined streams and brooks, which in turn snaked their way towards the Tyne. Above the trees, huge flocks of rooks and crows circled and cawed in a frenzy of nest-building and mating.

He started to relax. 'Of course you were, hinny,' he grinned. 'Same as I'm thinking at the moment: what a nice view.'

She flushed with delight but never took her eyes away from the landscape which tumbled down below them. 'It is rugged and natural but throbbing with passion beneath the surface,' she mused.

Aren't we all? he thought.

He followed the direction of her finger and pretended to take an interest in the view. Down at the bottom of the hill, the church tower rose above the tiled roofs of the old Roman town. The church bells rang in celebration of the resurrection of Christ. Somewhere in the distance a bull bellowed.

'Listening to that bull, it sounds to me that much of the passion has already surfaced,' he observed wryly. 'It seems as though everything on God's earth is straining to get closer to its mate.' He pulled himself back up on the wall. They were only inches apart; her right shoulder nearly rubbed up against his leg. He could smell the sweetness of the soap she used to wash.

Her eyes never left the scene below. 'On days like this, when there is a bit of sun in the sky, it is the best view in the world.'

'I am impressed, Miss Milburn,' he grinned. 'You have taught me to see this same old dale with a fresh set of eyes. From now on every time I glance down this hillside it will seem brand new to me, almost virginal.'

She glanced across to him unsure. Her eyes fell away from his face in confusion. Their conversation had taken an unexpected turn. 'You mock me,' she chided gently.

'A little,' he confessed. 'But kindly. You see, if you have never been beyond Corbridge, how will you know what to compare it with? Your enthusiasm for what you see here could be misplaced. It may not be all that good.'

'True,' she replied. 'But I know what I like.' She moved her head and shifted slightly away from him. 'I have heard about other places, of course – my brothers have described in detail the amazing sights they have seen in the New World but always they say the same thing about the Tyne valley: that there is no more beautiful place on earth. It really is God's Own Country.'

While she talked he studied her features. She was fine-boned and delicate in a way that was rare in farming stock. Her light blonde hair was swept back from her face and pinned up on the back of her head. It looked like finely-woven silk and gleamed silver-white in the sunlight. Her eyes were the same vivid blue as his.

'It sounds like you'd be sorry to leave it,' he observed.

'Leave it? I don't think I'll leave it.'

'Oh, that's a shame,' he said, lightly. 'I thought my good friend, Archie, wanted to whisk you away to the Americas with him. He plans for the two of you to join your brothers and make a fortune in the New World. I'm sure he mentioned it the first day I came to your home last year.'

'Archie's sweet,' she said, smiling.

'Archie's sweet on you,' he corrected her.

'I'll never leave my ma,' she said suddenly. 'I'll marry a local man.' She changed the subject so quickly, he wondered if he had heard that first comment. 'I have brought you a present. Ma knew you were here on your own this Easter. Knowing how you men never feed yourselves properly, she has baked you a pie.' She pulled back the cover of her basket. The delicious smell of a fresh-baked and succulent meat and potato pie wafted up to his nostrils.

'That was most kind of her,' he said.

'Here, have some,' she insisted. She broke off a piece and handed it to him. For a brief moment, their hands touched. Her skin was deliciously soft and warm. And so was the pie. His stomach rumbled with anticipation as he raised it to his mouth. His mother's cooking was the main thing which he missed up here at Thorn Tree.

'That's good,' he mumbled, in between mouthfuls. 'I'll swear your mother learned how to cook at the same kitchen range as my Ma.'

She pulled herself up onto the wall beside him and smiled at him as he ate. 'So, Mr Charlton, what amazing places in the world have you seen, on your many travels?' she asked.

'I've lived in Newcastle for a few years,' he told her. 'I've visited Gateshead and Sunderland – all of them dreadful and over-crowded.'

She laughed. 'So what do you think of our little neck of the woods?' she pushed. 'Is it not the most beautiful place in the world?'

'Absolutely,' he conceded.

'Even prettier than Ponteland?'

'Yes,' he said, and without thinking he added: 'And the women are far prettier, as well.'

She blushed at the compliment. 'So is that why you have come here, to Corbridge, Mr Charlton?' she asked, shyly. 'To look for a pretty wife?'

He could have kicked himself for his thoughtlessness. The promise he had made Archie seared through his brain and made him flush with guilt. *What was he doing flirting with the lass?*

'No, Miss Milburn,' he said sharply, as he leapt off the wall. 'Finding a wife is the last thing on my mind.'

And with that, he turned his back on her and strode off towards his farm.

Behind him, he heard her gasp at her rudeness.

In August, Jamie Charlton served three writs at the assizes against Michael Aynsley and his two sons for their slander against his good name the previous summer. Despite all the odds, Michael Aynsley was still alive. His stroke had left him a gibbering and drooling idiot who spent his days drifting in and out of consciousness and his nights raging incoherently in his sleep. But still he clung on to his life.

Aynsley did not attend the court hearing; and neither did either of his two sons. The magistrates duly awarded the damages of five pounds in all three cases to James Charlton.

Then, as Jamie walked out of the courtroom, they had him arrested and charged him – again – with the robbery of Kirkley Hall.

Wiser now, Jamie did not put up a fight. He simply passed on a message for Cilla to a startled onlooker whom he knew from Ponteland. Then he walked calmly with the gaolers to Newcastle Keep.

He was pushed into a cell with an elderly man who had been imprisoned for debt. The man's sobbing wife left just as Jamie arrived. She had brought him a plate of meagre food and a warm blanket to protect his arthritic joints against the creeping damp of the prison. Within seconds of her departure and that of the gaoler, Jamie had the plate of food off the old man – and his blanket.

Realising that he was no match for the strong labourer, the old man wailed and complained bitterly.

'Get used to it,' Jamie callously advised him, as he gulped down the old man's food.

'The ones that come in new, are fit and well fed…'

Wednesday 29th August, 1810

Detective Stephen Lavender returned to Newcastle for the trial of James Charlton. The chairman of the jury was Earl Percy, the eldest son of the Duke of Northumberland. The rest of the jury was made up of landed and titled men as he had predicted.

Building work was being carried out on the old court house in Newcastle so the trial was held at an alternative venue, in St. Nicholas' Church. The interior of the church was sombre and dark. Several images of Christ nailed to the cross looked down on Charlton as he sat impassively in the dock. The rows of pews which had been given over to the public were packed. This trial had attracted great interest in Newcastle and the surrounding area.

Detective Lavender and Constable Woods pushed their way through the heaving throng to a couple of cramped seats. Lavender scanned those assembled for Charlton's family and his flame-haired wife. The whispering and pointing crowd soon helped him to identify Charlton's mother and elder brother who sat pale-faced and strained amongst the masses who had packed into pews to watch the trial. There was no sign of Charlton's wife, Lavender realised with a stab of disappointment. Charlton's white-haired, elderly mother looked like she was struggling to hold back a tide of emotions and fidgeted nervously with her shawl. Her eldest son stared sourly ahead of him.

'It is just as well the venue of the assizes had been changed for this trial,' Woods observed. 'The old courthouse would have been too small for this crowd.'

The pew in front of them was crammed with journalists from the regional newspapers who had come well-armed with quills, notebooks, sheaves of paper and bottles of ink which balanced precariously on the bench beside them. Several young men who had arrived late and who were obviously apprenticed in the legal profession could find no seats amongst the shuffling crowds. They leaned casually against the walls of the church, affecting disdain and taking frequent pinches of snuff.

The prosecution made their case. Michael Aynsley was too unwell to attend, but the trial began with his statement and that of his son Joseph. Then one by one, the witnesses of the previous summer were brought in to give their evidence of Charlton's apparent wealth in the weeks after the robbery.

Finally, William Taylerson was brought to the witness stand and gave his damning account of the conversation he had held with James Charlton in Newcastle Keep. The last eight months had been good to Taylerson, who was now back to full health and wore a new set of clothes. This was his moment of glory and he knew it. Unaffected by the sullen hostility of the courtroom, he walked arrogantly to the witness stand and spoke his well-rehearsed speech, clearly and slowly:

'I, William Taylerson of Morpeth, do hereby swear on oath that last assizes I was a prisoner at Morpeth Gaol and in the Town Keep, charged with horse stealing. Here I saw the prisoner James Charlton and had a conversation with him. Charlton said that he was very happy not to have gone before his lordship in a trial by jury because he feared that his own conscience might have condemned him.'

'I then asked him why his conscience would have condemned him so long as he was clear. He made reply that there were more than sixty witnesses against him. I said to him, that I suppose no person saw you break into this house? He answered: 'No, there was not.'' There were audible gasps of shock from the public.

Unconcerned, Taylerson continued. 'I further said to him: 'Are you guilty of this crime?' He made answer: 'If I'd have known as much as I know now, I would not have returned a half-penny of the money.''

The public section of the court erupted with shouts of 'No!' and 'It can't be!'

The presiding judge, Baron Robert Graham, glared at the crowd over the top of his glasses, and the gallery quickly subsided into silence. This was no parochial magistrates hearing; no insubordination or contempt would be tolerated in the assizes.

Following a nod from the judge, Taylerson continued: 'I then asked him how he got into the house. And he answered that he tried many doors and windows, but they had a ladder…'

'They?' the judge queried.

'Aye, he said his next door neighbour and his wife, Priscilla, were with him.'

A murmur of shock now ran round the public gallery. John Charlton and Ann turned pale and for the first time the detective saw a flicker of emotion pass across the face of the accused.

Lavender frowned. This was a new development – and not one that he believed.

Blithely unaware of the reaction he was evoking, Taylerson continued. 'He said they entered the house by a broken pane in the window. His wife went in and let Charlton in. I then said: 'How did you see?' And he replied: 'By a dark pocket lantern.' So I then said to him that he must have known where the money was? And he said: 'I knew the house very well – as well as them who were born and bred in it.' And he told me that he had lived and worked there for over four years and he well knew where they kept the money.'

Taylerson seemed to dry up at this point and struggled to remember what he planned to say next. His lawyer prompted him: 'But did he confess to actually taking the money?'

'Aye,' Taylerson confirmed loudly. 'But he said tha he had great difficulty finding the money at first; there were many books and papers to turn over before he got to it at the bottom of the chest.'

'Charlton further said that he kept as much as bought him out of his troubles with his creditors. Then on the Saturday morning after the robbery, he got up between five and six o'clock and he came to Mr. Ogle's and he flung some of the money over the wall upon the garden walk.'

'That same day he paid a woman in Newcastle for some leather, and bought some cloth for sheets as much as came upwards of three pounds. He also bought some stockings and a silk handkerchief and the money he paid that day in the town was between fifteen and sixteen pounds.'

The public gallery shuffled uncomfortably on the hard church pews, stifled their indignation and waited for the cross-examination.

Mr. Blake went straight to the point: 'Let me get this correct, Mr. Taylerson. When you met my client, James Charlton, you were in Morpeth Gaol charged with horse stealing, is that right?'

'Aye, sir,' said Taylerson. He grinned smugly, revealing his blackened teeth.

'And you were sentenced to hang for the crime were you not? On account as it was the third time you had been called up in front of the bar for stealing horses; and the judge despaired of you ever learning the error of your ways?'

'Aye, I was,' the witness confirmed brazenly.

'Was? Taylerson,' queried Mr. Blake slowly. He placed as much emphasis on the word as he could. 'Was? Are you not facing the death penalty any more?'

A new and more intense silence now fell upon the people in that courtroom.

'Naw, I'm not,' said Taylerson, hardly able to conceal his jubilation. 'I've been reprieved.'

'When was your execution reprieved?'

'Last week.'

'Last week!' echoed the lawyer. 'Have you agreed to give evidence against James Charlton in exchange for your own life?'

'Aye,' the horse thief went on ignorantly. A growl of disgust rippled round the public gallery. '– I mean Nay! Nay! What I says is true! Charlton said he were the thief!'

'You're lying, man!' snapped Mr. Blake. His voice rose in disgust and anger. 'You've sold your soul to the devil and condemned an innocent man to death! You've exchanged your hanging for that of James Charlton's!'

When he was called upon for his defence, Jamie Charlton claimed he was innocent and then left himself in the hands of his counsel.

Several witnesses, including Mistress Dorothy Hodgeson, the servant at Kirkley Hall, were called forward for the defence who commented on the curious behaviour of Michael Aynsley at the time of the robbery and reignited the suspicion that the wrong man was in the dock. The defence suggested that Michael Aynsley had stolen the money while Mr Ogle was absent, knowing James Charlton had borrowed money so that he would get the blame.

Thomas Gillespy, the farmer from Haindykes who had employed Charlton as a barns man at the time of the robbery gave evidence that Charlton was always well-behaved, earned a great deal of money and had gone to work as normal the day after the robbery. The meat trader who had bought Charlton's calves confirmed the sale and the amount he had paid him.

Next, William Charlton took the stand.

Lavender observed him closely. This was the man who had wrecked the case he had so painstakingly prepared the year before with his claim that he had loaned money to his brother. The man standing in the dock was well-built and smartly dressed in a dark blue coat, boots and breeches. The strong jawline which jutted out from the top of his white cravat was clean shaven with just a hint of stubble. His features were wide set and above his broad forehead his black hair was pulled back and tied behind his head. His ice-blue eyes stared confidently at the jury as he gave his testimony.

He had clearly been carefully tutored by the defence lawyer since the previous hearing when his challenging attitude had landed him in gaol for contempt. Now his manner was calm and polite. He claimed that in the weeks leading up to Easter he loaned his brother twenty pounds. The prosecution was quick to point out that William had previously told several different stories, both about the days the money was lent and the amount the previous summer. William calmly explained the contradictions by saying:

'I was never before a magistrate before, and Mr. Aynsley threatened me so much at the last assizes, that I did not know what I was saying or doing and might have then given a different account and swear to it. I was so frightened that I clean forgot about the first ten pounds that I'd loaned my brother.'

Lavender doubted very much that such a man would be frightened – even by the blustering Michael Aynsley – but the prosecution lawyer accepted William's explanation without comment. William's voice was deep and slightly less accented than those of the other witnesses. His diction and grammar left Lavender in no doubt that he was intelligent and well-educated.

Meanwhile, a few pews away, John Charlton shook his head and his lips moved silently.

'He's saying a prayer for his brother's soul,' Woods whispered.

The young pickpocket, William Oliver, also formerly of Morpeth Gaol, was brought to the witness stand. He told the court how his old cellmate, Taylerson, had said that Charlton had got discharged without a 'bill' being found but that he, Taylerson, would gain his own liberty by fetching him in again.

'When I had said: 'Would you, for the value of your own liberty, hang another man?' Taylerson made reply: 'Aye, liberty is sweet'.'

The whole trial lasted fourteen hours; it finished at one o'clock in the morning. Many of the public had long since left by the time the jury retired to discuss the verdict, but the exhausted and loyal few who had seen it through to the end were not kept waiting long.

It took only five minutes for the esteemed jury to bring back the inevitable verdict:

'Guilty.'

Jamie stared at the jury. His mouth gaped open, as if he could not comprehend what had been said. William Charlton groaned and buried his head in his hands. Ann Charlton was wracked with sobs and collapsed into the arms of her ashen-faced elder son.

Before he passed sentence, his lordship Baron Robert Graham remarked that a variety of circumstances favourable to the prisoner had transpired and that he felt: 'there was still a mystery about the whole case that he could neither unravel nor understand.'

He suggested an appeal for clemency would be suitable in this case.

Then, against a background of muted sobs and the horrified wails from the public, he brought out the black cap. He told the prisoner to stand and passed the death sentence in the usual way:

'James Charlton of Milburn, you have been found guilty of stealing over one thousand one hundred and fifty seven pounds from the estate office of Kirkley Hall on 3rd April in the year of our lord 1809. It is now my duty to pass sentence.'

'James Charlton you are sentenced to be taken hence to the prison in which you were last confined and from there to a place of execution where you will be hanged by the neck until dead. Thereafter your body buried within the precincts of the prison. May the Lord have mercy upon your soul.'

CHAPTER EIGHTEEN

After the judge and the jury had filed out, Ann Charlton's sobs of disbelief and horror grew louder. Then the old woman started to yell.

'They'll not hang my son!' she screamed. 'They'll not kill my Jamie!'

She tore herself away from John's restraining arms and tried to reach Jamie in the dock. William rushed over to help John hold her back, while the gaolers hurriedly pushed their dazed prisoner towards a door at the back of the church.

As he disappeared out of sight, Jamie cast a last desperate glance over his shoulder. Ann let out the dreadful primeval wail of an animal in agony. It stabbed at the heart of everyone in the room. They averted their eyes, tried to block off their ears and scurried towards the exit and the blackness outside.

'Does this seem right to you?' she yelled hoarsely at the backs of the disappearing public. 'Is this justice? Should my son hang because of the testimony of a condemned felon who has been given his liberty?'

Her strangled and broken words echoed around the rapidly emptying church and went unanswered. Her despair subsided into wracking sobs as she collapsed into William's arms.

'Hush, Ma,' soothed William, his own voice cracked with emotion. 'We need to go home now.'

The journey back to Ponteland seemed interminable. They sat shocked – and for the most part silent – as the wagon rolled along the quiet moonlit lanes towards Milburn. Each one of them was gripped with the unspeakable horror which had overtaken their Jamie. Ann had now cried herself dry; she sat grim-faced in between the two men. In the light of the swaying lantern, she looked every one of her sixty-four years.

This could kill her, thought William who tried unsuccessfully to cope with the leaden lump that had settled in his stomach. Every time he thought about Jamie's neck snapping on the end of the hangman's noose, he was swamped by waves of nausea. At one point he leapt down from the wagon and vomited onto the verge of the lane. John and Ann said nothing. They just pulled over and waited for him before resuming the journey in silence.

Despite the lateness of the hour, Ann insisted that she was taken straight to Milburn to break the news to Cilla; she did not want her to hear it from anyone else. She was also concerned that the terrible news might shock Cilla into labour and planned to stay overnight with her. A candle-end spluttered on the windowsill of the cottage as the wagon quietly drew up outside. The men waited just long enough to watch Ann walk falteringly up the short path towards the door before they rumbled past on their way back to North Carter Moor. To William, it seemed as if his mother's shoulders were stooped beneath the weight of the dreadful burden of news she carried.

The exhausted brothers were silent as they completed the short journey back to the farm; both of them had been up since milking. It wasn't until the horse was stabled and they were alone in the farmhouse kitchen, picking at the cold platter left out for them by Susan, that John Charlton finally broke the silence:

'So our Jamie is guilty after all.'

'Of course he is not,' William replied sharply. 'Taylerson has been primed by the authorities. He would have said anything to save his own damned skin.'

'Taylerson seemed very clear in the account that he gave. He and Jamie had obviously spent a long time talking together. The man knew all about us – and Cilla's family from Stockton. We have to accept the jury's decision that our Jamie robbed Kirkley Hall.'

'Why? The only difference between now and the hearing last year is the evidence which the bastard Taylerson gave. Jamie was convicted on the word of a man who has sold his soul to the Devil and bartered his own freedom in exchange for his testimony.'

John had moved over to the fireplace to prod at the dying embers of the fire. Now he hurled the poker angrily onto the grate. The metallic clanging reverberated around the sleeping farm like the slam of Morpeth Gaol doors.

'Yes!' he yelled. 'And the only reason our Jamie got away with it last year is because you sold your soul to the Devil, perjured yourself in the eyes of God and falsely claimed that you had loaned him twenty pounds!'

In the silence which followed, William heard a muffled whimper from a child upstairs and the dogs start to bark in the barn.

'Accept it, William – he did it; Jamie robbed Kirkley Hall – and he has made a fool out of all of us ever since. Damn him.'

'No,' William pleaded desperately. 'He's an idiot at times, John – I know that as well as the next man – but our Jamie is no common thief.' There was a pain in his stomach which seemed to reach out and constrict the muscles in his throat when he tried to speak.

'We stood no chance against the evidence of that horse thief. Our Jamie has been a condemned man since he was seen throwing his money around in Ma Shotton's the night after the robbery. He's lived on borrowed time ever since then.'

John nodded grimly. 'Aye, borrowed time – and my charity. He's made a fool of us all.'

Now his voice rose again with anger: 'Today I heard someone refer to North Carter Moor as a viper's nest of trouble. A viper's nest! My farm? My family's home? We have all been tarred with the same brush; Jamie has dragged this family's reputation down into the gutter.'

'You have done more than any of us,' William acknowledged, graciously. 'For Jamie, Cilla and the bairns. You say people are turning on us now? There's been many a time I've heard folks say that if Jamie hadn't had the lawyer you paid for last year, he would have been convicted then.'

'It might have been better if he had,' John snarled. 'All he's done in the last twelve months is cause more trouble in the parish and beget another child! Another mouth for the parish to feed!'

'You can't turn your back on Jamie and Cilla now, John. Not now. We've got to show the world we still believe in him – even if you don't.'

'No. We do not. It ends here,' declared John firmly.

'So what is to be done?' William asked at length. Exhaustion and misery swept over him in successive waves.

'You will need to get another lawyer to make his appeal against execution. At least the judge said he was willing to recommend clemency in Jamie's case.'

'Aye.' William's voice threatened to break with emotion. 'At least that is something we can do. For I tell you John, every time I think of our Jamie pissing himself on the end of the hangman's noose, I feel sick to my stomach.'

John grimaced at the image but said nothing.

'He's our brother – whatever he's done – or hasn't done. We cannot abandon him now,' William pleaded.

'We must all be guided by God and our own conscience. This is God's will. You've obviously chosen your way and intend to follow Jamie on the path to perdition; yet again you stood up in court, swore on the Holy Bible and then lied in the eyes of God that you had loaned him money.'

'Oh, come on, John!' William snapped. 'We have never been a family of saints! Our Da' broke the law many a time. When he wasn't drunk or fighting he made this farm profitable by cheating on half his neighbours. We've always done what we had to survive – but since the time of the reivers we've always done it together!'

'That doesn't make any of the law-breaking or the perjury right,' John said coldly as he pushed back his chair and rose to leave.

'You'll not even join us in the appeal against his death sentence?' William asked frantically. 'Save his neck and get his sentence commuted to transportation?'

'No.' John was quiet but resolute. 'I'll not throw any more money away on that wastrel of a brother of ours. He's guilty, Will, accept it. He's made fools out of us all.'

With that John started to move towards the hallway. William felt as though he had been slapped in the face. What chance did Jamie stand of financing an appeal without his elder brother's money behind him? If John turned his back on Jamie now, their brother would hang for sure.

'What about Cilla and the bairns?' William asked desperately as John reached the doorway. His brother paused and glanced over his shoulder.

'I have given her a bit of money to tide her over for now but I cannot keep them any more. They'll have to go to the poorhouse.'

Damn you, thought William.

He only had a few hours of sleep before he set off to return to Corbridge. The family was just stirring as he left. He had no desire to see John again that morning.

William felt tired, depressed and miserable. He seethed with conflicting emotions: fury at Taylerson and the cruelty of the judiciary; terror when he thought of Jamie and the hanging which lay before him and grief-stricken with impotence when he thought about the fate of Cilla and her little children.

How the hell would she survive?

Paying for a barrister for Jamie's appeal would to cost a fortune. William was not sure if he and the rest of the family could afford it without a contribution from John. He did not make much money from Thorn Tree Farm. Yes, there had been some cash earned from the sale of livestock and wool but much of it had had to be reinvested in the stock and in repairs. He thought of the harvest waiting to be reaped and quickened his step. There always was the slim chance that their mother would be able to change John's mind, but he doubted it. He had never seen his older brother so resolute.

Back at Thorn Tree, his black mood overwhelmed him again. He threw himself into the harvesting with a vengeance. Archie and Old George quietly let him have his own way in everything and somehow managed to avoid getting in the path of his anger.

On the Sunday following the trial, he trudged moodily behind Archie up to the Milburns' farm after church. He did not particularly relish the idea of spending another afternoon watching his friend's hopeless attempts to win over the affections of Jenny Milburn but he did not want to be alone.

The visit brought him some comfort. Archie and Old George may have tiptoed around William for the last few days, but old Josh Milburn had no qualms about bringing up the subject of Jamie's trial after their dinner.

''Tis a disgrace,' he declared loudly. His clay pipe protruded from the side of his mouth and danced up and down as he spoke. ''Tis a disgrace that a man should be convicted on the hearsay of a convicted felon who gets his freedom as a reward. Your brother should never have been found guilty. Them magistrates have set a precedent, like, that will turn the assizes into a farce. Every bloody prisoner will now be giving evidence against his cellmate in the hope that he can escape the hangman's noose.'

'Thank you for your support.' William was surprised. 'I didn't think that many folks would see it this way – besides my family of course.'

'Oh, I'm not the only one to think so,' continued the old man. 'Jenny pet, fetch your old Da the *Courant.*'

Jenny Milburn brought over the newspaper from the sideboard and handed it to William. He was acutely aware that her lovely young eyes were full of sorrow and pity. He thanked her and looked away.

Jamie's trial had been reported in detail – and on the front page:

'The case of James Charlton has excited great surprise. It will be recollected that in the night of 3rd April 1809 the steward's office at Kirkley Hall, the seat of Nathanial Ogle Esq. was broken into, and robbed of £1157 13s 6d.

This money, excepting about £100 in small notes, was some time afterwards thrown over the garden wall, and recovered by the owner. Suspicion fell on Charlton, who was once a servant on the premises and he was committed to prison; but at the last assizes, the grand jury, after examining a vast number of witnesses, threw out the bill against him. Since this time,various reports respecting the robbery have been in circulation in the neighbourhood, and at these assizes Charlton brought three actions against Mr. Aynsley, Mr. Ogle's (then) steward, and two of his sons for defaming his character by this charge, and actually gained a verdict of £5 damages against them.

Yesterday se'nnight James Charlton was again apprehended; and on Wednesday, after a trial of 14 hours, found guilty principally on the evidence of WM. Taylerson, who received sentence of death at the last assizes for burglary and stealing horses, but has since obtained his majesty's pardon; and who stated that Charlton confessed to him, when he found that the bill was thrown out in 1809, that he, his wife, and another person committed the robbery; and this confession, which according to his evidence, he rendered complete by a most artful set of interrogatories, he asserted was made to him just after he had himself received sentence of death!

William was surprised but pleased; having the support of the *Newcastle Courant* would be good news for Jamie's appeal. It might even persuade John to help out with the cost of the defence lawyer again. *The Courant* was produced every Saturday and was Northumberland's main newspaper. Those flimsy sheets were read by just about everyone who could read, from the duke downwards. Its circulation even extended into the county of Durham.

For the first time in five days he felt vindicated in his loyalty to his brother. He would borrow the newspaper from old Josh and take it back to show his family when he next went over to Ponteland. If nothing else, it might make his mother feel better.

As it happened, they had some livestock to sell at Morpeth meat market that week. With the copy of the *Courant* in his coat pocket, William set off early to drive the animals to the loud and bustling market. He planned to get back as soon as he could and help Archie and Old George bring in the last of the harvest. He took the wagon and let the dogs herd the sheep beside him. He conducted his business quicker than expected and then decided to see if the gaolers could be bribed to let him in to see Jamie for a while.

A crowd of angry women were gathered beside the grim stone walls of the gaol. Their husbands stood some way off, unsure what to do. He was shocked to see Cilla in the centre of the crowd. She was hugely pregnant and deeply distressed. She had attempted to gain entrance into the gaol to see Jamie; the turnkeys had refused to let her in.

‘’Tis shocking!’ one woman declared loudly. ‘And her husband sentenced to death as well!’

‘Ah, they should let her see her man!’ sympathised another. ‘Try not to cry, hinny – it’s not good for the bairn.’

Instinctively, William strode into the crowd of women. Cilla saw him through her veil of tears and threw herself into his arms. ‘They won’t let me see Jamie!’ she sobbed.

‘For God’s sake, Cilla, how on earth did you get here? Tell me you haven’t walked all the way from Milburn in your condition?’

‘She got a lift in a neighbour’s wagon,’ one of the women informed him.

‘I’ll see what I can do,’ he said and extricated himself from Cilla’s arms.

‘’Tis his brother,’ he heard one of the women whisper. ‘Him that stood up for him at the trial.’

An expectant hush fell on the crowd as he walked towards the entrance of the grim building; the eyes of half the market place watched him.

The gaolers were having none of it. The noisy crowd which had gathered around Cilla beneath the prison walls had alarmed them. Even the glint of William’s money would not sway their resolve.

He led the weeping Cilla away from the prison and the crowd towards the hostelry were he had left his wagon. By the time he had harnessed the horse, she had stopped crying. She looked wretched: her eyes were deadened with misery, the eyelashes matted with tears and her face was bloated from weeping. Strands of damp hair hung down lankly and stuck to the side of her cheeks. His heart ached for her.

He harnessed the horse and they left the town. As soon as they were out of sight of the prying eyes of the gossips, he reined in the horses and took her in his arms. She sobbed like a child against his chest.

William just did not know what to say. He doubted that even the crumpled newspaper article in his pocket would do much to cheer her up. He felt helpless. Even if Jamie’s sentence was commuted to transportation, she would probably never see him again.

Gradually, her grief subsided and she indicated that they should return to Milburn. They travelled in silence for most of the way. She squirmed uncomfortably on the hard wooden seat of the wagon when the child moved within her.

What would become of her and the children?

He didn't know how long John's money would last but he guessed that she would be in the poorhouse before Michaelmas. It would be weeks – possibly months – after the birth of the child before she could work again and she would never be able to earn enough as a casual farm labourer to feed and clothe five children.

Her life was ruined.

He grimaced as stark realisation finally dawned on him; it would probably be better for her and the bairns if his Jamie was hung. At least then, she might be able to leave the poorhouse, marry again and find someone to take care of them. Alright, five children were a burden for any man to keep but she was still an attractive woman and a damned good housekeeper.

But if Jamie's sentence was reprieved and he was sent for transportation, she would be left married but not married. A woman alone for the rest of her life, unable to remarry and with her husband and provider trapped on the other side of the world. It was only at this point that the real cruelty of the transportation punishment hit him; it was more devastating for the convicts' wives and children who were left behind.

As the wagon crawled towards the tiny hamlet, he realised that he faced a decision that no man should ever have to consider. Should he find the money for an appeal and save Jamie's scrawny neck? Or should he let his brother hang and give Cilla and her children the chance of a decent life with another man?

He sighed when he realised that he was fooling himself; he could never live with Jamie's death on his conscience. Somehow he would find the money to pay for his brother's appeal and see him on his way to New South Wales.

He did not have the time to ponder this further. As they approached Milburn, they could see a smart black carriage in front of Cilla's cottage. Two men stood beside it, awkwardly watching their approach.

What now? thought William. *What now?*

As William helped Cilla clamber down from the cart, the stouter of the two men stepped forward, squinting at them through his spectacles. This man clearly enjoyed his food. His waistcoat buttons were straining across the huge stomach

'Mistress Charlton?' he asked. 'Mistress Priscilla Charlton?'

'Aye,' William growled. 'Who wants her?'

The visitor's round face broke into a beaming smile. 'Thank Goodness!' he declared enthusiastically. 'Thank Goodness you have returned. We were just about to turn back to Newcastle – and what a pity that would have been! It could have been a wasted journey!'

Cilla leaned against William and stared blankly at her visitor.

'I'm William Charlton – her brother-in-law. What can we do for you?'

'Of course I know who you are Mr. Charlton – I saw you at the trial last week. Let me introduce myself. I am Edward Humble of E. Humble & Sons, Booksellers and Stationers in Newcastle. My companion is Mr. Mitchell of the *Newcastle Courant.*'

William glanced at the thinner of the two men and recognised the pinched features and ink-stained fingers of one of the reporters he had watched scribbling down notes at Jamie's trial.

'I have a proposition to put to you both,' Humble continued. 'May we go inside?'

Cilla nodded and the two men followed the Charltons inside the cottage.

Without a fire and the chatter of the children, the cottage seemed dark and unusually quiet to William. Humble's bulky frame blocked out most of the light from the doorway. Cilla sank down into the chair by the empty grate and rubbed her swollen belly. She looked exhausted and confused.

William dropped down onto his haunches and struck a light beneath some kindling in the hearth from his tinderbox. A silence had descended onto the group as the two strangers took in the contents of the cottage. William became conscious how poor and meagre it must all seem to a wealthy man like Humble.

'Would you like some tea?' he asked as he stood up again. It wasn't his place to ask of course, but the mistress of the house had been struck dumb beside him.

'No, no,' Humble insisted. 'No. We have merely come along to impart unto you some excellent news!'

'Well, we could certainly do with some good news,' William replied.

'Firstly, Mistress Charlton,' said their visitor, as he cleared his throat. 'Myself and Mr. Mitchell would like to extend our sympathy towards yourself, your husband and family, regarding that travesty of justice which was enacted at the assizes last week. In short, your husband should never have been convicted of the crime on the word of the horse thief, Taylerson. We have nothing but compassion for the plight of your family, don't we Mitchell?'

The thin man nodded.

Cilla continued to stare blankly at her guest.

William found himself forced to respond on her behalf: 'That's most kind of you, sir.'

'Secondly, we are not the only ones to feel for the distresses of you and your family. In fact, such has been the reaction to Mr. James Charlton's trial, that a subscription has been opened for the purpose of defraying the expense of an application for his majesty's pardon of the prisoner, and also for the support of you, his family.'

'A subscription?' Cilla had found her voice at last.

'Yes, my dear,' the bookseller continued kindly. 'And several respectable individuals have already contributed.'

With that, he moved forward and held out a black leather purse. They could hear the coins chinking softly inside the bag. She tentatively took the purse from him, opened it and poured several gold and silver coins into her lap. She gazed at the money in surprise.

'In addition to this, my colleague Mr. Mitchell has written a pamphlet entitled: *'The Trial of James Charlton'*. We propose to sell this at my bookshops across Northumbria for eighteen pennies a copy. Mr. Mitchell has agreed to donate all the profits towards the subscription and, hopefully, this should raise a considerable amount.'

'That is very kind, Mr. Mitchell,' William said quietly.

Now Mr. Humble fished in his coat pocket and handed a small, closely printed booklet to the illiterate Cilla. She gazed at it uncomprehendingly before passing it over to William. Then she burst into tears.

Alarmed, Mr. Humble moved quickly to offer her his lawn handkerchief which he whipped from his pocket with a flourish. 'There, there, now, Mistress Charlton. I do apologise, I had no intention of distressing you further.'

'No, no – 'tis my condition, that's all,' Cilla struggled to explain through her sobs.

'We had no idea you were expecting a child, or we should perhaps have gone more cautiously. Is it your first child, perhaps?'

'No. 'Tis my fifth bairn.'

Mr. Humble's face registered concern. 'There are five children to be rendered fatherless by this miscarriage of justice?' he asked and glanced at his companion. As if receiving a pre-arranged signal, the reporter pulled a quill, a bottle of ink and some papers out of his coat pocket.

‘Yes. The others are with Jamie’s mother,’ Cilla informed them. ‘We have two more lads and twin girls…’

‘Twins?’

‘Aye, our Hannah and Mary – they adore their Da – and he adores them. They’ll miss him so much when…when he….’ Her lip trembled again with the words she could not bring herself to say. Somehow she managed to pull herself back from the brink of tears. ‘Our Jack is the eldest. He’s a good boy. Very bookish – his father had high hopes of making sommat of himself in the world…’

Talking about her children to the sympathetic Mr. Humble calmed Cilla and gave her more confidence. As the older man nodded compassionately, the reporter made notes.

Meanwhile, William glanced down at the first few pages of the pamphlet in his hand and tried to make sense of the development which unfolded before him. Two pages of the booklet were enough to convince him that the facts of the case had been dutifully recorded by Mr. Mitchell but the tone of the writing was indignant and angry: Jamie was described as *the unfortunate James Charlton;* he was a man on the receiving end of *unjust prejudice.* They seemed to genuinely believe and care that Jamie had been convicted unfairly.

William thought back to his time living in Newcastle when he was closer to the beating pulse of the county. He had heard talk about rich folks who set up charities, wealthy men who talked about prison reform and who entered politics and railed against unjust laws and the harshness of the penal system.

Well, whatever their motives, these men and their pamphlet were bound to upset the magistrates and judiciary who had condemned his brother. This was enough for Humble and Mitchell to find favour in his eyes. Any money which they raised for Jamie and Cilla was only to be welcomed, although he could not believe that anyone would pay hard cash to read about his damned brother.

As Cilla launched into yet another story about the antics of the twins, he cleared his own throat and interrupted:

‘This is most kind of you Mr. Humble, sir – and you too Mr. Mitchell. On behalf of Cilla, Jamie and our family I can only thank you for the interest you are taking from the bottom of my heart.’

‘Yes, thank you,’ stammered Cilla.

‘But who are these ‘respectable individuals’ who have sent us this money for Jamie’s appeal?’ he queried. ‘These folks will also need thanking.’

‘They are just ordinary Christians, like you or me,’ insisted Humble. ‘Many of them wish to remain anonymous. They are mostly folks who were at the trial – or have heard about it. Charitable men and women who are shocked at what happened to your brother; who feel he was wrongly convicted and that the judiciary has over-reached itself.’

Ah, thought William and he remembered Josh Milburn back in Corbridge.

He pocketed the leaflet to read to Cilla later and started to discuss the details of Jamie’s appeal with Mr. Humble.

On Saturday, 15th September, the *Newcastle Courant* ran the following advertisement on its front page:

James Charlton

At the request of several respectable individuals who feel for the distresses of the unfortunate James Charlton and his family, a subscription has been opened for the purpose of defraying the expense of an Application for his majesty’s pardon of the prisoner, and also for the support of his family – a wife eight months advanced in pregnancy, and four helpless young children. Subscriptions will be received by E. Humble & Son, Booksellers, Newcastle.

William did not see it until the next day when he and Archie visited the Milburns at their farm after church.

Josh, who seemed to have become his brother’s staunchest supporter, could not wait to discuss it with him.

‘It be obvious that many of the ‘respectable’ citizens of this county do not believe a word of that horse thief’s testimony. This’ll give them nobs on the jury summat to think about!’

The next week William bought his own copy of the newspaper and was startled to find out that the subscription had already raised thirty nine pounds, seventeen shillings and two pence. The names of most of his brother’s generous benefactors were listed, although, as Humble had predicted, some preferred to remain anonymous. By the 29th September the fund had risen to nearly fifty-nine pounds and a third edition of *‘The Trial’* by Mr. Mitchell was published. This pamphlet was now sold by twelve different booksellers across the North East: in Newcastle, Durham, Sunderland, Gateshead, North Shields, Morpeth and Alnwick.

He could not believe his brother’s good fortune

You lucky old bugger, Jamie. William grinned to himself.

Meanwhile, in Morpeth Gaol, Jamie had discovered a new way to make his life more comfortable as a result of his new-found notoriety. Several groups of curious strangers arrived at the gaol and requested to see the unfortunate prisoner they had read about in the newspaper. Well dressed, articulate and educated, they paid handsomely to gain entry. The bemused gaoler led them through the piles of filth towards Charlton's cell. Several of them had trouble with the stench and gagged into their perfumed handkerchiefs.

''Ere, Charlton! Get up! You've got visitors, man.'

Despite his hunger and wretched condition, Jamie staggered to his feet and smoothed down his wild hair and straggly beard.

'Oh, you poor fellow!' observed one of the guests. 'To have been snatched from the comfort of your own hearth and the warmth of your family and to have come to this!'

'Be strong, man,' said another as he handed him a hip flask of brandy. 'You have many friends on the outside.'

'Aye, so I've heard,' said Jamie. William had managed to get word to him about the subscription which Humble had set up on his behalf. 'If you gentlemen be amongst those who have given to the subscription which has been raised to pay for my appeal, I thank you from the bottom of my heart.'

'You poor man. How did it come to pass that you have been so cruelly used?'

''Tis a long, sad story, my friend,' Jamie said. 'Taylerson was not the only one who wronged me. I have been sorely abused from start to finish. Let me tell you about that fiend, Michael Aynsley, the steward of Kirkley Hall, because that's where my troubles began. The man is a devil – and the real thief who broke into Kirkley Hall...'

With his throat lubricated by several long swills of the brandy, Jamie told them a good story. After a dramatic and heart-wrenching account of the injustice which had been handed out to him – both before and after the robbery – the visitors all dropped coins through the bars of the prison into the filthy cap which he had laid on the stone floor.

As the autumn progressed, Jamie Charlton, the *'wronged prisoner'* in Morpeth Gaol, became a popular attraction. Crowds of wealthy men and women continued to visit the gaol and listen sympathetically to the distressed man as he relayed his tragic tale. By the time the first, deadly fingers of frost had started to descend through the high, narrow windows of the prison, Jamie had saved up enough money to pay the gaolers for the privilege of using the comfortable upstairs cell with the fireplace. Jamie now occupied the same bed and chair where his nemesis, Taylerson, had sat out the ravages of the previous winter.

Cilla gave birth to a baby daughter on 27th October. After a difficult labour, the child was born just before midnight. She was a feeble scrap of a little girl with the soft, dark hair of her father and brothers plastered to her tiny head. Cilla had lost a lot of blood and wilted in the bed with the child at her breast. Exhausted and depressed, she murmured that the bairn was to be named for her own sister: Isabella. The bairn was not expected to survive.

CHAPTER NINETEEN

Knowing that the misery and distress of Cilla and his brother had been temporarily eased by Mr. Humble's subscription, a relieved William was able to turn his attention back to his own farm in Corbridge. Life had to go on and he had problems of his own.

Despite all his curtness and rudeness towards the lass, Jenny Milburn still continued to follow him and take every opportunity to engage with him in conversation. He had recently been forced to take desperate measures to avoid her in Corbridge.

He and Archie had enjoyed a good dinner in The Angel. They had left the inn and parted company to pursue their business in the town separately. William paused for a moment to watch Archie cross the wind-swept street. Then he had spotted Jenny Milburn approaching him on his side of the road. She stopped a few yards away. Her pretty eyes glanced to Archie's retreating back. For a moment he thought that she might call after his friend but her gaze returned to him. Her face was illuminated with a beautiful smile.

He turned his back on her abruptly and tried to walk away. Then he spotted the usual crowd of whores standing in a group by the wall of the tavern. Bella Nimmo laughed and swayed drunkenly amongst them. Without hesitation he marched forward and seized her thin arm.

'Good afternoon, Bella,' he said pleasantly. 'Remember me? Will Charlton – Cilla's brother-in-law. Do you mind if we walk a while and talk about some family business?'

Without waiting for her agreement he slid Bella's arm through his and began to walk away, dragging the startled woman along with him.

'Keeping it in the family are you, Charlton?' one of the other whores called out behind them and the group dissolved into raucous laughter.

'Don't forget to give him a discounted price, Bella!' shouted another.

The drunk and confused woman beside him suddenly jerked him to a halt. She yanked back her arm and glared at him out of alcohol-glazed eyes in a face which was pale with lack of nourishment and marked with disease. She didn't look a bit like her twin close up, he realised. She also stank unpleasantly of damp, rotting clothes and unwashed bodies – hers and the bodies of the men she laid with.

'What you want?' she slurred. 'And where you taking me?'

Out of the corner of his eye, he was aware of Jenny Milburn, watching them from a few yards down the street. This group of whores were notorious in Corbridge. Church groups and committees had all petitioned the beadle to have them moved on or sent to a house of correction. Little Miss Milburn might have had a sheltered upbringing on her father's farm but even she could be in no doubt about the type of woman he was now talking to – and he was glad of it.

Resigned to carrying out this farce to the end, he fished out a ten shilling piece from his pocket. Drunk or not, Bella's eyes caught the glint of silver in an instant.

'I have something for you and your mother,' he said quietly. 'From Cilla. Look, is there somewhere we can talk? I have no desire to discuss this in front of so many gawping eyes.'

Now she had seen his money she was more agreeable. She nodded and led him down a narrow side alley, beside the inn. Shadowy and cramped, it was slimy with the recent rain and the discarded slops from the tavern. The overhanging upper casement windows of the dilapidated buildings were so close they almost touched. Sunlight struggled to penetrate the tiny gap between the upper storeys and the alleyway stunk to high heaven.

'Why's our Cilla sending me money?' Bella asked suspiciously. 'I'd heard her husband had got himself sentenced to hang.'

'Ah, but they have recently had some good fortune,' he explained. Confident that Jenny Milburn was now scurrying away as fast as her young legs would take her, he leaned against the dripping wall and told Bella about the subscription which had been set up to help Jamie and Cilla. He could sense that Bella did not understand a word he said but she was not a woman to look a gift horse in the mouth. As he finished his tale, she took his coin and glanced back towards the entrance of the alley.

'I'll take your money, no problem Will Charlton,' she commentated wryly, 'But I don't believe for one minute that it came from our Cilla – and what's that lass doing following you?'

He spun around. Jenny Milburn now stood at the entrance to the alley. She stared at them in horror. Her pretty face was etched with shock. For a moment William felt a stab of regret at what he had done – then his anger flared.

For God's sake! She's stalking me like a poacher following a stag! Why isn't she in Archie's arms?

Without warning, he seized Bella and pushed her roughly back against the grimy wall. Ignoring the diseased scabs around her dry mouth and her reeking breath, he kissed her as convincingly as he could, while his hand roamed down to cup her skinny arse. Taken by surprise, at first Bella let him fondle her but then she pushed him away.

'Gerroff!' she said angrily, 'what you playing at now? We haven't agreed on a price.'

A quick glance back up the alleyway confirmed that the kiss had been enough; Jenny had gone. He stepped back and sighed, relieved that his ploy had worked. Now he just had to deal with the drunken whore by his side.

'I apologise, Bella,' he said with forced cheerfulness. 'I don't know what came over me. It must have been your beauty.' He flashed her his best grin.

Bella eyed him suspiciously. He sensed that she knew he was using her. For a moment she was angry but when he smiled again she grinned back.

'For a moment there, I thought that you wished to take me down the aisle at Stamfordham church – like your brother did with our Cilla,' she flirted.

'I'd take you, Bella,' he smiled. 'But not in a church aisle. It's far too cold and draughty on the stone floor – and the vicar tends to object.'

She laughed now and started to relax. 'You're a rum one, Will Charlton, that's for sure. I don't know what you're playing at. What's wrong with that lass you were trying to avoid?' She jerked her thumb in Jenny Milburn's direction. 'She looks canny enough. Why are you trying to put her off, like?'

'She's not my type,' he said shortly.

'Aye – I've heard you prefer your women to be already wed,' she said slyly.

He blinked in surprise. 'She's just too young for me, that's all.'

Bella shrugged. 'That lass is old enough for thee to wed and bed – and I've no doubt she'll make a canny farmer's wife.'

Without another word she started to weave her way unsteadily past the piles of stinking refuse, towards the street.

Now that the harvest had been gathered in and sold and their barns were full of winter feed, William and Archie turned their attention to their sheep. A small portion of the ewes had already been tupped in August to produce lambs in late January but the bulk of the flock was to be mated in November to give birth in the April, when both ewe and lamb stood the highest chance of survival in the harsh climate which dominated those fells. The rams stamped in frustration in the holding pens as the wind blew scent of the ewes on heat over the hedgerows towards them.

William and Archie sat on the stone wall and cracked a few crude jokes as they watched the first ram do his work. Within seconds he had mounted the first, then the second and a third. Only then did he take himself apart from the group and graze awhile to rebuild his strength.

William thought of the process which they had set in motion and the exhausting spring they would face next year at lambing time. 'He gets all the pleasure – and we get all the work,' he smiled.

Archie did not smile back; he had fallen silent. He cleared his throat and said: 'I've been thinking,'

''Tis a dangerous habit,' William quipped.

Archie managed a half smile. 'Be serious for a moment, man. I've been thinking that we've a long, harsh winter ahead of us – and that it would be nice – I would appreciate – oh damn it! I've been wondering if it is time to approach Miss Milburn and…and…' His voice trailed away hopelessly.

'And ask her how she would feel about keeping you warm in bed on a night through the long, harsh winter ahead?'

Archie blushed to the roots of his hair and leapt off the wall. 'Damn you, Will! I hope to marry the girl!'

'You tend to find that the two go together,' William reminded him softly.

How can a man who is surrounded by rutting animals become so coy at the thought of swiving with a lass? he wondered. Archie was no blushing virgin; he'd enjoyed a girl or two back in their Newcastle days. But there again, Jenny Milburn was no ordinary lass.

'Aye, well, you're right there about the bed thing.' Archie was still flustered. 'But what I wanted to ask you is: do you think she'd say yes?'

Archie paused for a moment and William's smile faded as he struggled to find an appropriate response. Fortunately, Archie gave him an extra few moments to formulate his lie; his friend continued to pour out his feelings: 'I have courted her, the best I know how. She can be in no doubt of my affection. I hope that I am not flattering myself when I say she seems to hold a certain fondness towards me…'

His voice trailed away again and William felt his friend's fear of rejection. Archie had invested all his love and tenderness in the

Milburn lass. He wondered how he would react when she spurned him – as William knew she probably would.

He suddenly became conscious of the icy wind that streamed down from the fells. As he pulled up the collar of his coat he resisted the wave of sadness which threatened to swamp him. He knew he had done his best to honour the promise he had made Archie nearly a year ago about Jenny Milburn but he still felt unworthy. His trusting friend deserved better.

Maybe, just maybe, the shock of seeing William with a whore last week might have made Jenny more appreciative of Archie's innocence, affection and suitability as a husband and provider?

He knew that it wouldn't be ideal if she accepted Archie as her husband while she still held feelings for him; it might be a bit awkward when she came to live at Thorn Tree Farm as a new bride. But given time she would learn to love Archie. Of course she would: everybody loved Archie.

God knows they could do with a woman about the place to provide a few home comforts in their filthy and cluttered farmhouse.

Archie still waited for his answer.

'You'll have to ask her, man,' he advised. 'Find out how she feels – and put yourself out of this misery of not knowing. She could say: 'Yes.' Just think how pleased that'll make you feel.'

'Of course, of course,' Archie was relieved. His soft brown eyes shone with excitement: 'I'll ask her tonight.'

'No, Archie, go and ask her now – while the courage is still in you – but get a wash first and change your clothes. You stink like that horny ram you've been handling and women are fussy about things like that.'

'Of course – I'll go and wash up and change first.' Archie set off but then stopped in his tracks and turned back to William. Finally, he voiced the terror which lurked within him.

'What if she refuses me?'

William shivered again.

'How could any lass refuse you?' he joked, lightly. 'You're a good catch, Archie, and will make a great husband. Damn it, if she marries you, the lass will even still be able to go home and see her ma every day if she wants!'

'Yes, yes! I had not thought of that.' His confidence lifted by this advantage, Archie turned and strode purposefully down the hill towards the farm.

Archie was back at Thorn Tree Farm within an hour. He was a despondent man. Jenny Milburn had rejected his proposal of marriage.

'His Royal Highness, The Prince Regent, in the name and on the behalf of His Majesty, King George III, was graciously pleased to extend his Royal mercy to the said felon on condition of his being transported to the coast of New South Wales or some other of the Islands adjacent for the term of his natural life... '

On 11th January 1811, Jamie's sentence was commuted to transportation. William did not get to hear about it until several weeks later, when a letter arrived from his mother. They had suffered terrible snows again that winter and the men had been virtual prisoners as blizzard after blizzard had lashed against their hillside farm. It had been a struggle to keep themselves and the animals alive.

He saved the letter until last thing at night when he was settled with his pipe and his dwindling pouch of tobacco in front of the kitchen fire. Archie, who had been a saddened man all winter, had gone to bed early, as had Old George – so he was able to enjoy it in peace.

Ann told him about Jamie's reprieve in a couple of lines. They had all come to expect it, of course; the judge had recommended clemency at the trial and once the subscription had raised the funds to pay for the reprieve, it had only been a matter of time before it arrived. Jamie was to be taken by ship from Newcastle Keep to London in the spring. Here he would be held on a prison ship on the Thames before being transported to New South Wales. His mother's tone was brisk and factual. Life had moved on for all of them, it seemed.

Still, William breathed a sigh of relief. It was official; his brother was not to hang. God knows what fate would befall Jamie in New South Wales. He had heard terrible tales of the steaming jungle where convicts were forced to hack out a meagre existence. He knew they dropped like flies from the heat exhaustion, starvation and tropical diseases.

However, one thing he had learnt about his brother over the past two years was that he was also a natural-born survivor who had more than his fair share of luck. Of course, he would miss him. Hell, he'd missed Jamie's drunken, jovial company for months now. But one thing was for sure: Jamie would survive.

As the hail began its stinging rattle on the casement window, he scanned the letter for news of Cilla and the children and found a short mention at the bottom of the page. Cilla still lived in the cottage at Milburn. Her share of the monies raised by the subscription and the money made from selling Jamie's cattle had paid her rent until the spring. Since the birth of her child, Cilla had worked for several local farmers with the infant strapped to her back. Jamie's old employer at Haindykes farm often gave her a bit of work. His wife liked Cilla's help around the house. Ann Charlton did what she could to help her daughter-in-law and grandchildren.

William knew that this situation could not continue for much longer. It was only a matter of time before the rent was due again and Cilla would leave the cottage and go into the poorhouse. The support for Mr. Humble's subscription had now waned and the income had dried up. The good citizens of Northumberland had eased their consciences with their donations and had now returned to their lives and taken up other causes. It had been some time since Jamie had had any wealthy visitors in Morpeth Gaol. However, William had sensed that their help had benefited the family in other ways besides financial. The appeal had softened attitudes towards Jamie and Cilla and made folks more sympathetic to their plight: Jamie was still referred to as *'the wronged man in Morpeth Gaol'*. It seemed the only person in the parish left unmoved by this tragedy was their brother John, the farmer of North Carter Moor, who, according to his mother, still glowered and became angry whenever Jamie or Cilla's names were mentioned at the farm.

William folded his letter carefully back into its envelope and placed it behind the clock on the mantelpiece above the hearth.

He resolved to try and see Jamie one more time before he was transported. He was determined to ask him, once and for all, for the truth.

Had he robbed Kirkley Hall?

By the end of February the last of the snow had gone and the weather had become mild, almost balmy.

They had dropped down to one man at a time on watch in the field of pregnant ewes. However, the last few weeks of lambing had taken their toll; William was exhausted and began to nod off to sleep against the mossy edge of the stone wall.

He was woken abruptly by the sharp bark of one of his dogs. He scrambled to his feet and scanned the flock for any sign of trouble. There was none. The ewes continued to graze unperturbed. He glanced at the dogs and realised that they were barking at something over the wall. He shushed them. Then he heard it; the gentle sound of a human female grunting.

'If that's you, Archie, can you please get over here quickly and help me?' Jenny Milburn's voice sounded sharp and strained.

He scaled the wall quickly and dropped down onto the muddy lane at the other side. Jenny strained to hold onto a ewe's rear end with one of her tiny hands – the other was inserted into its uterus. The distressed sheep frantically tried to break free and the slip of a girl struggled to hold on. Despite the cold, sweat was breaking out on her pale forehead with the exertion and the front of her skirt was already covered with blood, mucus and faeces.

He positioned himself at the head of the ewe and steadied it.

She flashed him a look of contempt with her icy blue eyes. 'You could have come to this end,' she complained through gritted teeth.

'Why?' he grinned. 'When you're doing such a wonderful job?'

The next second, the lamb slithered to the ground, still wrapped in its silvery membrane. Jenny stepped back hastily as the afterbirth gushed out and splattered all over the lane.

William grabbed a handful of grass and ferns which grew by the edge of the wall and wiped down the newborn before pushing her towards her mother's teats. Jenny had sat down on a large boulder and pulled up more clumps of grass to wipe clean her arm and her clothes.

Satisfied that mother and baby were doing fine, Will sat on the grass beside her.

'That, Miss Milburn, was very impressive.'

Two pink spots of pleasure appeared beneath her cheekbones. 'Well, I am a hill-farmer's daughter,' she murmured.

'And does Old Josh have you out in the fields with him at lambing time?'

'Sometimes,' she smiled.

William scanned the empty road and his eyes came to rest on the ewe and her new lamb. 'Well, it's a good job that you were passing today – I've no idea how that ewe got out of the field. I'd fallen asleep on the other side of the wall.'

'I wondered what the strange noise was. It must have been your snoring,' she said wryly.

'Aye, more than likely.'

'You must have been sound asleep – I've been here for ages,' she added.

'And thank goodness you were. We're eternally grateful, Miss Milburn – myself and yonder ewe.'

She smiled and they fell silent for a moment.

There's not many lasses who could look that pretty covered in sheep shit and slime, he thought. A strand of silver blonde hair had escaped from her bonnet and waved gently down to her stubborn little chin.

His mother had a much-prized porcelain figurine of a woman which languished on the dresser at North Carter Moor. The statuette brandished a shepherd's crook and was draped in porcelain lace and pastel pink and blue frills. Ann Charlton called it a shepherdess. The rest of the family had always struggled with the difference between reality and the romantic notion which the statue represented.

Today, William could see the resemblance between the delicate figurine and this real-life shepherdess, with her porcelain complexion and slender figure. The main difference, he fancied, was that this lass had a backbone of pure iron.

'There's something I want to explain to you, Mr. Charlton,' she said quietly. 'About Archie.'

'Oh, yes?' He was guarded now. His own blue eyes fixed her with a steady gaze. 'What might that be?'

'I like Archie very much,' she began. 'He's become like – like another brother to me – but I didn't – don't – love him.'

The words came out in a rush and she looked at him nervously – desperate for him to understand. 'I knew he cared for me deeply – and it just wasn't fair. I could never have married him – knowing as I did that I would never love him back the same way as he loved me.'

They stared at each other for a moment. Then she dropped her eyes beneath his piercing gaze.

'You are his friend,' she murmured. 'I know you care about him. I thought that you deserved an explanation.'

'Well, at least you're honest, hinny,' he conceded, sadly. 'There's many a lass who would have looked at Archie and just seen the farm, the money and the home that he could provide. You were cruel to be kind, I suppose.'

'And then there was his dream to go to the new world…'

'I thought this might have been something that appealed to you, like,' he interrupted. 'Don't you want to go to the Americas and see your brothers again?'

'Not really,' she sighed. 'I belong here – in Northumberland. I could never leave my parents and live that far away from them. That was Archie's dream – never mine.'

He rolled onto his back and stared at the white clouds which skittered like daft lambs across the vast expanse of sky above them. 'It's not my dream, either,' he murmured sadly.

'I would have just held him back,' she continued. 'Will he still sell up and go to America now, do you think?'

'He's talked about nothing else since Christmas,' William told her as he sat up.

This was true. Finally facing up to the fact that Jenny Milburn would never have him, Archie had found solace in his American dream. Now there was a new urgency in his voice when he talked about it. He planned to go this year after the harvest was sold.

'And what about you, Mr. Charlton, will you go with him?'

He looked down into her earnest young face, framed by the soft white-blonde hair.

'I may have no choice,' he said, more sharply than he intended. 'I've only been here just over a year. I cannot afford to buy out Archie's share of the farm – and the few acres of land which I own will not produce a big enough yield to live on. Never mind the fact that the farmhouse which goes with them is just a ruined pile.'

'Well, I'm sorry to hear that,' she said simply. 'I will miss you – as will my father. I know he thinks highly of you and enjoys your company on a Sunday.'

He got to his feet and reached out to help her up. Her grubby little hand was tiny, her fingers long and slender. He felt the warmth of her hand in his and realised how good it was to touch a woman's soft skin again. It would be so easy to just pull her forward into his embrace. It took every ounce of self-restraint he had to resist the urge. Archie still came between them.

They stared at each other for a moment as he held her hand.

'You're a grand lass, Miss Milburn,' he told her, gruffly. 'And an amazing shepherdess. You'll make a wonderful farmer's wife one day. Somewhere out there is a lucky man whom you will make very happy. Sadly, it won't be Archie – or me. I think that our destinies lie on different sides of the world.'

She was unfazed: 'Call me, Jenny,' she said.

He should have realised that she was not the kind of girl to take no for an answer. She had obviously been indulged by her parents and her older brothers. She was the only daughter, the youngest child and a beautiful clever little woman: the darling of the Milburns' farm.

Two weeks later, Josh Milburn found him – alone – mending a wall in the far field. William greeted the older man warmly and shook his gnarled, arthritic hand. They chatted about the weather and heaved a mutual sigh of relief that the lambing was over for the moment; the second batch of lambs were not due until April.

'I've missed your company on Sunday at ours,' the old man admitted as he lit his pipe.

'We were snowed in for weeks,' William told him. 'And what with the lambing and the…and the…' His voice trailed away to nothing.

'…and the trouble between our Jenny and Archie?' Josh finished for him, gently. 'I guess it were awkward, like?'

'Yes,' William said simply. 'It was.'

'It must have been hard for the lad. It were clear to me and the missus that he were sweet on her for most of the years he's been at Thorn Tree.'

There was a silence for a moment as Josh puffed on his pipe. William deftly split a rock in half with his knife and placed it in the gap in the stone wall.

'Still, if they weren't right for each other – and she says they weren't – then it's probably for the best. The lass is old enough to know her own mind. Marriage lasts a lifetime and if you marry wrong then that lifetime can be longer than your stint in hell.'

William smiled. Old Josh and his missus were probably the happiest married couple he had ever met; far more so than his own strong-headed, argumentative parents. However, he accepted the suggestion that it had not always been a bed of roses between them. Life never was that simple, was it?

'Our Jenny says that Archie's leaving for America in the autumn?' Josh continued.

'Aye.'

''Tis probably for the best, it will give him a new start; a chance to forget our Jenny and mend his broken heart.'

'Aye.' William couldn't think what else to say.

'You've been a good friend to the lad, Will.'

'He's been a good friend to me. I drifted for years; taking a share of this farm has been the best thing I've ever done.'

'You're loyal to your mates – and that troublesome family of yours. That's a good quality in a man.'

'I do my best,' William said amused.

'Mind you, I think it may have caused you a bit of worry and cost you a bit of happiness, like – all this loyalty.'

William paused in his work and looked into the old man's lined, brown face. He was weathered like a piece of old leather.

'What are you getting at, Josh?' he asked. The old man was clearly leading up to something.

But Josh wouldn't be drawn and asked another question instead. 'Are you to gan with him, when he sails?'

'I don't have much choice,' William sighed. 'My fortunes are tied up with Archie's. I don't have the money saved to buy his share of the farm. God knows, I've tried. But every time I get some money saved there always seems to something to buy, or something which needs repairing around this place.'

'Aye, that's the way it is with hill farming,' Josh nodded sympathetically.

'If we go, we'll take over letters for your sons,' William offered.

'Well, I'm hoping that you won't go.'

'Oh?'

'For a start, you don't want to go.'

'True.'

'I don't want you to go either.'

'Thank you.'

'But mostly I don't want you to go for me daughter's sake.'

William stared.

'Me missus tells me that our Jenny has been pining for you, ever since she first clapped her eyes on you,' Josh explained. ''Tis you she's taken a fancy to – not young Archie. You must have had an inkling?'

'Yes, I did have an inkling,' William confessed slowly. 'And because of how Archie felt I kept out of the way.'

'Aye, that's what I thought were going on. As I said, your loyalty has cost you some personal happiness, like. But the lass turned Archie down. There's room for a new suitor in her life. You could come up to the farm on a Sunday again and get to know her a bit.'

'Josh, I'm trying to be honest here, with you,' he said, slowly. 'I think that Jenny is a wonderful young woman – I've nothing but respect and fondness for her. If I was in the position to take a wife, I wouldn't look any further than your daughter. She is everything a man, and a farmer, could want in a wife. But as I've already explained – when Archie goes, I have to go. Or else I have to go back to the poverty and hunger of labouring on other men's farms and that's no life to offer your daughter – or any woman for that matter.'

'There's many who live that way – your brother, Jamie and his family for one.'

'Aye,' William snapped. 'And look where that got them.' His face darkened.

'What about if I gave you the money to buy Archie's share of Thorn Tree Farm?'

William's eyes widened.

'I have a bit put by you see, for the missus and I, in the future – and a bit for Jenny of course. She's me only daughter, Will. It's important to me and the missus that she's settled and happy. You'll understand this right enough when you've a bairn of your own.'

'You're offering me a loan to keep me here?' William was confused.

'Naw, lad, I'm offering you a *dowry,*' the old man said wryly. And he named his figure.

William was stunned. He put down his knife and the stone he held. His mind raced. With Josh's money and his own savings, he would only need to find another seventy pounds to buy out Archie's share of the lease and stock. Could he borrow this amount from John, perhaps? Or even the bank down in Corbridge?

It was a chance in a lifetime. All he had to do was wed the pretty Jenny Milburn and then he would be able to stay on at Thorn Tree and have his own farm of 500 acres. He'd finally be his own man. He was too stunned to even speak. It was not every day that a man came and offered you both his beautiful daughter and a whole stack of money to go with her.

'Anyway, think it over and sleep on it, Will. Do what's best for yourself and I'll trust that it is best for my Jenny as well.' The old man tapped out the remaining ashes in his pipe on the stone wall beside them and prepared to go.

'Oh and there be one or two other thing as well: firstly, not a word of this little chat of ours to either of the women in my household, eh?'

'You have my word,' William promised.

'Secondly, it may be that if you wed our Jenny, you will have to put up with us living with you. My son has also a mind to wed this summer and the lass he's taken a shine to is not to the liking of my missus. Naturally, he'll bring her to our farm to live and I can see some trouble there in the future between the women.' The old man sighed. 'I think we'd both be happier living with you and our Jenny in our old age.'

William smiled. 'You'd be welcome at Thorn Tree, Josh – you and Mistress Milburn.'

'That's what I thought you'd say, lad.' The old man nodded satisfied. 'Now have a good think about what I've said – put yourself first for once.'

That night William could hardly sleep for excitement. He felt released from the uncertainty which had clouded his future for months. He laid awake making plans for the farm: he was certain that the farm could support more cattle; he would cut the number of sheep and adapt the older barn for milking. They'd have to go careful for a few years mind, while they paid back the loan and the interest.

He could not believe his luck. He had heard men joking over their ale in the taverns about old men who had tried to pay younger men to marry their ugly daughters. He smiled when he realised that nobody would believe him if he ever spoke of the 'arrangement' old Josh had offered him concerning the pretty Jenny.

Jamie would have loved this development and would have ribbed him for years about it. *Oh, Jamie…*

It was only when the darkness began to lift, in the hours before dawn that he found himself thinking seriously about Jenny Milburn herself. A picture of her hopeful little face swam into his mind and he felt slightly guilty when he realised that he did not love her with the same burning passion which he had harboured for the feisty Sarah. Nor did she stir him to distraction the same way Cilla had stirred him to lust two summers ago. His preference definitely was for an older, more sexually experienced woman. But then again he had a disastrous history with women; the fact that Jenny Milburn was different was probably a good thing. It was confusing. After more than a year of telling himself that Jenny was not for him, now the lass was being thrown at him. However, what he had said to Josh about respect and fondness had been true. He tried to picture himself married to Jenny Milburn – taking her gently in the large bed in the main bedroom, and living and working with her day after day on the farm. There'd be children, of course, to bind them together and probably her aged parents living with them as well.

It was not a bad picture of the future, he decided. He knew he would be a kind husband and hoped he could be a faithful one. He didn't drink excessively, fight like his Da or gamble like their Jamie.

He worked hard and could provide for them all. The fondness and respect he held for her would blossom into love as they lived together. He had heard it often did.

By dawn he had made his decision and knew how he would make it work. The biggest problem was Archie. The thought of losing his friendship saddened him, but like Jamie, Archie would leave him soon anyway. He would never see Archie again after he emigrated: nor would he ever see Jamie again after he was transported. What was he supposed to do? Mope around Northumberland for the rest of his life grieving for the two of them? No. It was time to move on and stake his claim to his own happiness.

That Sunday as they trudged down the muddy lane to the church in Corbridge, William told Archie that after the service he was going back to the Milburns to see Old Josh.

Archie glanced at him sharply. He was not fooled. 'Do you intend to try your luck with Jenny Milburn, Will?' he asked.

He nodded. He saw the pain flash across Archie's face and watched him struggle to come to terms with this new development. He felt for him. 'I did what you asked, Archie,' he said. 'I stayed out of your way while you were courting her.'

Archie said nothing. He just pulled his collar up tighter round his face against the wind and quickened his step away from William. His face was rigid.

William sighed. Life would to be awkward at Thorn Tree Farm for the next few months until Archie's departure.

However, the welcome he received up at the Milburns' farm after church soon put all thoughts of Archie out of his mind. Josh's wife welcomed him like a long-lost son. Jenny flushed with excitement; her eyes shone with happiness every time he looked at her. Old Josh just smiled knowingly. He chatted with the old man and Jenny's older brother about farming. He flirted with her mother and was charming, attentive and gentle with Jenny.

After lunch he took her for a walk around the fells. It was damp and drizzling and difficult to walk over the sodden ground but they hardly noticed. It felt good having a woman on his arm again and quite a novelty having the blessing of her parents. The rain came down heavier and they found shelter in an old barn. They were cold and they hugged each other for warmth. She melted into his arms and he kissed her soft lips. She gave no resistance as his hands gently explored the soft contours of her body. He was pleased with what he felt beneath her clothing. She flushed with excitement and he felt himself stirring with pleasure.

Suddenly nervous about frightening his little virgin, he pulled away. ‘Let’s get to know each other properly, hinny. We’ve got all the time in the world.’

CHAPTER TWENTY

With a rattle of chains, Jamie slumped on the wooden chair across the table in the cramped interview room in Morpeth Gaol and winced. Despite spending most of the winter in a private cell, with extra food and firewood, the last ten months in prison had not been kind to him. His body was stiff with inactivity, the constant damp had set off rheumatism in his joints and he was verging on the edge of malnutrition. He was thirty-seven years of age but he knew he looked like a man well into his fifties with long, unkempt greying hair and gaunt features. He had avoided the ravaging fever which had swept through the main cells of the prison on the ground floor during the winter but the gaol had still taken its toll on him physically.

Across the table, Magistrate Clennell glared at him with distaste. 'You'll be sailing down to London next week, Charlton,' he informed him abruptly. 'From here, you'll be taken by cart to the docks in Newcastle and then chained into the hold of a ship bound for Woolwich on the Thames. Once at Woolwich you'll be held on a prison hulk before you are transported to New South Wales.'

Clennell paused, waiting for a reaction. There was none.

'It has been decided that you are to be given one more chance to confess.'

Suppressed laughter escaped from the back of Jamie's throat. Clennell chose to ignore it. 'You have been convicted of the burglary at Kirkley Hall,' he continued. 'After next week you will never see your home or Northumberland again. It is only right that before you go, you should tell the truth. Continuing to proclaim your innocence of the crime achieves nothing but distress for those closest to you.'

Still Jamie said nothing.

'So why not confess, Charlton? Stop the lying and clear your conscience, for once and for all – get it off your chest, man. Confess.'

'I didn't do it; I never robbed Kirkley Hall.'

'I see,' Clennell said coldly. 'Still the same stubborn, foolish man you always were. You disappoint me, Charlton.'

The magistrate walked over to the filthy window of the office and stared out of a cracked pane into the bustling marketplace outside. He appeared to be thinking deeply. The two gaolers stood impassively behind the prisoner. It had started raining. Jamie could hear the folks in the market scurrying about like ants trying to get out of the rain and cover up their stalls. He recognised all the sounds from outside now. As he lay festering for month after month in his cell, he amused himself with listening to the sounds drifting into the gaol through the high windows. He could recognise individual stallholders from their voices. He knew what they sold and how much they charged. He knew where they came from and where they went.

'Let me tell you about the prison hulks, Charlton,' Clennell said suddenly.

'They are stinking, rotting war ships moored in the centre of the Thames, only accessible by boat. Sometimes a convict tries to escape by throwing themselves overboard but even the strongest swimmers are washed away to their death by the tide, or dragged down to the bottom by the weight of their chains. Can you swim, Charlton?'

'Yes.'

'Then the gaolers had better make sure that you wear extra heavy leg irons. I'll write to them advising it.'

There was no reply.

'Conditions on board the prison hulks are grim. If you thought that life here in Morpeth Gaol was rough, you are in for a shock when you get down there. Why, Morpeth Gaol is like Newhamm Edge coaching inn compared to what awaits you in London.'

Jamie heard one of the gaolers laugh. He was clearly enjoying this.

'Each ship is crammed with about 600 fettered prisoners,' Clennell continued. He turned away from the window and stared at Jamie as he talked. 'There is serious overcrowding. The conditions are grim: dysentery and gaol fever are rife. Many men – and women – die in agony, unnoticed; their cries for help go unheeded. Every now and then the gaolers go down below and instruct the other convicts to carry out the bodies which are later dumped into a pauper's grave. On a still summer's day, the appalling stench from these ships can be smelt from bank to bank across the Thames.

'The prisoners are given the thinnest clothing to wear; although many end up half naked when the other convicts steal their clothes. And the food? The food is terrible – not like the delicious fare that they serve to you here in Morpeth.'

Again the gaoler laughed out loud.

Clennell continued: 'Prisoners are fed a diet of brackish water, mouldy biscuits, ox cheek soup and pease – which they fight over. Many catch rats or frogs and eat them raw to get some meat.

'During the day you will work in chain gangs dredging the Thames or helping to build the arsenal at Woolwich. It is heavy manual work made all the harder because you will be poorly clad and poorly fed.

'At night…at night you will be left in the company of some of the cruellest, hardest, most desperate men in the country. These criminals are not casual opportunist thieves like you, Charlton, or the motley collection of sheep rustlers and lunatics with whom you have shared your cells here in Morpeth. These men are murderers, cut-throats and rapists; they use anything they can lay their hands on to attack and maim each other. The gaolers close the hatches and leave them to it; they never venture below at night – fearful for their own lives. The conditions are brutal – sometimes bestial – on board the prison hulks, Charlton.'

He paused to allow his words to take effect. 'How do you think you will fare down there?'

Jamie stared impassively ahead at the wall of the room. His face was like a mask. If anything that Clennell had said had bothered him at all, it did not show. His emotions were veiled.

'I'll survive,' he said at last.

Clennell chose his next words carefully. 'Yes, you might – but would your wife?'

Jamie glanced up sharply. 'What did you say?'

'I asked if your wife would survive in those conditions? And all your little children, of course – we must not forget them. When she's convicted they'll have to accompany her.'

'What are you talking about?' Jamie snapped. The colour had started to rise beneath the filth on his neck.

'Your wife, Charlton. Your beautiful, gentle wife – and your innocent, little children. You see, if you won't tell us what really happened on the night of the Kirkley robbery, then we'll have to assume that Taylerson's version was correct and that you robbed the Hall with your wife and some undisclosed neighbour.

'We've made enquiries, of course about whom your helpful neighbour and accomplice could have been, but we have been unable to find him. Fortunately, we know exactly where your wife is.'

'You'll go after Cilla and the bairns?' Jamie was aghast.

'We'll have no choice, Charlton. The law is the law. Burglary is wrong and criminals must be found and punished. The children are innocent of course, but they usually accompany their mothers to gaol. Some of them will perish in prison but a few do survive for transportation.'

He paused again. Jamie said nothing but now Clennell had his undivided attention. The magistrate pressed his point home.

'Of course, many of the women turn to prostitution to survive. It is regrettable of course, but it can ensure their survival. For a few favours here, and a few favours there, the women can earn themselves extra food rations and a few home comforts – like blankets. Your daughters will grow up in that environment.'

Jamie turned pale.

There was not a man in the room who did not know what he was talking about. One of the gaolers leered and said that it might be worth his while to: 'take a trip down to Lunnen and get a job on one of these floating prison ships.'

Clennell snapped at him to be quiet. The other gaoler, Simeon Hawkes, said nothing.

'So, what do you think about confessing now, Charlton? Will you reconsider?'

'You'll do that to me bairns? To Cilla? Just to get at me?' Jamie's eyes glowered with hatred, his voice was choked.

'Oh, it's not about 'getting at you', Charlton. No, this is about getting at the truth; the truth about the Kirkley Hall burglary. You were convicted by a jury of your peers of your crime. You are guilty. All we need now is for you to tell us the details; was your wife there with you, or not?'

Clennell waited a moment for his words to sink in. Then he leaned forward.

'It's in your hands, Charlton. You have tonight to think about it. Tell us in the morning what really happened the night that Kirkley Hall was robbed. Otherwise we'll assume that Taylerson's account was correct – that your wife was your accomplice – and we'll arrest and charge her.'

Jamie did not sleep that night. His moods swung violently from raging fury to despair. He had thought that there was nothing left that the sods could do to him. How wrong he had been. He had been stripped of everything: his liberty, his pride, his reputation, his life and his family. Now he had only one thing left in the world – the shadow of doubt that hung over his conviction. Yet still the bastards came after him for that. Clennell, Aynsley, Lavender and Taylerson. Each one of them seemed hell-bent on trying to destroy him.

But what should he do?

He tried to weigh up the alternatives. Maybe, just maybe, this was an empty ploy? After all they hadn't moved against Cilla so far – and they'd had the best part of a year to arrest her. Should he risk it? But what if Clennell's threat was real? There was still plenty of time for them to arrest her and make her stand trial at the next assizes. They had moved on him pretty fast last August. If they did arrest her after he was gone, would he ever even hear about it?

For a brief moment he fantasised about Cilla and the bairns turning up in New South Wales and them all being reunited as a family on the other side of the world. Then he brought himself back to reality. They could be living in that vast continent for years before he found them. The picture that Clennell had painted in his mind tortured him. How many of the bairns would survive life in gaol and transportation across the world? He imagined finding only half his family alive and that half traumatised by brutality and rape – possibly even the lads. How could he live with their censure and blame?

Halfway through that interminable night, the gaoler, Simeon Hawkes, wound his way down the narrow passageway between the cages. His lantern flickered violently in the draught, illuminating the rotting piles of straw strewn across the flagstones. The other prisoners lay slumped in heaps in their cages. Only Jamie remained upright, staring moodily into the darkness.

Hawkes stopped before the entrance to Jamie's cage and held up the light.

Jamie blinked and nodded gruffly in the gaoler's direction. Hawkes was the most sympathetic of the turnkeys. William used him to send letters, food and money to Jamie.

'What are you going to do, Charlton?' he asked.

Jamie shook his head, mournfully. 'I can't believe that they are still coming after me and mine. Not after all this time. Why? What does it matter to them? They got their bloody conviction last year.'

'Ah, but it came at a price,' Hawkes said wisely.

'What do you mean?'

'That fuss the newspapers made – the subscription that was set up for you – it upset a lot of people. It was said that the duke himself flew into a mighty rage and demanded that they used the thumb screws on you to get you to confess.'

Jamie winced.

'The support you got after your trial was a solid gesture across the whole county. It told the authorities that no-one believed you were guilty. The magistrates, jury and judges at your trial lost face. They had all been sullied by that trial. This matters to likes of Clennell and the duke.'

He paused as another prisoner emitted a resonating snore from the next cell.

'Tell them what they want to hear, Charlton. That's my advice. You've got nothing to lose – you're ganning to Botany Bay whatever happens. And if you confess, you'll not only be saving your wife and bairns from gaol – you'll probably get to keep your thumbs as well…'

Jamie shivered and thought miserably about Cilla and the children. This was one last service that he could do for his family before he left them, he supposed. He could never undo the damage that he had done to their lives but he could stop it getting worse. Even though the gall would stick in his throat, he knew that Hawkes was right: he only had one choice. He would have to confess. As Hawkes started to move away, he called him back.

'Tell that bastard magistrate gadgie that I'll do want he wants. I'll sign a bloody confession and admit that I robbed Kirkley. There's one condition, mind. I want to see my family again before I go to Lunnen. They cannot deny me that.'

5th June 1811

Bad weather had delayed the sailing of the convict ship bound for London. As a result, the authorities delayed taking James Charlton's confession until the week of the Quarter Sessions when all the magistrates were in Morpeth.

The day before he was due to be transported, they came to take him over to the Black Bull to sign his confession. This was the first time he had been outside for nearly a year; the fresh air smelt strange and filled him with a rush of longing for his freedom. The brilliant sunlight blinded him. He had managed to get word to Will and Cilla, through the gaoler, Simeon Hawkes, that he could see them before he left. He thought he heard William shout his name as he shuffled over the cobbles. He blinked frantically but he could not make him out in the crowd.

He could hardly walk with the leg irons and half stumbled, half fell into the private room Clennell had organised for the confession.

It was crowded; there were over half a dozen men already in the room. He recoiled in horror and baulked at entering.

The bastard's turned me into a spectacle like a bloody side show at Stranghow Fair, he thought.

His resistance was futile. The gaolers shoved him inside and forced him down into a chair behind a table. To his right sat a clerk with a pile of parchment, inkwell and a quill. Thomas Clennell sat opposite. The magistrate looked grimly satisfied.

'Well, Charlton,' he said. 'I'm glad to hear that you have finally come to your senses and that you are prepared to confess to the robbery at Kirkley Hall before you leave. Not before time, mind you. You stirred up a lot of trouble with your stubborn refusal to admit to the burglary.'

Jamie sat in stony silence.

'As you can see, an occasion like this warrants the presence of all three of Northumberland's magistrates as witnesses. To your left is the Reverend Ekins and behind you is Sir Charles Lambert Monek. Everyone is here to bear witness to the fact that you gave this confession voluntarily before you left.'

Clennell paused, checked that the scowling prisoner before him was still listening and then glanced in dislike at the younger man who stood nervously behind Charlton with a quill twirling in his blackened fingers.

'The young man behind you is Mr. Mitchell, a reporter with the *Newcastle Courant.* As the *Courant* has taken such an active interest in your case,' Clennell continued ironically. 'We have summoned him here today. We thought it fitting that he should be here to witness the event, for the benefit of his readership – who have, of course, been totally misled by the *Courant* in their support of you and your family.'

Jamie made no effort to turn around and look at the man that Clennell was introducing but he was conscious of him shuffling uncomfortably from foot to foot. Another gadgie who doesn't want to be here, he thought.

'Your confession will be printed in full in this weekend's newspaper for the enlightenment of those misguided fools who supported you and just in case anyone misses this week's newspaper, a pamphlet will be printed containing your confession and distributed free of charge onto the streets of Newcastle.'

'So Charlton. The clerk here is ready to take down everything that you tell us. What have you got to say?'

An expectant hush fell on the room, the clerk picked up the quill but Jamie continued to sit in brooding silence.

'Come on, man!' Clennell snapped. 'We haven't got all day.'

'I'm thinking of what to say,' Jamie said. He was deeply uncomfortable with everyone in the room hanging on his every word. Half of him wanted to tell them all to bugger off.

'The truth, man! The truth!' the Reverent Ekins suggested.

'We shall start it off for you,' Clennell informed him.

'The confession of James Charlton respecting the Kirkley robbery... ' he dictated to the clerk.

The clerk dutifully began to scribble down his words. The nib of the quill rasped against the surface of the parchment. Jamie watched as the man worked. Suddenly he had an idea. 'I'll write it,' he said simply.

'You can write?' the Reverend Ekins queried.

Jamie threw him a thinly disguised look of anger. 'Yes, I can write,' he informed them sharply. 'And read.'

Clennell looked like he was about to refuse when the other magistrate, Sir Charles Monek, leaned over and intervened.

'It would be better to say that he not only voluntarily made the confession, but that he wrote it in his own hand. 'Twould carry more weight with the local community.'

And any man who can still hold a quill and parchment obviously still has his thumbs, Jamie thought, cynically.

Clennell nodded and agreed to Monek's suggestion. However, there was no way that the prisoner could handle the quill and parchment in his current condition; the confession would quickly become as filthy as Charlton himself and would be unreadable. Clennell called for a bowl of hot water and some soap.

When the water arrived Jamie found some pleasure in its warmth and the sweet smell of the soap. He washed the grime from his caked hands. The towel was black by the time he had finished. He would have liked to have slipped the remaining soap into his pocket but there were too many pairs of eyes watching his every move.

When he picked up the quill, Clennell dictated to him the first sentence but then he settled back in his chair to wait like the rest. Jamie was pleased. He had no desire to entertain these men with the story he was about to tell; they could sit in bored silence while he wrote. Writing his own confession gave him more chance to think. This had to be worded right.

'The confession of James Charlton respecting the Kirkley robery with perticlers of the circumstance on the evening of the third day of april 1809 to the best of my knowledge. After leving my work I had a desire to go to newhamedge to get a pot of beer to refresh my self...'

Clennell leaned over, read what he had written and snorted in pious disgust.

'...but on returning home sumthing struck my minde I had a desire to go to Kirkley hall and sumthing was so pressing upon my minde tho with all the resistance I cold make to the contrary I could not pas it by tho I had three times taking the other rode to go home and there was still sumthing prest upon me that at last I took the Kirkley rode...'

Let them think that Old Nick was in Kirkley that night, leading me into temptation, thought Jamie, half smiling. Folks always enjoyed the appearance – or the suggestion – of the devil in any story.

Clennell had seen the half smile that had lifted Jamie's blistered lips. He reached over and snatched the paper from him.

'Stop this procrastination, Charlton,' he snapped, 'and get to the point.'

'... On my coming to Kirkley I walked down by the south side of the hall and then returned back to the coal house and went over the roof of the storehouse and broke a paine in the window by which I entered the office. Having tinder flint and steel and a candle I struck a light and I then began to search the room after making a great deal of search I could find nothing but books, having found no money as I expected, but something turned ne round and led me to the place whear the money was, which was in a press in the office in a small box with a number of books over all I then removed the books and then took the money and came away and went to my own house...'

As Charlton continued to scratch away with the quill, the tension in the room visibly relaxed. The reporter from the *Newcastle Courant* settled himself down on a vacant chair. The noise from the crowded marketplace drifted into the room. Dark clouds were gathered in the distant sky. There would be a storm later when the heat broke; already Jamie could hear the distant rumble of thunder.

He struggled with what to write next.

Cilla. I have to mention Cilla and show that she was innocent in all this.

'...My wife woke when I came in and told me that I had stopt late I told her that it was but ten o'clock I then went to bed not saying

anything to my wife what I had been about Next morning I went to my work again and continued day after day till Friday night On Saturday morning I had a desire to go to Newcastle and I went by Kirkley and laid the parcel of money which was found later...'

It became easier now that he felt that he had removed Cilla from all blame and his thoughts began to drift towards his family, whom he hoped waited outside to see him. It was a good to think about them; it made this humiliation easier to bear.

He had never seen the new bairn of course, but he had heard that Baby Bella was a little trouper who had fought off all manner of dangerous childish ailments during the winter. It would be nice to get a picture of her face in his memory before he left.

Keep fighting, little one, he thought.

'...I cannot now remember the sumes of money which I kept except that there were several five pound notes but as to them I am not certain of the number...'

Young William had been just a chubby toddler when he had last seen him; a fat, healthy bairn with rosy cheeks, large startled eyes and a piece of bread and jam permanently clutched in his pink fist. He'd be four years old now and had probably lost some of his puppy fat.

Will he recognise me now? he wondered.

The twins were nearly seven. Mary was a pretty, sweet-natured girl. Hannah was a wild one. She had a stubborn, independent streak and preferred tearing around the countryside with gangs of lads rather than helping her mother and sister in the home.

Don't wear out your ma's patience, girls, he thought. Heed what she tells you and try not to cause her grief.

'...I think their was one pound thirteen shillings and sixpence in silver likewise one guinea and one half guinea three seven shilling peaces in gold...'

Unaccustomed to writing so much, he had to pause and rub his aching hand. Clennell leaned forward but then fell back disappointed into his chair when Jamie said: 'I ain't finished yet.'

As he picked up the quill again and dipped it in the ink, he thought of his eldest son. Ten year old Jack was the only one of his children to have really understood what had happened:

Don't hate me, lad, he thought sadly.

Jack. The apple of his eye. Jack – the lad with a golden eagle for a friend.

Be good to your ma; look after her, and the little ones. You will have to be the man in the family now, Jack…

'For God's sake Charlton, hurry up!' Clennell snapped. 'We haven't got all day to sit here.'

Jamie sighed and dipped the quill in the ink again.

'...the notes which I kept ...'

Now what should I say I did with the notes?

He grinned again as an idea came to him but he was careful to keep his head bowed over the parchment so that Clennell did not see.

'I put them in to a hole in the wall within the chimney in my own house which none of my family new aney thing about my putting it their, a short while after I had a minde to take it out again but to my great surprise I found it all brunt to mush so that I got not the least gud of it...'

That'll give them all something to laugh about, he mused to himself. If any bugger thinks I'm daft enough to stick paper money up a chimney, they don't know me. Our William will enjoy reading that. It won't take him long to realise that I'm lying.

He paused again for a moment and thought fondly about his brother. He had been a good friend and brother had Will – far better than he had deserved. Jamie felt wistful when his mind skimmed through the adventures they had shared as boys – and later as grown men. Those days were over now. No more poaching together in Ogle's rivers, chatting up the lasses at Ma Shotton's or brawling with the Aynsleys.

'Have you finished yet?'

'One more sentence,' he said.

'...this is all the account I can give about this business and I likewise declare that I had nobody along with me when I committed the robery...'

And that's for you, Cilla, my darling. Live long, hinny. Enjoy life and think of me fondly from time to time.

CHAPTER TWENTY-ONE

William had received a message from Simeon Hawkes telling him that Jamie was to be sent for transportation on the 6th June and his family could see him for the last time on the 5th. William was surprised by this apparent act of kindness; normally the prisoners were just shipped off without any chance of saying goodbye to their relatives. Although part of him dreaded saying farewell to his brother, he knew he could not let this opportunity pass. He sent a hurried note over to his mother, to let her know that he planned to come and that he would transport her, Cilla and the bairns in his wagon to Morpeth. Not for the first time he wished that Cilla could read and write.

Ann Charlton did not join them. She was too ill and upset; she told William that she had already resigned herself to the fact that her second son was lost to her. So he went to Cilla's cottage alone.

He arrived in Milburn to find all the children outside with large pile of carpet bags stacked against the garden fence. Everyone was busy trying to round up the chickens to pass onto a waiting neighbour. His arrival caused a temporary halt in the chase. The twins threw themselves into the arms of their favourite uncle, delighted to see him. Young Jack shook his hand, awkwardly. His shy, little namesake ran to hide behind his mother's skirts.

Cilla looked well. She had regained her figure since the birth of her last child and was dressed out in her best dark blue and green checked dress and matching blue bonnet. She also seemed relaxed and almost excited. She gave him a hug and laughed as he joined the children in the chase to catch the elusive hens.

Once the birds had been rounded up and paid for, she gave the baby to one of the twins and then took out a large iron key. She locked the door to the cottage and placed the key beneath a flowerpot.

'We're moving on,' she explained to a surprised William – who had never known them lock the door to that cottage.

'The rent is due again at the end of the week but I've decided that there is no point in dragging it out any longer. I've sold everything – even the beds – and we will go to the poorhouse tonight. It seemed the right time to go – what with Jamie leaving tomorrow. It'll be a new start for all of us. There's no point in putting off the inevitable any longer.'

Not exactly a very pleasant 'new start' for any of you, he thought as he lifted the children and their bags into the back of the wagon, but he was impressed with her cheerful attitude and courage.

'I hope that you've got your money stashed somewhere safe, Cilla,' he commented. 'They're a right load of thieves in that poorhouse, by all accounts.'

'Oh, your Ma's looking after most of it for me,' she told him. 'The rest is sewn into me undergarments.' She patted her bosom and winked at him. 'They'll have to strip me to find it,' she said.

She and Jack climbed up onto the seat beside William, and Mary handed up the baby. Cilla smelt good. The three younger children clambered into the back of the cart. They were all very chatty – apart from young Jack who sat moodily beside his mother.

The trees dripped were heavy with summer dew that morning. Wisps of mist still lay in the hazy bluebell strewn dells and low lying fields beside the road. It won't last for long, thought William. Above them the sun was breaking through the clouds and the day promised to be scorching hot.

As the wagon rolled on through the leafy lanes towards Morpeth, they exchanged news and gossip about the family. So far neither of them had mentioned Jamie.

'You look a bit thinner, Will, since last time I saw you,' she observed gently.

'Well you're looking a lot thinner, since last summer,' he grinned.

She slapped him playfully. 'Well, of course! I've had the bairn! I'm not one of these women that keep their fat after the bairns are born.'

A man and a woman in a dog cart drove towards them. William realised with a start that it was Sarah Robson and her husband. Sarah was holding a baby while he drove the cart.

William tensed with the awkwardness of the situation. He did not know what reaction to expect. The last time he had seen Sarah she had been spread out beneath him, half naked, on the table in that deserted farmhouse. He had a fancy that her husband knew that as well.

Both of them were dressed in the black clothes of mourning. They stared sombrely ahead as the two vehicles passed on the road. Neither of the Robsons acknowledged the Charltons and no one in the two vehicles spoke a word. As she passed he compared her to Jenny and he wondered what he had ever seen in that hard-faced, manipulative woman. He had no regrets.

Cilla was more interested in the baby in Sarah's arms. 'Why, that bairn even looks like you!' she quipped dryly, after they had passed.

'Cilla!'

'Well it's true what the gossips say, isn't it?' she grinned. 'You used to meet up secretly with Sarah Robson and you fathered their son, didn't you?'

'I'm saying nothing,' he retorted.

Cilla enjoyed his embarrassment and had no intention of letting him off the hook. ''Tis said that the old doctor has never been able to satisfy a woman – even his first wife. I'd love to know what they are saying to each other, right now – now that they've just seen you.'

'Seems to me, that you've turned into a right nosey old gossip yourself lass.'

'Well, we've got to have a little pleasure in life, haven't we? Talking about pleasure – have you met up with another lass, yet Will? We girls from Corbridge are the best looking in the world, of course. You must be spoilt for choice over there for a pretty lass to walk out with.'

'Maybe – maybe not…' he teased.

William was saved from further interrogation by the commotion which broke out behind them among the children. The eagle had been spotted. It circled the treetops high above them.

'Look, Ma!' shouted Hannah. 'The big bird's come to say 'goodbye' to us!'

William reined in for a moment and they all watched as the raptor wheeled and dived on the thermals above the treetops.

''Tis an omen,' said Cilla softly. ''Tis good luck for our future. Say 'goodbye' to the big bird, children,' she instructed them. The little ones waved dutifully and called out to the eagle.

Jack did not join in. He slouched miserably on the seat beside his mother. 'He's been following us for ages,' he said sharply. 'He's wondering where we are going. He won't understand why we have left.'

The anger in his voice and the strangeness of his comment made William glance down at his nephew. He remembered how emotional Jack had become when the eagle had appeared at Henry's wedding.

There is more to this than meets the eye, he thought. He resolved to speak to the lad later, to try and find out the meaning behind his words.

They arrived at Morpeth marketplace just in time to see Jamie dragged across to The Black Bull. William called out to him but Jamie didn't seem to hear him; he had trouble walking, his eyes squinted tight against the harsh sunlight.

He looked wretched. Cilla turned pale when she saw the state of him and the older children became distressed.

'What'll we do now?' she asked once Jamie and the gaolers had disappeared into the inn and she had calmed the children.

'Wait here,' he said. 'I'll try to find out what is happening.'

He walked over towards the inn and met one of the gaolers coming out. It was Simeon Hawkes. William was pleased; he had successfully slipped Hawkes several bribes during the last year in order to gain a few minutes' visit with his brother.

'Oh Will, it's you.'

William got the distinct impression that Hawkes wasn't pleased to see him. He avoided looking William in the eye.

'What's happening, man?' William asked quietly. 'I thought you said we were to be allowed to see our Jamie before he left.'

'You may be. You may not be…' the gaoler said awkwardly.

'Why has our Jamie been taken into the inn?'

'Them there magistrates wanted to see him – I cannot tell you why, so don't ask. This whole thing has got too much for me now.'

The magistrates? Clennell and the others? Why?

'What new devilry is this?' William demanded.

The gaoler ignored him and turned to go. Then suddenly Hawkes stopped and turned back. 'I'll tell you what, Will. If they don't let you see him today, I'm driving the prison wagon to the docks tomorrow. We'll take the Newcastle Road at first light – they don't sail till the afternoon tide.'

'So?'

'Meet us on the road and I'll let you have a few minutes with him – no funny stuff mind – I'll be armed.'

William smiled. 'I won't to try to set him free,' he said. 'I'm no gaol breaker.'

The man laughed shortly. 'You never know with you Charltons. Bloody bad uns – the lot of you. The gaolers at Hexham still talk about how that horde of Charlton reivers came to break Topping Charlton out of their gaol.'

William smiled. 'I know that old story. Those gaolers just turned and ran away. I think you're made of sterner stuff.'

Hawkes flushed at the compliment. 'Well, after all he's been through, I reckon your brother deserves to see his wife and bairns for one last time.'

When William returned to Cilla he found her alone with the baby. She looked sad.

'The other bairns wanted to go off and play – there didn't seem much point in stopping them,' she explained. 'I don't know when they'll next get a day out like this. I don't suppose they'll get much freedom at the poorhouse.'

They won't get much of anything, he thought sadly. Food, freedom or fun.

He led her across to a couple of empty ale barrels which lay abandoned in the shade of the tavern. From here, they could sit and watch the entrance to the public house. He had started to sweat with the heat and appreciated the shade. It became very close and humid; thunder rumbled ominously in the distance. Ignoring the curious stares of the passers-by, he told her what the gaoler had said.

'I have no idea what is going on,' he added. 'He wouldn't tell me.'

'I wonder if it's something to do with Michael Aynsley dying,' she murmured thoughtfully. 'You don't suppose Aynsley came over with remorse and confessed to the robbery on his deathbed, do you?'

'Aynsley is dead? When did this happen?'

'About three days ago,' she told him. 'I thought you might have heard?'

He shook his head. He heard no news up on his remote hilltop farm.

'He never recovered from that first seizure. He's spent most of the last year and a half dribbling like a bairn in a chair by his son's fireplace. I thought I'd tell our Jamie before he left – I thought it would please him to know Aynsley was dead, like.'

'Jamie won't be pleased to hear Aynsley died peacefully in his own home with his family around him,' William said grimly. 'I think Jamie would have preferred a far more violent end for Michael Aynsley than that.'

'Still, do you think Aynsley might have confessed to the robbery on his deathbed?'

'No,' William said smiling. 'We are not that lucky.'

He suddenly had a great sense that an era of his life was ending. Archie would be gone soon and with his brother's imminent departure and the death of Jamie's nemesis, the old steward, it was like arriving at the end of a section of a book. A whole new chapter of his life lay before him, a life which he would share with Jenny and their children on his own farm. Finally, the tentacles of Ponteland, which had repeatedly drawn him back into the murky depths of the parish, seemed to be falling away.

'It took me all winter to come to terms with what had happened to us,' Cilla said. 'I could not understand at first how God had been so cruel to me and Jamie.'

William settled down to listen; they had plenty of time by the look of it.

'The money which Mr. Humble gave us helped make the days more bearable but my nights were long, black and lonely, Will.'

'I can imagine it must have been difficult, Cilla,' he murmured.

'The bairns were sick, one after the other – with one ailment after another – I had to drag myself round to see to them all – especially this little one.' She nodded down at the contented and pretty dark-haired baby in her arms.

'There's many a time I thought I would lose her last winter; there's many a time I just wanted to curl up and die myself.'

She spoke calmly now but William did not doubt the depth of her despair.

'Then I started to realise something. Although God had taken Jamie away from us, he had given us Bella in exchange. He had sent us Mr. Humble and kept us all alive through the winter for a reason. I don't know what plans God has for us all in the future, Will. But we are all alive – and healthy – for another year. And whatever may happen in the future, I have much to be grateful for. I still have all my bairns to love and care for and they still have me.'

William smiled and, ignoring those around them, he put his arm around his sister-in-law and gave her a hug.

He knew and she knew that she would see very little of her children once they entered the poorhouse. She would be worked to the bone and the older children kept separately from her. More worryingly, he also knew that most of the parish whores were poorhouse women. He dreaded the thought of her whoring like her sister but part of him knew it would probably become inevitable.

'I think about Jamie, from time to time,' she told him. 'But not so often now.'

'The man I loved, the father of my bairns, was lost to us last summer. To be truthful, Will, I barely recognised the man they just dragged across the marketplace as my husband. You see, it really didn't matter whether he was hanged or transported – he was still lost to us.'

She paused for a moment and gently stroked the cheek of her sleeping child.

'It was hard coming to terms with the idea that he would never walk in the door of the cottage again, with that daft grin on his face. It was hard knowing that he would never throw his hat on the table, sweep the twins off their feet and throw them up into the air. It was hard realising that I would sleep in a cold, empty bed for the rest of my life.'

William sighed. He did not know what to say. She had distanced herself from the man who was still alive and was talking about him as if he was already dead. It was probably for the best that she could do that. He just wished he could.

'I try not to be downhearted, Will. I try to keep cheerful for the bairns.'

They sat in silence for a moment and then she said: 'Will, if that gaoler can be trusted, I think I'd rather say my 'goodbyes' to Jamie on the Newcastle Road tomorrow, rather than in front of all these Morpeth folks.'

'You know what, Cilla,' he replied, as yet another stranger threw them a knowing glance, 'I think I agree with you.'

The magistrates never had any intention of letting Jamie see his family.

As soon as the confession was signed and witnessed, Clennell ordered the guards to take him straight back to his cell in the gaol. He was to receive no visitors.

Jamie cursed and protested loudly and was beaten for his language and belligerent attitude.

Confused and upset, William and Cilla were forced to watch helplessly as the gaolers dragged a furious and bloodied Jamie back to the prison. They had no opportunity to speak to him. William tried to gain them admittance to the gaol but he was refused.

By now all the children had returned and had picked up on the despondent mood of the adults. They clamoured plaintively for food and started arguing with each other.

William had business to conduct in Morpeth but, seeing Cilla so dejected by this latest setback, he decided to stay and help.

'Right, who wants a picnic down by the river?'

'A picnic?' queried Cilla in surprise.

'Yes! Yes, Uncle Will!' shouted the bairns in unison.

‘We’ll have a picnic to remember,’ William said, ‘Jack and I will go and get some scran and then we’ll eat by the river and play games.’

‘I have brought some food, Will,’ Cilla said.

‘Oh we need a lot more for a party,’ he informed her frivolously.

He and Jack bought some hot pies, bread, cheese and a flagon of ale from the marketplace. They went down to the river bank where Cilla and the younger children waited on old coats spread out on the grass. The children fell on the food ravenously. It lifted all their spirits.

Now bursting with energy, the older ones began racing and chasing around them. William left Cilla to change and feed the baby while he joined in their games. The children shrieked with laughter as he caught them and tossed them in the air and then joined them in rolling down the grassy bank. Away from the prying eyes of the townsfolk, he felt relaxed and happy. He should have been on his way back to Corbridge by now but he didn’t care.

He took the bairns to the bridge and they threw sticks into the river. They rushed from one side of the bridge to another as their ‘boats’ bobbed erratically along the dark, bubbling surface of the water. They were so absorbed with their game, they did not realise the sky had darkened overhead.

Suddenly the thunder broke deafeningly above them and the first huge spots of rain dashed down upon their heads. The children squealed.

‘Quick! The church!’ William yelled. Shrieking and laughing, they scrambled to pack up their things and rushed towards the gloomy coolness of the nearby church. William tossed his namesake onto his shoulders and grabbed a twin in each hand. They all tumbled through the door of the church, drenched but grinning. The bairns began to play hide and seek amongst the pews, while he and Cilla stood in the porch and watched the lightning flash overhead. William could feel the air freshening around them as the humidity was dispelled. He welcomed it.

‘When this finishes,’ he told her, ‘you and the bairns can go back to the wagon and wait for me, while I sort out a bit of business. Then we’ll go down the Newcastle Road and make camp for the night.’

‘We’re going to sleep out?’ she asked, surprised.

‘Well, unless you’d prefer our John’s grudging and pious hospitality at North Carter Moor? I can’t think of anything better now that you’ve given up your cottage and sold all the beds. It’ll be a clear, warm night after this storm has passed. The ground will dry quickly.'

'It'll be fun for the bairns,' she said.

'It'll be fun for me too,' he added. 'I can't remember the last time I slept beneath the stars – although I've no doubt our Jamie was beside me at the time.'

They found a quiet spot on a bend in the road a couple of miles outside of Morpeth, close to a stream. Apart from the odd stagecoach rumbling past, William did not think they would be bothered by much traffic and they were too close to the town to be pestered by highwaymen and thieves – not that they had anything for anyone to steal.

With Jack's help, William unhitched the horse and settled it down for the night. They scoured the wood for dry tinder and then lit a fire. Cilla produced an old pan and a couple of chipped cups out of her luggage. The twins fetched water from the stream and Cilla boiled it for tea. They all settled down around the fire to eat the food that was left over from earlier in the day. Cilla took off her bonnet and let down her hair. It bounced down to her waist in waves of gleaming copper.

The children were tired now. As the daylight faded, they sat sleepily around the crackling fire and listened to Uncle William's stories. He told them about the strange and wonderful animals he had worked with on farms. But their favourite stories were about the wild pranks he used to get up to with their Jamie on the moors around North Carter Moor when they were young lads. The baby, young William and Mary were soon fast asleep. Jack continued to listen silently, while Hannah yawned and pestered him with questions.

They laid out the tarpaulin from the cart onto the ground beneath it. Then they lifted the sleeping bairns and laid them a row, like meat sausages on a griddle, beneath the shelter of the wagon. It was a warm night and they all slept in their clothes. Eventually even a reluctant Hannah was settled down next to her brothers and sisters and was lulled to sleep.

William lit his pipe and sat thoughtfully beside the fire. It was wonderfully peaceful. In the distance he heard a fox bark. Closer by was the gentle hooting of owls and the occasional flutter of bat wings. The stars erupted overhead like diamonds in the black velvet sky.

Her children settled, Cilla appeared out of the gloom. She slid down onto the ground beside him. He had assumed that she would sleep with the bairns and her sudden appearance beside made him shift uncomfortably.

'Thank you, Will,' she said simply. 'Thank you for everything. Thank you for today. Thank you for always being there for us and thank you for everything you have done for our Jamie.'

'It's nothing, hinny,' he said quietly.

'I need to ask you for a couple more favours like,' she murmured huskily.

'Oh yes, woman?' he said, slightly worried. 'What are you wanting now?'

'I want to ask you to take our Jack with you back to Thorn Tree. Give him a home and get him to help you on the farm – carry on with his education, if you can. You've been as much a father to him as our Jamie has over the last two years – and Jack worships you.'

'I don't know about that last bit,' he said, embarrassed. 'But we could do with his help on the farm – he's always been good with animals. In fact, I intended to suggest it in the morning – but I didn't know how you felt about being separated from your firstborn son?'

'They will all leave me someday,' she sighed softly. 'Are you sure Archie won't mind?'

Archie would not care. They rarely spoke these days except about the details of the sale of the farm to William. A few more months and Archie would be gone. Jenny Milburn might be surprised at the sudden appearance of his nephew at Thorn Tree Farm but he knew that eventually she would come to love the lad as much as he did.

'I need to ask you another favour,' Cilla continued.

Again he went rigid – with alarm.

'I want you to tell me about that Jenny you've been courting,' she smiled. 'I've heard she's a bonny lass.'

He exhaled with relief and smiled into the darkness. So much for his 'private' life. If Cilla knew, then no doubt so did his mother and most of Ponteland. He told her the story of how Archie had been rejected and how old Josh Milburn had offered him a dowry to marry Jenny. Then he told her of the growing love he felt for Jenny and how he felt a warm glow of satisfaction every time he thought about his future wife and their life together.

'This has worked out well,' Cilla commented with satisfaction. 'Jamie would have loved that story; how you had been offered money to marry Josh Milburn's pretty daughter.'

‘He would have ribbed me for years,’ smiled Will. They both fell silent and William realised that they were talking about Jamie in the past tense again. The man still breathed and walked on God’s earth, but he was lost to them both forever.

‘Do they have the same stars and the same moon on the other side of the world?’ Cilla asked.

He looked up at the gleaming moon and the myriad of stars pricked out in the blackness above them.

‘I’m not sure about the stars but it’s the same moon. Why?’

‘When I see Jamie tomorrow, I shall tell him to look up at the moon in New South Wales and think of me. I shall do the same for him over here.’

CHAPTER TWENTY-TWO

6th June 1811

Tom Philips shivered as he crouched uncomfortably in the dark of a shallow pit beside the riverbank and he cursed his foolishness in letting the turnpike keeper talk him into this mad scheme. His muscles ached, his body was damp from the loamy soil, the pungent smell of wild garlic made him feel nauseous and he was starving. On top of this, it had now started to drizzle. He glanced up through the lattice cover of woven twigs and branches above his head where the rain dripped through. As he did so, he caught sight of the gleaming silver scales of the salmon they had poached the night before for bait. It glistened in the first, drizzly rays of dawn.

Bugger the bloody eagle, he thought. I'd like that for me breakfast.

Beside him on the sodden ground was the cage that he and Rob Wilson had made for the bird. Wilson took up most of the room in the pit. He was sprawled out asleep and softly snoring. Philips envied the man's ability to nod off in such an uncomfortable position and resented his presence at the same time. It was only his appalling poverty and the fear of the ex-soldier's brutal anger which stopped Philips sliding silently out of the pit, taking the fish and disappearing back home. This was the third night they had waited for the raptor to take the bait and he was sick of it. They had used a dead rabbit as bait on the first night but some bloody fox had sneaked along and whisked it away.

Casual farm work had become more and more difficult to find in these parts. The duke's reward – now raised to twenty-five guineas – for the capture of the golden eagle tantalised men like him. Last winter his elderly mother had taken a fever and developed a hacking cough. Philips had pawned the pocket watch sold to him by Jamie Charlton, to pay for medicines. It had worked that time; his mother had survived. Now they were slowly starving to death.

Wilson had spent some time in America as a young soldier with the duke's 5th Foot Regiment of the Northumberland Fusiliers. He claimed he had learnt this trick of catching eagles from the savages over there. He'd told Tom they used the tail feathers of the birds to decorate their headdresses. So four days ago he had come along with Wilson and dug the five foot wide pit while the older man weaved together the foliage which made up the cover. That first night he had been hopeful – until the fox had stolen the bait. Now as he sank into the wet mud left by yesterday's downpour, he was despondent. He was convinced he had wasted his time.

Dawn crept slowly through the lattice of greenery above his head. Suddenly the light dimmed as a shadow floated across the sky above. Philips heard rustling and glanced up. He could just see the golden brown head of the eagle as it walked towards the edge of the pit.

Unable to believe his luck and alarmed at the sheer size of the bird, he nudged Wilson, who woke immediately. Phillips gestured upwards. The ex-soldier silently twisted himself into a crouching position.

The raptor came up on the edge of the pit, quite to its edge, and appeared to be studying the dead fish.

Neither man moved. Philips swore he could hear the beating of his own heart as they waited for the bird to come into range of their hands. One false move and it would flee.

Suddenly, Wilson raised his hands and thrust them forward through the canopy and seized the eagle's legs. The flimsy cover crashed down around them in a shower of twigs and leaves as he started to drag it down into the pit.

The startled bird spread its wings and tried to soar away but Wilson had a firm grasp on the raptor's legs. The eagle swiped its wing and broke his nose. Wilson swore but held on.

Next, the raptor swooped with its razor-sharp beak to slash the hands which restrained it, but in the last second the bird diverted its attack onto the terrified white face of Tom Philips which peered up at him from the pit. It gouged a huge chunk out his face, narrowly missing his eye. Blood poured. Philips screamed. He rolled away, clutching his head.

Now Wilson struggled alone with the mighty bird. His muscles bulged as he hauled the creature down towards the cage. Using his foot, he viciously pushed the body of the bird towards the open door. With one final savage kick, the raptor and its flailing wings were squashed into the cage and the door slammed shut. Sweat poured from Wilson's contorted face and mingled with the blood from his broken nose.

The eagle began to quiver and pant. Wilson fell back against the slimy wall of the pit, swearing. Meanwhile, Tom Philips clutched at the gaping flesh of his shredded face and sobbed like a baby.

It was the drizzle falling softly on his face which woke William.

For a split second he couldn't remember where he was and why. Then a searing pain in his stiff back reminded him that he had spent the night out in the open, sleeping on the hard ground.

I'm getting too old for this, he thought.

Cilla was already up, wrapped in her shawl against the weather and feeding the baby under a nearby tree. She smiled across to him. The other children stirred beneath the cart. He sat up groggily and tried to gauge what time it was. If the prison wagon left Morpeth at first light, then they probably wouldn't have long before it got here.

Good. Let's get it over with.

He took himself down to the stream, relieved himself and splashed ice-cold water onto his face.

In the cold light of a grey, drizzly dawn, things looked very different.

Yesterday he had felt exhilarated with the excitement of having a day – and a night – away from the grinding drudge of his life at Thorn Tree Farm.

This morning he couldn't wait to get back.

After Cilla had returned to sleep with the bairns beneath the wagon, he had lain awake for hours, his mind in turmoil. Over and over again he tried to think of ways to help them. But it was hopeless: he could not support them all at Thorn Tree Farm.

Old Josh's words came back to him: 'put yourself first for once.'

The old man was right. No matter how much William loved them, Cilla and her bairns were, and always had been, Jamie's responsibility – not his. Jamie had let down his family and it was not his place to try and pick up the pieces. They were destined for the poorhouse and he was destined to marry Jenny Milburn. Their lives was set on a path which he could not – would not – alter.

Suddenly, he became aware of a commotion over at the road.

A strange sight met his eyes. Rob Wilson and Tom Philips were walking towards Morpeth carrying a heavy contraption between them. Both men looked bloodied and ragged. Philips' face was tied up in his blood-stained shirt. They had long poles slung over their shoulders and suspended on these poles was a large, wooden cage. At first he William could not see what type of creature they carried, but when he did his blood froze. It was that damned eagle.

Jack.

It was too late. The boy had already seen their captive. Jack scooped up a handful of stones and ran towards the men, screaming abuse at the top of his voice.

'Let him go, you bastards! Let him go! You cannot take him!'

The rocks showered down onto the heads of the startled men. The cage crashed to the ground. Wilson and Philips threw up their arms to protect themselves from the onslaught.

'He's the 'lucky bird', for Christ's sake! You cannot take him away to a cage, you greedy buggers!'

Now the other children ran up screaming. Hannah stooped to gather stones as she ran. Rob Wilson moved menacingly towards Jack. 'Stop it! You little sod!' he yelled, as he whipped off his belt.

He grabbed hold of Jack and swung him round by his ear. Jack screamed louder and lashed out at the ex-soldier with his fists and his feet, but he was no match for the burly man. The other children screamed in horror as Wilson raised his belt.

William got there just in time.

He grabbed Wilson's arm and the two men became locked in a furious battle of strength. Jack broke away and William forced himself between the boy and Wilson.

'Enough!' he yelled angrily at the top of his voice.

The sound of their beloved uncle shouting finally silenced the screaming children. They froze to the spot. For a moment, no-one spoke and no-one moved.

'Enough,' William said again, quieter this time. 'He's just a lad, Wilson – and he's fond of the bird. Let him be.'

Rob Wilson glared furiously at William. 'He'd better not cross my path again or I'll thrash the living daylights out of him,' he growled angrily.

'He won't.'

Wilson glanced around at their camp and an ugly smirk distorted his face when he saw the frightened Cilla, standing a few paces behind William. 'Stepping into your brother's shoes, are you Charlton? Taken up with his wife, have you?' he leered.

'We are waiting to say goodbye to our Jamie,' William said quietly. 'He's been sent for transportation today. The prison wagon will be here soon.'

'Aye, I'm sure you are,' Wilson snarled. He turned away, picked up the poles and slung them back over his shoulders. The side of his head dribbled with blood where one of Jack's rocks had found its mark. The two men slunk away; their captive swaying silently between them in its cage.

Young Jack was inconsolable. Distressed and confused by their older brother's grief, the younger ones ran crying back to their mother. Jack sobbed and ranted incoherently in William's arms. 'It's all lost. We're all lost now.'

William held him and said nothing. There would be plenty of time to talk to the lad during the long drive back to Corbridge.

Suddenly, the prison wagon rumbled around the bend in the road.

'Quick, Jack,' William said. 'It's your da. Pull yourself together lad. Don't let him see you like this.'

The young boy wiped his sleeve across his tear-streaked face and steeled himself for his last conversation with his father.

The prison wagon was a large metal cage on top of a wooden cart. It was open at the top to the elements. Behind the bars were slumped three or four dejected wretches in chains, already soaked to the skin from the drizzle. Beneath the grime every one of them was pasty white with lack of sunlight.

As the cart passed Wilson and Philips with their strange load, Jamie glanced out of the bars. He was riveted by the bloodied and gashed face of his old friend, Tom Philips, who had betrayed him in court in the forlorn hope of claiming the reward money. Jamie worked out what happened immediately. A wound like that would fester and kill the man. He felt no pity. The eagle had got revenge for both of them.

Jamie and the eagle stared at each other through the bars of their cages. Neither blinked as the cold golden eyes of the raptor met ice-blue eyes of Jamie Charlton.

They've hunted for both of us for years, he thought. Now we're both captives, being transported along the same road.

True to his word, Simeon Hawkes reined in the horses and pulled over when he saw William, Cilla and the children.

William walked towards the head of the horses and paused to have a brief word or two with the gaoler. Cilla and the bairns moved quickly down the side of the cart towards where Jamie already reached out his manacled hands towards them. The gaoler pocketed the coins.

William fished out a handful of coins from his pocket and gave them to Hawkes.

'Thanks for this,' he said. 'We're grateful.'

'We haven't got long, mind.'

William nodded.

'Like I said before, the man deserves the chance to say goodbye after all he's been through,' said Hawkes.

'You think he's innocent then?' William asked. He didn't really care, but felt he ought to make a bit of conversation while Cilla and the bairns said their farewells to Jamie. He watched Cilla lift the younger children up to the bars of the cage to kiss their father. She had started to cry. So much for her attempts to distance herself from her feelings about her husband.

The gaoler laughed. 'Well, I did think he were wronged, like, but now he's gone and confessed to the robbery, I realise that he might have had me fooled as well as the next man.'

William was horrified. 'He's confessed to the bloody robbery?' he gasped in disbelief.

'Aye, yesterday. That were why we had to take him to The Black Bull – so he could write out his confession in front of them magistrates.'

William's mind reeled. *After all this time – over two years – the stupid bugger had gone and confessed?*

'Why?' he gasped.

But Hawkes would not be drawn to say more.

William's mind still struggled to grasp the full implication of what he had just heard. Was it possible? Had the daft bugger robbed Kirkley Hall after all?

Did this mean they'd come after him for perjuring himself at Jamie's trial? Could they prove that? What about John and his mother up at North Carter Moor and all the other poor sods who had supported Jamie over the last two years? What would happen to them now?

He felt an overwhelming desire to get home. Rob Wilson's leering comments had already unsettled him; now he felt uneasy and threatened. But first he had to say goodbye to his wretch of a brother. A tearful Cilla beckoned him to join them.

'Will! Will!' yelled Jamie as he approached. 'Cilla's just told me that Aynsley is dead!'

Aynsley. Always Aynsley. Always his bloody obsession with Aynsley.

'Aye,' he replied quietly. 'The parish has got rid of both you troublesome bastards in the same week.'

Jamie thought he was joking and his parched mouth cracked open into a grin. The stench from the prisoners was nauseating – even out here in the open.

'They say that New South Wales is hot – but I bet it's a lot hotter where that old devil has gone! May he rot in hell!'

William was silent. Wave after wave of conflicting emotions washed over him. He wanted to throttle his brother with one hand – and yank him out of that prison wagon with the other. This wasn't right; Jamie should not be in there. He reached out. With a rattle of chains, Jamie grabbed his hand in his own bony claw and clutched it hard.

'You take care of yourself over in the wilds of Corbridge,' Jamie told him. 'Watch out for them women – they're a wild bunch.'

Cilla made a strangled noise beside him; he could not tell if it was a sob or a laugh. He felt his anger subsiding.

'You take care of yourself,' William said awkwardly. A lump rose in his throat. 'Keep yourself alive and try to write us a letter now and then to let us know how you're getting along.'

'Now, where am I going to get a quill and ink in New South Wales?' Jamie asked, amused.

'Steal it,' William advised. 'But don't get caught this time.'

Jamie laughed and pulled him closer to the bars of the cage. 'You've been the best brother a man could ever have, Will – and I mean that. Without your help in court I would have been condemned the first time I was arrested. You gave me another year with my family, another year of my life, and I thank you for that.'

William could barely speak. He was close to womanish tears. 'So why did you do it?'

'What?'

'Confess.'

'I had to. They threatened to come after Cilla. They said they were going to charge her with being an accomplice.'

For a moment, William was confused. Then Taylerson's words came flooding back to him: *'He said his next door neighbour and his wife, Priscilla, were with him.'*

It all made sense now. Jamie would do anything for Cilla and hang the consequences. The last of his anger subsided. He understood. His unpredictable brother had always been constant in his love for his family.

'I've one last favour to ask.'

'Oh, yes?' William smiled sadly. 'If it's to break you out, Jamie, I'm afraid the gaoler is armed and I'm not.'

Jamie never laughed. His face was deadly serious.

'Cilla says that you're taking our Jack back up to your farm at Corbridge?'

He nodded.

'I'd like you to take them all. Cilla and the little ones as well. Take her as your wife, Will – with my blessing. I've always known that you fancied her. For God's sake you only got involved with that red-headed Sarah Aynsley because she looked a bit like Cilla. Well now's your chance; take her as your own.'

William froze. He felt Cilla stiffen beside him.

'I can't, man. There's another lass…'

Disappointment flashed across Jamie's face. He let go of William's hand and shifted sulkily back inside the cage.

'Well, that's that then,' he said bitterly. 'They're condemned to the poorhouse.' His face was as hard as his voice.

Suddenly the creaking wagon lurched forward and the children wailed and clamoured to be lifted up to kiss their father again. For a moment, William stood silently amidst the outpouring of emotion around him.

As the vehicle began to rumble away, his brain kicked back into life. He began to jog alongside the cart. Cilla and the bairns ran with him, stumbling, crying, clawing at the side of the wagon, desperate to prolong their last moments with Jamie.

'Did you do it?' he yelled.

'Do what?'

'The robbery at Kirkley Hall. For once and for all, Jamie – tell me the truth!'

The driver spurred on the horses and he struggled to keep up. Cilla and the children fell behind and collapsed, sobbing, onto the ground. The swaying wagon sped away from him with a clatter of hooves.

'Did you rob Kirkley Hall, or didn't you?' he roared.

As the driver whipped the horses into a gallop, he heard his brother's voice for the last time:

'Does it really matter now?'

Author Notes and Acknowledgements

During the five years it took us to research the story of Jamie Charlton and his Regency miscarriage of justice, my late husband, Chris, and I were bowled over by the kindness of all the people, mostly strangers, who went out of their way to help us. I especially need to pay tribute to Harry Coxon at this point – a man whom I have never met. Harry responded to a query of mine on a genealogical message board back in 2004. It was Harry who first gave me the startling news that my husband's ancestor was a convicted felon, sentenced to transportation to New South Wales. That one short Internet post from Harry sent Chris and I on a fascinating journey of discovery which eventually resulted in this novel. Thank you, Harry Coxon.

Many other people have also gone out of their way to help us gather up the remaining information about this two hundred year old mystery. These include: Karen Benoy (nee Charlton), the late George Bell and John Turner of the Ponteland Historical Society. Karen fished out the original court case records for us from The National Archives. George, a professional genealogist, was also investigating the fate of dodgy Geordie criminals and he helped us solve the mystery of what ultimately happened to James Charlton. The information provided by John Turner was invaluable for filling in the gaps and he alerted us to the fascinating story of the subscription which the indignant folks of Newcastle set up to help James Charlton and his family. John also provided us the photograph of the original Kirkley Hall which sadly burnt down in the 1930s. This Victorian photograph was turned into my book cover by the very clever David Harland at *Q Design* in Middlesbrough.

Without the unswerving support and encouragement of two of my friends, Zena Breckner and Sam Blain (Cultural Attaché for Boosbeck), this novel would never have been finished. Both volunteered to read it, chapter by chapter and gave me invaluable feedback and help. They nagged me, criticised me and encouraged me in the way that only good friends can. Very often I forced myself to sit down at the computer and get on with it only because I knew they were waiting for the next instalment. More often than not, it was their praise which motivated me to run back into the study and write some more.

I also need to thank Jill Boulton who shared her experience and skill as a professional editor and journalist. Jill has been an invaluable help with the marketing of this novel. I would also like to thank Redcar Writer's Group and my brother, Matthew James – who were subjected to an earlier version of *Catching the Eagle* – and my many friends on redcar.forumotion who supported and encouraged me every step of the way.

But I owe the biggest thanks and the most grateful acknowledgement to my late husband, Chris, who was always supportive. He was with me every step of the way through those years of research. It can't have been easy to be married to a writer. It must have been quite lonely at times when I disappeared into the study to write, night after night, month after endless month. Without Chris' unerring love and support, I could never have written this book. He quietly enjoyed my success and I know he was proud of me when the book was first published. I know that it meant a lot to him that we were able to tell the world the truth about his much-maligned four times great-grandfather. *Catching the Eagle* is also part of his legacy to his children; they now have a printed history all of their own.

If you would like to know more about how Chris and I stumbled across our Regency convict and researched his sorry tale of injustice, then please check out my non-fiction genealogy book: *Seeking Our Eagle.* This is the non-fiction companion to *Catching the Eagle.* I am currently researching and writing the second part of Jamie Charlton's story, which follows his life after he was transported.

For anyone interested in the further adventures of that Regency crime-fighting duo, Detective Stephen Lavender and Constable Woods, there is a new series of novels called: *The Detective Lavender Mysteries.* Their first case takes them back to Northumberland to investigate the strange disappearance of a beautiful heiress from her locked bedchamber: *The Heiress of Linn Hagh.* The first chapter is reproduced at the end of this book for your enjoyment.

Finally, to you the reader. Thank you for reading my book. I hope you enjoyed it – and if you did, please take a moment to leave me a review at your favourite retailer.

Best wishes,
Karen Charlton,
Marske-by-the Sea, North Yorkshire.
20th May 2014

Also by Karen Charlton
SEEKING OUR EAGLE

Seeking Our Eagle is the perfect, non-fiction companion piece for Karen Charlton's historical novel, *Catching the Eagle.* It is in itself a remarkable story. Written with honesty and humour, this factual book shows how the Charltons shook their family tree until a Regency convict fell out.

Seeking Our Eagle takes us on a fascinating journey back through three hundred years and the turbulent lives of seven generations of their family. Illustrated with poignant photographs, it shows how the Charltons first became interested in genealogy and gradually uncovered their history. The author reveals how she eventually stumbled across the Northumbrian skeleton in their closet, researched his sorry tale of injustice and turned it into a novel.

Illuminating the importance of family in all our lives, *Seeking Our Eagle* is an entertaining and informative read for anyone interested in genealogical research or social history, and for those writing historical fiction.

REVIEW

SEEKING OUR EAGLE

Family Tree genealogy magazine - April 2013

Karen Charlton has such a great response to her debut novel, 'Catching the Eagle', about her husband's ancestor Jamie Charlton, who, after some historical detective work, they came to believe was wrongly convicted of burglary in 1809, that she has penned this delightful 'how we did it'. Here she details her family history and creative writing journey that led to the publication of her novel...

...In this funny, honest account of how she and husband Chris came to breathe new life into Jamie's story and clear his name, Karen reveals the trials and tribulations of her quest, visiting graveyards and farmsteads with amazingly well-behaved young children in tow! Her methodology is laid bare as she reveals how her fictionalised family story was finally accepted for publication.

A refreshing insight into the writing process for wannabe family history authors, readers entertaining similar aspirations can learn much from Karen's experiences.

Karen Clare, *Family Tree* magazine - April 2013

Seeking Our Eagle is available on Amazon and from other reputable retailers.

Also by Karen Charlton

THE HEIRESS OF LINN HAGH

The First Detective Lavender Mystery

Northumberland, 1809: A beautiful young heiress disappears from her locked bedchamber at Linn Hagh.

The local constables are baffled and the townsfolk cry 'witchcraft'.

The heiress's uncle summons help from Detective Lavender and his assistant, Constable Woods, who face one of their most challenging cases: The servants and local gypsies aren't talking; Helen's siblings are uncooperative; and the sullen local farmers are about to take the law into their own hands.

Lavender and Woods find themselves trapped in the middle of a simmering feud as they uncover a world of family secrets, intrigue and deception in their search for the missing heiress.

Taut, wry and delightful, *The Heiress of Linn Hagh* is a rollicking tale featuring Lavender and Woods—a double act worthy of Holmes and Watson.

The Heiress of Linn Hagh is the first in a series of Regency mysteries featuring Detective Stephen Lavender and Constable Edward Woods.

'Worthy of Agatha Christie' – www.crimefictionlover.com

'Fabulous, rollicking tale of intrigue and family secrets' – B.A. Morton, author of *Mrs. Jones, Molly Brown, Wildewood & Bedlam*

'Atmospheric mystery' – Cathy G. Cole. *Kittling Books*
'A romp of a whodunit' – Moonyeen Blakey. Author of *The Assassin's Wife.*

Published by Thomas & mercer, *The Heiress of Linn Hagh* is available from Amazon in paperback, audiobook and eBook formats.

THE HEIRESS OF LINN HAGH
Chapter One

London - October, 1809

The two-wheeled hackney carriage sped down Mile End Road towards Whitechapel, weaving in and out of more sedate vehicles, farm carts and barrow boys. It churned up the stinking waste and sprayed the startled pedestrians.

Beneath the hackney's black hood, a dark-suited man gripped his walking cane and braced himself as the carriage lurched violently from side to side. His sharp eyes scanned the crowds, seeking out familiar faces.

A never-ending tide of soot-blackened shops, brothels, dilapidated taverns and coffee houses flowed past the carriage as it raced through the crowded streets. The man caught glimpses of shadowy figures lurking in the gloom of dank alleys between the buildings. The cries of the street vendors mingled with those of the drunks, rearing horses and the constant rumble of wheels and clatter of hooves over the cobbles. For the man in the hackney carriage, it was noisy, drunken and out of control.

It's good to be back, Detective Lavender decided.

When they slowed for the Whitechapel tollgate, he caught a familiar flash of scarlet. He rapped on the hood above him with his cane.

'Driver, stop here.'

In the centre of a ragged crowd of onlookers were two members of the Bow Street Horse Patrol. Instantly recognisable in their blue greatcoats and scarlet waistcoats, they had dismounted from their horses. One of them was Constable Woods. The officers circled a curvaceous and extremely drunk young woman, who appeared to be on the point of passing out. Lavender climbed down from the hackney and watched the developing scene from the edge of the crowd.

Suddenly, the woman's legs buckled beneath her, and she lurched towards the older, stockily built man. Constable Woods caught hold of her beneath her stained armpits and broke her fall.

Now on her knees, she flopped forwards and vomited down his breeches.

'Gawd's teeth!' he exclaimed. 'The doxy's gone and spewed down the leg of me damned boot.'

The crowd roared with laughter.

Woods frowned, lowered the limp woman onto the ground and whisked out his handkerchief to wipe his uniform. He glanced up sharply at his companion, who hovered nervously above the prostrate female.

'Get on with it, Officer Brown—search her—you know what you're looking for.'

The younger man dropped down onto one knee and tugged at the drawstring of the faded reticule, which was half-trapped beneath her body. She let out a great snore before obligingly rolling away into the pool of her own vomit. Her skirts were halfway up her legs, revealing the gaping holes in her stockings and the flapping sole of her boot. Officer Brown retrieved the tatty cloth bag, yanked it open and held up six shillings, a few pennies and a half crown piece.

'It's not here, Constable Woods,' he said. 'I think the strumpet has already drunk it away.'

''Tis not very likely in a mere two days,' Woods barked. 'I said search *her*—not fool around with her purse, you saphead.'

The crowd laughed again, and some wag made a wisecrack about how the red, beaded bag matched the young officer's pimply complexion.

It was at this point that the man from the hackney carriage stepped forward and joined his colleagues.

'Is there anything I can do to help, Constable Woods?' he asked. The bemused spectators regarded him curiously. One or two of them started with alarm and scurried away, but few in the mob recognised him these days.

Woods beamed in delight.

'Detective Lavender!' He shook his hand vigorously. 'Well met, sir! It's been too long.'

'I agree. So, what do we have here?'

'We have been searching for this thieving trollop since yesterday.' Woods sighed. 'It's claimed she stole money from a rich merchant a few nights ago—while he slept in a bed in a bawdy house . . .'

'I think I know where the money is, sir!' the young officer interrupted, from his position on the ground. 'I heard the paper rustle when she moved.'

'Where, lad? Where?'

Constable Brown pointed nervously to the woman's ample breasts. 'I believe it's down there—between her habit shirt and the bosom of her gown.'

'Well, get it!'

The young man blushed. His hand trembled above the two wobbling mounds of female flesh and the gaping cleavage.

'Go on, son!' someone jeered in the crowd. 'Give her a good fumble!'

There were howls of laughter.

'Oh, for Gawd's sake!' Woods snapped. He stepped forward, stooped low and thrust his hand down the bodice of the unconscious girl. He had a good rummage around.

The crowd loved it.

'Whayy!'

'Try the other end!'

'Don't forget her placket!'

'I'm glad to see that you've not lost your touch with the ladies.' Lavender grinned.

Undeterred by the irony of his colleague or the raucous leering of the mob, Woods' ruddy face was a picture of studied concentration.

When he finally pulled back his hand from the woman's stained underclothes, he held up a crisp one hundred pound banknote. The crowd around Lavender emitted a sharp collective intake of breath, and the laughter subsided.

'That lush will get more than a whippin' fer being drunk and disorderly,' Lavender heard someone whisper.

'Is the rest not there?' Disappointment flashed across Officer Brown's face.

'No. The trollop must have given it over to someone else fer safe keepin' .' Woods straightened up. 'Never mind—if the numbers match those retrieved from the bank, then this should be enough to convict her. Let's get her back to Bow Street.'

The problem of how to transport the inebriated thief now made the constables pause. Lavender knew that normally they would have clapped her in irons and made her trot behind the horses.

'If I sling her over the front of me horse, she'll probably slide off and crack open her skull on the cobbles,' Woods commented.

'Perhaps I can be of assistance,' Lavender volunteered. 'I've a hackney carriage standing by, and I'm on my way to Bow Street myself. Place her in the foot well. Woods, tie up your horse at the back of the carriage, and travel with me—there's a thing or two I want to discuss with you.'

Woods nodded, lifted the woman and carried her towards the hackney.

'Cor! She don't half reek,' he complained, his broad nose wrinkled in disgust.

Woods had no difficulty with carrying the woman. He was as strong and as agile as a twenty-year-old. His large build and great strength were fed by a legendary appetite. Woods did have a bit of trouble manoeuvring the woman's dead weight to fit her into the tight space on the floor of the carriage, but he succeeded in the end.

The trollop didn't get any more attractive on closer acquaintance, Lavender decided. Her hair was dishevelled and matted at the back like a bird's nest.

Woods clambered into the vehicle beside the detective, and the hackney swayed alarmingly with the extra weight. Lavender was squashed on the shallow seat, but despite this he was glad of Woods' company. He enjoyed working with him and made a point of singling Woods out when a case needed an extra pair of hands. Woods was honest, humorous and had the common touch, a quality Lavender lacked. Besides which, Lavender was not thrown about so much in the swaying hackney now that he was wedged between Woods and the side of the hood.

'She's in for a shock when she wakes up in the cells at Bow Street,' the constable commented.

'What is the full story? Who is she?'

Woods glanced down, and Lavender saw pity flash across his weathered features. 'She's Hannah Taylor, a known prostitute and petty thief. She's been up to the beak before and went to a correctional institution. She must have thought she'd struck it lucky when she ran into this drunken merchant. He'd just returned to London and was flush with money and well in his cups. While he snored off the drink, Mistress Taylor, here, lightened his load to the tune of two hundred pounds. She took a one hundred pound note and two fifty pound notes from his pocket book and disappeared.'

'It's a shame that she doesn't have the other two banknotes on her.'

Woods nodded. 'She'll have to be questioned about their whereabouts. The merchant gave a good description of the woman who robbed him—I had an inkling the thief was her. He has also retrieved the numbers of the banknotes from Down, Thornton and Gill. Once we're back at Bow Street, I should be able to match the number on the note with one of the numbers the merchant got from the bank. She'll be headin' fer Botany Bay this time—at the very least.'

'That's good work,' Lavender said. 'However, you might have to let the blushing Constable Brown drag her to the gaoler back at Bow Street. I need your assistance on another case or two.'

Woods' eyes lit up. 'Heaven and hell! Where are we off to this time?'

'Back to Newcastle for a start. Magistrate Clennell has been in touch with Bow Street. Apparently, there is some more evidence come to light regarding the Kirkley Hall burglary.'

Woods' face fell with disappointment, and Lavender understood why. That damned case had been the bane of their lives earlier in the year. Both of them had been convinced they had found the thief, but the suspect, James Charlton, had been as slippery as a jellied eel and had avoided being sent to trial at the August Assizes. It was one of the few unsolved cases in his career as a principal officer. Their only consolation was that they had retrieved most of the stolen money—from beneath a redcurrant bush in the grounds of the Hall.

'And in addition to that,' Lavender continued, 'an heiress has mysteriously disappeared in neighbouring Bellingham.'

'An heiress, eh?'

'Yes.'

'Isn't it usually the case, when these pretty young gals disappear, they have eloped with some spongin' rake?'

'Yes,' Lavender confirmed. 'However, I understand there are unusual circumstances surrounding this case—and I've been asked to travel to Northumberland to solve it.'

'Requested by name?'

Lavender nodded. 'It would seem the girl's concerned uncle is a close friend of Mr Clennell, the magistrate, and that the uncle is also familiar with the particulars of the Kirkley Hall robbery. Despite the fact that we failed to secure the conviction of James Charlton, we're still famous in Northumberland for recovering most of the missing rent money.'

Woods chuckled. 'So this uncle thinks that because we found the rent money, we should be able to find his missin' niece?'

'Exactly. Are you willing to accompany me, Constable Woods?'

Woods glanced out of the carriage and seemed to be pondering for a moment. Lavender knew that Betsy, his constable's wife, would play merry hell at another lengthy absence. Their oldest two sons were a handful and difficult for Betsy to cope with on her own. Lavender knew the family well, and if the truth were to be told, he was a little scared himself of the quick temper and sharp tongue of the tiny Mistress Woods. Yet he suspected that she wouldn't complain about the extra money her husband would earn in expenses.

'What're these mysterious circumstances surroundin' the gal's disappearance?'

Lavender smiled and his face lit up like a mischievous schoolboy's.

'Oh, nothing I'm sure we can't handle, Ned. Apparently, the girl vanished from a locked bedchamber.'

Woods' greying eyebrows rose sharply, and a wide grin broke across his broad face.

'Is that all? Shouldn't take us long to fathom this one out, should it? We'll be back in Bow Street within a fortnight . . .'

Praise for
THE HEIRESS OF LINN HAGH

Worthy of Agatha Christie

"Forget the wham, bam, slash you ma'am of modern-day crime thrillers and return to a more sedate era in 'The Heiress of Linn Hagh', an engaging novel set in a time when ladies wore bonnets, highwaymen terrorised coach travellers and the Bow Street Runners were still, well, running.

Detective Lavender has no time for superstitious nonsense and is soon demonstrating a Sherlock Holmes-like determination in his pursuit of the truth. He's a well-conceived character, and in Constable Woods the author has created a perfect foil. Where Lavender broods and thinks, Woods is a man who would rather deal in practicalities. In short, they're a double act made in crime fiction heaven.

The plot has more than a touch of the old fashioned whodunit about it, and, in particular, the scene where Lavender reveals to an incredulous audience how the heiress got out of the locked room is worthy of Agatha Christie.

There's plenty of historical detail to give the story an authentic feel, and the wide-ranging cast of characters are well drawn and highly believable. Charlton is a skilled writer... It takes a lightness of touch to keep the reader intrigued without making them feel bombarded with historical context, and the author achieves this with aplomb."

Sandra Mangan
www.crimefictionlover.com

Atmospheric mystery

"Karen Charlton's 'The Heiress of Linn Hagh' is an absorbing glimpse into a Regency England far from London. Detective Stephen Lavender and his partner, Constable Woods, must deal with people who dislike any sign of authority – farmers and gypsies – and as they delve deeper into the facts of the case, they begin to understand why. I loved the way Lavender conducted his investigation and how

he pieced the clues together. The camaraderie and humor he and Woods share is welcome relief from their dealings with suspicious townsfolk and supercilious gentry.

Although there was little doubt as to who instigated Helen Carnaby's disappearance and why, Charlton really made me wonder just how far those people would go to get what they wanted. All in all, a most satisfactory case for the detective...Charlton hooked me with her eerie, suspenseful tale and I didn't want to be pulled away from it for a second.

Now after seeing how Lavender and Woods can solve a case, I have only one thing to say: I want more!"

Cathy G. Cole - *Kittling Books*

Made in the USA
Charleston, SC
02 November 2015